DOUBLE DOG DARE

A MILWAUKEE GROWLERS BOOK

TRACY SOLHEIM

PRINT ISBN: 978-1-949270-19-8

Cover design by Lee Hyat Designs

To the ladies of Talking Volumes—past, present, and future. Thank you for the gift of your friendship.

And for the wine. Always the wine. :)

CHAPTER ONE

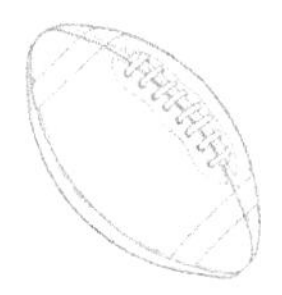

LUKE KESSLER ZIGGED when he probably should have zagged. Not that it mattered. Despite an overzealous blow from one of the linebackers, the ball remained clutched tightly to his chest, not a blade of grass coming in contact with it. He wasn't known as the man with the surest hands in professional football for nothing.

Now, if he could only get his lungs to work as well as those hands. The turf felt like cement when his flank slammed into it. He wouldn't be surprised if he'd bruised a kidney. Rolling onto his back, he worked to quell the panic that always accompanied having the wind knocked out of him. He'd been playing football for more than half his twenty-eight years, and it still scared the shit out of him whenever this happened.

His teammates huddled around above him, their shoulder pads and helmets nearly blocking out the bright blue Wisconsin sky. From what he could make of the expressions behind their grills, they weren't all that concerned about his welfare. Instead, they were like a pack of hyenas poised to pounce on a dying gazelle, waiting for him to say something.

Or swear, most likely.

He should have known they'd hit him hard so he'd lose his

dare. Before taking the field, he'd challenged them not to utter a single expletive during practice. He hadn't counted on them being so bloodthirsty. Not during the pre-season. He would have grinned with appreciation at their zeal had he not been so busy trying to breathe.

"Jesus," he wheezed at last.

Fortunately for Luke, he hadn't stated anything in his dare about using the Lord's name in vain. Not that he'd mind donating twenty bucks to the local SPCA for the offense. He was just relieved to be among the breathing again and very grateful for the heated discussion among his teammates about the rules of the challenge.

Mostly because it gave him a chance to further catch his breath.

"Dammit, you shitheads!" Trey Van Horn, the Milwaukee Growlers quarterback, yelled as he shoved his way through the circle of muscle surrounding Luke. "Save the savage hits for our opponents, will ya? Take it easy on Kessler. He's the runt of my receiving corps. I can't have him on IR before the season even starts."

Their teammates snickered like a bunch of tweens in a sex-ed class. At least they'd gotten someone to swear. Van Horn let out an exasperated sigh at their behavior. The quarterback was all business when it came to football. Not that anyone complained. The stud was one of the most accurate passers in the league. And even though he wouldn't ever admit it out loud, Luke was Van Horn's favorite receiver. Probably why his QB's "runt" remark didn't bother him so much.

Not that much, anyway.

Luke stretched his arm into the air. The ball was still gripped within his long fingers. "What I lack in stature, I make up for in ferocity," he croaked. "And you owe forty bucks to the dogs and cats of Wisconsin awaiting adoption."

Van Horn shook his head in disgust and snatched the ball

from Luke's hand. "Put it on my tab," he said before stomping back to the line of scrimmage.

The rest of the guys chuckled as they trailed after their leader, leaving Luke still flat on his back and, gazing up at the cloudless, late-summer sky. A hand came down from above while the sun's glare blacked out the rest of the body attached to it. But Luke would know that mitt anywhere. It was the size of a T-bone steak, and it belonged to Hall of Famer Lenny Washington. Known to everyone as Wash, the Growlers' receiver's coach boasted an impressive array of statistics for receptions during his storied career, the likes of which Luke could only dream of ever achieving.

Every day, Luke pinched himself for his stupid luck of having the man as his mentor and coach. Most guys with Wash's fame would have taken advantage of the variety of opportunities afforded to him in retirement, leaving the gridiron in their rearview mirror forever. But not Wash. He loved the game too much not to share the knowledge that had made him the G.O.A.T.

"I'm too ugly for 'Dancing with the Stars,'" Wash joked at the time.

Luke suspected the real reason was the man was embarrassed by his slight stammer. But it was that embarrassment that had likely propelled him to glory. No doubt he'd spent most of his life trying to prove himself. *To prove to everyone that he was more than his life's circumstances.*

Luke could relate. He knew all too well the internal demons that could drive a man to the top of his chosen profession.

"Why must you constantly be t-tossing out dares at everyone?" Wash asked after helping Luke to his feet.

"Just trying to bolster team camaraderie before the season starts." He winced at the pain in his side.

"Just trying to get your ass b-broke," Wash mumbled.

Luke gave his mentor the side-eye. Wash sighed as he reached for his wallet and pulled out a twenty.

"What are you complaining about? I'm giving back to society." Luke reached for the money. His grin turned into a grimace brought on by the movement.

The coach shot him a questioning look.

"It's nothing."

"Mmmhmm," the other man replied. "Go see the trainer so that 'nothing' doesn't turn into something. And s-stay out of Coach Gibson's way. He's had it with your hijinks today."

Forty-five minutes and some serious stretching and ultrasound later, Luke was surprised to see so many of his teammates still hanging around the locker room. The team's young punter, Kane Palmer, was standing at its center, looking like a deer caught in headlights.

"Dude, whatever you do, make sure the diamond is pure," one of the guys was saying. "Women have a sixth sense about that shit. They can spot a fake from a mile away."

"Yeah, but you need to make sure it's not one of thosc blood diamonds," another teammate chimed in. "You don't want the woke mob coming down on you."

Woke mob? What the hell?

Steve Jacobs, the senior member of the Growlers receiving corps, stepped up beside Palmer and draped an arm over the punter's shoulder.

"Stick with me, kid." Jacobs pointed to the two caret studs he wore in his ears. "I've got a guy who will hook you right up."

"You getting your ears pierced, Palmer?" Luke headed to his locker and began changing into his street clothes. "You better bring someone with you to hold your hand. I seem to remember you nearly fainting when the team physician was doling out flu shots last year."

Laughter engulfed the room.

"Something worse than that," Van Horn said. "It seems our boy is getting married."

"Seriously?" Luke should not have been surprised. Palmer's college girlfriend had been a regular fixture at team functions last season, despite the fact she was still in school back in Oklahoma. That familiar gnawing began in his gut as his teammates talked about rings and vows and everything else that implied commitment. He hated the jealousy that bubbled up whenever he was confronted with the topic. "Either she's marrying you for your money, or you knocked her up. Which is it?"

The locker room was suddenly as silent as a tomb.

Shit.

Why was it that Luke's normally impenetrable filter never worked in this situation? Years of therapy, and he still couldn't control the knee-jerk reaction he had to the word marriage. He needed to do a better job at hiding his anger.

His teammates looked at him with varying expressions of surprise. Luke was typically the Growler's affable peace-maker. Sure, he could tease as well as the next guy. But he drew the line at insulting any of his teammates.

Until today, apparently.

"Ignore me. That was a dickhead thing to say," he backpedaled. "Must have hit my head when you tackled me. I'm sorry, Palmer." He nodded at the punter. "Congratulations. Shaina's a lucky girl."

It was another long moment before the fraught silence evaporated, and the debate about diamonds filled the locker room again. Luke kept his mouth shut and finished dressing. Van Horn gave him the stink-eye from his locker across the aisle.

"What?" Luke snapped.

The quarterback shook his head.

"Van Horn is speechless because normally it's him dissing marriage," Declan Fletcher, the Growler placekicker, commented from his chair directly beside the quarterback. "It's not like you to be sour on matrimony."

Luke wasn't "sour on matrimony." At least on most matrimony. Just one marriage in particular. Or should he say one "non" marriage. But he didn't need the two brainiacs on the team suddenly psychoanalyzing him. He paid good money to a professional to do that.

"Just unsuccessfully trying to make a joke, that's all. I didn't want these guys going at each other's throats about stupid diamonds."

It was a lame excuse. Judging by the silent look the other two men exchanged, they knew it, too. Luke needed to change the narrative.

"The ring is important, Palmer," he called out. "But have you given any thought to the proposal?"

The men in the locker room turned their attention to Luke, a mix of suspicion and curiosity on their faces.

"No. I haven't gotten that far," Palmer replied. "I figured I'd ask Fletcher to help me out."

This brought on a chorus of guffaws from their teammates.

"Fletcher? Hell, no," Luke shouted over the din. "The dude never proposed. His marriage was arranged in his lawyer's office so he could avoid deportation back to Scotland."

The placekicker shrugged. "Aye, it's true. But it did the job. I'm still with the team, happily married to the lass for real now, with a bairn on the way."

Luke shook his head. "Shaina is going to want something more. The grand gesture. Leave it to me. I'll help you with this. We'll give her a proposal that will be the envy of social media."

Palmer's face lit up with a grin. "Hell, yeah! Shaina is all about being an influencer."

Van Horn snorted as he lifted his gym bag over his shoulder. "I'd ask to see his references first, Palmer. I mean, how many times has Kessler proposed to anyone?"

"Yeah," Jacobs added. "When did you suddenly become the Love Doctor? You pick your women based on a standardized chart of qualifications. You don't even care about chemistry. Have you even picked out your Seasonal Arm Candy yet?"

Antonio McGraff, the rookie receiver the Growlers drafted a few months ago, let out an astonished snort. "'Seasonal Arm Candy?'"

"That's what I said, *McGruff*." Jacobs deliberately mispronounced the rookie's name. He was bent on hazing the kid who threatened to dethrone him as the team's return man. "Get your ears checked, Crime Dog."

Van Horn took pity on the rookie. "Right about this time of year, Kessler picks one woman to be his main squeeze for the season. She has to meet certain requirements that he keeps to himself. But once he picks her, he sticks with her no matter what. We suppose it's so he can focus on his game without having to wade through the clubs for a booty call."

"It's not like that," Luke protested.

Although it was sort of like that.

Except for the booty-call part. He had a bit more respect for women than these guys gave him credit for. But the motives for his dating behavior were genuine. Not that it was his teammates' business.

And Van Horn was one to talk. He only dated women who could further the political career he was dreaming of after football. Last season, he'd dated the daughter of a United States senator. The woman was smart, gorgeous, and a manipulative bitch who'd gone so far as to try to break-up Fletcher's marriage.

"That's the stupidest thing I've ever heard," McGraff said. "What if after a few dates, she's not worth the effort?"

Van Horn shrugged. "The thing you need to know about Kessler is once he's made up his mind, he never backs down. Ever. Even if the woman has a bad habit of taking food off his plate."

The locker room echoed with laughter again.

"Ohh," one of Luke's teammates called out. "Remember the one with the laugh like a mule?" He brayed loudly, causing several of the guys to double over.

"Or the one who never had an opinion about anything," another guy weighed in.

"Switzerland," his teammates chorused.

"Blonde, blue-eyed, and cold," someone added.

"What about the tennis player who grunted like she was serving every time they had sex," another player said.

Whoa.

That had to be a lucky guess, because there was no way he'd told anyone that.

"So, who's it gonna be this year, Kessler?" Palmer asked.

"And don't say you haven't picked her yet," Jacobs said. "Regular season starts next week."

His teammates were a damn bunch of old ladies. Luke shouldn't give them the satisfaction of knowing they were right. Except he didn't have anything to hide. He may be a bit Machiavellian when it came to his personal life, but he had good reason to be.

Outperform the negative.

"The morning meteorologist from Channel 11," he answered, seeing no need to avoid the inevitable. They were going to find out this weekend anyway. He'd invited her to the team's season kickoff picnic.

Luke's announcement was met with a concert of wolf whistles.

"The one you act a fool with every Tuesday during your dog adoption pleas?" Fletcher asked.

Luke nodded. The striking blonde was the ideal choice. She was comfortable in the lime-light, intelligent, and, best of all, not needy. She fit all his qualifications to a tee. Especially the one about it not hurting when she eventually left him for someone else. He'd already had too much of that in his life. That's why he made it a point to date women with one foot out the door. Women who weren't necessarily interested in a committed relationship. They were either focused on their careers or on landing someone else. Someone with more to give.

Love didn't fit into his qualifications. Ever.

"Hot damn, man," Jacobs crowed. "I'm pretty sure half the male population of this city wakes up to that woman, if you know what I mean."

The guffaws grew louder. Luke shook his head. Life in a locker room could get pretty raunchy some days, but there were certain subjects Luke couldn't stomach. Growing up in a house with two women, he'd had the lesson about not objectifying the female sex drilled into him since birth.

"Let's show some respect, assholes." He grabbed his gym bag and headed in the direction of the door.

He was nearly to his car when he noticed McGraff on his heels. Luke tapped the key fob, unlocking his Ford Dually pickup.

"Something on your mind, Tony-O?" Luke asked, using the handle the media had dubbed McGraff during his playing days at LSU.

"Yeah. What's up with Jacobs? Why has he got it out for me?"

Luke dumped his duffel in the back seat before turning to the rookie. Here was a guy with more natural athletic talent in his pinkie finger than Luke would possess in his entire life. The kid had the chops to become a legend in the game. And with Lenny Washington guiding him, that was likely going to happen.

He should resent the rookie. McGraff would almost certainly take away some—if not many—of Luke's receptions as the season progressed. And it royally pissed him off that he had to work ten times as hard as the rookie to stay in the league. Except Luke had always been a team player. It's what made coaches keep him on the squad.

Outperform the negative.

But that didn't mean other players wouldn't be resentful. Especially a receiver whose legs had ten more years' worth of miles on them. Like Jacobs. Nope. That particular veteran was not going to go easy on the pup.

Luke crossed his arms over his chest. "Welcome to primetime, McGraff. Up until now your teammates worshipped the ground you walked on. You were the star of the show. The reason they won. Here, everyone is playing at a high level. You can be a threat to a guy's bank accounts. You get what I'm saying? Suck it up. Play hard every down, and the respect will come. You'll see."

The rookie's face grew hard. He sucked in a breath before turning to glare back at the building. "I don't need a stinking fan club, Kessler. I know how good I am. All I'm asking for is some damn hospitality, that's all. This team is one huge fucking clique."

He stormed off before Luke could reply.

Palmer jogged over. "What's eating him?"

"A bad case of rookie anxiety."

"Huh. I never really felt that last year."

Luke chuckled. "That's because you were our punter, for better or worse."

"Speaking of for better or worse," Palmer said. "Were you serious about helping me with the proposal?"

He wanted to say no, but he'd already opened his stupid mouth. And he had been rude to the guy. "Sure. You need to come up with a grand gesture, and I'll help you execute it."

The air went out of Palmer's grin. "I was kind of hoping you'd come up with something."

Figures. If it didn't involve a ball, Palmer didn't have much of an imagination. Luke sighed. "Okay, but I'm going to need a bit more to go on. I'll need to know what Shaina likes."

"Let's go putt a few balls, and I'll tell you all about my best girl."

The punter was obsessed with the game of golf. He spent all

his free time on the course. Luke wondered if the dude knew that marriage would likely curtail that activity.

Not his problem.

"No can do." Luke climbed into the driver's seat. "I promised my Gram I'd stop by today." It was a lie, but he didn't want to spend the entire afternoon listening to Palmer wax on about his fiancée. He'd chat up Shaina to get some ideas when he saw her this weekend. "See you at the picnic."

Driving away from the practice facility, he decided a visit with his Grandma Grace wasn't a bad idea. He'd moved her from Boise and into the Sunset Glen senior living community last week. Every time he called, she claimed to be acclimating just fine. Rather than take her word for it, he'd go see for himself.

CHAPTER TWO

"THE JUDGE CAME by this morning. She was looking for you."

Summer Pearson stumbled at her best friend's words before quickly catching herself. She adjusted the leash with her free hand, glancing around to see if anyone had witnessed another one of her bouts of lack of coordination. Fortunately, the walking trail around the senior community where her grandparents lived was deserted. She pressed her cellphone back to her ear.

"She honestly seemed shocked you skipped town," her friend continued.

"Oh, for heaven's sake, Paige, I didn't 'skip town.' The Judge knows exactly where to find me. Heck, I'm fairly certain the address is saved in her car's GPS." Summer tugged on the leash, but the little black French bulldog wouldn't budge. The dog was mesmerized by a butterfly hovering over some liriope. "Are you sure you're only fifteen pounds?" she grumbled.

"I don't think she believed you'd go through with it. Honestly, neither did I," Paige said.

"What? You're the one who convinced me to do it. You practically kicked me out!"

Paige's tone became defensive. "That's not how it went down.

I told you to stop drowning yourself in Ben and Jerry's while you cried along to a soundtrack of Adele songs. Three months on the sofa feeling sorry for yourself wasn't doing you any favors. I did *not* tell you to run off to Milwaukee and take a job substituting at the elementary school where your grandparents used to teach."

"You would have had to kick me out anyway. I ran out of money, remember?"

"No one told you to give all your YouTube riches away."

"I didn't deserve them in the first place." Summer pulled on the leash again, this time with success. Milli lost interest in the butterfly, except now she was sprinting toward a squirrel. The squirrel sized up the dog and quickly scampered up a tree. Milli barked at the retreating bushy tail as she loped after it. Summer nearly turned her ankle trying to keep up. "At least I'm not on the sofa," she said.

Although the sofa sounded pretty nice right now. How could one tiny dog be so strong? And how could she be so out of breath? She glanced down at the sweatpants she was wearing. It was eighty-five degrees, but none of her shorts seemed to fit. Maybe Paige had a point about the three months of Ben and Jerry's.

"Summer." Her friend's voice grew softer. "I only meant you needed to get on with the next chapter of your life, to find a way to pivot. I didn't mean you should leave Chicago. I could afford to carry you. Besides, there are substitute jobs here. And I'm sure if you talked to Principal Kliphuis, she could find something you could do at Preston while you figure out what comes next."

Six years ago, Summer and Paige began their teaching careers at Preston Academy, a prestigious private school in Oak Brook, a suburb of Chicago. The two women knew each other from their days at Northwestern and decided to become roommates when they started teaching. They'd been best friends ever since.

"I can't go back there." Summer's heart began to race, remembering the going-away party the teachers and staff threw for her and how she'd brazenly bragged that she would remember them all when she hit it big. Except that she hadn't hit it big. She hadn't even hit *it* at all. Her cheeks burned at the memories. There was no way she would return to the school like a runaway dog with its tail tucked between its legs. "They've already hired someone to replace me."

Paige groaned. "That man is a blowhard. Did you know he insists even the staff call him Dr. Dixon? Everyone calls him Dr. Dick behind his back. It's only a matter of time before someone calls him that to his face."

A laugh escaped before Summer could smother it. She had no right feeling smug that her replacement wasn't as popular as she had been, no matter how pleasant it felt to her bruised pride. "In his defense, he does hold a doctorate in music. Never mind his years of experience playing in various orchestras." She swallowed the lump of jealously that formed in her throat.

"I give him one year," Paige said, her voice ringing confidently through the phone. "All it will take is for his ego to grate on one parent. You know how the board kowtows to those who pay the tuition. At least you won't have to worry about keeping the board of directors pleased in a public school."

"I don't think I'll have to worry about too much parental involvement either," Summer replied. "Not a single parent stopped by the music room at the open house today."

"See. Yet another reason why you're wasting your talents there. Don't those people realize who is teaching their children?"

Summer shook her head. If she had any talent, she wouldn't be walking her grandmother's dog in Milwaukee. She'd be in Vienna.

"It's serendipity, Paige. My grandmother gave the best years of her life to this place. These days, music is a luxury in most public elementary schools," Summer explained. "The principal had to fight to get funding for a long-term sub when the music teacher went on maternity leave. The school board would just as soon let the program die and use the money elsewhere. My grandmother has already lost so much. I can't let her legacy die."

Paige let out a sympathetic sigh. "I get it. How is Grandma Bonnie doing?"

"As well as can be expected. She seems content here. The community is beautiful, and they take wonderful care of her. It helps that my grandfather is onsite now, too. He doesn't live in the memory care building with her, but the apartment he has is nicer than a lot of the ones in Chicago. This place has its own gym, a barber shop, a card room, and even a bar. Plus, he gets two meals a day at the restaurant. He's living large."

Milli picked that moment to do her business beneath a rhododendron. Summer dropped the leash so she had a free hand to retrieve the plastic bag she'd brought with her. She grimaced as she pulled the bag over her fingers and grabbed the still-steaming pile.

"Gross," she murmured, grateful she had bought the scented bags from the pet store.

The little dog sat in the grass, proudly eyeing the gift she had left, her pert black nose lifted slightly in the air. One of her ears bent forward adorably while her stumpy tail swished over the grass.

"*Tous es bon chien,* Milli," Summer praised her.

"Are you speaking French to that dog?" Paige sounded as though she thought Summer had lost her mind.

It was a possibility.

"Milli Chanel is a purebred French bulldog. It's only fitting that I speak to her in her native tongue."

"This is exactly what I was afraid of," Paige said. "You've only been living with the Princess for a week and her pretentiousness is already rubbing off on you."

The "Princess" was Summer's cousin, Lizzie. Only a few months apart in age, they were worlds apart in personality. When they were both students at Northwestern, more than one person had remarked that Lizzie should have been the Pearson named Summer. The blue-eyed blonde was bubbly, sunny, and always the life of the party. Summer, on the other hand, was more of a hurricane run amok. A ditzy klutz who liked to hide behind her dark hair and coffee-colored eyes.

"What's it like sharing a house with her?" Paige continued.

Both Summer and Lizzie found themselves in need of a place to live at the same time. Lizzie's now ex-boyfriend took a job in New York, leaving her broken-hearted and homeless in Milwaukee. Their grandfather needed someone to look after his home while he decided whether living in a senior community would suit. He'd offered the Craftsman bungalow where both girls' fathers had grown up as a rent-free refuge for six months. It was a win-win for everyone.

"It's not that bad. I have many fond memories of being in that house with my grandparents. It's like slipping on an old pair of jeans," Summer replied. "And Lizzie's work schedule is so crazy. She spends the rest of her time working out or getting some sort of beauty treatment. I won't see her that often."

"She's not still crying in her Prosecco about Josh leaving her?"

"Surprisingly, no. She's already landed someone new. Someone she claims will keep her in the public eye."

Paige snorted. "As long as she's the center of her universe."

"As long as her ego gets fed, you mean. It's the only way I'll be able to survive six months living with her."

"And then you're coming home?"

"It's what I promised The Judge. I sit for the LSAT in November. She's arranged an internship in the courts while I apply to law school."

"But is that what *you* want?"

Summer swallowed roughly. "My mother is right," she said softly. "I'm not cut out to be a serious musician. I need to get on with my life. Besides, I've wanted to be a lawyer like my parents since kindergarten. Teaching at Preston was only supposed to be how I spent my gap year before law school. I got side-tracked, that's all." Sidetracked by a dream she'd failed at. She sighed. "My mom is one of the most respected judges in the city. That's not a bad pedigree. People always tell me I'm the spitting image of her. Why not *be* her?"

"Um, I mean this in the best possible way," Paige said. "But you are nothing like your mother. If I didn't know better, I'd say you and Lizzie were somehow switched at birth because your cousin is more like The Judge in personality than you are."

It wasn't always that way, she wanted to argue. But she was suddenly aware that Milli was no longer beside her. "Holy crap. I've lost my grandmother's dog. I'll call you back." She hurried along the path. "Milli!" she shouted, but it came out more like a strangled wheeze. Her lungs burned as she tried to push her out-of-shape body to move faster.

She couldn't lose the dog. Milli was the only thing from the past Grandma Bonnie remembered. Summer feared that if the dog disappeared, so too would her grandmother.

Struggling to run in flip-flops, she barely managed to round the corner of the path. It opened up into a large grassy area in front of the parking lot for the independent living apartments. Up ahead, a giant dog was grunting furiously at something. Summer screamed when she realized the beast was on top of Milli.

"Get off her!"

Reaching into her pocket, she pulled out her keys and pressed the alarm meant to protect herself from attack. The high-pitched siren startled the big dog, making it jump away with a yelp. Summer scooped up Milli and wrapped her arms around her. The tiny dog was trembling, but she barked and struggled against Summer's hold, foolishly trying to get at her tormenter.

The bulky mutt hurried toward them, intent on finishing what he started, no doubt. He licked his chops at Summer, and she froze. The beast bearing down on her was a pit bull. A student at Preston had been mauled by one of those dogs a few years back. The poor child lost an ear.

Milli wasn't the only one shaking now.

"Monty!" a man yelled from the vicinity of the parking lot.

The large dog took two more steps in Summer's direction before turning and sprinting toward the male voice. Summer released a breath that sounded more like a sob than she would have liked. Milli whimpered in her arms.

"It's okay, *mon petite*. That big bad dog won't hurt you again."

Milli gave her a look that was more miffed than relieved. Fickle animal. Some girls just didn't know what was good for them.

The man responsible for the beast approached from the parking lot. Summer was suddenly trembling for a different reason. Of course, the guy had to be ridiculously hot. Fortunately, Summer had put some effort into her hair today, thinking she'd have a line of parents hurrying to the music room to meet her. She'd even applied mascara and lip gloss. *Un*fortunately, the sweatpants and oversized T-shirt she changed into after school made her look like a dumpy circus clown.

The beast's owner wasn't much taller than she was. Given how his Boise State T-shirt stretched over his chest, he was definitely in better shape, though. He had on neon blue basketball shorts and sneakers. Peeking out between the two was a pair of nicely muscled calves dusted with sandy brown hair. He wore a baseball cap backwards on his head. Summer always found that look ridiculous.

Until she saw it on this guy.

A pair of reflective wraparound sunglasses set atop his aquiline nose. For some reason, Summer very much wanted to see his eyes. His square jaw was shaved clean. When he opened his mouth to speak, she caught a glimpse of perfectly straight, white teeth.

"Sorry 'bout that, eh. There's usually no one walking on the trail," he said. "I hope Monty didn't frighten you."

Frighten her? His dog had *terrified* her. Not that she was sharing that bit of info with him.

"Your dog violated Milli," she said instead.

He unleashed a slow, devastating smile. One that made her weaker at the knees than his beast of a dog. Clearly, man and beast both considered themselves lady killers.

"Now, Monty, I told you to at least buy the ladies a drink first." He tugged on the dog's ear. Monty leaned his giant head against the man's thigh with a satisfied grunt.

Annoyed at his flippant remark, Summer ground her teeth. "That's disgusting. No wonder your dog has despicable manners. There are leash laws around here. Especially for dogs like yours."

"Whoa." The guy put both hands up, palms out. There was a leash dangling from his long fingers. "I apologize. I shouldn't have made a joke. It was offensive. And you're absolutely right about the leash laws." He bent over and snapped the leash to Monty's collar, mumbling something about his funny bone being broken today. "He's been cooped up all day, and, like I said, there's usually no one out here this time of the afternoon."

She clutched Milli tighter. "Well, *we* were out here this afternoon."

Jeez, Louise, she sounded starchy. How had that happened? She was always the cool teacher. The one who gave every student a second—sometimes third—warning. Since when had she become so high and mighty?

The sexy smile was gone. Not that she blamed him. She was being a bitch.

"Yeah, I sincerely apologize," he said. "Monty was neutered by the shelter before I adopted him. He still gets a bit frisky when he sees a pretty girl, though. He's harmless otherwise. Not all Pitties live up to their bad rap." He rubbed the dog's head. "This one is blind in one eye and afraid of loud noises. He'd rather lick you to death than bite you."

She felt like the biggest fool. Summer had never been much of a dog person. Growing up, The Judge had no time for dogs in the house, no matter how hard Summer and her brother pleaded for one. Still, you couldn't be too careful. How was she to know Monty was harmless? And why should she believe some studly rando about his dog?

She squared her shoulders. Tightening her grip on Milli, she gave man and dog a wide berth as she walked past them. "All the same, he should be leashed. I'd prefer not to be licked to death, either. Lord knows where that tongue has been."

His only response was a swift nod when she swept past him.

"There you are." Her grandfather was striding across the grass. "Fred said he heard someone yelling for Milli. Everything okay?"

No!

She was speaking French, for crying out loud, to her grandmother's dog. She was acting like a prudish old lady with a stick up her butt in front of a stranger. Paige was right to worry. Summer was losing her shit.

"Everything's fine, Papa Harry," she lied. "Milli took off after a squirrel while I was picking up her poop." As soon as the words were out, she realized she was no longer holding the offending bag. "Oh. I must have dropped it when I was chasing her."

"I'll pick it up," Monty's owner said. "We are headed that way for a quick run."

Summer sighed in defeat. She'd hoped the guy had already moved onto the trail, allowing her to put the whole embarrassing incident behind her.

"Thank you, son," her grandfather replied.

At eighty-one, Harry Pearson was still broad-shouldered and vital. Beneath his full head of thick gray hair were the same sparkling blue eyes as his granddaughter, Lizzie. The former P.E. teacher laughed loud and often. To him, everyone under the age of fifty was either son or sweetheart. He got away with it because everybody adored Papa Harry.

"Hold on," Papa Harry continued. "I know who you are. You're Grace's grandson. She's been bragging about you all week. Of course, most of the folks here are already big fans of yours."

Big fans?

The smile was back on Monty's owner's face, albeit a lot less sexy than the one he'd aimed at her earlier. This one was his gracious smile, apparently. The one he reserved for "big fans." Summer was suddenly very curious about the man standing in front of her.

"Grace and I have been having a fine time getting acclimated to this place," Papa Harry continued. "I only moved in a few weeks before she did. And you don't have to worry about a thing. I've been looking in on her. I'm across the hall if she ever needs anything."

Summer ignored the quick squeeze she felt in her heart at the thought of her grandfather hanging out with another woman. Of course, it didn't mean anything. Papa Harry gave up his home to move to an apartment clear across town so he could be with his wife of nearly sixty years. Theirs was the kind of love that transcended time. He was being his normal affable self to this Grace woman, that was all.

"I appreciate it," Monty's owner said. "Most of her friends in Boise had moved or were . . . gone. It's a big deal, her moving to Milwaukee. I'm hoping she'll have more social interaction here. All I want is for her to be safe and to enjoy life."

Well.

Her heart squeezed a second time because, dang, that was kind of sweet. He rescues dogs and takes care of his grandmother. Now she was even more embarrassed for her snotty tone earlier.

Summer's gaze drifted to his mouth. There was something playful about those lush lips of his. The way they appeared as if he was reining in a grin that threatened to escape at any given moment. Minutes ago, she couldn't wait to get away from this guy. Now, however, she found herself being drawn in by his smile and wanting to know all his secrets.

Too late, he was already jogging along the path, Monty by his side. She gave her head a firm shake. That guy wasn't going to share his secrets—or anything else—with her. No doubt he thought she was a shrew and he couldn't jog away fast enough. She'd likely never see the guy again.

"I wish you'd change your mind about the band, Sunshine," Papa Harry said as they made their way to the memory care building.

He'd been calling her by the silly nickname since she was a toddler. As she got older, she suspected he used it simply to annoy The Judge. Her mom was always complaining that the name "Summer" was too whimsical, and she must have lost her mind to let her husband talk her into saddling her daughter with it. No one would take the child seriously, she argued. Everytime Papa Harry called her Sunshine when her mom was around, he would wink at Summer as if it were their private joke.

"It'll be a fine way for you to meet people, helping out with the band," he continued.

For thirty-five years, her grandfather and his friends played in a rag-tag pep band for Milwaukee's professional football team, the Growlers. Unfortunately, so had most of the band's other members. The only "people" Summer would meet likely no longer had their own teeth and went to bed at nine.

She linked her arm through her grandfather's. "Not to sound ungrateful, but I'm only here temporarily. Most of my free time needs to be spent studying for the LSAT."

Her grandfather opened his mouth, no doubt to make some comment about law school. She was grateful he still supported her dreams. It was no use, though. She'd already made up her mind. Summer was through with dreaming.

She spoke before Papa Harry could. "Besides, I wouldn't want to break anyone's heart when I head back to Chicago."

Papa Harry snorted, seeing right through her ploy. "Not everyone in the band is a geezer like me. For your information, the director is only thirty. And he's single. And a firefighter. I know how you gals can't resist a man in uniform. Besides, I already told him all about you."

"Papa Harry!"

"Relax. I merely pointed out that you are a whiz at arranging music. He said he would love any help he can get. No one is saying you have to marry the guy." He winked at her. "Or watch Netflix and chill with him."

Summer nearly stumbled for the second time this afternoon. "Please tell me you do *not* know what that means."

Her grandfather was suddenly sporting a smug smile. "I'm old, but I'm not dead, missy. And I thought you might enjoy having someone else to pal around with besides your cousin."

When he put it that way, of course, she would. Anything to keep from getting sucked into Lizzie's orbit was a win in Summer's book. Papa Harry knew both his granddaughters too well.

"You're a sweet man. You know that?"

He opened the door to her grandmother's apartment. "It comes with the job description for grandfathers."

Milli jumped from Summer's arms and headed straight for Grandma Bonnie's lap. Grandma Bonnie sat in a chair in front of the room's window, gently cradling the dog in her sun-spotted hands. She was dressed in pink slacks and a matching blouse. Her white hair was gathered in a perfect chignon at the base of her long, elegant neck, showing off her ever-present pearl earbobs. Her grandmother had always been a stickler about looking presentable, even when she was ill.

The sound of her grandmother's laughter filled the room, making Summer sigh with delight. This was the silver lining to her taking a job in Milwaukee. She was able to take care of the two people who had guided her through the most trying times in her life. Things may not have gone her way three months ago, but being able to spend the next couple of months in her grandmother's company was the perfect consolation.

"Oh, there's my best girl," Grandma Bonnie said to the dog. "Thank you for bringing her to tea, Grayson."

Except for that part.

It still took Summer's breath away when her grandmother called her husband by her son's name. Especially since that particular son—Summer's dad—had been gone for almost eighteen years. She glanced over at Papa Harry, but he didn't react. Instead, he made his way over to his wife, leaning down to kiss her on the cheek.

What would her father look like today had he lived? She liked to think the man she remembered tossing her in the air would still be as handsome and virile as Papa Harry had been in his fifties. He would certainly have been as kind.

Choking down the lump in her throat, she stepped further into the small apartment and braced herself for what came next.

"It's nice of you to join us, Victoria." The forced expression in her grandmother's faded blue eyes told Summer the older woman didn't think it was "nice" at all.

Not that Summer enjoyed having her grandmother confuse her with her mother. It wasn't until Alzheimer's set in that Summer realized how much Grandma Bonnie disapproved of The Judge. Her grandmother had always been gracious towards her daughter-in-law—at least in Summer's presence. Obviously, Summer wasn't the only one who had issues with her mother. Too bad they couldn't compare notes.

Squaring her shoulders, she put aside her heartbreak at being erased from her grandmother's memory banks and stepped into the role that was her family's reality now.

"You're looking lovely today, Bonnie."

CHAPTER THREE

SUMMER POURED herself a second glass of wine, telling herself she deserved it. She was celebrating surviving her first week in Milwaukee.

"One down, sixteen more to go." She raised a glass at her reflection in the oven door and toasted.

"What did you say?" Lizzie called from the larger of the home's two bedrooms.

Her cousin had staked her claim to the room their grandparents once shared, arguing she had more stuff than Summer. Since Summer left most of her belongings in the apartment she shared with Paige in Chicago, she conceded the point.

Besides, arguing with Lizzie was like spinning in a circle. The thing about Summer's cousin was, in spite of being hugely egocentric, she was genuinely nice to everyone. It was impossible to disagree with her. Or deny her anything. And everyone knew it. The world was well and truly Lizzie's oyster.

Paige and Summer spent years studying the phenomenon of Princess Lizzie, but they couldn't figure out how she did it. Her cousin was well aware that she was gorgeous and clever. But instead of lording it over other people—women especially—she treated everyone as if they were her best friend. It was no wonder television viewers adored her.

"Just talking to Milli," Summer replied.

At the sound of her name, Milli lifted her head from the dog bed in the living room where she'd been snoring seconds before.

Cover for me, Summer mouthed.

Great, now she was conspiring with a dog. Maybe that second glass of wine wasn't such a great idea after all.

"Did Grandma ask about me?" Lizzie called out.

Somewhat ironically, but not surprisingly, the only one of her five grandchildren Grandma Bonnie remembered was Lizzie. She woke up every weekday morning to watch her granddaughter deliver the weather forecast.

"She wondered why you weren't on this morning."

"She knows I'm not on the news on the weekends," Lizzie replied.

Except their grandmother didn't know that. She had no concept of the days of a week any longer. Lizzie claimed she didn't want to remember Grandma Bonnie in this state, so she rarely visited her. Neither did she bother educating herself about Alzheimer's. It was less painful for her to be ignorant.

Summer took a healthy swallow of her wine. Different strokes and all that.

"Are you excited about school starting next week?" Lizzie asked. "It can't be too different than what you're used to."

Except it was. At Preston, music was an integral part of the development of the well-rounded student. Parents didn't balk at paying fees that included money for state-of-the-art musical instruments and recording equipment. At her new school, many of Summer's students who enrolled in beginning band and orchestra couldn't afford to rent an instrument. As a result, the school had a small cache of donated instruments for students to borrow. But after spending her weekend inspecting and cataloging those instruments, Summer discovered a lot of them were woefully inadequate. Many were missing pieces, broken, or just plain worn out.

When she'd approached the principal about the situation, the woman basically told her, "good luck with that." She did hint, however, that if Summer could convince her locally famous cousin to participate in the school's career day, she'd sift through other school accounts in an effort to find more money for instruments. It had taken a few moments for it to dawn on Summer that career day at her new school would be vastly different from at Preston's. There, most of the parents could rearrange their day to speak to their child's classmates about their fabulous careers as a cardiologist, a professional athlete, or a restauranteur. They even had a network news anchor come last year.

Given how many parents showed up for back-to-school day last week, she doubted the pool of parents willing to participate was very deep. Having the local meteorologist would be a coup for the school. As far as Summer could see, the situation was a win-win for the Pearson cousins. Lizzie would get an afternoon of adoration, and Summer would hopefully get funds to repair and replenish the school's instruments.

She wandered down the hall into Lizzie's bedroom. Her cousin's bed was littered with clothes as she tried on and discarded what looked like everything in her closet.

"I thought you were going to a picnic?"

Lizzie's reflection in the mirror rolled her eyes at Summer. "It's not any ol' picnic. This picnic is hosted by the owner of the Milwaukee Growlers. The team and their families will all be there. You wouldn't believe how those WAGs dress. It's the place to be seen this weekend."

"'WAGs?'"

"Wives and girlfriends," her cousin clarified. "I guess I'm kind of one of those, even though this is just a date." She grinned and shrugged her shoulders. "For now."

"That would make you a WAD. Wives and dates." Summer chuckled at her own joke.

Lizzie narrowed her eyes. "Not funny." She pulled a sky-blue sundress over her head, turning side-to-side in the mirror as she smoothed down the skirt with her palms.

"That looks nice on you."

It wasn't a lie. Everything looked nice on Lizzie thanks to fabulous genes from her mother's side of the family and hours spent in the gym or at the spa. But Summer had another agenda here.

"You think so?"

"It's perfect. Understated but very classy," Summer added.

Lizzie bounced up on her toes. "It is, isn't it? Thank you for helping me decide." She skipped over, wrapped her arms around Summer's neck, and pulled her in for a hug. "This is going to be so much fun living together. It's almost like we're sisters."

Summer returned the hug. She mouthed a silent prayer that maybe this time, it would be like that.

"Hey, I have a favor to ask," she began. "I'm trying to fit in among the staff at the school. The principal asked if I would invite you to speak at career day."

Her cousin groaned as she dropped her arms. "Ugh. Papa Harry asks me that every year."

"He does? Then why don't you do it?"

"Because the only other time I spoke to kids, it was a bunch of kindergartners who had just polished off cupcakes after a birthday party. Unbeknownst to the woman who was substituting that day, one of the kids had a gluten allergy."

"Uh, oh."

"Yeah. The kid hurled all over my Marc Jacobs boots. And then . . ." Lizzie lifted her hand to cover her mouth.

But no additional explanation was necessary. Summer could guess exactly what happened next. Her cousin was one of those people who only had to hear someone puke to then puke herself. "Say no more."

"It was humiliating," Lizzie whispered. "Kids screaming and crying. I lost my lunch all over a rug shaped like a dinosaur that one of the moms had made."

Well.

As excuses go, hers was a pretty solid one. Still, there was no guarantee it would happen this time. She tried another tack.

"My Swarovski tear drop earrings would look great with that dress."

Lizzie looked up from the pile of shoes she was rifling through in the bottom of her closet. "Is that a genuine offer, or are you trying to bribe me?"

"Both. Is it working?"

Her cousin plopped down on the bed and pulled on a pair of Steve Madden wedge heels. Summer sat down beside her, leaning her head on Lizzie's shoulder.

"Come on, Liz," she said softly. "Do it for Grandma Bonnie. You know what the school means to her. And Papa Harry is letting us live here rent-free. It's the least we can do to pay them back for all they've done for us."

"There's no 'we' here," Lizzie grumbled.

"I'll accompany you on the recorder to drown out any sounds the kids might make. I can play some weather-themed music."

Lizzie laughed. "That I'd like to see."

"Then you'll do it?"

Her cousin sighed dramatically. "I guess. If it means you and Papa Harry will stop asking. But I want every kid vetted for stomach issues before I get there."

Summer would have spilled her wine when she threw her arms around her cousin's shoulders, except she'd somehow already drained the glass. "Grandma will be so proud of us."

"Don't forget you promised me earrings," Lizzie said.

"Right." Summer swayed after popping up too quickly. "BRB."

She dashed into her room and grabbed the earrings when the doorbell rang.

"Oh no," Lizzie cried. "I'm not ready yet." She snatched the earrings from Summer's hand. "You have to stall him. I still need to finish my hair."

Summer looked down at the baggy flannel boxers she'd pulled on earlier when she got home from making the final preparations in her classroom. Had she even remembered to shave her legs today? Yesterday? The T-shirt she wore was tied in a knot at her waist, revealing the Ben and Jerry's induced swell of her belly. No way was she dressed to greet anyone, much less a hot jock.

"Oh no," she said. "I'm locking myself in my bedroom until you leave."

"I just agreed to your big ask," Lizzie hissed. "This is mine in return."

She slammed the bathroom door in Summer's face and locked it. Milli was barking like a fiend in the living room when the doorbell rang again. *Crap.* There was no time to wrap herself in a Snuggie.

Or refill her wine glass with liquid courage.

With a resigned sigh, Summer made her way to the front door. Milli's toenails were tapdancing on the oak floors as the dog prepared to launch herself at whoever was on the front porch. Summer positioned her leg awkwardly to prevent Milli from escaping and opened the door, revealing an unexpected familiar sight—none other than Monty's owner. She bit back a groan at the sight of the mouth she'd been having some serious dreams about last night. The eyes she'd been wondering about yesterday were hazel. And currently very bemused.

"You," she said, sounding just as priggish as she had the day before.

Monty's owner shoved his hands into the pockets of his sharply pressed khakis. "Uh, I hope I've got the right address. I'm looking for Elizabeth Pearson."

Of course, he was.

Summer was suddenly appalled she'd been fantasizing about her cousin's date.

"She's expecting a football player." In for a priggish penny, in for a priggish pound.

He rocked back on his heels. "Number eighty-one in your Growler's program and number one in fans' hearts. And the league's leading receiver, two seasons in a row."

"Wow." That explained Papa Harry's "big fan" comment from yesterday.

Milli whimpered as she clawed at Summer's leg to escape. No doubt the silly dog wanted to roll over and expose her lady parts to her lover's owner.

"*Asseyez-vous et comportez-vous,* Milli," Summer commanded. The dog neither sat nor behaved. Instead, the wee beast continued to struggle to get free.

Number Eighty-One chuckled. "I'm pretty sure the only French that dog understands is French fry."

Summer bristled with indignation. How dare he fat-shame her grandmother's adorably pudgy dog. "I'll have you know that Milli Chanel understands French perfectly. She's brilliant."

He cocked an eyebrow at her. "You don't say."

Crouching down on his haunches, he stared into Milli's eyes. Summer swore the dog sighed.

"*Voulez-vous manger vieilles chaussures,* Milli?"

Mother of God. The man was fluent in the language of love, not to mention bread and chocolate. Summer was shocked her panties hadn't spontaneously combusted as the perfectly accented words sensuously rolled off his tongue.

Milli seemed to be having the same reaction. The dog's eyes practically rolled back in her head as though he'd asked if she wanted cheese on her burger rather than if she wanted to eat old shoes.

Satisfied he had proved his point, he stood up with the lithe grace of a natural athlete and smirked at her. "I rest my case."

Milli whimpered at the loss of Monty's owner's undivided attention.

"Oww!" Summer yelped when the dog's claws broke the skin on her leg.

She hopped on one foot to the kitchen, leaving the guy to fend for himself with the little hussy that was her grandmother's dog. She snagged a paper towel and held it to her shin while pouring herself another glass of wine with her other hand. Who said she wasn't talented?

"They aren't acting in the movies. It actually does hurt like hell when you put alcohol on an open wound. You might want to hold onto something."

Great. Number Eighty-One made himself at home and followed her into the kitchen, cradling Milli in his arms. The dog was purring like a cat as she tried to burrow into his neck. Not that Summer could blame her. She'd gotten a whiff of him when they were at the door, and he smelled delicious. Like fresh soap and her grandmother's fabric softener.

Without the silly ball cap, his dirty blond surfer hair was finger-combed into a semblance of a style that made him look carefree and boyish. Add to that his lush lips, and the man was lethal to female hearts everywhere.

And he was all Lizzie's.

Summer downed half the glass of wine in one swallow.

He grinned at her. Not the potent smile he'd nearly taken her out at the knees with the day before. This was the gracious one reserved for his "big fans."

"That works, too." He stroked Milli's ears. The dog moaned as though she were in the throes of passion. "So. You and Elizabeth. You're sisters?"

"Cousins." She continued to press the paper towel to her leg while willing Lizzie to hurry up.

"Ah." He nodded. "I never connected the dots. I guess I don't even know Harry's last name. But he spent all afternoon bragging about his granddaughter, Summer, the talented cellist, and YouTube star. He never once mentioned Elizabeth." He tilted his head slightly. "I tried to find your YouTube channel, but the site says it's no longer available."

His comment stunned her, causing her to sputter mid-swallow. Damn straight her YouTube channel was no longer available. The thought of the millions of people watching her most embarrassing moment over and over again in perpetuity was unbearable. The idea that the hunky football player cuddling her grandmother's dog might have seen it had her stomach in knots.

"Papa Harry was talking about me? To you? Whatever for?"

Milli was snoring against his shoulder now. His fingers gently stroked the dog's fur as he carefully rested a hip against the counter. "He and his friends were in the pub at Sunset Glen talking about their plans for the Growler's pep band. They're playing at the picnic this afternoon. He said you might be joining them this season. He seemed pretty excited about it."

"Oh, no." She shook her wine glass at him. "He's trying to fix me up with their director. No way am I joining their band."

"That's too bad." He sounded genuinely disappointed. Of course, that could have been the effects of the wine she was guzzling. "Fans love the band. So do the guys on the team. They're what make Growlers home games so unique. "

He was calling her out for dissing the band. She was sure of it. Honestly, though, what business was it of his what she did or didn't do with her life? She opened her mouth to ask him that, but, thankfully, Lizzie appeared, saving her from making yet another prissy comment.

His mouth curved up in an appreciative expression when his eyes landed on Lizzie. Summer bit back a sigh because her cousin was, as always, gorgeous. Looking at the two of them together made her stomach sink. They looked like Malibu Ken and Barbie. Their children would be stunning.

Summer tossed back her wine glass, but it was empty. How had that happened? She debated pouring another glass but held off. Mainly because she still had to walk Milli, and the last thing she needed was to break an ankle drunk-dog-walking in the dark.

"Oh, Milli, get down," Lizzie scolded the dog. "You'll get hair all over Luke's shirt."

Her cousin was less of a dog person than she was, but in her case Summer wanted to be one. As far as she was concerned, one of the perks of staying in her grandparent's house was taking care of Milli.

She doubted Lizzie knew about Monty. Not her problem. She'd find out about the beastly lug when she moved from WAD to WAG status. What Summer wouldn't give to be a fly on the wall when that went down, though. She stifled a giggle at the thought.

Malibu Luke carried the still sleeping dog into the living room, where he gently deposited her onto her bed, giving them a nice glimpse of his drool-worthy butt. While his back was turned, Lizzie turned to Summer and shot her a questioning look. Summer shrugged. Lizzie mouthed, "Isn't he hot?"

So hot that the room was spinning.

Summer managed a quick thumbs-up before he turned back to them.

"Did you two get acquainted?" Lizzie asked.

"Actually, we met yesterday." He aimed another one of those gracious smiles in Summer's direction. "My grandmother and your grandfather are neighbors."

Lizzie's eyes went wide. "Seriously?"

Luke looked pleased while Lizzie looked. . .panicked.

"We'll have to join them in the pub for trivia night some evening," he suggested.

Lizzie didn't go to Sunset Glen. Ever. It was too difficult for her. Summer decided a rescue was in order. After all, her cousin had agreed to speak at career day.

"She doesn't get to see my grandparents that often," she said. "Her schedule being what it is, our grandmother is sundowning during the only time of day she can visit."

Lizzie's shoulders relaxed. "Um, yeah. And Papa Harry and I have a standing lunch date every week. It gives us an opportunity to visit while he gets a meal out."

Luke nodded. "I'm sure he enjoys that. Maybe my Gram and I can join you one day?"

Lizzie beamed at him. "We'd love to have you join us."

Summer bit back a snort. Lizzie would love any opportunity to be out and about with a nationally-known star. Especially since it helped her celebrity status in the process. No doubt Papa Harry would enjoy it, too, being such a "big fan" of Luke.

Except Summer was uncomfortable with the idea that it could be misconstrued as the two of them going on a double date with Papa Harry and Luke's Gram. Of course, it wasn't. But her grandparents' friends and neighbors wouldn't know that. She didn't want them to get the impression her grandfather was less than devoted to his wife. Because there was nothing further than the truth.

"Nice to see you again," Luke was saying as he led Lizzie to the door.

Summer saluted them with her empty wine glass. "Say hi to Papa Harry."

Lizzie halted in her tracks. "Papa Harry?"

"Didn't Luke tell you? The Growler pep band will be entertaining you at the picnic."

She could see the moment Lizzie realized her grandfather and his friends would be "chaperoning" her all afternoon. Papa Harry and his cronies could be a tad overbearing, but they meant well. At least Summer knew they did, but Lizzie didn't seem to think so. Her cousin's lips curled inward. "I forgot he was still involved with that group."

"It'll be fun at the games this year. Now that I know the guys, maybe they'll take requests when I score," Luke joked.

"Right. They'll be at the games, also," Lizzie said. "Fun." Her tone indicated she thought it would be anything but fun.

"I'll be there with them, too." That had to be the wine talking because Summer had no intention of working with the Growler pep band. It took her a full two seconds to realize she'd just said the exact opposite though.

Lizzie looked at her askance. Luke, however, was sporting that killer smile from yesterday. The one that made her want to do whatever it took to keep him smiling at her like that forever. And then he winked at her. As though by agreeing to play in the pep band, she'd passed some kind of test.

Or dare.

CHAPTER FOUR

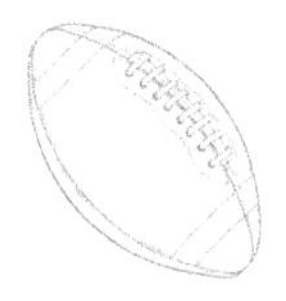

MONTY TROTTED beside Luke as they rounded the corner of the mile-long walking path at Sunset Glen. The community's Labor Day cookout was in full swing under a tent at the other end of the path. Luke decided to skip the pool party Jacobs and his wife threw for the receiving corps every year, instead hanging out with his Gram. After all, spending time with her was why he'd relocated her from Idaho.

That and she needed looking after.

Gram was reasonably healthy and agile for a seventy-eight-year-old woman. With the exception of her heart. It was three times too large. Not physically, but his father's mother had a habit of letting people take advantage of her. She was a sucker for every scam wrapped in a sob story.

Her generosity was one of the things Luke loved most about her, though. She'd been there for him when his parents were too absorbed in their own complicated love lives—both of them choosing someone else over him. Her home in Boise was a safe haven for a rebellious teenage boy who didn't understand why he wasn't lovable. But Gram loved him unconditionally, then and now. And for that, Luke would do whatever it took to make the rest of her life easy and peaceful.

That included moving her some 1,700 miles from the only place she'd ever lived. Luke's father, Grace Kessler's only child, lived in a sprawling house located in a gated suburb outside Dallas. He'd offered to move Gram into a guest house on his property, but she'd refused, saying it was too warm for her blood in Texas. Luke suspected that was simply a convenient excuse. Gram may have her son's college and pro-football jerseys hanging on her walls, but that was about all she could endure of his presence these days.

Luke could relate.

He and his father hadn't seen eye to eye since Luke followed in his footsteps and tried out as a walk-on for Boise State's football team. Jake Kessler feared his son's lackluster football skills might tarnish the older man's image. Not that he told his son that. Instead, his dad claimed to be worried about Luke's mental health when his son didn't make the team. After all, Luke didn't grow up playing the game as he had. Hockey was the game boys gravitated to in Canada.

Little did his father know, but the fact he believed his son *wouldn't* make the team was the tipping point in Luke's decision. His father's dismissive attitude spurred Luke to not only make the team but to be their best player, as well as a three-time All-American. And Gram was right there beside him the entire way. His biggest cheerleader.

Proving people wrong was Luke's greatest life skill.

Monty whined beside him before jerking ahead on the leash. The dog's tail thumped against Luke's thigh when he reined Monty into a semi-respectable heel.

"What's got you all excited, eh?"

The dog surprised him by replying with a bark. It was immediately answered by a much shriller one. He couldn't help but smile. It seemed his dog was smitten with the little French bulldog belonging to Elizabeth's grandmother.

"You have great taste, buddy. She's a good choice."

Just like Elizabeth.

She'd been the perfect date for the team's picnic, just as he'd known she would be. Some women were intimidated when interacting with the players and their wives. Not Elizabeth. She'd charmed them all with her sunny personality and natural poise. While he'd spent much of the picnic chatting up some other guy's soon-to-be fiancée, Elizabeth didn't complain. She'd been content to mingle without having him glued to her side all afternoon.

Other women he'd taken to team functions were all about the PDA, hanging off him at every opportunity. Elizabeth blushed gorgeously when he'd taken her hand in his in front of everyone, but she was reserved with any other outward displays. He got the sense she was more private, which suited him just fine. She certainly didn't hold back on her response to his kisses later in the evening.

There had always been a flirtatious spark between the two of them whenever he appeared on the morning news to promote a dog that needed adopting. He was relieved to discover the chemistry between them wasn't simply for the benefit of the television cameras. The next several months definitely looked promising.

Milli bounded into view. Summer was tripping over her flip-flops, trying to keep up with the tiny dog. Luke bit back a laugh. It amazed him that one of Harry Pearson's granddaughters could be so polished and put together while the other was such a hot mess.

The two dogs were on a collision course. Luke took pity on Summer and yanked Monty into a sit beside him. Summer managed to overtake Milli and scoop the dog into her arms at the last possible second. She skidded to a breathless stop a foot away from Luke and Monty.

This time he did laugh. Monty wiggled beside him. Summer narrowed her eyes at both of them. This close, he could see tiny flecks of gold sparkling in their coffee-colored depths. Her eyes were warm and soothing.

"What's so funny?"

Too bad the rest of her wasn't warm and soothing. Why was it that this woman wanted to bust his balls with every encounter?

"I find it funny that a grown-ass woman can't seem to control a dog."

"I can control her just fine." She gestured at Monty before seemingly realizing how close she was to the larger dog and taking a step back. "Except when your sex-starved dog is around."

Milli lunged at Monty with a whine that sounded more like a wail.

"I'd argue that your dog is hornier," he said.

She rolled her eyes. "Typical male. It's always the female's fault."

His gaze shot to her lips. She was always so busy using them to snipe at him, that he never noticed how full and pink they were. He let his eyes roam lower. She had ditched the hobo clothes today in favor of a cute red, white, and blue sundress. The striped fabric enhanced her luscious curves.

For fuck's sake.

He had no business checking out Elizabeth's cousin.

"If you'll excuse us, we'll be on our way. Enjoy your walk," she said before lifting her chin and flouncing past them. Milli glanced back over Summer's shoulder, making eyes at Monty. The idiot dog whimpered when Luke tugged him in the opposite direction.

Seconds later, the sound of Summer's screech filled the air. Luke and Monty hurried back down the path.

"Ow, ow, *ow*," she cried as she hopped toward one of the benches spread out along the trail. "Son of a biscuit."

Milli protested with a yelp when Summer nearly plopped down on top of her.

"What happened now?" Luke demanded.

"Go away!"

Shit.

Was she crying? He dropped to his haunches in front of her and grabbed her bare foot. A spiky ball from one of the sweet gum trees along the trail was embedded into the arch.

"This might hurt."

"Don't—ouch!"

He tossed the offending thing back into the brush. Both dogs followed it with their eyes but thankfully remained where they were. He rubbed his thumb over the bottom of her foot, applying pressure to where the thorn had entered to quell any bleeding. A long moment later, he lifted his gaze to her face. A pair of dilated pupils stared back at him. He froze when she bit her lip.

She came to her senses before he did.

"Are you trying to look up my dress?" she accused with that prim schoolmarm voice of hers.

He swore beneath his breath because, for a moment there, he was actually considering that very thing. And because he enjoyed pushing her buttons, he let her know.

"Summer Pearson, if I were going to look up your skirt, you'd know it. Because you would be begging me to do that and a whole hell of a lot more."

The blush was back. This time not only on her cheeks but her neck and chest as well. She opened her mouth before quickly closing it again. He skimmed his palm up her calf before lifting her leg and draping her injured foot over the opposite knee.

"Sit. Stay," he commanded the three of them before going to retrieve her missing flip-flop. When he returned, he crouched back down and slipped the star-studded thong onto her foot. "There you go, Cinderella. You're ready for the ball."

"Thank you," she whispered.

He lifted his head to meet her gaze. Her eyes held a look of sheer terror. For a split second, he wondered what he'd done now. But then he saw that Monty was resting his massive head on her thigh. It was the dog that frightened her.

"Monty, off." The dog didn't listen. "He's worried about you." He reached up to grab the dog by the collar, but she swatted his hand away.

"No."

Then she cautiously laid her palm on top of Monty's head. Sighing, the dog shoved in closer. Milli whined, wanting in on the action. Luke snatched her up instead.

"Nope. We're going to finish your walk while these two get acquainted."

He took the dog several yards down the path. After a few minutes of dawdling, Milli finally relieved herself, and the two returned to the bench. Summer and Monty hadn't moved. Her hand stroked from the top of his head down to his shoulder blades. Monty's eyes were closed, and his breathing was even, as though he were asleep. That was *not* a slither of jealousy tightening up Luke's groin. He lifted Milli onto his lap and joined Summer on the bench.

"You didn't have to do that," she said softly, her eyes still trained on Monty. "Walking her is the only exercise I get in a day."

Luke snorted. "First of all, this dog doesn't walk. She stops and starts. You're not going to get any real exercise that way. Secondly, you should never walk a dog in flip flops."

She did lift her chin then, shooting him a look through her lush lashes. "I've never had a dog before. I didn't know there were rules."

Whoa. Was that actual flirtatious charm Summer was throwing his way? Apparently she could use those full lips of hers for something other than snark. He was surprised how much he liked it.

He shook his head to regroup. Summer was Elizabeth's cousin. Elizabeth was his Seasonal Arm Candy.

For crying out loud.

Now he was using the condescending label his teammates created. *Damn it.* Elizabeth was *not* a booty call. She was an attractive, well-respected, intelligent woman. Someone to help him fill up his free time during the season while everyone else he knew enjoyed their families.

He jumped to his feet, frustrated at the route his mind was taking.

"Not rules. Simple common sense. But if there were rules, you wouldn't be walking anywhere without a damn keeper," he replied testily. Monty lifted his head and gave Luke a dirty look. Milli squirmed in his arms. "I hear the band starting up. I need to make sure Gram is down at the party. Are you okay to walk?"

"Oh, for crying out loud." She stood up from the bench. "It was only a sticker."

"Well, you screamed as though a snake or something worse had bitten you." He grabbed Monty's leash and headed back toward the community center, Milli still in his arms. Behind him, Summer mumbled something that sounded a lot like "jackass." He looked back over his shoulder at her. She stuck out her tongue.

"Can I have my grandmother's dog back?"

"That depends on whether or not you trip and fall in the next fifty feet. It's a good thing the Growler's band doesn't march. You'd be the laughing stock of Milwaukee."

She was beside him in a flash. "And that's your fault, too!"

"Too? What the hell are you talking about?"

"I had no intention of joining the band, and you knew it. Then I was suddenly in it. All because of you."

Luke stopped short. "Hold up. How does that have anything to do with me?"

She mashed her fists into her hips. "You dared me."

He laughed. She ground her teeth. He laughed harder.

"You did. And you know it. If you hadn't goaded me, I would never have told Lizzie I was joining the band."

Luke wanted to wipe his eyes, but both hands were holding a dog. "Sweetheart, I didn't make you do anything. That was all you." He grinned at her. "And the wine."

He moved on down the path, still grinning ear to ear. She tramped along beside him.

"I'll admit the wine played a small part," she surprised him by saying. "But you were goading me when you were waxing on about how wonderful everyone thinks the Growler band is."

"They do, and they are."

She might have snarled beside him. The sound made him laugh again.

"How about this? I dare you not to have fun being in the band," he said, issuing another challenge with bravado. Luke excelled at throwing out dares and challenges. It was what kept him relevant among his teammates. Not that he wanted to be relevant with Summer. He enjoyed frustrating her, that was all.

She reached over and plucked Milli from his arms. "Of course, I'll have fun. Fun is my middle name."

He was doubled over with laughter now.

"What's so amusing this time?" she demanded.

Luke held up a hand while he tried to catch his breath. Milli and Monty looked between the two humans as if they were watching a tennis match.

"You are." He grabbed his side. "I hate to break it to you, but your middle name isn't 'Fun.' It's 'Stick in the Mud.'"

Summer screwed up her face. "My fifth graders aren't as obnoxious as you."

She clutched Milli closer and stormed ahead. Monty pulled on the leash to follow.

Luke chuckled as he and Monty moved to catch up. "Your cousin doesn't have any issues with my charming personality."

Summer made a sound deep in her throat but said nothing. What the hell did that sound mean? They walked a little farther, and she still said nothing. Alarm bells starting going off in his head. Elizabeth was into him.

Wasn't she?

"She doesn't," he insisted.

Summer shrugged half-heartedly.

She was punking him. She had to be. There was no way he could be that far off base here. Elizabeth was into him. She certainly kissed him like she was. He'd kissed a few women in his day and definitely knew when they were interested.

He stepped in front of Summer, halting her progress. "What exactly did she say?"

"Nothing." Another shrug. "And that's not like her. There was no blissful afterglow either. Probably because she was home before her eleven o'clock curfew."

He blew out a frustrated breath. "Maybe I'm not one of those guys who sleeps with a woman on the first date."

Summer snorted and stepped around him. "Said no man ever. And that is not what I was insinuating. Lizzie can't help but dish about the guys she dates ad-nauseam. This morning, she was mum. I know this may be a blow to your ego, but you might not have shown her your best moves last night. You're going to have to try harder, bub."

The woman had more than one screw loose. That's all there was to it. She was just yanking Luke's chain. Probably because she was jealous of her popular cousin.

She took a few steps before turning back around. "Oh, God. Maybe you didn't show her your best moves because you're not into *her*. Wow. Two in a row. There's a first for everything." She closed the distance between them. "Please, all I ask is that you break it to her gently. She's still a bit fragile after the mess with Josh. And I really need to make it through the next sixteen weeks in relative calm."

He looked down to where her fingers were now clutching his forearm. His skin sizzled at the connection. She followed his gaze before abruptly jerking her hand away.

Jesus, he needed to get away from this woman before she dragged him aboard the crazy bus she was driving.

"I'm not planning on ending anything," he stated firmly.

Summer slowly nodded. They were steps away from the tent where the residents had assembled for the cookout. They stood there in charged silence for a moment before being interrupted by one of the residents.

Scratch that.

Not just one of the residents but the nosiest one around. If they were doing a reboot of "The Golden Girls," Mrs. Hilbert could easily be cast as Sophia. The always elegantly dressed septuagenarian was petite, quick with the wisecracks, a busybody, and never without a designer bag.

"There you are." Mrs. Hilbert offered her powdered cheek for Luke to kiss. The older woman was responsible for arranging Declan Fletcher's marriage. She was also the mother of a prominent sports agent who represented a few of the Growlers.

"Hey there, Mrs. H. How are you?"

The woman eyed both Luke and Summer shrewdly. "I'm doing well. I was chatting with your grandmother. We are so excited to have Grace living here. She's going to fit in wonderfully."

Her words should have been music to his ears. But coming from Mrs. Hilbert, the statement sent a shiver up his spine. The woman was trouble with a capital "T." She carried a flask of Fireball whisky in her purse, for crying out loud. She and her geezer squad were always getting into some sort of jam. He wasn't sure Gram could handle some of the wilder residents.

She turned her rheumy gaze toward Summer. "You must be Harry's other granddaughter. At least one of you comes around to visit. Here, give me that dog. Your grandmother is getting anxious for her."

"I can take her," Summer said.

"Nonsense." Milli went to Mrs. Hilbert as though the woman had kibble in her purse along with the Fireball. "You two stay here and finish—" She looked over at Luke. "—whatever this is."

Summer stared after Mrs. Hilbert's retreating back. "She misspoke about Lizzie. She doesn't come because she can't."

"Yeah. Her schedule. You mentioned that."

She drew in a deep breath. "It's not easy watching someone slip away. Especially when that person played such an important role in our lives. My grandmother is the anchor for all of us. She demonstrated the living embodiment of love every day. There isn't a more giving person on this earth." She pinned him with a beseeching look. "It's not Lizzie's fault she handles things the way she does. Be kind to her, okay?"

With that, she hurried off after Mrs. Hilbert. As exasperating as the screwball woman was, he had to admire her for standing up for her cousin. Obviously, he was off base about her being jealous of Elizabeth. Which meant she might have been telling the truth. Luke needed to up his game.

Challenge accepted, Summer Pearson.

CHAPTER FIVE

"We should be sipping wine on the terrace right now," Paige declared. "It's our first day of school tradition."

Summer held the phone with one hand while tugging on a piece of rope she'd bought at the pet store with the other. Milli pulled on the rope's other end, snorting and snuffling furiously. She laughed at the little dog's embarrassed grunt when she fell back on her tail, the rope smacking the wee thing right on the white heart-shaped spot on her chest.

"At least you get to have tea with Grandma Bonnie," Paige went on.

"If she wakes up from her nap on time. She's been sleeping a lot more lately. But I'll Facetime you. Then I can be jealous that you're drinking wine while I'm making do with tepid Earl Gray."

Summer dropped the pull toy so she could swipe at a bee buzzing toward the dregs of her frozen custard. She justified the pitstop at Kopp's as a necessary compensation for missing happy hour with her best friend. Milli circled twice before happily sprawling out with her chew toy on a beach towel Summer borrowed from Papa Harry's linen closet. After yesterday's mishap on the walking trail, she decided that a little picnic on the grassy area next to the senior community's pool was a better way to give Milli some exercise.

"So, tell me everything," Paige demanded. "Start with breakfast."

Summer snorted. At Preston, the parents catered a breakfast for the staff to kick off the year. No such luck at her new school. Someone brought in a box of donut holes, but there had been nothing left except some crumbs by the time Summer found the teacher's lounge.

"Things are a lot different in public school," she said. "I barely got time to shovel down my lunch."

"What about the other teachers? What are they like?"

"Fortunately for me, my reputation did not precede me. Not big YouTube music fans, I guess. To them, I'm a long-term sub who won't be teaching there by the time they come up for air during the holidays. Although the resource officer winked at me as I was leaving today."

"Yeah, that's not creepy at all."

"I think I won a few of them over when they found out Lizzie is coming to speak at career day next month. Honestly, I think the teachers will be more in awe of her than the kids."

"What's the scoop on this football player the Princess has lured in? What's he like?"

Arrogant. Annoying. Manipulative. Exasperating.

And ridiculously intriguing.

And the real reason she and Milli were avoiding the path today. She needed to keep her distance from Luke Kessler. The man got under skin.

Not to mention he was off-limits. Luke was dating her picture-perfect cousin. She had no business fantasizing about him while in the shower. Or anywhere else, damn it.

But there had been a moment yesterday when she'd sensed *something* from him. Something that felt an awful lot like longing.

Which was impossible because, once again for the back of the class, he was dating the perfect Pearson granddaughter.

The successful one.

The one who never, ever, choked.

"Summer?" Paige's voice helped to refocus her meandering thoughts.

"Uh, he's okay. You know, if you go for the whole spoiled jock thing."

"Mmm. I googled him. He's not just okay. He's freaking hot. Those eyes. And that smile. Yum. But please make me feel better by telling me that he has bad breath or grunts or something."

"Haven't gotten close enough to smell his breath," she lied. She knew for a fact that Luke Kessler smelled fantastic. It was so unfair. "And I hate to disappoint you, but he speaks in full sentences."

In French, also.

"Sheesh. The Princess did always rebound well. Do you think she can hook us up with tickets to a game?"

Summer rested back on her palm. "Actually, it looks like I'm not going to need a ticket to get into the games. I'm going to be helping out with the Growler pep band."

She was still reeling with how the whole thing came about. But once she'd committed to it, her mind began to whir with musical arrangements and possibilities. Of course, it wasn't the same as arranging music for the string ensemble she'd been performing with for the past five years. But she'd done her student teaching for a high school band director who'd given her carte blanch to create tunes for the school's pep band. This would be similar.

"A pep band?" Paige croaked. "You're a cellist. A very successful cellist at that. One with serious OCD about the humidity and temperature where you store your instrument. I'm having trouble visualizing you in the stands during a Milwaukee snow storm playing Bach."

"I'm not a cellist any longer, remember?" Summer explained. "And I'll be arranging the music and directing. Not playing."

Paige sighed. "I guess it says something that you haven't totally given up on your music."

Not her music.

Just her dream.

"Although I'll pass on sitting with you at the games. Silver foxes aren't my thing," her friend added. "Maybe the Princess can introduce me to someone else on the team."

"They're not all in AARP." At least she hoped her grandfather hadn't lied to her. "Did I tell you the saxophonist who organizes the pep band is a fireman? A single fireman. I'm meeting him for drinks tomorrow night."

Mike Runson had sounded genuinely relieved to hand off arranging the music to Summer. He had enough on his plate trying to keep the rowdy band members in line. From what he described, the geriatric set could be as uncooperative as hormonal teenagers.

They'd talked on the phone for nearly thirty minutes the night before. Her grandfather was right, as always. It would be nice having people her age who share a common interest to hang out with. And if the guy turned out to be as friendly as he sounded, all the better.

"Ooooh. Now you're talking," Paige said. "Okay, find out if he has any cute friends, and I'll consider sitting with the band at the games."

"Deal." Summer's phone buzzed with a reminder. "Crap. I've got to get moving if my grandmother is going to spend any time with Milli. I've got an LSAT study group meeting at Marquette tonight I need to get to."

"Ah-ha! There's the roommate I know and love. Overscheduled and thriving again. And to think I was worried the sofa had zapped all of your overachieving juju. For what it's worth, I still think you'll be wasting your talents on torts and briefs instead of treble clefs and concertos."

"Yeah, yeah. I'll call you tonight for a 'Bachelor' recap." Summer sprang to her feet and shoved her phone into her pocket. "Come on, mon Cherie. Let's go see Grandmere."

Trotting beside her, the dog proudly carried one end of the rope toy in her mouth while the other end dragged along the grass. They'd almost made it to the memory care building when the woman from yesterday called to Summer from across the narrow parking lot.

"Yahoo!" The petite woman was rather spry for her age, dashing across the blacktop without looking. "Oh, I'm so glad I caught you."

Milli tried to bark a welcome, but she couldn't do it with the rope in her mouth. Summer wrapped the dog in the beach towel and lifted her into her arms. She quickly realized her mistake when Milli shook her head, beaning Summer in the eye with the toy.

Just the look Summer was going for at her meeting with a group of undergrads tonight, a shiner.

"Ooh, that's gonna leave a mark," the other woman pointed out, needlessly.

"Um, did you need something?" Summer asked with a bit less tact than she should have. But, hey, her eye stung something fierce.

"As it so happens, I do. I need you. Well, you and your cello."

That got Summer's attention. "I'm sorry?"

"I'd like to hire you to play the cello this Friday night at happy hour," the woman said matter-of-factly. "How much do you charge for, say, an hour?"

More than you can afford, Summer wanted to say. But that would imply she still performed. And something told her the woman standing before her was as persistent as Milli with her chew toy. So, she opted for the truth.

"I'm sorry, but I can't."

The lady narrowed her eyes. "Can't? Or won't?"

Summer had judged correctly. There was nothing sweet about this particular little old lady. "Who are you, exactly?"

She pressed her glasses to the bridge of her nose. "My apologies. I'm Mrs. Hilbert. One of the residents here. Your grandfather plays poker with my boyfriend, Fred."

Boyfriend?

Well, wasn't that freaking great? This old broad could get a guy while Summer and Paige were still drowning in the dating pool.

"Then you should ask my grandfather and his jazz quartet to play at happy hour," she suggested. "They will keep things lively."

This time she rolled her eyes at Summer. "A jazz quartet? No one wants to hear the Boogie Woogie at a wedding proposal."

"A wedding proposal?" *Seriously?*

Mrs. Hilbert crossed her arms over her chest. "Yes. That's what I've been trying to tell you. Sharon is going to propose to Gary on Friday night. And she wants some romantic music playing in the background. Some Mendelson or Pachelbel."

"*She's* proposing to *him*?"

"It's not like she's got all the time in the world to wait for him to get around to it."

Well, then.

Something fluttered deep in Summer's chest. Sharon and Gary didn't have all the time in the world. She had only to think of her grandparents to know that. Summer was convinced it was her grandfather's unwavering love that kept her grandmother strong in the face of literally losing her mind. Didn't everyone deserve a love like theirs? Especially later in life?

"That's very sweet," she replied, because it truly was. It still didn't sway her, however. She sighed with regret. "But I can't do it." The idea of playing in front of people again had a cold sweat breaking out on the back of her neck. "I can ask around to see if I can find someone else available if you like."

"No." Mrs. Hilbert all but stomped her foot. "I don't 'like.' Your grandfather said you are *You Too* famous, whatever that means. And that you were invited to perform with the Vienna Symphony Orchestra."

Damn Papa Harry. "Do you see me in Vienna?" Summer asked tersely.

"Oh, posh on those snooty Viennese. What do they know? Have you seen the size of the sausages they serve there? Puny. No bigger than my thumb." She held out her gnarled thumb for comparison. "Nothing like the brats we serve. Now, those are some wieners, I tell ya."

Summer choked out a laugh. The woman had her wanting to check the back of her head for injuries, because everything that came out of Mrs. Hilbert's mouth blindsided her.

"I appreciate your interest, Mrs. Hilbert. I really do. And I certainly want Sharon and Gary to have a special proposal. But I'm being honest when I tell you this is not a case of 'won't.' It's 'can't.'"

Milli must have sensed her distress, because she dropped her rope and nuzzled Summer's neck. Mrs. Hilbert stepped closer, laying a hand on the dog's back.

"Come on, Toots, you've got to get back on the horse sometime. A talent like yours is not something to waste. And it wouldn't be as though you are giving a performance. I won't pay you if that's what is making you nervous. Just you playing your cello in front of a bunch of seniors. Half of them can't hear, and most of them don't know a dang thing about that Hickory Dickory Dock app, much less how to watch a *You Too* video."

Heaven help her from this woman. Summer meant to shake her head no, but Mrs. Hilbert saw her slight hesitation and went in for the kill shot.

"Your grandmother will be there. I'm sure she'd love to hear you play."

It was only after Summer agreed that she realized the shrewd biddy had effectively maneuvered her into playing for free.

That night, the nightmares started.

"This morning's rehearsal when exceedingly well," Summer's brother, Sterling, remarked.

He and Summer were waiting in the green room of the Mozart Hall in the Vienna Concert House. Excitement pulsed through her hearing the hum of the audience as they filed in to take their seats.

"The director mentioned the possibility of extending the tour from six months to nine, possibly a year," Sterling continued.

A whole year sitting in with the Vienna chamber orchestra as they toured Europe and the U.S., playing the music she loved. Talk about a dream come true. She blew out a breath to steady her nerves.

"The chair of the music school at Northwestern also reached out today," her brother said. "They'd love to talk to you about putting together a course on building your brand on YouTube. It seems you've started a trend. We should talk about it before you speak to him, though. It could be a lucrative additional revenue stream we haven't considered. I don't want you to give anything away."

She laughed. "How much of a cut are you taking from my earnings, anyway?"

Sterling grinned, the dimples he'd inherited from their father winking at her. After misspending his teenage years, he'd barely made it into the University of Illinois. Once there, he'd lived by the adage "C's get degrees" and continued to fully enjoy all that college life had to offer. Much to their mother's disdain.

But then he'd surprised them all by actually getting into law school and graduating. Not at the top of his class as their parents had, but that didn't matter. He'd made a name for himself during his internships, landing a plum associate's position at one of Chicago's premier law firms. When Summer's YouTube channel took off, she'd enlisted his help with keeping track of the financial and legal end of things.

"I'm pretty sure I'm not taking enough of a fee," he joked. "Who knew how much you could make having a YouTube side-hustle. Playing the cello, no less."

She'd fallen into the whole YouTube thing. On a lark, she'd taken her cello to a friend's birthday picnic in Grant Park. Paige filmed her playing various covers of current hits. Several guests asked if they could have the recording. A friend created a YouTube channel, and before Summer knew it, she had a couple of thousand followers. Several of the channel's followers made requests for particular songs, and the audience grew. Soon she was taking her cello to various places in Chicago and recording songs. An impromptu Christmas concert in the snow saw her audience climb to six figures, and she was suddenly an Internet sensation. Two years later, she had well over a million followers and an income that surpassed anything she made in the classroom or playing in the ensemble. And now, an invitation to guest star with one of the top chamber orchestras in the world.

"The Judge will have to take my career choice seriously now," she told her brother.

Sterling's face softened. "She's never dissed your career, Squirt."

Summer gaped at her brother. His smile was resigned as he nodded.

"Okay, maybe a smidge. But she looks at the world differently than you or I." He sighed. "Losing Dad changed her."

"That's the understatement of the century."

"She wants to see both our futures secure. There was a time when she wasn't sure she could provide for us. I'm not saying she's right. Just that I can finally understand where she's coming from." He placed his hands on her shoulders. "She's stinking proud of you. You should have seen her at the hotel this morning. She was telling perfect strangers about her 'gifted' daughter."

"I still can't believe you both came."

"I can't believe you thought we wouldn't." He brushed a kiss over her forehead. "Now, go out there and live your dream. If anyone deserves this, you do."

One of the stage directors stuck his head into the room. "We will be ready for you in five minutes, Ms. Pearson."

"I better go find my seat. The cameras are all set up. They're only allowing us to Livestream the first song, but it will be the crown jewel in your channel. People who've never been to an orchestra concert will be snatching up tickets right and left."

Sterling gave her a quick salute and was gone. Summer figured she ought to find a restroom before she took the stage. She hurried to the ladies' lounge, but a pair of raised voices in the hall stopped her in her tracks.

"You are denigrating the reputation of our chamber by allowing this woman to play with us," a thick accented male voice said.

"This chamber can't exist on reputation alone. Fewer and fewer people are coming to see us play. We need to reach a newer, younger audience to keep our music alive," another man argued.

"And you think bringing in a woman who has no pedigree, and no real performance background will give us that?" He made an ugly sound with his throat. "She is a gimmick. Not an artist. Mongrels with no musical education like her videos, and you think that represents talent? You are demeaning the expertise of all the other musicians who belong in those chairs with this performance."

The blood was rushing through her ears so loudly, she didn't hear the rest.

"Ms. Pearson?"

Summer turned to find the stage director waiting for her.

"We are ready for you," he announced.

She opened her mouth to tell him she wasn't ready, but no sound came out. He smiled encouragingly at her as he gestured to the stage door.

"If you'll follow me."

And like a lamb to slaughter, she did, numbly finding her chair to the left of the director, and front and center to the rest of the orchestra.

The same musicians that her performance was demeaning.

A gimmick.

The man's cruel words washed over her. Her palms began to sweat, making the curl of her cello slick. Her bow slid between her fingertips.

No pedigree.

Mongrels.

Suddenly she was lightheaded, the bright stage lights blinding her as the curtain went up. The applause felt like cannon fodder against her now throbbing head. The director was moving to his podium. He nodded at Summer. The red lights on the cameras indicated they were broadcasting. The music began to flow behind her. Her heart pounded so loudly she assumed it would drown out the song. Too soon, the director pointed his baton at her.

But Summer didn't move.

She woke with a start, her body drenched with sweat. Sucking in a lungful of air, she tried to get her heart rate down from Olympic sprinter-level to couch potato zone. From her spot at the end of the bed, Milli squinted at her with one eye as if to let Summer know she was peeved at having her sleep disturbed.

"You have a perfectly fine bed of your own," she choked out.

The dog rolled over and put her back to her. Summer flopped back down onto her pillows. She was sharing her bed with a dog. Worse, it wasn't even her bed. It was a bed in her grandparent's house. This was what her life had been reduced to.

"I can't do it," she said to the ceiling.

But that busybody, Mrs. Hilbert, wasted no time telling Papa Harry.

"Your grandmother lives for your music. This will be so wonderful for her," he'd told her. "She'll be tickled pink to hear you play in person."

Your grandmother lives for your music.

Doing whatever it took to make her grandmother's last years pleasurable was the main reason Summer had come to Milwaukee. After all, her grandmother was the reason Summer fell in love with music in the first place. And she would do just about anything to see Grandma Bonnie smile. Even, apparently, if it meant the possibility of humiliating herself again.

CHAPTER SIX

THE MOOD in the locker room was light after Friday's practice. Tomorrow the Growlers would have a brief run-through in the afternoon before heading to the hotel near the stadium downtown. Luke loved those Saturday nights together, bonding with the guys over cards, college football, and video games. After years of searching, he'd found his tribe. The place he finally fit in. And, if he was lucky, he had seven more months to enjoy being a part of something.

Not only that, but he'd been able to debunk Summer's accusation that Elizabeth wasn't into him. He'd sent flowers to the station Tuesday morning. She showed them off to her morning viewers and on her social media feeds, complete with the requisite heart emojis. Because of her early schedule, he'd had to settle for lunch on Tuesday as their only date this week. She'd chosen a stuffy country club restaurant where they could barely get a bite of their food before someone stopped at their table to say hello and snap a selfie with them.

It seemed Elizabeth was more than eager to fill up her social media feed with photos of them together. Including one of her kissing his cheek. Fine with Luke. One of the reasons he chose the women he did was to paint a portrait of the upbeat, well-adjusted sports star. Dating successful women like Elizabeth made him look like he belonged. It allowed him to flaunt in the faces of those who had denied him their love when he was a child that he had survived anyway. And he was doing pretty damn great, thank you very much.

Tonight, they were invited to have dinner with Fletcher and his wife. Elizabeth had texted him a picture of herself in a very sexy dress that might be over the top for dinner but definitely suggested he was getting dessert. He was looking forward to the evening. Elizabeth was a fabulous conversationalist who could charm the kilt off the studious Scot. Afterward, Luke would take his time undressing Elizabeth. Her nutjob cousin was wrong to even try to put doubts in Luke's head.

He whistled the Growler's fight song as he grabbed his gym bag and headed for the exit.

Wash poked his head out of his office as Luke went past. "You got a minute, Kessler?"

"For you, Coach, I have two."

He dropped his bag into one of the two chairs in front of Wash's desk before plopping down into the other one.

The receivers' coach shook his head, taking the seat behind the desk. "The apple doesn't fall far from the tree. Both you and your father are smart mouths."

The mention of his dad had Luke instantly tensing up. Wash had been on the receiving end of many of Jake Kessler's passes when the two played together in Dallas. Some people around the league whispered that it was Wash who made Jake Kessler such a successful quarterback. The man had the hands of an octopus, catching anything thrown in his direction and making it look like the ball was supposed to be thrown to that spot.

Luke spent years dissecting the game films. He didn't have to whisper that Lenny Washington was the reason his father was cited as a Hall of Fame candidate. He knew it was true.

"Time's a tickin'." Luke forced his tone and his body to appear relaxed.

"H-hot date with the meteorologist tonight?"

Relaxing came a bit easier with the subject change. He was counting on things getting pretty steamy after their dinner. "As a matter of fact, I do. But I need to stop over at Sunset Glen to check on Gram before that."

Coach Washington nodded with a grin. "You're a good man."

Luke nodded along with him, making a grab for his gym bag as he did. "Well, nice chat."

"Hold up, funny man. As much as you d-deserve the compliment, that's not why I called you in here."

Luke was afraid of that.

"I have a request."

From the way he said it, Luke suspected that whatever words came out of Wash's mouth next wouldn't be a request. They'd be more of a command.

"I need you to room with McGraff instead of Jacobs."

Definitely a command. And not one with which Luke was comfortable. One of the perks of being a veteran player on the team was rooming with another veteran. Rookies roomed with rookies. Period.

Luke wasn't normally one to buck the system. In this case, though, he decided to test the waters. He liked rooming with Jacobs. Despite his showboat personality, the guy was a family man with very few annoying quirks.

McGraff, on the other hand, was fresh out of college with wild oats to sow. Luke may appear nonchalant about the game, but he took football—and his game prep—very seriously. He didn't need any room parties keeping him up all night.

"Why?"

Wash ran his fingers over his brow. "Because the boy has a ch-chip on his shoulder so huge he should be s-stooped over like a damn hunchback. Coach Gibson wants to n-nip it in the bud.

We figure some of your can-do attitude might rub off on the kid."

"There's nobody else you could buddy him up with?"

Wash arched an eyebrow at him. It was definitely out of character for Luke to protest a "request" from any of the coaches, much less the Growler head coach, Heath Gibson.

"What would you have me do? Make him b-bunk with Jacobs?"

Luke groaned. "That would be a disaster." One that would likely spill over to the field. Not what the Growlers needed to kick off their season.

"Mmmhmm."

"Fine." Luke released a beleaguered sigh as he stood up. "But I'm not making any promises."

"You did to me." Kane Palmer stepped into the doorway. "You're going to help me propose to my girl, remember?"

With the bad news delivered and the outcome he wanted, Coach Washington waved both men out of his office. Luke hefted his bag back onto his shoulder.

"I said I would," he told the punter. "Have you ever known me to go back on my word?"

"Nope." Palmer grinned and slapped him on the back. "So watcha got planned?"

They stepped outside, and Luke pulled on his sunglasses. Not only to protect his eyes from the late-day sun but to keep Palmer from seeing the truth. He didn't have anything planned. Despite spending thirty minutes trying to weasel something out of the guy's girlfriend last weekend, he was no closer to coming up with the perfect proposal than when he brashly offered to help. He was beginning to think neither lovebird had a romantic idea in their head.

Of course, neither did Luke. Romance wasn't his thing. Love wasn't his thing. It was for everyone else. Just never for him. If he'd learned anything growing up, he'd learned that.

"When will you have the ring?" he deflected.

"I'm headed down to Chicago to pick it up Tuesday. It's a beauty."

"I'm sure it is." Luke unlocked his truck. Palmer wasn't the type to sit around and wait for the right moment. And there was always the possibility the airhead would lose the ring before putting it on Shaina's finger. Which meant Luke would have to come up with something quickly.

"Have you asked her dad's permission?" he said.

Palmer rocked back on his heels, a cat-ate-the-canary grin on his face. "Yep. And they're coming in next weekend for the game. I'd like to pop the question while they're here so we can have one of those glitzy after-parties, you know? With all my friends and teammates."

Shiiiiit.

That meant he needed to come up with something fast.

"We'll finalize the details tomorrow night," he promised, hoping like hell he could devise a suitable idea before then. There was always Google. "I'm on it," he said to Palmer as he climbed into his truck.

Still grinning, the punter saluted him. "You're a good man."

That was the second time someone had said that to him in the last five minutes. Too bad being "good" had never been enough.

After a quick pitstop home to change his clothes and feed Monty, he pulled into the parking lot of Sunset Glen. Despite it being barely five, the main building was bustling. Residents were shuffling around the lobby on their way to the bar in the center's atrium, where Friday happy hour sounded like it was in full swing. Luke decided that was as good a place as any to look for Gram.

As soon as he entered the atrium, he spotted her. The smile on her face was dazzling. He couldn't remember the last time he'd seen her so content. It gave him a tremendous sense of relief that he'd made the right decision to bring her here.

But it was the object of Gram's smile that had him stopping in his tracks. Summer Pearson was seated on a small stage at the front of the atrium, a cello nestled between her knees. Eyes closed, her head gently bobbed to the incredible sounds she created each time she stroked the bow over the strings. The Frank Sinatra song she was covering echoed off the high ceiling.

Luke couldn't take his eyes off her. There was something so damn erotic about the way she was caressing the instrument. The way it seemed to be an extension of her body. The way she was practically making love to it in order to coax out the beautiful sounds.

Fierce desire suddenly washed over him. The desire to feel her hands gliding over his body. To be the lucky shit between her legs instead of that cello. To have her coax a benediction of ecstasy from his lips.

What in the hell?

He was fantasizing about kooky Summer of all people. The hot mess cousin of the perfect woman who was likely going to be a sure thing tonight. Luke sucked in a ragged breath. It had been a while, that was all. But he was going to remedy that situation in a matter of hours.

With Elizabeth.

Not Summer.

He forced his gaze away from her and glanced around the atrium. It seemed the rest of the audience was enjoying the concert as much as his gram. Heads were nodding, toes were tapping, and there was even a couple swaying together near the stage. Some of the staff were handing out glasses of what looked like champagne to the residents.

Summer finished her song with a flourish, and the crowd applauded. Harry Pearson and his friends let out a few catcalls making her blush. Mrs. Hilbert stepped out in front of the crowd.

"Isn't she wonderful?" she asked. The residents cheered. "Thank you, Summer, for helping us celebrate Gary and Sharon's engagement this evening." She gestured to the couple who'd been dancing together. Both of them beamed at Summer before returning their gazes to each other. "Now, let's all raise our glasses and toast the happy couple."

Hold up.

Did she say those two geezers just got engaged? And Summer was serenading them with her cello? He felt the smug grin tugging at the corners of his lips. That was it. The answer to his dilemma was sitting right in front of him. Smart-mouthed Summer Pearson and her cello.

He could hire her to play while Palmer proposed. It was simple yet sophisticated. Shaina would eat it up. Now all he had to do was find some romantic spot in Milwaukee to pull it off. Assuming, of course, he could convince a usually crabby Summer to go along with his plan. The woman had the annoying habit of doing the opposite of what he expected.

Then again, Luke loved a challenge. There wasn't a dare he could resist. And Summer Pearson was a dare wrapped up in form-fitting black pants and a peek-a-boo white blouse. He was suddenly looking forward to the verbal sparring that was sure to come.

Donning his game face, he headed over to her. She didn't look up, her focus on gently wiping down the bow. "That was amazing," he said truthfully.

She started at his words. When she glanced up, she looked slightly awed herself. As though she didn't know she was capable of making such beautiful music. "Um, thank you," she replied before lovingly tracing the curly top of the cello with her fingertips.

He ignored the tightening in his groin. "Your grandfather wasn't exaggerating about your talent."

Her lips curled up into a sly grin. "Couldn't picture me as anything more than a klutzy drunk, huh?"

"No."

She arched an eyebrow at him.

Damn it. She was twisting his words. "I meant 'no' as in that's not what I thought."

Chuckling, she bent over to tuck the instrument inside its velvet-lined case, giving him a bird's eye view of her rounded ass. A sheen of sweat formed along his shirt collar.

For the love of God, you've seen plenty of women's asses before. Get a grip, man.

He tore his eyes away and got down to business.

"It just so happens I'm looking for a musician to accompany a wedding proposal next weekend."

She shot up straight, an astonished expression on her face. "Proposal?" she wheezed. "Don't you think you're moving a bit too fast?"

It took him a moment to realize what she was insinuating. He jerked his hands up, palms out. "Whoa. Not what you're thinking. It's one of my teammates. He's proposing to his girlfriend."

"Ah-ha." She blinked her eyes as if to clear an image from her head. "That makes more sense. Okay."

He let out a relieved breath at her "okay."

"Great."

She aimed another one of those prissy looks at him. "Great what?"

Luke shoved his hands in his pockets. He was beginning to feel like he was on Mr. Toad's Wild Ride, and he didn't want to lose any extremities. Especially not his moneymakers. "Great, you'll do it."

"I didn't say that."

Had he actually been looking forward to conversing with this woman? "You just said 'okay.'"

"Not 'okay' I'll play for your friend's proposal. 'Okay' that you're not marrying Lizzie."

Wait. *What?*

"What's that supposed to mean?" he demanded.

She lifted her cello case and shrugged. "I don't have to worry about you becoming part of the family."

He might have felt the blow in the area of his heart, but a lifetime of rejection had walled it off from insults like that one.

Focus, dumb ass.

This wasn't about him. It was about getting her to play for Palmer's proposal. And he wasn't losing this round. Not to Miss Priss here.

"Now that we've got that settled," he ground out. "How much will it cost me to have you play at my buddy's proposal?"

"I don't play in front of an audience." She stepped around him and headed out of the atrium full of partying seniors.

What the ever-loving fuck?

He charged after her, ignoring Gram's wave.

"Correct me if I'm wrong but weren't you playing before an audience just now?" he argued.

She glanced back at the seniors around the bar and blew a kiss to her grandfather. "They don't count."

Luke's temple was beginning to throb. "I'm sure they appreciate you thinking that about them."

Shots fired.

She stopped so abruptly that he nearly bruised his balls on the damn cello case.

"Look, you said next week, right?" she snapped.

He nodded.

She shook her head. "Next week is impossible for me. I've got parent-teacher night and a county-wide elementary band meeting another night. The rest of the week is taken up with my LSAT study group." She resumed her march out of the building.

He was going to need a neck brace after this conversation.

"LSAT? You're going to law school? But your grandfather said you're a musician. You teach music, and clearly—" He gestured back to the bar area "—you're damn good at it."

She stopped beside a red VW bug. "Dreams don't always

provide stability. A direct quote from Her Honor, Victoria Pearson." She proceeded to strap the cello into the passenger seat.

"Let me guess. Your mother?"

She tapped her nose.

"She doesn't support your desire to be a cellist?"

"Oh, she did when I was younger. She was all for it, in fact. Private lessons. Summer camps. The whole nine yards. But only as means to enhance my college application. Once that goal was achieved, she insisted I be more realistic with my ambitions."

"Your mom sounds like a ball-buster."

She looked off into the distance. "Not really. It was a solid plan. I wanted to be a lawyer like her. And my dad. But then..." She brushed her fingers along the cello case.

"Then, you fell in love with music," he finished for her.

She shrugged. "We can't always get what we want."

"Yeah, I can relate," he surprised himself by saying.

Summer cocked her head to the side and studied him for a charged moment. "I find it hard to believe you aren't doing exactly what you've dreamed of doing since you were a boy."

If she only knew the things he'd dreamed of as a kid. Football had been low on his radar, that was for sure. Mostly because no one expected it of him. That didn't mean he hadn't exceeded everyone's expectations, though. Using grit and determination, he'd outsmarted them all.

He suspected the woman standing defiantly in front of him could do the same. And damn if he didn't want her to. "You have to tune it all out," he told her. "Don't let their noise drown out your dreams. Outperform the negative."

Her lips parted, but nothing scathing came out before she quickly closed them again. He wasn't sure, but he thought she might be counting to herself silently. She murmured something before tossing her hair back. "Appreciate the pep talk, thank you. Now, if you'll excuse me, I need to hurry to meet my date." She glanced at her watch. "I don't want to keep him waiting."

"A date?" The words were out before he could stop them. *Why wouldn't she have a date?*

She rolled her eyes at him. "I'm sure that's hard for you to believe. Not everyone thinks I'm a 'stick in the mud.' And before you ask, yes, I'm having drinks with an actual red-blooded male. We were supposed to get together earlier this week, but he had to use *his* muscles to save some lives. He's a fireman."

He didn't like the sly smile that played around her lips when she announced her date was a fireman. He especially didn't like the stirring deep inside him at the thought of her going out with anyone else. Summer Pearson was nothing but a sassy pain in his ass. Why would he want her when her more affable cousin was waiting for him?

Summer's VW bug drove away with a sputter before he realized he hadn't gotten her to agree to play for Palmer's proposal. He couldn't help the smirk that formed. Damned if she hadn't bested him at his own game. There were likely other cellists he could hire. Hell, he could afford to bring in an entire orchestra if he wanted.

Except he wanted Summer Pearson.

To play the cello while Palmer popped the question, he reminded himself.

That. Was. All.

She might have upped the ante, but Luke was game for the challenge. He was looking forward to it.

CHAPTER SEVEN

MUCH TO SUMMER'S DELIGHT, Mike Runson turned out to be as appealing in person as he was on the phone. He was handsome in a rugged, outdoorsy sort of way, complete with broad shoulders and beefy biceps to match his thick thighs. He wore his dark hair in a military cut that flattered his high cheekbones and blue eyes. Best of all, he didn't take himself too seriously.

Unlike a certain infuriating surfer-boy football player with a Napoleon complex.

Don't let their noise drown out your dreams.

Outperform the negative.

Luke Kessler had some nerve. Who did he think he was, quoting advice from pillows his grandmother had likely embroidered? According to Google—*yes, she'd stalked him*—Luke was the son of a former professional football great. Every door along the way to the pros had likely been held wide open with a red carpet rolled out for him to stroll up to the elite echelon of Jockdom. What the heck did he know about people trouncing on his dreams?

I can relate.

Except there'd been a hint of pain in his eyes when he'd

spoken those words. Summer was familiar with that look. She'd seen the same thing often enough when she looked into the mirror. That brief glimpse into the secrets behind his ready smile had her biting back her sarcastic retort earlier. For a moment, she thought there might be something more than their grandparents or Lizzie connecting them.

Then he'd made the snarky comment about her having a date. Summer quickly remembered what a jerk he was, sexy smile or no.

"You up for some live music?" Mike asked, bringing her back to the present. "There's a bar a few blocks from here with open mic night the first Friday of every month. I can't promise there won't be a trainwreck taking the stage, but most of the performers are decent."

Summer glanced at her watch. Had they been sitting on the restaurant's patio for over two hours? During that time, they'd talked about everything and nothing while polishing off a pitcher of beer, a plate of cheese curds, and some sliders. Now they had reached the moment of truth in the date where she could still end things graciously by pleading an early morning tomorrow, a headache, or some other made-up excuse.

"Why not?" she replied, because she was enjoying herself for the first time in months.

She was *not* prolonging her date because she didn't want to risk running into Lizzie and Luke at home. At least, that was what she told herself.

The bar he led her to was filled with an eclectic mix of people, many of whom seemed to know Mike well, judging by the cheer that went up when he followed Summer through the door.

"Yo, Mikey!" the bartender bellowed. "Where have you been this week?"

"In case you've forgotten, I have a job, Marty," Mike replied as he guided Summer to a pair of empty stools at the end of the bar.

The place was built into the basement of a mid-century

building that still housed a bank on the first floor. There were three stories of law offices above that. Behind the stage was a round vault door, opened to reveal shelves that once likely contained stacks of bills or even gold. The shelves were now lined with wine bottles that had string lights inside of them. A catwalk surrounded the main floor. Small tables were placed against the railing, with every table seemingly occupied. There had to be over a hundred people crowded into the bar.

The bartender put two bottles of water down in front of them. "You two are right on time," he said. "No one will believe who is about to sit down at that piano. I should have charged a freaking cover tonight."

"I told you before, Marty, if you're gonna charge a cover, you can't charge for popcorn," Mike joked.

The bartender snapped his towel in Mike's direction before nodding toward the stage. The lights in the bar dimmed. "Shut up and listen, smart ass. You're going to wish you were as talented as this guy."

A keyboard stood alone in the center of the stage, two spotlights illuminating it. A murmuring among the crowd began as a man took the stage. He wore a pair of joggers, white tennis shoes, and an oversized hoodie. A baseball cap sat low on his forehead, obscuring his face. A massive gold cross dangled from a chain around his neck, sending off arcs of light every time one of the spotlights landed on it.

The crowd quieted when he took his seat at the keyboard. Summer spun her barstool around to get a better view. A familiar fluttering began in her stomach as she watched the guy hesitate for a moment too long. From her vantage point, she could just make out his lips moving.

He was praying. Summer was sure of it. A wave of panic washed over her as she began to pray furiously with him, hoping against hope that he wouldn't choke.

Her prayers were answered a minute later when his fingers

landed on the keyboard. The syncopated notes of a ragtime piano arrangement filled the air, startling her with its brilliance. It took Summer a few bars to recognize the classic hymn, "Ode to Joy," a favorite of Grandma Bonnie's. Moments later, the bar patrons cheered when he launched into a rousing cover of the Super Mario Brothers theme song.

From there, he jumped to Stevie Wonder tunes, spurring several couples to get up and whirl around the center of the bar. The crowd sang along boisterously to his rendition of "Sweet Caroline." He covered a Coldplay song next before smoothly transitioning into a Bach concerto that had Summer nearly swooning at his mastery of the classic. He closed out the set with the Beatles' "Let it Be."

Raucous applause erupted as the last note sounded. Summer jumped to her feet, clapping furiously. She was in complete awe of his talent. For his part, the guy acknowledged the audience with a quick tap to the bill of his cap before sauntering backstage with such swagger that left her even more in awe of him. For nearly forty-five minutes, he'd owned that bar and its patrons, ensnaring them with a raw talent and confidence that was hard to come by. Suddenly, she was desperate to know this man.

Maybe his confidence would rub off on her.

"Is there a backstage?" she asked Mike.

He nodded. "But there are two more acts tonight."

Her posture must have conveyed her impatience because he led her backstage without further protest. The pianist was already pushing on the stage door leading outside.

"Wait!" Summer cried.

"I'm not looking for any groupies tonight," he murmured as the door opened to the night.

For heaven's sake. Were all the men in Milwaukee this pompous?

"Good thing then, because I'm not interested," she said.

Behind her, she heard Mike chuckle.

The pianist stopped his flight, slowly turning to face her. His eyes went wide against his dark skin when they landed on her. A slow smile formed on his lips. "Well, if it isn't the YouTube cellist, Summer Pearson, as I live and breathe," he said. "So this is where you ended up."

Summer wasn't sure whether to be flattered that he recognized her or not. Probably the latter, given his reference to how low she'd sunk. Suddenly she regretted coming backstage.

"Don't get any ideas about talking him into joining your Growler band, you two," the bartender announced from somewhere behind them. "Our friend here already has a gig for the games."

The pianist chuckled. "Wow. From Vienna to the stands at pro football games. If I ask nicely, will you play my favorite song every time I score?"

Summer's stomach and mouth dropped at the same time hearing the guy parrot Luke's words from days earlier.

"Whoa." Mike edged past her with his hand extended. "You're Antonio McGraff, that new receiver they picked up in the first round. Man, you've got some serious talent. On and off the field."

No! The brilliant pianist was also a professional football player? That explained the arrogance, at least.

Antonio looked at Mike's hand for a strained moment before finally offering a fist bump instead. Mike was practically giddy at having been touched by the other man. Summer rolled her eyes.

"That didn't work for Kessler," she snapped. "And it's not going to work for you."

Mike arched an eyebrow at her. It was his band, after all.

Antonio's grin grew wider. The rest of his features relaxed, revealing a face much younger than she initially judged him to be. He crossed his arms over his chest and propped a shoulder against the doorjamb. "Not a fan of Kessler's charms, huh?"

She snorted. "He has charms?"

She ignored the fact that Luke was sweet to his grandmother.

And dogs. And that he wanted to help his friend propose, which was over-the-top charming, if she was being honest.

"Maybe I do have time for a groupie tonight," Antonio said.

Summer ground her teeth. "That's not why I came back here."

"Why did you come back here?" he asked softly.

Her frustration waned. "Because." She sighed heavily. "You've got an amazing talent and . . . no fear." The last two words came out as a whisper.

He uncrossed his arms, suddenly looking uncomfortable. "Yeah, well, looks can be deceiving." He stepped away from the door. "I'm not into sitting around a bar drinking. I hear there's a great pizza place near here. Would you guys want to share a pie with me?" He aimed a shy grin in her direction. "Kessler's charms are supposedly legendary. I gotta know how you resist him."

Summer returned the smile. "That would be great." Too late she realized she should have consulted Mike before answering. She turned quickly to face him. "Um, I mean, if you want to?"

"You two musical geniuses go ahead," he said magnanimously. "I've got an early day tomorrow giving a tour of the firehouse to a bunch of Cub Scouts."

A half-hour later, she and Antonio were seated in a back booth at The Pizza Pub. Antonio was devouring slices of pepperoni pizza as quickly as Milli snarfed up her treats. Summer nibbled at her slice.

"That wasn't well done of me, was it?" she asked.

Antonio paused with a slice of pizza halfway to his mouth. "Huh?"

"Leaving Mike back there." She cradled her head in her hands. "He must think I'm awful."

"He could have come if he wanted to spend more time with you."

Summer narrowed her eyes at him. "Way to make a girl feel better. Tell me, did you suffer from the same head injury as Luke? Is being a prick a prerequisite for playing with the Growlers?"

Antonio laughed so hard people turned to stare at them. "How do you know Kessler, anyway?" he asked once he stopped snorting.

"His grandmother lives in the same senior community as my grandparents." She waved a hand in the air. "He keeps popping up like a bad penny every time I go there."

"He does love his 'Gram.'" Antonio placed his pizza slice back on the plate. "Can't fault a guy for that."

Summer rested her chin in her hands. "Do you have a 'Gram?'"

A bashful smile broke out on his face. "Great-Granny Pearl. She practically raised me. My dad works on the oil rigs. My momma works in the school office. Pearl raised my momma too."

"You miss her." It wasn't a question. The expression on his face told Summer all she needed to know.

"Mmm. I miss them all. I've got three younger sisters and a little brother still at home. Except for some away games in college, I've never traveled that much. Never really been away from my parish." He shook his head as if he'd revealed too much and snatched up his slice of pizza again. "It was Pearl who taught me to play. She plays the organ at church."

Summer suspected there wasn't much Pearl had to teach Antonio. It didn't take a trained ear to know he'd been born with a rare musical talent.

"Your performance tonight was amazing. You have an extraordinary gift."

He shrugged.

"Why would you waste it by playing football?"

He eyed her shrewdly. "I have multiple gifts, and one pays more than the other."

"But you don't know that."

"Let me rephrase that. One has a more instantaneous payoff." He looked down at his pizza. "My dad's got stage-four lung cancer. He never smoked. They say it came from exposure to something on the rig." He cleared his throat. "I need to make sure he gets the best care. To make sure my mama and Granny Pearl are taken care of. My sisters and brother too. My dad provided a solid life for us." He shrugged. "It's my turn to step up."

A familiar chill washed over her as his words sparked her memories of the dark days when her father fell ill. Gray Pearson had been out for his daily run when he felt a pain in his side and collapsed. Doctors discovered he had liver cancer. He was gone weeks later. There was nothing to be done.

Her mother was devastated. The Judge's wealthy family had cut her off years earlier when she gave up law school to marry Summer's dad rather than the turd they had picked out for her. Like Antonio, she'd taken the easiest path to provide for her two children. For The Judge, that path led to returning to law school. For Antonio, it was the football field.

He was doing the right thing.

She forced her lips into a cheerful smile. "Well, there is a lot to be said to being a famous athlete. You do get the best seating at restaurants."

"I wouldn't know. This is the first time I've eaten out since I've been here. I usually order in," he said matter-of-factly.

His words surprised her. "The guys on the team don't go out on the town eating pizza, drinking beer, and thumping their chests?"

He snickered. "Oh, I imagine they do. Except not with me. They're all tight, you know. Cliquey."

Summer's mouth dropped open in surprise. The teacher in her wanted to take all those buffoons to task. Didn't they know Antonio was lonely? But she knew enough about the macho traits of the male species to realize he was concealing it from his teammates. From what she'd sensed in the short time she'd known him, Antonio wouldn't want anyone to fight his battles for him.

"I'm new to Milwaukee myself. And there are a bunch of

restaurants I've been anxious to try. Maybe we can explore the city together?" she suggested.

The expression on his face mimicked those of her students when they really wanted to do something but were too cool to admit it. She was afraid she might have overstepped until another one of those boyish grins broke out on his face.

"Once word gets out about how poorly you treat your dates, you'll be untouchable. I guess I can take pity on you, so you don't have to eat alone," he quipped.

Summer tossed a pepperoni at him. He caught it mid-air with reflexes so quick, it surprised her.

"Maybe you are gifted at two things," she said.

He smirked at her. "Are you hanging out with me so that maybe some of my mojo will rub off on you, and you'll be able to perform again?"

She slumped back against the padded booth. "I played tonight. At the senior community. I had two panic attacks before Mrs. Hilbert gave me some Fireball from a stash she keeps in her purse. It felt right to make music again. But I was playing for people I basically know. A toothless crowd of critics." She chuckled. "Literally and figuratively."

"It's a start."

"But what if that's as far as I go?" She voiced aloud the question that had been dancing in the recesses of her brain since Antonio had taken the stage that evening. Watching—and listening—to him command the room had rekindled her desire to perform. It was an aching need she never thought she'd feel again. But what if she never found the nerve to walk into a room and play for strangers again?

You'll be a lawyer, that's what. Her mother's words echoed in her head.

Summer never told anyone about the horrible things she'd overheard in Vienna. Besides, they were a convenient excuse. If she were truly confident in her abilities, something like that wouldn't have derailed her in the first place, she reasoned.

The Judge never asked her what happened. She simply bundled her daughter up in her arms, loaded her on a plane, and took her home to Chicago. It was only after a couple of weeks on the couch that she'd given Summer the "it's time to get on with your life" pep talk. Surprisingly, her mom had been open-minded enough to entertain any suggestions Summer had for her future. Except Summer had been too raw to suggest anything. She'd failed epically at the only thing she'd ever wanted. The gavel came down almost immediately. Barring any other options, the law it was.

"Great-granny Pearl always says, if plan A doesn't work, there are plenty more letters in the alphabet."

"If only it were that simple." She looked up from her hands she'd been wringing to find him staring at her intently.

"Nothing worth having is simple. Trust me." He tossed the crust to his slice of pizza onto the pan. "Next time I want to try that steak house the baseball players all tweet about."

Summer was eager to continue soaking up Antonio's music vibe, even if she never was going to perform like that again. She'd found a kindred spirit in the young man. "We can go tomorrow night."

He shook his head. "No can do. The team stays in a hotel the night before games. They like to keep an eye on us."

Strangely, Summer's first thought was of Monty. "Who takes care of Luke's dog?"

"I hope he doesn't bring that beast with him. Kessler is my assigned roommate."

It was ridiculous of her to worry about Luke's dog. The two were practically joined at the hip. Of course, he would make sure Monty was cared for while he was away.

"You better bring earplugs. Luke looks like somebody who snores," she joked.

Except he didn't really. But he was probably a blanket hog or something. The unbidden image of Luke Kessler tangled up in the sheets, his muscled arms and legs stretched across the mattress, his hair all mussed up, had her thighs clenching together suddenly.

Antonio shook his head. "Nah, Kessler won't snore. He's too in control for that. But Mr. Positivity likely sings in the shower."

"Yes," she added. "And badly if I had to guess."

They both laughed. "I'll let you know on Sunday."

CHAPTER EIGHT

Luke normally took the first bus to the stadium on game day. Getting there before the crowd gave him a chance to check out the turf in relative obscurity. He didn't like to rely on the training staff to tell him which cleats to wear. While on the field, he would take his time visualizing the game plan and the routes he would run for each play. Then he would return to the quiet locker room to mentally prepare for the beating his body was likely going to take. His pregame ritual hadn't changed since he'd moved up to the pros.

Today, however, he'd hung back at the hotel to wait for Palmer. The two hadn't gotten a chance to iron out the details for his proposal last night. The punter was excused from curfew to attend a middle school football kick-off banquet where he delivered the keynote. Luke was pretty sure the Growler's community relations office considered it a match made in heaven given Palmer's juvenile personality.

It was a calculated risk to mess with his routine, except he was already out of sorts. His weekend had not gone the way he expected it would. Starting with Elizabeth flaking out on him Friday night. She'd departed the dinner party early—and alone—

because she unexpectedly had to fill in for the weekend meteorologist Saturday and Sunday morning. Sure, she'd left him with a very passionate kiss and the promise that she'd be off Monday and Tuesday. Neither one did nearly enough to ease his pent-up desire, however.

And then there was McGraff. The dude had been like a shadow from the moment they'd arrived at the hotel. A very sulky shadow. Luke tried to cut the kid some slack. It was his first regular-season game, after all. When he'd offered to go over the plays with him last night, the little shit stuffed in his earbuds and played video games on his tablet. Thankfully, he had taken the first bus to the stadium.

The second bus was always the more crowded of the two. Most guys preferred to get as much rest as possible before a game. This being the first game of the season, the mood among the players was upbeat and relaxed.

Luke headed to the back where Palmer was yucking it up with his long-snapper. Unfortunately, there wasn't a vacant seat near the punter. He settled for the empty one next to Van Horn. Across the aisle, Fletcher had an open seat, also. Luke had no desire to rehash Elizabeth's abrupt departure from the Highlander's penthouse last night, though. The quarterback was the lesser of two evils.

Van Horn looked up from his tablet. "What are you doing on this bus?"

Apparently, Luke had chosen poorly.

"This is the Growlers' team bus. I play for the Growlers. Simple enough for you, eh?"

The quarterback narrowed his eyes at Luke. "You always ride the first bus. Religiously. You're fucking with your routine, hoser. On game day. I don't like when players fuck with their routine. It doesn't bode well for the game we are about to play."

The bus began to move. Resisting the urge to flip his teammate off, Luke jumped across the aisle and dropped into the empty spot next to the broody Scotsman. Fletcher had the nerve to chuckle.

"What's wrong with him?" Van Horn demanded of the kicker.

"He's got blue balls." Fletcher replied loudly enough for everyone on the bus and in the cars beside them to hear.

For fuck's sake. All Luke wanted to do was cross off his obligation to Palmer and get on with his life. He glared at Fletcher, but it was too late.

"Who's got blue balls?" one of the idiots at the back of the bus called.

"Kessler," Fletcher continued. "It seems his Seasonal Arm Candy isn't such a sure thing after all."

Laughter from his teammates filled the bus.

"That better not be messing with your head, Kessler," Van Horn said. "I need you on your game today."

"There's nothing wrong with my head," Luke ground out. "Either of them. I'm riding this bus because I needed a word with Palmer about his damn proposal."

"You're off the hook, old man," Palmer announced. "I came up with an idea all on my own. I'm taking my girl axe-throwing on Friday night. I'm thinking of attaching the ring to the board."

"Jaysus," Declan mumbled beside Luke. A chorus of groans erupted around them.

Luke turned back to face the punter. "For real? I think you might want to give that idea some more thought. I'm fairly sure women want something a bit more romantic than axe-throwing."

Palmer shook his head. "My girl loves that kind of thing. She's better at it than I am."

"You sure you want to marry a woman who can wield a dangerous weapon like that?" one of the guys asked. "You better not piss her off."

Their teammates broke out in another round of laughter as the bus pulled into the tunnel beneath the stadium.

"It's not your problem anymore," Fletcher said to Luke as they made their way to the front of the bus. "The fool's gonna do what he's gonna do. Let it go."

His head was telling him the same thing. *One less thing to worry about.* Even better, he wouldn't have to spar with Summer Pearson any longer.

A wave of disappointment washed over him at that particular thought. He justified it by telling himself it was because she was a challenge, and he didn't like to lose the opportunity at besting her. It certainly had nothing to do with the way his nerve endings danced when she touched him.

"Forget about Palmer," Van Horn commanded. "We've got two hours until kick-off. Get your head in the game." The quarter-back led the way into the home team's locker room.

The trainers had laid out the locker room by uniform number. Each player's jersey hung beside a cubby marking the spot the players would use to dress for the game. Luke wandered down the row until he reached his jersey hanging between McGraff's and Jacobs'. The rookie sat on the folding chair, thumbing through the game program. The training staff put one in each player's cubby before every game. Luke lifted his copy and handed it to McGraff.

"You'll want to keep that one for yourself," he said. "But your parents will want one too. Take mine."

The kid hesitated for the briefest of moments before taking the program and shoving it inside his duffel. "Thanks."

Luke shucked his street clothes and wrapped a towel around his waist. He liked to start his pre-game prep with a shower. It helped him to clear his head so he could focus. He turned toward the showers just in time to see McGraff reach for one of the chocolate chip cookies left in Jacobs' cubby.

"No!" Luke shouted before tackling the rookie to the floor.

"Get the fuck off me!" McGraff yelled as the two men wrestled.

"Did the Crime Dog go after one of Jacobs' cookies?" someone asked as the players in the locker room gathered around.

"Holy shit, that would have been a disaster," another guy murmured.

McGraff nearly kneed Luke in the nuts in his struggle to get free. Still, Luke managed to pin him to the floor. "Calm down and listen carefully. Jacobs religiously eats three chocolate chip cookies before every game. Not one. Not two. Three. Three cookies the team special orders for him and only him. He eats them right after he finishes getting taped. No one touches his cookies. You got it?"

Shoving with all his might, McGraff was able to dislodge Luke and spring to his feet. He eyed the rest of the quiet room before marching toward the tunnel leading out onto the field.

Fletcher reached a hand down to help Luke up. "The lad didn't know."

Luke rewrapped his towel around his waist. "Yeah." He stared down his teammates. "It was an honest mistake. Nothing happened. There's no reason for Jacobs to ever hear about it."

The rest of the guys nodded in agreement. They were all eager to keep the peace in the locker room. Luke headed for the shower, eager to finally get into his pre-game mode.

Thirty minutes later, he was showered, taped, and ready to head out to check out the turf when his phone buzzed with a text. It was a photo of Gram and Elizabeth with the Growlers' owner, Mrs. Ciaciura. At the picnic last weekend, Elizabeth had charmed the team owner. Mrs. C. invited Elizabeth and Gram to sit in her box for the first game. Elizabeth looked ecstatic. His grandmother looked like she was enjoying herself, if not a tad overwhelmed. Which was odd since she'd met the team's owner several times over the years. This wasn't even Gram's first game in Milwaukee.

"Where's McGraff?" Coach Washington startled Luke with his question.

"You asked me to room with him. I didn't realize that included babysitting him."

Wash shot him a menacing look. "I want to go over routes with him before things get crazy in here. Go out and see if you can find him. Tell him I want to see him."

The coach turned on his heel and headed toward the offices lining the back of the locker room before Luke could lodge a protest.

Luke swore loudly. He should have come on the early bus. *Damn Palmer.*

He charged through the tunnel and onto the field. His shoulders relaxed as soon as his feet hit the turf, however. There was nothing like the feel of opening day. The flags lining the upper deck seemed to be flapping a welcome-back salute at him. The warm breeze off the lake carried in the mouthwatering scents of food fans were grilling at the tailgate outside the stadium.

Several of the opposing players barked in his direction. His reputation as the protector of stray dogs was well known throughout the league. Luke gave them a jaunty wave before heading toward the middle of the field, where one of the trainers was guiding Van Horn through a series of stretches.

"Here's the Director of Dares himself. The stakes are high on opening day. What have you challenged your teammates with today?" the trainer asked.

"The lineman with the cleanest pants at the end of the game owes a hundred bucks to Fletcher's Mathletes," Luke said distractedly.

The trainer grinned at Van Horn. "Your boy is making sure you're well protected today."

"As he should," Van Horn grunted.

"Have you seen McGraff?" he asked the quarterback.

Van Horn glanced up at him from the turf. "What's he done now?"

Shit. Van Horn hadn't been in the locker room when the kid went for Jacobs' pregame snack. That meant someone snitched. No wonder Wash was looking for him.

"You should know by now that nothing is secret in a locker room," the trainer said. He jutted his chin toward the end zone and the section of the stands that was home to the Growlers' band. "No need to worry, though. I'd say your boy isn't suffering too badly. He seems to have found a hottie to console him."

Luke spied McGraff near the entrance to one of the tunnels used to bring cameras and equipment onto the field. He was smiling down at a woman dressed in a Growlers T-shirt and khaki shorts that did a great job of accentuating shapely legs. Her wavy chestnut hair was pulled back in a ponytail. It bobbed up and down along with the hand she was wildly gesturing with. Both she and McGraff laughed when she nearly knocked over a microphone in her exuberance. She was too slow in righting the microphone, though, toppling over a row of water bottles set out for the band. A pile of sheet music suddenly fluttered in the breeze when she tried to save the bottles.

The woman was a hot mess.

A very familiar hot mess.

"What in the ever-loving hell," Luke said under his breath as he marched in their direction.

McGraff had wrangled up most of the sheet music by the time Luke arrived. Summer, however, was on her hands and knees chasing water bottles that threatened to roll onto the field. Luke stepped in front of her and stopped one of the bottles with his sneakered foot. When she glanced up, her startled expression quickly changed to the annoyed one she seemed to reserve only for him.

"Don't you touch him!" She jumped to her feet, trying in vain to juggle the water bottles in her hands. Giving up, she dropped them to the turf before stretching out her arms and blocking a chagrined-looking McGraff with her body.

Did she seriously think she needed to protect the rookie from him? Luke arched a brow. McGraff averted his eyes.

Just as he thought.

The kid likely told her an abbreviated version of what went down in the locker room earlier. He'd deal with McGraff later. Right now, he had questions. Lots of them. Starting with what was he doing with Summer.

"Care to explain how you two know each other?"

McGraff leveled a hard gaze back at Luke. "What business is it of yours?"

It was none of Luke's business.

None. At. All.

Except the way these two were carrying on before he showed up had his gut twisted up in knots. And he didn't need any knots in his stomach with kickoff an hour away.

"It's not his business," Summer chirped. She crossed her arms beneath the generous bosom her T-shirt was stretched over nicely. "But if it will make you go away and stop bullying Antonio, we met Friday night."

Stop bullying Antonio? Was she high?

Then something more concerning registered.

"Wait." He gestured to McGraff. "You said you were meeting a fireman."

She opened her mouth to say something before seeming to think better of it. Her lips turned up into a smug smile. "A girl can have more than one date on a Friday night."

Behind her, McGraff smirked.

Summer and Antonio?

It wasn't only his gut tied up in knots now. Luke's temple began to throb.

"Coach Washington wants you in his office. Now," he barked at the rookie.

Summer slapped her palms against her thighs with a groan. "There you go again. Acting like a bully."

Again with the bullying bullshit. "When have I ever bullied you?" he demanded.

"Oh my God, practically every time you speak to me."

Luke rested his hands on his hips. "Name one time."

Her hands were on her hips now. "The other night. You tried to bully me into playing for your friend's proposal."

He heaved a sigh. "For the record, I wasn't bullying. I was pointing out why every one of your excuses was lame. But the problem has been solved. Palmer has decided to propose at a bar while throwing axes."

The idea still sounded idiotic to Luke. Since he never intended to propose to anyone himself, however, he had no license to throw shade on the punter.

"Now *that's* lame," McGraff said.

"Isn't it?" Summer wrinkled up her nose. "Is this guy a lumberjack or something? No woman should be proposed to while axes whiz past her." She turned to McGraff. "I know. You should offer to play keyboard. Maybe some folksy love song or something. It would make the whole thing feel more romantic."

Mother of God. He needed a roadmap to understand this woman's thought process.

The scuttlebutt around the league was that McGraff had majored in music. Last month at training camp, he'd whipped off a few tunes on a shabby upright piano in the dorms. Luke had to admit his performance was decent. But how did she know that?

"I'll play if you do." McGraff's suggestion had Luke rocking back on his heels. "We could do a duet. 'Endless Love' or something."

Summer shook her head vehemently and grimaced. "Don't tell me that's your Great Granny Pearl's favorite song?"

What the fuck? She knew his grandmother's name?

"Come on." The rookie reached for her hand and gave it a squeeze. Luke's jaw clenched at the intimacy of the gesture. "You know you don't want Palmer to ruin the poor woman's proposal.

It'll be fine. I'll be there to support you all the way. We'll be a team."

Her face softened, and she placed a palm on McGraff's chest. Luke swallowed the growl that forced its way up from his belly when she touched his teammate.

"You're sweet," she practically cooed. "But if I agreed to play at all, we'd be doing something much hipper."

"Nobody is playing anything," Luke roared. "Except for a damn football game." He leveled a finger at McGraff. "You. In Coach Washington's office. Now."

They both aimed dumbfounded looks at him before McGraff found his sulk once more. With a nod at Summer, he pulled away and headed for the locker room. Of course, Miss Priss couldn't leave it at that.

"Wait," she called after him. When she caught up to him, she stretched up on her toes and kissed him on the cheek. "Have a great first game, Antonio. You're gonna rock it."

Jealousy, fierce and furious, gripped Luke. When had anyone ever sent him off to a game with that kind of exuberant affection or caring?

"He's lonely," she said softly once McGraff was several yards away. She turned back to Luke. "He misses his family."

Luke knew how that felt. He'd been missing his family for as long as he could remember.

"He's not as worldly as he'd like everyone to think," she continued, closing the distance between them. "He's simply trying to fit into his new life, and it's hard for him. You should let him play at your teammate's proposal. It would go a long way to making him feel like a part of the team." She glanced back toward the tunnel McGraff had disappeared into and sighed. "If he says he'll only do it if I perform with him, I guess I'll have to. It's important that he not be so lonely."

Her compassion gutted him. Why did this woman never do or say what he expected?

She placed her fingers on his forearm, causing the nerve endings beneath his skin to pulse. "Please, Luke."

Those big caramel eyes of hers slayed him. He took hold of her wrist and tugged her toward the equipment tunnel behind the bandstand. "Come with me."

Surprisingly, she didn't protest. She did continue to plead McGraff's case, though.

"You'd be doing a nice thing for your teammate by including him. Both your teammates, as a matter of fact."

He released her wrist and pressed a finger to her lips. "Hush."

"But—" she murmured against his skin.

He would have laughed at her tenacity. Instead, he did the most reckless thing he'd done in his life. He kissed her.

The moment his lips met hers, whatever remained of his brain cells—and his well-honed control--scattered across the stadium. Luke could not have cared less. He was too intrigued by the taste of her. The feel of her soft lips opening without fuss beneath his. The sweet curves of her body that his hands were suddenly exploring.

That trademark obstinance he needed from her to stop this madness was nowhere to be found. Instead, she kissed him back like she did everything else, with reckless abandon and passion. Her fingers slipped beneath his T-shirt and skimmed across his skin. One of them moaned. He was pretty sure it was him because, *damn,* Summer Pearson turned him on like no woman ever had.

Had he been thinking clearly, that very fact would have scared the bejesus out of him. But he wasn't thinking clearly. He never seemed to be able to when this woman was involved.

Luke tilted her head back to gain better access to her sweet, warm mouth. They both grew more frantic as their tongues and their bodies collided. Summer sighed into his mouth, making him incredibly uncomfortable in his football pants and pads. She pressed her palms to his chest and backed him against the concrete wall. He was palming her lush, round ass when a voice echoed off the walls like a referee's whistle.

"What the hell, Kessler!" Van Horn shouted.

It took a moment for the quarterback's words to permeate the sensual fog surrounding Luke. Not so for Summer. She quickly detached herself from his arms, jumping back wearing an astonished, what-have-I-done look. Her panicked breaths filled the tunnel as she swiped furiously at her swollen lips.

For the first time in his life, Luke didn't have a ready comeback or pithy comment to soothe things over. He was frozen against that damn cold wall. Summer avoided making any kind of eye contact with him or Van Horn. His asshole teammate didn't have the good grace to leave. Instead, he stood there like a pissed-off father who'd caught a boy taking advantage of his teenage daughter.

The truth of it was, the quarterback was right. Luke owed Summer an apology. He opened his mouth to do just that, but she wasn't interested in hearing anything he had to say. A gulping sob escaped her mouth before she slapped a hand over it and dashed out of the tunnel, nearly blindsiding Van Horn in her haste to escape.

Luke swore violently when he finally regained the use of his limbs. He charged after her, only to be stopped short by Van Horn.

"You've got bigger issues to deal with right now," the quarterback said.

"Have I ever not been prepared for a game?" Luke snapped. He hadn't. For much of his life, Luke made it his business to be prepared for anything.

With the exception of the last few minutes.

He needed to find Summer. He needed to apologize for taking things way too far. Not that Van Horn would understand. The quarterback was more machine than man, thinking only of football and how best to win every game. It wasn't in his nature to exhibit empathy for anyone else. And Luke wasn't in the mood to listen to one of his speeches. Nothing his teammate said would deter him from seeking out Summer and making things right.

"Your father is in the locker room. He brought your brother with him."

Except maybe that.

CHAPTER NINE

"YOU MIGHT HAVE MENTIONED Dad was coming to the game." Luke was having a hard time tempering his tone with Gram.

It wasn't fair of him to take out his frustrations on her. But his father's sudden presence in the broadcast booth was the icing on the cake of a shitty day. A day in which Luke had dropped more balls than he'd caught. Fortunately, one of the few passes he managed to hold onto was for the winning touchdown.

Growler fans had already forgiven him. Van Horn and Wash, not so much. Before Luke could escape the locker room, the quarterback had issued a summons to study game film back at his place that night. As if Luke wanted to relive any part of this day. Or be subjected to his father's on-air commentary of his performance. Fortunately, he had the excuse of having to drop Gram back at Sunset Glen first. Hopefully, that would give him enough time to regain his runaway composure before heading to Van Horn's.

"I had as much idea he was coming as you did," she replied tersely.

He puffed out a breath. Of course, she didn't. Jake Kessler was as stealthy as a damn crocodile. He loved the element of surprise.

As if showing up when Luke or Gram least expected it would make up for all the other days, months, years of radio silence.

"They sure didn't bother staying long. It would have been nice to spend some time with Brady," Gram added. "I hardly know him. He's all grown up now."

Luke ground his teeth together as he steered his truck into the parking lot of the senior community. At eighteen, his half-brother wasn't exactly "all grown up." But having won the lottery of the Kessler gene pool, Brady towered over Luke. If that wasn't enough, the kid possessed a laser-sharp passing arm, making him one of the country's top college prospects at quarterback. With his mammoth shoulders, blond hair, and blue eyes, he was their father's "mini-me" in every way that mattered.

While Luke was a potent reminder of Jake Kessler's greatest mistake.

"You should take dad up on his offer and go visit," he suggested. "You could go to one of Brady's games."

Luke couldn't help the all-too-familiar guilt that always accompanied any discussion of Gram's other grandchildren. It was his fault she barely knew Brady or his younger sister, Layla. Their father would have likely brought them around more often if Luke had been able to tolerate life in Canada rather than decamping to Idaho and Gram's house whenever he got the chance. Instead, Jake took his wife and kids on vacations around the world. Better to expose his kids to Christmas in the tropics or summers on Lake Como than Idaho with the son he never wanted.

Except he had wanted Luke once.

Memories of fishing with his father on Redfish Lake and camping trips in Gram's backyard flashed before Luke's eyes. He'd been the center of his dad's world back then. Those summers spent together seemed as if they were from another universe. A universe before Jake Kessler became a megastar in the league and the husband of an oil heiress.

He shifted the truck into park with more force than was necessary.

As if sensing his thoughts, Gram reached over and patted his hand. "I'd rather watch you play football," she said.

He rested his head back against the leather, hating that she felt she always had to choose him. Hating that his parents chose other people over him. And selfish enough to be grateful to have Gram in his corner. He lifted her hand to his lips.

"You're a treasure, you know that?"

"Mmmhm, I'll bet you say that to all the girls."

Her remark immediately had him thinking of his pre-game fiasco. Guilt squeezed at the back of his neck as he hurried around to the passenger's side to help Gram out of the truck. He needed to find Summer and clear the air.

Except he wasn't sure how he would do that. Or what he would say. Kissing her had been a mistake.

Even if it didn't feel like one.

Luke was guiding Gram toward the building when the howling reached his ears.

Gram's eyes widened. "Monty."

Shit.

He hurried Gram inside. When the elevator doors opened to the third floor, Monty's baleful howls filled the hallway. Worse, the hallway was also filled with aggravated residents, including the community's beleaguered looking executive director.

"Afternoon, folks." Luke wasn't one of those players who used his celebrity status to game the system, but desperate times and all that nonsense. "How about that game, eh?"

"Could have used some more fantasy points from you," one of the old men grumbled.

Luke bit back a groan when Mrs. Hilbert made her way to the front. He should have known the busybody would be the ringleader of Sunset Glen's noise police.

"Now, Fred, the boy was getting the kinks out this afternoon.

It was the first game of the season. We can all cut him some slack." She smiled at Fred before turning to Luke and narrowing her eyes. "But you're not getting any slack when it comes to that beast."

"I think I can take it from here," the director said as he stepped in front of Mrs. Hilbert. "Why don't you all head over to the main building? One of the local wine stores is hosting a tasting tonight. I'm sure you don't want to miss that." When none of them budged, he added, "It's free."

That did the trick. Mrs. Hilbert led her merry band toward the elevator without so much as a goodbye. Only the director and Harry Pearson remained. Summer must not have told her grandfather what transpired between her and Luke earlier that day, because the guy didn't give Luke a second look. Instead, he was smiling softly at Gram.

"Would you like to join us, Grace?" Harry asked. "I'm happy to wait and walk you over?"

Gram looked between Luke and the director with a wobbly smile on her face. "Um, perhaps I should stay here and sort this out?"

"No need," the director said. "I'm sure your grandson and I will be able to resolve this on our own."

His tone indicated that the solution would likely involve a check with a few zeroes at the end of it. Luke sighed. He would do whatever it took. This was Gram's new home. No way was he —or his dopey dog—going to screw things up for her.

"We can't have you missing free wine." Luke leaned down and kissed her on the cheek. "I'm going to grab Monty and take him home. I'll call you tomorrow."

Her eyes were shining with relief. "In that case, I'd love some wine, Harry."

Monty's howls grew even more mournful as Harry led Gram to the open elevator. The doors had barely closed when the director started in.

"We have specific guidelines for pets belonging to residents. No dogs over thirty pounds. And absolutely no pit bulls."

"Monty is my dog," Luke explained. "Gram was watching him for me last night. I've only had him a few months. I haven't worked out a plan for him when I'm playing yet. Gram enjoys the company. She's good with him."

The director cleared his throat. "Your grandmother may think she's good with your dog, but he nearly pulled her down last night when she was walking him. We're lucky she didn't break a hip."

Luke's mouth was suddenly painfully dry. That was a scenario he never considered. Jesus, he was an idiot.

"And he obviously can't be left alone," the director continued. "As you can hear, he's quite a nuisance."

"Yeah." Luke dragged his fingers through his hair. "My apologies. I'll make other arrangements for Monty from now on. I'll personally apologize to the residents for disturbing their peace and quiet."

"No need." The director's affable grin returned. "You're paying for the wine tonight."

Half an hour later, Luke pulled into Van Horn's historic mansion overlooking the shoreline of Lake Michigan. Monty crawled onto Luke's lap in his exuberance to get out of the truck. Van Horn was going to blow a gasket at him for showing up with his dog in tow, but Luke didn't give a shit. The dog was so distraught at being left alone in a strange place that he had practically glued himself to Luke's thigh the moment he liberated him from Gram's apartment. No way could he leave him by himself again.

Besides, this wasn't a social visit. Van Horn had commanded Luke to be here. If the quarterback objected to Monty coming also, they would happily leave.

"Let's hope he throws a tantrum about his hardwood floors.

Then we can go grab a couple of drive-thru burgers." Luke rubbed Monty's ear. The dog responded with a lick to the face.

"You better have food," Luke demanded when Van Horn opened the door. "I'm starving."

The quarterback stoically watched Monty trot in beside Luke. Monty sniffed the air for a long moment before making a beeline toward the kitchen.

"I don't have anything suitable for that thing to eat," Van Horn said.

Luke lifted the reusable bag with Monty's bowl and dinner in the air. "Don't worry. We knew this would be BYO-dog food."

He stopped short in the doorway to the large breakfast area where Monty was resting his snout on Fletcher's enormous thigh. The placekicker was absently rubbing the top of the dog's head while watching several of the late games playing on four different television screens mounted to the wall. A knot of tension settled in the back of Luke's neck. Fletcher wasn't here to study game films. Hell, the broody Highlander rarely paid attention during practice.

Van Horn was up to something. Fletcher tossed a tortilla chip into the air. Monty scrambled to catch it, his lips smacking before the chip landed on the floor in front of him.

"Your dog looks a lot like you did today," Van Horn said.

Fletcher chuckled, tossing another chip at the dog, who, of course, missed it.

"What is this, an intervention?" Luke demanded, his normally endless patience running low.

Fletcher smirked at him. "Oh, don't mind me. I'm not here to find out why you were sucking face with a woman who isn't your Seasonal Arm Candy. Although that would explain your date's abrupt exit from dinner the other night."

For fuck's sake.

Luke rounded on Van Horn. "Gossip much?"

"When it impacts this team, yes." Van Horn snatched the bag

from Luke's hand and proceeded to pour food into Monty's bowl. He filled another plastic bowl with water and placed both by the back door. "Come and get it, Cujo."

"We're not staying," Luke snapped.

"Your beast says otherwise," Van Horn replied.

Monty's stubby tail shook as he nosily tucked into his dinner.

Luke mumbled a stream of obscenities. Reaching into the fridge, he helped himself to a beer. He screwed off the top and took a long swallow before dropping into the chair opposite Fletcher.

"I don't have all night," he said. "Why don't you get whatever it is off your chest so you can go to sleep feeling all sanctimonious?"

Fletcher and Van Horn held another one of their silent conversations, pissing off Luke even more.

"Who I do and don't kiss is none of your damn business," he snapped again. "My personal life is just that. Personal."

"It becomes our business when it affects your performance during a game," Van Horn replied equally as testily.

Luke jumped up from the chair, ready to grab his dog mid-chew and leave the two assholes to unpack someone else's life.

"Sit back down, Luke," Fletcher said calmly. "Please."

Monty finished his dinner with a loud belch. The dog lapped up the entire bowl of water before wandering over to the mudroom door, where he proceeded to scrunch up the throw rug and lay down with a grunt. Literally seconds later, he was snoring.

All three stared at the dog in wonder for a brief moment. Van Horn placed a bowl of salsa on the table next to the chips and took a seat.

"I ordered wings," he said. "They'll be here in fifteen."

Luke's stomach rumbled. He grabbed a handful of chips and returned to his chair.

"This isn't about the woman you were giving mouth-to-mouth to in the tunnel," Fletcher said. "You're right. That is none of our business."

Van Horn snorted as if he disagreed. Fletcher's glare kept the quarterback from saying anything more, however.

"This is about your father," the placekicker announced. "And don't insult us by lying and saying it isn't. It doesn't take a Ph.D. from MIT to know the fool rattles you every time he shows up."

Luke nearly chuckled at Fletcher describing his father as a fool. Jake Kessler was beloved both inside and outside of the game. Leave it to the Scotsman to see through the man. Still, it wasn't in Luke's best interest to tarnish the family brand.

"I wasn't expecting him, that's all." Luke washed the chips down with a long pull of his beer.

"He never seems to tell you when he's coming," Fletcher observed.

"So? Sue me because my old man and I aren't buddy-buddy like you and your—" he made air quotes with his fingers "—*da*."

"He'd have to sue me too, if that's the criteria," Van Horn murmured.

Luke looked at him in surprise. The elder Van Horn attended many of the Growlers' games. Every time Luke had seen the quarterback with his father, things had looked very jovial.

"Don't forget, Van Horn is careful about cultivating his public image," Fletcher reminded Luke. "Can't have the future voters knowing he thinks his da is a philandering ass."

"Huh." Luke munched on another chip.

Van Horn crossed his arms over his chest and leaned the chair back on its two back legs. "The Ciaciuras can pull some strings to ensure your father never wanders into the locker room again. Even with a press pass."

Wow. These two were serious about keeping the locker room Zen if they were willing to use the nuclear option with his dad. As much as Luke would love to put their suggestion in motion, he would never give his old man the satisfaction of knowing how much his defection affected him. Affected his life. Luke hadn't created his carefully curated public persona for himself. The smokescreen was there so his dad could see that Luke was surviving very well without him, thank you very much.

"Don't you think that's a bit drastic just to ensure I don't have another game like today?" he asked.

Fletcher slapped a hand on the table. "Jaysus. This isn't about your play. This is about you. You get more enjoyment from playing this game than any player I know. And that parlays to the rest of the team around you. It's a bloody shame to have your father ruin that."

Luke looked from one man to the other. *Were they serious?*

Van Horn nodded as though Luke had asked the question out loud. "You'd do the same for anyone else on this team," he said. "In fact, you'd do more. In case you didn't realize it, you are the glue that holds this team together."

Well, shit.

The doorbell rang, shattering their unforeseen Oprah moment. Monty scrambled to his feet, letting out a few confused barks as he tried to recall where exactly he was.

"Come on, Cujo," Van Horn called to the dog. "Let's go get our wings." They started down the hall before the quarterback stopped abruptly. "Don't go getting a swelled head now, Kessler. You're still down for a half-hour of extra practice for every ball you dropped today."

Fletcher chuckled. "Now you can tell me what's going on with the lass," he said once Van Horn was out of earshot.

Luke dragged his fingers through his hair. How could he tell his teammate what was going on with Summer when he couldn't figure it out himself?

"Nothing. Just a stupid lapse in judgment. It didn't mean anything." The lie hung up in his throat like a boulder.

The kicker studied him as if he were attempting to work out one of those tricky math calculations he made up for his Mathletes. Luke tried not to squirm beneath Fletcher's steely gaze. Doing so would give too much away.

"Have a care," Fletcher said finally. "It doesn't take much for those—" He formed air quotes with his fingers "—lapses in judgment to turn into a whole lot more."

"There isn't going to be anything more," Luke insisted. "Like I said, it was nothing."

Fletcher snorted. The corners of his eyes crinkled with resignation. "I reckon I uttered those exact words no more than a year ago. You may think it's nothing until it turns into something. Something you can't live without."

Luke let the implication of Fletcher's statement sink in. Against all odds, the kicker had fallen in love with his pretend wife. She had somehow softened Fletcher's rough edges and gruff demeanor. He was definitely a happier man with Andi in his life.

But Fletcher was worrying for nothing. Luke wasn't going to fall in love with anyone. He had gotten this far in life without love from anyone but his gram. He didn't need a woman's love to complete him.

An unbidden vision of Summer and her wobbly smile flashed before his eyes. She knew how to use those lips of hers for more than sass. His junk grew hard thinking about the way she responded to his kisses. Shame quickly washed away his lust. He had never been the type of guy who would carry on with one woman while he was dating another one.

He squeezed his eyes shut, trying to conjure up the image of Elizabeth. The woman he should be lusting over. The one he should be kissing in dark places.

Too bad he failed miserably.

CHAPTER TEN

SUMMER'S BUTT cheeks were growing numb sitting in the Lilliputian plastic classroom chair. Shifting slightly, she kept her smile focused on the student massacring "Hot Cross Buns" with his recorder. She might have clapped a tad too enthusiastically when he finished.

"That was wonderful, Trevor. I can see you practiced over the summer."

The young boy drew his shoulders up proudly. "My dad told me to share the music with our neighbors. He gave me a dollar every time I practiced outside."

Summer smothered her laugh. "I'm sure your neighbors appreciated that."

The boy nodded at her with a toothy grin.

"Your sister is waiting to walk you home, Trevor," the principal announced from the doorway. "Hurry along."

"Thank you, Miss Pearson," Trevor said. "I'm gonna go home and practice some more. I'll make you proud tomorrow. You'll see."

Summer waved goodbye, too choked up to reply. She was astounded at the joy these kids found in music. There had been students at Preston who had a similar love of music, but so many of them took the opportunities handed to them for granted. Not here. Her students showed their gratitude every day with their smiles, their hugs, the homemade gifts they brought her, and their willingness to try.

If anyone knew how music could transform a life, it was Summer. After her father died, she became a bitter, lost ten-year-old girl. The mother she'd known had seemingly died, too, leaving behind a determined woman with the single focus of providing for her children. But here in this very classroom, Grandma Bonnie had rescued Summer, with music. More specifically, with the cello. It wasn't lost on her that she'd been given a wonderful opportunity to show her grandmother how grateful she was by paying it forward.

And darn if it didn't make her heart feel amazing. If only the rest of her body felt the same. Smoothing her skirt with her hands, she tried not to groan as she got to her feet. It had been a long day—a long few days, in fact. With the limited number of instruments, she was forced to hold many of these assessments after school. Between the extra hours in the classroom and her LSAT prep study group, she was exhausted. Tonight, she was looking forward to going home to enjoy a relaxing soak in the tub before working on song arrangements for this weekend's game. Gathering up her things, she headed out of the classroom.

Unfortunately, her principal was still hovering in the doorway.

"I've been thinking," the woman began.

Twenty-eight years among the living had taught Summer that nothing good ever followed that phrase. She mentally braced herself for whatever was coming next.

"Wouldn't it be fabulous if we had a mini-concert for the guests coming in to speak to the students on career day?"

"Uh—" Summer stammered. Surely the woman understood it wasn't that simple throwing together a concert with elementary school kids. They needed an entire semester to learn the few songs they played for the holiday concert in December. And even then, it was a miracle if the parents could recognize the tune without the cheat sheet disguised as a program. Career day was a mere two weeks away. She was asking the impossible.

Her astonishment must have been written all over her face because the principal waved her hand. "Nothing too elaborate. It's the first month of school, after all. But maybe something on the recorder. Something worthy of a light, feel-good, fluff segment on the morning news. Your cousin is bringing a film crew with her, isn't she?"

So that was it.

Summer highly doubted her cousin planned on publicizing her appearance at the school. The principal didn't know how lucky she was to get Lizzie by herself.

"Because it would be nice publicity for our meager Title One school," the principal continued. "And positive things always come out of positive publicity."

Summer didn't need her own cheat sheet to understand that "positive things" meant "more resources." At Preston, all the principal had to do was send home a letter to parents, and, *voilà,* whatever needed to be funded was instantly flush with cash. Not so in this school. She had to hand it to the principal who seemed to know every trick in the book.

But she had a point. Summer could only imagine what she could do if there were more instruments for the kids to play. More sheet music for them to learn. She had it within her power to make that happen. To make career day a resounding success. All she had to do was kowtow to Lizzie, yet again.

It's for the kids. And Grandma Bonnie.

"I'll see what I can do."

The principal responded with a satisfied grin. "I know you will. You're doing fantastic with the children, by the way. Your grandmother would be so proud."

WHILE THE WEATHER REMAINED NICE, Summer walked the five blocks to and from school each day. The brief amount of exercise wasn't exactly making a dent in her Ben and Jerry's padded hips, but at least they weren't getting any wider. And there was the added benefit of the fresh air, which always helped her think.

Today on the walk home, she was desperately trying to come up with a way to persuade Lizzie to bring a film crew to career day. Of course, whatever scenario she came up with would mean she'd have to *speak* to her cousin. Summer had been avoiding her since Sunday. The guilt and shame she felt threatened to overwhelm her. She hadn't even told Paige what she'd done with Luke Kessler. Her face burned even now, thinking about the way she'd behaved with him the other day.

She stomped her bootie-clad feet for several steps. It wasn't like she initiated it. The skunk had kissed *her*.

Except she hadn't done anything to stop him.

Worse, she hadn't wanted to.

Instead, she'd opened her mouth and her arms wide, inviting him in to do with her whatever he wished. For crying out loud, she was no better than Milli, rolling over on her back and exposing her lady parts to any male that approached. And Luke Kessler was definitely a dog. Ravaging her while he was dating her cousin.

But, *damn,* the guy could kiss.

She'd heard talk of toe-curling, panty-melting kisses before. Mostly on Netflix or in the romance novels Paige devoured, but still. She never thought they were possible in real life.

Until a few days ago, that was.

A lusty groan escaped her mouth at the memory of the way his mouth stoked her body to near orgasmic heights. She looked up to see a UPS driver standing beside his truck at the curb. He was glancing at her strangely. Summer's cheeks burned even hotter. She tucked her chin and hurried along the next block toward her grandparent's house.

She was so busy keeping her head down that she didn't notice the odd assortment of cars parked out front. It wasn't until she walked through the front door and Monty nearly took her out at the knees that she realized she had company.

Her grandfather and two of his friends were sitting around the table playing cards. Several beer cans and a half of a pizza were also on the table. Milli sat at Papa Harry's feet, waiting for a scrap of food to fall onto the ground. Monty circled Summer's legs, woofing with excitement.

"Summer!" Papa Harry shouted. "You're home. Come sit in for a hand."

Monty headbutted her thigh for attention. Summer cautiously patted the top of his head once. The dog sighed and leaned into her. He really was a sweet thing. His owner, not so much. She glanced around the room, looking for Luke, but he was nowhere in sight. The breath she didn't realize she was holding whistled past her lips.

"What's going on?" she asked.

"We moved our game here today," Papa Harry announced as if that explained everything.

So much for a quiet bath.

"What fun," she replied because, really, what could she say? It was his home. If he wanted to throw an impromptu poker game here, who was she to object?

She dropped her book bag on the sofa and helped herself to a slice of pizza. It had been five hours since her measly lunch of yogurt and an apple, after all. She wondered where Lizzie was hiding. And why was Monty here? Perhaps her cousin was out with Luke somewhere, and Papa Harry was watching his dog.

That sinking feeling in her stomach was hunger. *Nothing else,* she admonished herself.

Monty followed on her heels when she went into the kitchen

to grab a seltzer water from the fridge. The door leading in from the garage opened suddenly, causing Summer to collide with a warm, hard body. One that felt and smelled familiar.

Luke juggled a glass jar between their bodies. Summer sucked in a breath when his fingers grazed her hip and the underside of her breast. The pizza she was holding landed with a slap against his rock-like pectoral muscle. Their bodies were so close together that their noses nearly touched. She could feel her heart pounding. Or maybe that was his. A wave of need washed over her, and she would have leaned into him and made a fool of herself again had Papa Harry not walked into the room.

"Summer! Are you throwing food?" her grandfather teased.

She jumped back, the remnants of the slice of pizza dangling from her fingertips. Monty squeezed in between their legs to gobble up the pepperoni that had dropped to the floor.

"It was my bad, Harry," Luke said. "I wasn't watching where I was going when I came back in." He held out the jar to her grandfather. "You were right. There was one left hiding in the back of the beer fridge."

Papa Harry let out a delighted whoop. "Hey, fellas. Who wants some raisins?"

He disappeared back into the dining room to the cheers of his buddies. Summer stepped around Monty and grabbed a paper towel off the roll. She wet it down and turned back to him. Her hand reached out as if to wipe off his chest, but there was danger in that move.

So. Much. Danger.

She tossed the paper towel to him instead. He caught it easily and began dabbing his Henley. Her fingers twitched to replace his. She grabbed a glass out of the cupboard and filled it with tap water to give them something to do.

"I always thought raisins were a kid thing," Luke murmured to his chest as he wiped it a bit more vigorously. "Who knew?"

"They're soaked in gin."

His head snapped up then. "Seriously?"

One of those slow, devastating smiles began to form on his lips. Summer swayed on her feet before forcing herself to look away. She guzzled the glass of water to cover her moan. The sounds of cards shuffling and the plastic chips clattering against one another filtered in from the other room. Inside the kitchen, however, the charged silence hung heavy between them.

"Summer," Luke eventually said, the word sounding more like an exasperated sigh.

Here it comes. The big letdown. Her breath got tangled up in her throat, and her stomach lurched.

"No," she whispered before shoving her way past him and out the back door. The screen door slammed behind her. Monty pushed it open a second time and followed her out into the yard. She strode over to the hand-made swings hanging from the branches of the two oak trees in the yard. Summer's father and uncle made them at scout camp decades earlier. Papa Harry had replaced the nylon roping once or twice since then, but the weathered wooden seats still bore his sons' initials.

Monty wandered off to explore the far corners of the fenced-in yard while Summer dropped down onto one of the swings. She viciously traced the dirt beneath the swing with the toe of her bootie while drawing a lungful of air and blowing it back out again.

"Is that helping?"

The sound of Luke's voice so close had her nearly jumping out of the swing. Only her death grip on the nylon rope kept her from pitching forward, face-first into the dirt. She should have known he'd follow her outside. He needed to make his excuses for his behavior the other day. To tell her how he was amped up for the game and his testosterone got the better of him or something else equally patronizing like that.

Except she didn't want to hear excuses coming through that

mouth, the one she'd been dreaming about since the day they met. She decided to beat him to the punch instead.

"The other day was a mistake," she announced as she jumped from the swing and spun around to face him. "I'm not sure what came over me. But I do know it's never going to happen again."

She could tell by the way he braced back on his heels ever so slightly that she'd caught him off guard. He opened his mouth before snapping it closed again.

Some part of her deep down hoped he'd deny it. That he'd tell her the only mistake was that he was chasing after the wrong Pearson. That he wanted her. Then he would take her in his arms and kiss her like he had the other day.

But of course, he didn't.

Why would he when he could have Lizzie, the perfect Pearson?

His lips formed a hard line as he stared her down. He didn't like having the tables turned. Too bad. Summer marveled at her poise. Chock up one positive to her public humiliation.

"And I would appreciate it if you would forget it ever happened," she added. "I don't want Lizzie hurt by something stupid I did."

He crossed his arms over his chest. "'Something stupid?'"

"Well, yeah. Epically stupid."

The sound of him grinding his teeth together escaped his lips. "First of all, what happened between us is just that, between us. Secondly, Elizabeth and I—"

Whatever he was going to say was interrupted by the screen door opening, followed by Milli's excited yips.

"Luke! What a surprise. I thought we were meeting later."

Lizzie was using her chipper morning TV voice. The edge in it was likely only detectable to those people who knew her best. Like Summer. She could relate to her frustration. *He and Lizzie what?* What was Luke going to say? She nearly stamped her foot in frustration again.

He aimed one of his gracious smiles—the one Summer was beginning to hate—at Lizzie. “I ran into your grandfather at Sunset Glen. He invited me over for a game of poker with his friends. I thought I’d hang out here until you were ready for our date.”

Lizzie toyed with her ponytail. She was dressed in only the finest workout clothes, bought to showcase the perfectly toned ass that had all kinds of creeps commenting on her social media accounts. Her face was flawless, as though she hadn’t even broken a sweat during her likely two-hour barre class. Still, knowing her cousin, Lizzie was thrown off her game by not having an extra hour of privacy to make herself even more camera-ready for the paparazzi she hoped would follow her and Luke on their dinner date.

Not that she’d let him know that. Lizzie tweaked his shoulder. “Be sure not to lose too much money to Papa Harry, though. I’m counting on you taking me to Bacchus tonight.”

Luke didn’t flinch when Lizzie dropped the name of one of Milwaukee’s most exclusive— and expensive—restaurants. He looked down at his pizza-stained shirt. “I guess I need to go home and change then.”

Lizzie bounced up on her toes and pressed her lips to Luke’s cheek. “Come back in an hour, and I’ll be ready.”

That would give her enough time to alert social media to her plans for the evening, Summer thought to herself. Her cousin was one of those minor celebrities who lived for the attention from her fans.

Luke whistled for Monty. The bulky dog lumbered out from beneath the holly bushes at the back of the yard, making a beeline for Lizzie’s crotch.

Lizzie squealed and jumped behind Luke. “What the hell is that?”

Her tone had the dog reversing course where he plopped down on Summer’s foot with an affronted whimper. Summer’s fingers absently found his head and began scratching him there.

Luke's gaze traveled from Summer's hand to her face, clearly surprised she would touch his dog on purpose. "This is Monty. He's my dog," he added with a tone that sounded clipped.

Summer almost felt sorry for him.

"Oh." Lizzie recovered quickly, as always. "I guess I didn't know you actually adopted one of the dogs you championed yourself."

"He was kind of hard to resist."

As if on cue, the dog farted. Luke glared at him. Summer dipped her chin to hide her chuckle. Lizzie shot the pooch a disdainful look.

"Yes, I can see that," she said as she stepped out from behind Luke.

"Um." Luke shuffled from foot to foot. "Your grandfather offered that I could leave Monty here on game weekends. I left him with my Gram last weekend, and he almost got them both kicked out. It was because he doesn't like being cooped up in small places. There's a yard for him to roam around here, and Milli would be good company while everyone is at the game."

"Here?" Lizzie's voice rose an octave. "With me?"

Summer wished she could have secretly recorded this exchange to share with Paige. Her roommate would be doubled over by now. Lizzie barely tolerated Milli living with them even though it was the dog's own home. She would never agree to watch Luke's dog, no matter how many five-star restaurants he took her to.

Or whatever other method he used to persuade her.

Summer's mouth went dry at the thought of what Luke and her cousin may or may not be doing behind closed doors. Her ridiculous jealousy wiped away any tinge of guilt she might have at using the situation to her advantage.

Wouldn't her principal be excited when Summer told her there would indeed be a film crew at career day? And now,

Summer had the perfect opportunity to make it happen—by coming to Lizzie's rescue.

"I live here, too," she chimed in. "I can look after Monty."

Lizzie's head snapped in her direction, her eyes wide with panic before resigned relief settled there.

Luke's shoulders relaxed. He eyed Summer warily. "You're sure?"

She buried her fingers deeper into the dog's fur. Monty groaned with pleasure.

"We'll be fine," she replied.

"Of course, we will," Lizzie said. She nodded slightly at Summer as she looped her arm through Luke's. "Now that that's settled, we should get changed for our dinner. We don't want to miss seeing who else is dining there tonight."

Lizzie led Luke toward the back door. With a sigh, Summer followed. She'd get her pound of flesh from Lizzie later. Both dogs scrambled between her legs to reach the kitchen before her. She had to stop short at the threshold because the room was suddenly more cramped than usual.

"Antonio!" she cried with delight. "What a nice surprise."

"It seems all the Growler receivers are surprising women today," Lizzie mumbled.

Luke and his teammate exchanged a frosty glare. Antonio's face softened when he glanced in Summer's direction, however. His eyes fairly danced with delight.

"I need your help," he said. "I got asked to play at the proposal. I said I'd do it only if I could bring you. I thought you could help me arrange the songs."

A warmth settled in the vicinity of Summer's chest. She looked over at Luke. He'd done this. He'd done what she asked the other day. He'd done what needed to be done to make Antonio feel part of the team. She offered him a slight smile, but he remained stoic, his gaze still trained on Antonio.

"What kind of proposal?" Lizzie demanded. "A wedding

proposal?"

"Yeah," Antonio replied. "One of the Growlers."

Lizzie clapped her hands together. "Who?"

"It's on the down-low," Luke answered before Antonio could spill the beans.

"Oh." Lizzie executed a near-perfect pout.

"It's happening Friday night," Luke explained. "We are all invited to the after-party. You'll get all the details then."

"How fun," Lizzie said. "Maybe I can shoot some video for an exclusive."

"No video," the two men said at the same time.

Both knew her feelings about performing in public, and she was grateful for their quick defense. The pleasant feeling in her chest spread throughout her body.

"I would never be that insensitive to include you in the video, Summer," Lizzie countered. "Besides, you won't be staying for the after-party anyway."

And just that quickly, the warmth evaporated.

"Actually, she'll be my date," Antonio announced. He lifted his chin at Luke in challenge.

Summer could have sworn Luke let a teeny growl. She heaved an exasperated sigh. Whatever was going on between the two teammates didn't involve her. There was still very much a "he and Lizzie," judging by the looks of it. Whatever he was going to say earlier couldn't be what she was hoping for. Better to escape this conversation with her dignity intact.

"Why don't we get started then?" she said to Antonio. "Have you had dinner?"

The receiver smiled smugly at Luke. "There's a rib place everyone is talking about. And I've been here for two months without ever trying any of those cheese curd thingies."

"Well then, we better remedy that right away." She tossed Malibu Ken and Barbie a wave before exiting the kitchen with Antonio.

CHAPTER ELEVEN

"You would be surprised how challenging it is to make the weather forecast sound unique each time you give it. Especially when you have to deliver the same exact forecast three times every fifteen minutes," Elizabeth was saying.

She was chatting with several of the WAGs at one of the long tables located in a courtyard overlooking the "throwing lanes" in the axe bar. The lanes were constructed like narrow barn stalls, with the bottom half built from local Wisconsin timber while the top half was segments of a chain-link fence. Wood shavings covered the floors of the lanes, muffling the clank of the axes that didn't meet their target.

String lights crisscrossed the outdoor tables casting shadows over Luke and his teammates in the fading twilight. The beat from the music below floated up to the patio. Luke anxiously jiggled his leg against the table.

"What the hell are you so nervous about?" Fletcher asked. "You're not the one tying on a ball and chain."

"Does this seem like a romantic way to propose to a woman?" Luke demanded of the kicker.

Van Horn cracked a peanut and tossed it into his mouth.

"What do you know about romance? Have you been watching soap operas with your Gram again?"

Luke flipped them both off. The truth was, he could give a crap about the romance. He only wanted Summer to have a positive performance tonight. Even more, he wanted his teammates to hear her, to be entranced by her mastery of the cello the same way he had been when he first heard her stroke her bow over the strings. It was important to him that she felt worthy. That whatever made her question her abilities be forgotten.

The patio was filled with athletes who were constantly striving to be at the top of their game. They would recognize a like-minded soul—even if her pursuit was a different one. They would appreciate her talent, and he'd make sure they told her. Each and every damn one of them.

He told himself he wanted these things for Summer because she was Lizzie's cousin. And Harry's granddaughter. The older man was quickly becoming a fixture in Gram's life. Gram would want Summer to be successful as well.

Those were the only reasons he was championing Summer, he lied to himself.

Luke swept his hand around the bar, a half-flight below them. "Where exactly is he going to propose?"

"I'm guessing in front of those two hundred roses," Fletcher replied, nodding to a roped-off area in the corner. Dozens of roses made up in the shape of an arbor stood by a keyboard and a chair.

Van Horn shook his head. "I'm pretty sure he stole that idea from another player in the league."

"He's going to do it in front of all of us?"

The quarterback and kicker exchanged another one of their looks.

"No wonder Palmer fired you," Van Horn said.

"Apparently, this is how it's done these days," Fletcher added with a shrug.

Luke ignored both men the moment he spotted Summer making her way up the steps, her cello case in her hand. She was wearing a billowing, sleeveless red dress that cinched at the waist, showcasing her curves. The dress ended mid-calf, exposing clunky red wedge shoes with straps that wrapped around her slender ankles. She'd piled her hair up in an elegant knot. But true to her nature, several wisps refused to be tamed. The evening breeze whipped them against her mouth. She swiped at one furiously, losing her balance in the process and nearly toppling backward down the steps.

He bolted forward from his seat to rescue her. But he was too late. He should have guessed McGraff would be right behind her. Summer laughed happily when the rookie wrapped his hands around her waist and righted her. They climbed the final two steps joined together like that. The feeling of having his shoulder pads laced too tight suddenly came over Luke.

Too bad he wasn't wearing shoulder pads.

Summer's gaze flickered around the patio. Despite her laughter, Luke could see the tension bracketing her mouth. The rigid way she held her body. She didn't want to be here. But she'd come because the rookie had asked. Not because Luke had practically begged her. And somehow, that burned worse than her calling their kiss "stupid."

Their kiss was reckless, yes. But certainly not stupid. Mind-blowing was a more apt description, if he were to analyze it. Which he wasn't.

Luke was still standing frozen in the center of the patio, looking like an idiot, when Fletcher's wife, Andi, hurried up from the bar below.

"They're coming," she announced breathlessly.

Fletcher was by her side instantly. "You shouldn't be racing up the stairs in your condition, lass."

Andi patted her husband on the chest. "I'm having a baby. Not an organ transplant. I'm fine."

The kicker mumbled something under his breath. His wife met his gaze and gently stroked his biceps. Fletcher's shoulders relaxed. A soft smile formed on Andi's face. Luke's throat tightened at the intimacy of their exchange.

"We need to take our seats and pretend everything is normal," she said.

Elizabeth came up beside Luke and threaded her arm through his. Luke realized he didn't remember what his date was wearing. He smiled as he let his gaze wander over her leather leggings, high-heeled booties, and a flowing sleeveless blouse she'd covered with a jean jacket. Chic and perfectly acceptable.

So why hadn't he noticed earlier?

Andi headed in their direction.

"And you." She slapped Luke playfully on the arm. "What a coup of you to get Summer Pearson to play for them. Shaina is going to lose it. How did you pull it off?"

"She's my cousin." Elizabeth chimed in before he could answer.

Andi's eyes went wide as she looked from Elizabeth to Summer and back again. "Oh, wow. I didn't think Summer was from Milwaukee. What a coincidence."

Elizabeth smiled. "We are a multi-talented family."

"You can say that again." Andi's phone chimed. She glanced at the screen before nodding to Summer. "Places, everyone. Remember to keep your faces averted and act like you don't notice them. It's pretty dark up here. Hopefully, she won't notice us before the big moment."

They found seats at the tables in the shadows.

"Like she isn't going to notice a bunch of musclebound guys trying to look inconspicuous in these uncomfortable plastic chairs," Van Horn murmured.

Elizabeth giggled. Andi put her finger to her lips, trying to quiet them both. And then the music began. The lilting sound of Summer covering Train's "Marry Me" slowly quieted the crowd.

Luke couldn't help the grin that tugged at his lips at the pride he felt for her. As he suspected, she'd captivated his teammates and their partners within the first few notes. McGraff joined in, but he was careful to maintain an accompanying roll, letting the spotlight shine on Summer.

An older man crept closer, his cellphone camera directed at her. Luke rose from his chair, but Andi's fierce grip on his forearm stayed him.

"That's Shaina's dad," she whispered. "He's filming it for them."

If Summer saw the man, she didn't miss a beat. Her eyes were closed as though she were one with her instrument. Luke made a mental note to talk to the guy later about editing her image out.

Andi gave his arm another squeeze. Her eyes were sparkling with delight. "She's amazing. Antonio, too."

"She absolutely is," he murmured.

The music enveloped him. Luke didn't recall seeing the couple enter the patio. Or Palmer getting down on one knee. His gaze was fixed on Summer only.

Shaina's squeal pierced the night air, and the crowd cheered. Summer and McGraff launched into Bruno Mars' peppy tune "Marry Me," followed by their rendition of "You're All I Need to Get By." Palmer and his now-fiancée made the rounds of the patio. The punter launched himself at Luke.

"Dude, how did you know my girl was a fan of Summer's? This was better than I could have imagined. You brought the magic. It's a night she'll never forget," he gushed.

A crowd gathered around Summer and McGraff. Their teammates slapped the rookie on the back, accusing him of holding out on them. Summer slipped away to one of the tables, where she carefully returned her cello to its case. Elizabeth was busy using her phone to interview the newly-engaged couple for the morning show. Luke wandered over to Summer. A wistful smile graced her lips, similar to the one she wore after performing at Sunset Glen.

Almost as if she couldn't believe the beautiful sounds her cello produced.

His hands suddenly ached to touch her for some inexplicable reason. He shoved them into his pockets. "Thank you," he said quietly, fully expecting her to remind him she hadn't played at his request.

She surprised him yet again. "Thank *you*." She jerked her chin in McGraff's direction. The rookie had donned a pair of sunglasses and was taking requests from their teammates.

Luke shrugged. "He'll be regretting it in a few weeks. Those guys will have him playing for them at every hotel bar where we stay now."

Her smile lit up the night. "A talent like his deserves to be showcased."

"But not yours?" He was suddenly desperate to know why she was so adamant about not playing in front of anyone. Especially given her amazing ability.

Her smile dimmed immediately. "There's no comparison. I'm a fluke. A poser. I don't have the training needed to make it in the music world."

"Bullshit," he snapped. He sincerely hoped it wasn't Summer's mother who had spouted that nonsense to her. Not that he hadn't heard the same type of things from his own parents about football. *Outperform the negative*. "And whoever told you that, had their head up their ass."

Her eyes went wide at his comment. She bit her bottom lip. "Tell that to the chairman of the board of directors for the Vienna Chamber Orchestra."

Shit.

That explained a lot. Luke took a step closer to her, hoping his presence would comfort her somehow. "They didn't know what they were talking about."

She arched an eyebrow at him, responding with a clipped tone. "Would you tell that to a team owner or a coach who said that to you?"

"Worse. I said it to my father when he told me I wasn't good enough." He hadn't intended to say that. Luke never shared that conversation with anyone outside his shrink's office. "And it's his words that propelled me to be the best at this game that I can be."

Her face immediately softened. She inched forward, closing much of the distance between them. "That's horrible. I mean the part about your dad. The part about you succeeding despite him, well, that's amazing."

"You could, too." He reached for her hand, jerking back seconds before their fingers touched, when he remembered where they were.

Her eyes were suddenly shiny. She shook her head. "It's not that simple," she whispered.

Luke wasn't sure if she was talking about her music or something else. Before he could ask her to clarify, they were interrupted by some guy wearing a T-shirt with the bar's logo on it.

"Summer," he said. "I thought you must be up here. No one else in Milwaukee plays the cello like that." The dude glanced over at McGraff and grinned. "He keeps popping up in front of a keyboard."

Summer wrapped her arms around the guy's shoulders and gave him a quick hug. "What are you doing here, Mike?"

Mike hooked his thumbs through his belt loops and sidled up next to her. "A buddy of mine from the station moonlights here. When one of the Growlers rented the place out for the night, they needed extra Axe-perts who wouldn't be starstruck by the players." He shrugged. "So here I am."

"'Axe-perts?'" Luke said.

The guy looked Luke's way. "We coach customers on how to safely throw an axe."

Luke swallowed a snort. Evidently, he hadn't been around a

team of testosterone-fueled competitive jocks. He doubted his teammates would take direction from this guy or anyone else.

The guy stretched out his hand. "Lieutenant Mike Runson of the Milwaukee Fire Department. I'm also the director of the Growlers pep band."

That explained his connection to Summer. And the team. Judging by his body language with Summer, Mike was probably the fireman she went out with last week. Luke shook Mike's hand a tad more firmly than was necessary. "And an Axe-pert."

The fireman grinned back at him with a firm grip of his own. "*Axe*-actly."

Summer groaned at his pun. "Do you think I could throw one?"

Runson eyed her from head to toe with a wolfish gleam in his eye. "I'd be happy to teach you. But open-toed shoes aren't permitted in that part of the bar." He reached a hand out to her. "Come on. They keep some extra sneakers in the office for the ladies. You can store your cello there."

The fireman was poaching her right out from under Luke's nose. He opened his mouth to protest, but Summer must have read his mind.

"You should see if Lizzie wants to give it a try," she said, reminding him which Pearson he'd brought to the bar tonight. She bit her bottom lip again. "I'm sure she'd enjoy it if you showed her how."

The patio felt a bit chillier when she and Mike disappeared down the stairs. Elizabeth was busy typing something into her phone. When she looked up and smiled at him, Luke had to force one in return. That calm he felt, knowing his emotional life was under control, was suddenly nowhere to be found. Instead, he felt restless and edgy.

And desire.

Too bad it was for the wrong woman.

CHAPTER TWELVE

SUMMER FELT a bit ridiculous wearing a pair of borrowed sneakers. At least the bar owner kept clean socks in his office, too. When it came right down to it, though, she would wear Mike's firefighter boots if it meant she could hurl something against the wall. Her emotions were so all over the place she wanted to scream. Throwing a lethal weapon at a target was the next best thing.

All day, she'd been a nervous wreck about playing her cello in front of strangers. Famous strangers with verified social media accounts. Many of whom could ruin her all over again with a single click. She'd spent most of last night googling the best illness to feign.

But in the end, she couldn't let Antonio down. Not when he needed this acceptance from his teammates. Not that he couldn't win them over with his incredible talent. He needed a crutch tonight. And somehow, she was that crutch. She'd almost asked him to swing by the liquor store so she could buy a bottle of Fireball. Mrs. Hilbert's remedy had worked so well the other day.

Yet, once she'd forced her legs up the stairs and into her chair, once her fingers gripped the curl and the bow was dancing over the strings, Summer's nerves vanished. She was back in her happy place. The one place where she could forget the world around her and immerse herself in sound. The fact that others claimed to feel pleasure from listening was the icing on the cake.

Right up until she finished.

She remembered why she wasn't ever going to play in front of an audience ever again. Her hands were shaky, recalling the shame and humiliation of her failure in Vienna. And then the bone-deep sadness began to creep back into her soul. The truth was, she missed making music for others' enjoyment as much as she would miss a limb were it to be amputated.

And it hurt just as much.

And damn Luke Kessler with his platitudes and confessions. *And his smoldering looks.* Damn him for making her think she could easily have it all again. For making her *want* it all again.

For making her want *him*.

She gripped the handle of the axe, dropping the blade behind her shoulder as Mike had instructed her. Clenching her teeth, she imagined Luke's face plastered to the bullseye and tossed the axe with all her might. Behind her, Mike cheered at the sound of metal splitting wood. It wasn't a bullseye, but she'd hit the target.

Her toss didn't make her feel any lighter, however. "I want to try it again," she insisted to Mike.

He cocked an eyebrow as he handed her another axe. "You're as passionate about ax-throwing as you are about music." He leaned forward, his fingers brushing and lingering against hers before he relinquished the handle. "It makes me wonder what else you're passionate about, Summer," he murmured.

It was all she could do not to roll her eyes. Why, when she was suffering an existential crisis, were men suddenly coming out of the woodwork? Except there was a lot to like about Mike. He was a nice guy. Uncomplicated and stable. Fun to be around and interesting to talk to. Reasonably handsome and hardworking.

Too bad Summer wasn't attracted to him.

Instead, she was lusting after a certain set of lips that half the time she wanted to smack. Maybe less than half the time now that she knew how sweet they tasted. Or how amazing they felt against her lips. She groaned. The man was exasperating.

And dating her cousin.

While at the same time toying with Summer.

She hurled the axe at the target, this time missing the bullseye by a quarter of an inch. Someone whistled behind her. Summer turned to find a small crowd observing her. A crowd that included a petite pregnant woman, a dark-haired man with captivating gray eyes, and the object of her frustration, Luke Kessler. He whistled his appreciation again.

The dark-haired man groaned. "Jaysus. You call that an axe?" He pointed to the target at the end of the lane. "That's no axe That's a bloody hatchet. At home, we use those to cut our meat for dinner."

"I didn't realize there was much cutting involved with haggis," another man joked.

Summer felt her cheeks go hot when she recognized the broad shoulders, and chiseled chin of the team's quarterback, the guy who had walked in on her and Luke at the stadium. For his part, the quarterback acknowledged her with a discreet nod. The pregnant woman shushed them all and stepped forward.

"Ignore my husband," she said to Summer. "He loves to play the Highlander whenever he can." She extended a delicate hand. "I'm Andi Lar—I mean Fletcher. Andi *Fletcher*." She chuckled softly. "I hope I get that right before the baby is born."

Her husband made an animal-like sound behind her. Andi's eyes twinkled. Summer liked the woman instantly. She pumped Andi's hand up and down.

"Lucky for you, the baby won't notice if you mess up. When are you due?"

Andi rested her hand back on her belly. "Not for another three months. An early Christmas gift."

"That's wonderful. Congratulations."

An unexpected pang stabbed Summer in her chest. She'd always assumed she'd be a mom one day. After she had established herself in her musical career. Managing a family would be easier when she could set her own schedule. Except now her future was a jumbled mess with three years of law school looming on the horizon. Her mother had juggled law school and children after losing her husband. Just not always successfully.

"I was wondering," Andi said, interrupting her spiraling thoughts. "Can I hire you to play at the grand opening of my shop next month?"

Her shop? She was having a baby *and* opening a store?

"It's a small place adjacent to my friend's salon," Andi explained. "I craft soaps and lotions and other spa items. We sell them online, but I've been getting a lot of demand from people who want to see the items in person. We're having a soft opening in two weeks and then a grand opening in October." She shook her head as if she found the idea of such pomp and circumstance ridiculous. "Clive—my friend with the salon—has gone slightly overboard, and it will be more like a party. But I think it would be wonderful to have live music. And yours fits my brand perfectly."

Summer felt her throat tighten up while her brain scrambled for some way to get out of this gracefully. These propositions were getting out of hand. Damn Paige for pushing her off their sofa. No one would make these requests if she were safely ensconced back in Chicago enjoying a tub of Ben and Jerry's.

"She doesn't perform in front of people."

Everyone turned to look at Luke, most of them wearing the same incredulous expression he wore when she said those words to him. He ignored them all. His inscrutable gaze never wavered from Summer's face. What was he up to now? And who was he to speak for her?

"It would be my pleasure." It was as if the words came from an alien inside of her, because that wasn't what Summer meant to say at all. Heck, she didn't even know *what* she meant to say. But it certainly wasn't that. "Um, if I'm free, of course," she backpedaled.

"We are flexible with the date," Andi said, her pleasure lighting up her pixie-like face. "We can certainly work around your schedule."

Sweat began to bead at the back of Summer's neck. What the hell had she done? "And I have to ask that you don't publicize that I'll be playing there. Or film it." *Great.* Now she sounded as eccentric as Mrs. Hilbert. "I'd prefer to be in the background. The event should be about your store, that's all."

"Of course," Andi replied. "Whatever you want. Perhaps we can get coffee next week, and discuss your fee."

Summer clasped her hands behind her back to keep from wringing them. "I don't play professionally any longer. There's no fee necessary. It'll be my pleasure."

Or death by nerves.

Andi's husband eyed her shrewdly. "Lass, her company makes decent money. You spent years training professionally to get where you are. We can afford to pay you what you are worth."

What you are worth.

Summer swallowed a nervous laugh. She wasn't a trained professional. Far from it.

She is a gimmick. Not an artist. Mongrels with no musical education like her videos, and you think that represents talent? You are demeaning the expertise of all the other musicians who belong in those chairs with this performance.

The ugly words echoed in her head, the memory making her palms sweaty. Any performance she would give was not worth anything. And there was no way she'd take a dime from this woman.

"Like I said, it would be my pleasure," she repeated firmly.

"Make a donation to your favorite charity in my name if you wish."

"Score one for Professor McMath's Mathletes," someone called out. The crowd around them laughed and cheered.

"Or Kessler's rescue mutts," another voice said.

Her eyes darted around the bar looking for an inconspicuous exit, when her gaze collided with Luke's. The asshole was smirking at her, his eyes shining with triumph. And that was when it hit her. He'd effectively goaded her into saying yes to Andi's plea. *Again.*

Turning on her heel, she marched down the lane and yanked one of the axes out of the target. Just her luck, a chunk of the wood splintered off and became lodged in her palm.

"Ow," she cried before she could stop herself.

Luke was beside her in an instant. He reached for her hand. She yanked it against her body, trying to squelch the blood with her other hand.

"Let me see it before you bleed all over that fabulous dress," he commanded softly.

The compliment stunned her into giving him her hand. She jumped when his thumb made contact with the chunk of wood wedged halfway into the skin.

"She okay?" Mike asked as he hurried down the lane. He grimaced when he got a look at Summer's hand. "There's a first-aid kit in the staff bathroom. Come on."

Andi offered her help when they passed by her. A wiser woman would have ditched Luke and taken her up on the offer. It seemed Summer wasn't very wise though. She pasted on an embarrassed grin and shook her head, letting Luke lead her by the hand to the back of the bar.

Using a keycode, Mike opened an unmarked door next to the office. Inside the tight bathroom was a steel cabinet. He pulled out a first-aid kit from inside and set it on the corner of the sink.

He was rifling through its contents when someone yelled his name.

"Shit. Your friends are getting crazy. Can you handle this?" Mike asked Luke.

"It's a splinter for crying out loud," Summer groaned.

Both men stared at each other for a long moment before Luke spoke. "I got her."

Something in his tone had her nerve endings jumping to attention. Mike looked like he might argue until a loud noise in the bar had him dashing out of the bathroom. Luke kicked the door closed behind him. He turned on the water with his free hand. Positioning himself behind her, he wrapped his arms around her waist before gently guiding her palm beneath the spray of warm water.

She sucked in a breath when the water jostled the splinter.

Or maybe it was the warmth of his muscled body pressing up against hers that had her breathless.

"Easy," he said, his breath fanning her cheek. "I'm going to see if I can get it out in one piece."

He carefully maneuvered the jagged piece of wood from her palm and held it up for her inspection. Then, he tore off a few paper towels and pressed it to her wound.

"Sit," he said, indicating the closed toilet. "Press hard with the paper towel, so it stops bleeding."

She did as he asked, peering through her eyelashes at his sure hands, rummaging through the first-aid kit. He pulled out a tube of antiseptic and a large band-aid before crouching down on his haunches. Lifting the paper towel from her fingers, he inspected the wound.

"This may sting," he said right before he slathered the antiseptic on her palm.

If it did sting, Summer didn't notice. Her skin was too busy basking in the warm caress of Luke's touch. He tore the bandage open with his teeth and pulled it over her palm, gently pressing the ends against her skin.

Rocking back on his heels, he smiled at her. "All set."

She traced the bandage with her thumb. "You missed your calling. You should have gone into nursing."

"One nurse in the family is enough." He sprang to his feet and began to reassemble the first-aid kit.

"Your mom is a nurse?" Now that she thought of it, nothing she'd googled about him mentioned his mother. Only his superstar father.

"Her wife is a nurse."

Summer let that tidbit sink in while he returned the kit to the cabinet. His family situation certainly wasn't uncommon these days. She was curious now what sort of role Jake Kessler played in Luke's life.

"Anyway, your hand will heal in time for you to play your cello at Andi's grand opening."

She shot up from the toilet, her pique from before returning in full force. "I knew it! You did it again!"

He was wearing that panty-melting smile of his when he turned around. "Me? What did I do?"

Summer lunged forward, pressing her finger into his chest. "You know *exactly* what you did. You manipulated me into playing for Andi. You practically dared me in front of everyone out there. You're despicable."

His eyes were dancing. "There's the sassy Summer Pearson I know, and lo—"

The air in the small room stilled. Summer was suddenly having trouble drawing in a breath. Had he been about to say what she thought? She searched his face for clues, but he was quicker. Pressing her back against the door, he leaned in and kissed her soundly.

The moment his lips met hers, whatever questions she had regarding what he was about to say disappeared. She simply melted into him, trying to stem the hunger that had been building since he'd kissed her days before. He opened her mouth with his lips, and their tongues collided. She arched against him, tangling her fingers in his hair in an effort to get closer.

Luke nipped at her bottom lip. "What are we doing?" he asked, sounding genuinely bewildered.

She scraped her nails against his scalp, trying to lead his lips back to hers. "You started it," she murmured.

"Mmm," was all he said before his mouth found hers again.

The skin on her legs suddenly met with cool air. Summer sighed into Luke's mouth when she felt his fingers graze against her thigh. Before she knew it, he had hiked her dress to her waist. He slid his hard thigh between hers, and Summer suddenly trembled with need. His fingers found their way beneath her panties, digging into her skin as he urged her on. She was so close.

"Luke? Are you in there?"

They both froze at the sound of Lizzie's voice.

Mother of God. She'd done it again. Gotten swept up in Luke Kessler's charm until she was practically dry-humping him in a public bathroom. What the hell was wrong with her?

Summer shoved his chest as she mouthed a litany of curse words. He grimaced at the movement. She glanced down. He was in no condition to receive visitors. *Well, then.* At least she wasn't the only one getting carried away. But she would delve into what that meant later. They had to move before Lizzie came face-to-face with their deceit.

She gestured frantically toward the steel cabinet. He nodded as he opened one of its doors and crouched down with his back to her as if looking for something. Summer smoothed down her dress and, saying a silent prayer that Luke hadn't left any bite marks, pulled open the bathroom door.

"Luke's right here." She tried to make her voice sound innocent as she waved her injured hand in front of her cousin's face, hoping to block her view into the bathroom. "He was bandaging my hand."

Lizzie examined Summer's palm skeptically. "I heard you got hurt. I didn't realize it was that bad."

"It wasn't very deep. I'll be fine."

"Kessler excels at kissing booboos and making them all better," a man drawled from the darkness of the hallway.

Holy hell. It was the quarterback again. The guy seemed to have a sixth-sense whenever she and Luke were in a compromising position.

The quarterback stepped into the light. "He's practically the team nursemaid."

"That's...sweet," Lizzie said.

"You're being a dick tonight, Van Horn," Luke said when he emerged from the bathroom, fully recovered from their escapade.

"I'll be nicer when you stop dropping my passes." He looked over at Summer. "All joking aside, I wanted to make sure you weren't badly hurt. Palmer is freaking out about it."

She waved her injured hand. "All good. It's only a scratch."

Van Horn nodded. "Glad to hear it. You have an incredible gift, by the way. It was a treat hearing you play tonight." He looked back at Luke then Lizzie before shaking his head and wandering back down the dark hallway.

Summer decided he had the right idea. "I'm going to grab my things from the office and call an Uber. You two enjoy the rest of the party."

"Don't be silly," Lizzie surprised her by saying. "You can ride home with us. Luke is going that way anyway. I'm ready to call it a night also. I've been up since three-thirty." She turned to Luke, who, for a brief moment, looked as perplexed as Summer felt. "You don't mind, do you?"

Summer minded. She minded very much, in fact. She was confused, horny, and emotionally drained. All she wanted was to be alone before she burst into tears of frustration. If her cousin knew she climbed Luke like a tree every time they were alone together, she'd mind, too.

Lizzie linked her arm through Summer's as if it was already decided that Luke would drive them both home. Someone should probably make her aware the guy she was dating was a philandering tool. Except there was no way Summer could tell her without implicating herself.

Shame washed over her, making her ribs unbearably tight. Not only was she a fraud, but a traitor. Luke certainly hadn't forced himself on her either time. She enthusiastically welcomed what he offered without a care about Lizzie. And that made *her* the real tool.

She risked a glance at Luke. If he felt any remorse at all, it didn't show in his expression. Instead, he looked cool and collected, damn him.

"I don't mind at all," Luke replied, giving Lizzie his "big fan" smile.

CHAPTER THIRTEEN

"SUMMER!"

The sound of Lizzie shouting her name jerked her from a restless sleep. She checked the clock by her bed. Seven-fifty. Practically noon for Lizzie. Summer, on the other hand, preferred a bit more rest on a Saturday morning. Especially after she'd spent most of the night sleeping in fits and starts, trying to reconcile whatever it was that was going on between her and Luke.

The guilt ate at her. She should just come clean to Lizzie and let the chips fall where they may. But that would require courage, and Summer had left all of hers in Vienna. She grabbed her pillow, pressed it to her face, and screamed into it. Milli jumped from the bed in a huff, annoyed at having her sleep interrupted.

"Summer!" Lizzie called again, this time from the end of the bed.

Lizzie sounded agitated. *Holy hell.* Could she somehow have figured out about her and Luke? Summer swallowed the bile that rose up in the back of her throat. Perhaps it was for the best. Her conscience was going to kill her anyway.

She slowly lowered the pillow. But instead of being furious, her cousin was practically giddy, jumping from one foot to the other in her delight. Milli yipped, excited by whatever had Lizzie all jazzed up.

Lizzie laughed at the dog. "Oh, you sweet thing! I have the best news."

Cautious relief washed over Summer. Whatever it was, Lizzie didn't suspect her betrayal. Technically, however, the betrayal could—and should—be laid at Luke's feet. He'd started it both times, after all. She never stood a chance against his potent sex appeal. Not a woman alive would.

At least that was what she'd been telling herself for the last ten hours.

She got the sense Luke was as conflicted by the situation as she was. And then there were the parts of his past he had revealed. And what he almost said. Frustrated, she balled her hands into fists, wincing when the skin pulled along the cut on her palm.

Summer sat up in the bed when her cousin lifted the dog, allowing Milli to lick her face. "Who are you? And what have you done with my cousin?"

Lizzie laughed. "Your cousin is about to become a star."

"You're already a star."

"Not only in Milwaukee, silly. A star on *national* television."

Nothing Lizzie was saying made much sense. Summer was just relieved Lizzie wasn't coming for her head on a platter. She threw back the sheets and swept her legs out of bed.

"Hold that thought," she said. "I have to pee."

"And I have to pack," Lizzie called as Summer raced to the bathroom.

Milli barked with glee, running in circles, trying to decide which woman to follow.

Five minutes later, after letting Milli out to relieve herself, Summer headed for Lizzie's room. Her cousin was furiously packing an overnight bag—most of the space taken up with hair product and makeup. Milli wandered around the room, inspecting Lizzie's shoe collection. Summer took a swig from the coffee cup on Lizzie's dresser.

"Hey!" Lizzie cried.

"You woke me up early on the weekend. I should get some compensation." She took another sip. "What exactly is going on here?"

Lizzie did that hopping thing again, this time while clapping her hands together. Milli barked along with her. "Oh, Sum. It's so exciting. I'm going to New York to fill in for the weekend meteorologist on the 'Weekend Show.'"

Well.

That certainly wasn't what Summer expected when her cousin barged into her room moments ago. "Seriously? How did that happen?"

Lizzie tossed a camisole into the suitcase. "You're not the only one in this family who can work career magic using social media," she replied.

And we all know how that turned out.

She didn't bother voicing the words, because she knew her cousin well enough to know they would fall on deaf ears. "Go on."

"I've been promoting myself more on different platforms. Not only weather stuff but other relevant news items. Like last night's scoop about Kane Palmer's engagement. It got over a hundred thousand views before midnight last night."

Summer recalled the high she used to get watching the likes and views from her videos go up. It was incredibly addictive. "And?"

"My contract with WMIL is up at the end of the year. I've been sending demo tapes all over. One of them went to the 'Weekend Show' just for giggles." Lizzie grinned as she shrugged. "They reached out to me this morning asking if I could do a last-minute fill-in for tomorrow's show. It had to be last night's post that got their attention." She gripped Summer's shoulders. "Their meteorologist is *pregnant.* You know what that means. They'll be looking for someone to fill in for her for six months. This could be my ticket."

"Wow, Lizzie. That's awesome."

And it was. She ignored the twinge of jealousy she felt knowing her cousin was succeeding in her dream while Summer had failed miserably. Lizzie took her job very seriously, and she'd worked hard to get ahead in a competitive field. Not only that, but viewers connected well with her. She had the ratings to prove it. Summer may be locking lips with Lizzie's boyfriend, but she wasn't so horrible that she begrudged her cousin this opportunity.

Lizzie squealed. "It is awesome, isn't it? And to think, Josh said I'd be stuck in mid-America forever. Ha!"

And the plot thickens. "Hold on. This isn't about Josh, is it?"

"No, of course not." Lizzie busied herself with closing the suitcase.

Summer wasn't sure she believed her. "What about Luke?"

Lizzie stilled for a brief moment. "Oh, crap. I forgot he's bringing his ugly dog over here to stay tonight."

Summer took exception to Lizzie's description of the dog. Okay, sure, Monty was ugly, but in an adorable kind of way.

"Although, I'm not the one who volunteered to watch the dog." Lizzie rounded on Summer. "You were."

"I said I would, and I will," Summer replied. "But it's gonna cost you."

Lizzie's hands went to her hips. "What do you want now?"

"Bring a camera crew to career day, and we'll call it even."

"What for?" Lizzie demanded.

Summer traced a pattern on the rug with her toe. "Well, think of it as adding to your social media resume. A fluff piece about the popular meteorologist talking weather with kids from a low-income school."

She could see the moment the idea registered with her cousin. Lizzie nodded. "That would work. Deal." She yanked her suitcase off the bed. "Papa Harry is bringing the dog over later today."

Luke wasn't bringing the dog over himself? Summer couldn't decide if she was relieved or hurt. "Why would Papa Harry have Monty?"

Lizzie shrugged again. "You know Papa Harry. He probably offered. He's spending the day showing Luke's Gram some of the sights around town."

Excuse me? "Papa Harry is showing Grace around town?"

"Yep. It's cute that he's found someone to spend time with."

"Cute? Papa Harry is *married*. He shouldn't be 'spending time' with another woman."

"He's allowed to have friends, Summer. And it's not like Grandma Bonnie is providing him with any companionship. She doesn't even know he's there." Lizzie checked her phone. "My Uber is five minutes away. Can you tell Papa Harry and Grandma to watch me tomorrow morning?"

Summer silently counted to ten, trying to drag air into her lungs. She probably should have paid attention those few times Paige dragged her to her yoga classes. But it was no use. Her Chakra had left the building.

She trailed Lizzie to the front of the house. "But what about Luke?" she repeated.

Lizzie checked her phone again. "Luke? Oh, crap. I won't be back in time to take Grace to the game tomorrow. Can you ask Papa Harry to drive her over?"

The last thing Summer would do was ask Papa Harry to spend any more time with Grace Kessler. She pushed that thought aside, however, because she was more focused on the other aspect of Lizzie's statement. "Wait. You haven't told Luke about this yet?"

"Everything happened so quickly. I haven't had time to tell

anyone except you. Besides, it's not like we are in each other's pockets or something."

"But you're dating. You're his WAG, remember?"

Lizzie rolled her eyes. "It's not like I need to be anymore. He's a great guy with lots of yummy charm, if you know what I mean. And he knows how to treat a woman."

Summer resisted the urge to agree as Lizzie went on.

"But I'm not ready to jump back into a serious relationship. It was mostly access to other celebrities in town I was using him for."

Using him.

A wave of nausea rolled through Summer, followed swiftly by anger. How dare she "use" Luke. It wasn't until Lizzie had given her a quick hug and dashed out the door that she realized she'd been feeling guilty for kissing Luke for no reason. He wasn't her cousin's boyfriend. At least not in Lizzie's eyes.

So where did that leave Summer?

She slid down onto the floor. Milli jumped into her lap. "I should have stayed on the sofa in Chicago," Summer whispered into the dog's fur. "I don't even know where to go from here."

Milli barked once.

"I assume that means you want your breakfast?" The dog yipped again. Summer sighed. "I guess that's as good a place to start as any."

"I CAN'T BELIEVE the Princess is going to be on the 'Weekend Show' tomorrow morning," Paige said.

"I can't believe most of what happened today," Summer replied on her cellphone.

She was sitting cross-legged on the sofa, her notecards from her LSAT study group spread out beside her. Her wine glass needed refilling, but she'd made a promise to herself to be responsible tonight. She was caring for an extra dog, after all. Monty and Milli were dozing on the floor with their backs pressed together adorably.

"Are you sure you don't want me to drive up?" Paige asked. "I can be there in two hours."

As much as Summer wanted to say yes, she'd already declined the offer twice. If Paige were here, Summer would never be able to keep from telling her about Luke. She wasn't sure why she was holding back—especially from her best friend. Except she had no idea what was going on between her and Luke herself. No way could she explain it to Paige yet.

"I'm fine. Really."

Paige scoffed. "That's a lie. I know this whole thing with Papa Harry has upset you."

That was an understatement. Earlier, Papa Harry had arrived with Monty. *And Grace.* Of course, Luke's grandmother was nothing short of lovely. Summer was almost ashamed that she was predisposed to dislike the woman. But the way Papa Harry had shown Grace around his home set her on edge.

"It's just that I got this strange vibe," she told Paige. "It felt as though he wanted her to like this house. As if she might live here someday, you know? I'm sure I'm overreacting." At least that was what her brother had accused her of when she'd called to tell him Lizzie's news, only to end up venting about their grandfather. "My grandparents' love story is remarkable, you know? My grandfather was a shell of the man he once had been when he returned from Vietnam. He tells everyone that had it not been for my grandmother's steadfast love and devotion, he would have lived a very different life. One that would not have ended well." She swallowed the sob that threatened. "He adores her."

"Of course he does," Paige insisted. "He moved out of their house to be closer to her every day. But honey, Lizzie has a point. The woman he knew and loved isn't exactly there any longer."

"Whose side are you on?" Summer demanded. *"Until death, do us part."*

Paige sighed. "You're right. Your grandfather would never do anything to hurt his wife or embarrass your family. He's one of the few honorable men left out there. You simply need to trust him." Her tone turned bitter. "Speaking of 'until death do us part,' my dad is getting remarried."

Summer suddenly felt awful for getting testy with her friend. Paige barely knew her dad. A career military man, he'd been deployed to the Middle East multiple times when she was young. Her parents' marriage never really had a chance to grow before it ended in divorce when Paige was six. Her dad continued his military service, living all over the world. Paige's mother never let her visit, because he was always in a war-zone. As a result, father and daughter were now estranged.

"How did you hear that?" she asked.

"Can you believe he sent me a message on social media?" Paige's laugh was humorless. "He claimed he didn't know how else to get in touch with me."

"Wow."

"Yeah. He's a sheriff in some podunk town in North Carolina. He says his fiancée has five kids. Can you believe it? He made a big deal about me having half-siblings. My guess is he probably saw I was a kindergarten teacher, and wants my help with babysitting. As if."

"Dog sitting is much easier."

Monty thumped his tail as if he knew Summer was talking about him.

"Tell me again why you are watching Lizzie's boyfriend's dog?" Paige asked.

He's not Lizzie's boyfriend, she wanted to shout. But then what was he?

"Because she's not here to do it herself," she said instead. "And

I've got nothing better to do on a Saturday night. It's only me and my notecards."

"What about the fireman?"

Mike had called earlier asking if she was free tonight. After the past couple of days though, Summer needed the solitude to get her thoughts in order. Not only that, but she didn't want to lead him on. She liked him, but only as a friend. She'd told him she had to study, which was the truth. Not that she was getting much studying done.

"I'll be home in a few months," she told Paige. "It would be silly to start something here."

Her friend made a sound like she didn't believe her. Summer's phone dinged. A text from Antonio popped up on the screen. She swiped over to it. It was a photo of him playing piano for his teammates in the hotel bar. His grin was effervescent. She smiled along with him as she "loved" the image. Another text quickly followed.

Still no evidence of kessler singing in the shower but I'm on the case. :)

Summer nearly laughed before an image of a soaped-up Luke sprang to mind. She'd had her legs wrapped around his muscled body last night, her fingers gripping his very fine ass. Suddenly, she was hot and bothered all over again, remembering how fiery their kiss was. She grabbed a notecard and began fanning herself.

"Summer, are you listening to me?" Paige demanded.

"Sorry." She sent Antonio a thumbs-up sign, instantly regretting it when she heard the swoosh of the message sending. She didn't need to know if Luke sang in the shower any more than she needed to be fantasizing about him there.

"I said, while you're ignoring the potential for three-alarm sex with a fireman, I've met someone promising."

That got her attention. "What? Who?"

"He's the uncle of one of my students. The girl's parents are divorced, and the uncle helps out when it's dad's week to have her at his place. He's charming and funny, and his niece obviously adores him. I swear I felt sparks when we first met." She could hear the smile in her friend's voice. "He lives in Champagne, but he's working on a project here in Chicago. He stays with his brother when he's here. He's coming back into town tomorrow night and he asked me if I'd like to grab a late dinner with him."

"Well, look at you. Sparks and everything. I hope you said yes." Summer chewed on her bottom lip. She couldn't very well bring up the situation with Luke now. It would sound like she was trying to one-up her friend. "I'm excited for you." And she meant it. Paige was attractive, thoughtful, and deserved someone special after growing up under the thumb of a bitter mother. "I can't wait to hear all the details."

They made plans to talk again after Paige's date the following evening. Summer shuffled through her notecards, but she couldn't seem to focus on anything other than the image of Luke Kessler in the shower. She pressed her head back against the sofa and groaned in frustration.

Monty rose from his spot on the floor and lowered his giant head onto her leg. The dog moaned when Summer scratched behind his ear. Not to be left out, Milli scampered onto Summer's lap. Both dogs eyed her sympathetically.

Either that or they were hungry.

"How about we make some popcorn?" she suggested. "That might make us all feel better."

At the word "popcorn," Milli was already halfway to the kitchen.

CHAPTER FOURTEEN

LUKE HAD NEVER CONSIDERED himself a coward. Growing up in a rural Canadian town, he'd endured endless bullying thanks to his small stature. Not to mention the fact he had two mothers. Every time, though, he stood his ground and took whatever his opponents dished out. He was proud that he never went quietly, always countering with a wisecrack or a dare that, more often than not, earned him a fat lip. Once or twice, however, his mouthiness bought him a reprieve.

In rare instances, he'd been forced to use his swift feet to outrun an opponent. But he never considered that cowardice. He was simply using his natural talents to preserve the orthodontia that had cost his moms a fortune.

Today, however, standing in the Growlers' end zone an hour before kickoff, he was feeling like every inch of a coward. He'd been avoiding the Pearson women. Well, not Elizabeth since she'd flown off to New York without so much as a text. His teammates were the ones to let him know she was guest forecasting on the "Weekend Show." He was grateful for the timing however, because he wasn't exactly sure what he'd say to her.

Hey, I kissed your cousin, and, well, she turns me on more than you do. A lot more.

I can't see you anymore because your cousin makes me crazy.

Your cousin makes me want things.

None of those was appropriate. And frankly, the last one scared the shit out of him. Luke had purposely structured his life so that he wouldn't get snared in any of the trappings a relationship might bring.

Specifically love.

He'd seen the destructive power of that particular four-letter word first-hand, growing up with a mother who always had more love for her partner than she had for him. And a father who'd dropped him like a hot potato when he'd found someone else to cherish. Luke wasn't naïve enough to believe that love wasn't a positive experience for most people. All he had to do was look at Fletcher and the effect Andi's love had on him, for starters. He'd merely learned early on true love wasn't meant for *him*.

Desire, however, was another matter altogether. Lust and passion didn't have to necessarily mean love. He considered himself a connoisseur of desire. And never let it be said that Luke Kessler didn't give women as much satisfaction as they gave him.

But that was where he drew the line. At mutual satisfaction. He wouldn't offer a woman anything more. And he sure as hell didn't want them *wanting* anything more.

Hence the reason he'd chickened out of dropping off Monty with Summer yesterday. He couldn't trust himself not to say or do something stupid. The desire he felt for her was off the charts. He'd spent the last two nights fantasizing about the things he wanted to do to her. Except, that was all it could be—fantasy. He couldn't risk getting intimate with Summer. He couldn't risk her seeing the depth of his need. He couldn't risk the pain that would surely come when she eventually discovered she loved someone else more than him.

"Hey, Kessler!" Luke turned to find Patrick Conway, the broadcast voice of the Growlers, baring down on him. "Gotta sec?"

"Sure."

Patrick had been covering the Growlers games for close to thirty years. The guy was practically an institution. As a result, he was no spring chicken. Patrick hadn't passed up many of the free eats the team provided in the press box, either. He held a finger up at Luke while he recovered his breath from his slow jog across the field.

"I know I should probably go through the proper channels to ask this," Patrick said. "But I didn't want to start down that road only to find out this is something you wouldn't want to do. Someone in community relations would end up twisting your arm to do it anyway, and I'd hate myself for putting you in that position."

Luke nodded. It was rare the team forced a player into a public appearance, but it happened. He appreciated Patrick's thoughtfulness.

"My wife is chairing an auction for the Humane Society—"

"Say no more. Whatever she wants, I'll do it."

Patrick chuckled. "You haven't heard the ask yet."

"I don't need to. You know how I feel about animals. Does she want a signed jersey? A signed ball? A check? Does she want me to emcee?"

"She'll take any and all of those from you, especially the emcee part. You're a lot handsomer in a tux than I am," Patrick said. His gaze darted toward the turf for a second. He wore a chagrined look when he glanced back up. "But she was looking for something unique. Something a bit rarer here in Milwaukee." He sighed. "She was wondering if you might be able to get a ball signed by your father. He's on the shortlist for the Hall of Fame this year. And his connection to you makes him relevant here in town. It would bring in a lot of money."

Luke held himself very still. He'd gotten very adept at not reacting when someone brought up his father. Years of practice will do that to a man. Never let them see you sweat and all that bullshit. Most of all, he never let them see his annoyance. Besides, Patrick's wife was correct. A ball signed by his dad would be rare at an auction in Milwaukee. And the Humane Society would be the beneficiary.

"You got it," he managed to get past the disdain clogging his throat. "Shoot me an email with all the details, and I'll get it there. And count me in for a contribution too."

Patrick looked relieved. "That's awesome. She'll be delighted. You know what they say, happy wife, happy life."

Luke nodded and took a step closer to the tunnel leading to the locker room. The sooner he got out of this conversation, the better. He needed to get his head clear for the game. His father had already ruined his concentration last week. No way was Luke going to let his old man do it again this game.

"Luke! Over here!"

Gram's voice had him turning back to the bleachers where the band sat. She waved from her seat next to Harry Pearson. The two of them looked very chummy sitting together like that, almost like a couple returning to their high school football stadium later in life and rekindling a long-dormant attraction. Luke shook his head at the fanciful thoughts as he jogged over to them.

"I got you a perfectly nice seat up with Andi and the WAGS in one of the boxes upstairs," he said to her. "What are you doing out here?"

"Enjoying some Vitamin D." She smiled broadly. She always did prefer to be outdoors. "I'll save the warm seats for later in the season."

She had a point.

"This way, if you catch a touchdown at this end, you can toss me the ball," she quipped. "I've always wanted to be on a highlight reel."

He felt his shoulders relaxing, knowing he'd done the right thing moving her to Milwaukee. She seemed to be fitting in beautifully. To hell with his dad. Luke had been the one to rescue Gram.

He'd been the one she had chosen.

"I'll see what I can do," he said with a wave.

When he turned to head back into the locker room, he nearly collided with Summer. She was standing in the end zone like some wannabe Amazon warrior, her feet spread wide, hands on her hips. This week her hair was tied up in a braid at the side of her head. She had a Growlers' logo painted on one cheek. The cute shorts were back, exposing those legs he'd had his hands all over the other night. The memory of her firm, smooth thighs had his fingers twitching for a reenactment. Until he noticed she'd paired the shorts with fucking McGraff's jersey.

That fact should not have bothered him as much as it did.

"Your dog snores," she announced, her tone frosty.

Luke smothered a laugh. Snoring was an understatement for the sounds that came out of the mutt when he slept. "I asked the vet about a C-pap machine, but they don't make them for dogs. Who knew?"

Summer wasn't having any of his jokes. Her eyes narrowed beneath the fringe of her auburn lashes. "I'm glad you find this so amusing."

He sighed. "I don't. I appreciate you keeping Monty last night. It wasn't fair of Harry to force him on you. I'll set something else up for the rest of the season."

She harumphed. "Did I say I wouldn't watch him? I think you could have given a girl a heads up, that's all."

As usual, he was having trouble following the trajectory of her ping-ponging thought process. Not that he cared. She was adorable in her indignation.

Jesus. Now he was using the word "adorable" to describe a woman. What the hell was wrong with him?

"Or maybe your grandmother could have told me about the snoring," she said. "When she came with *my* grandfather to drop him off."

Luke suddenly felt like he was about to take a hit on his blind-side. There was something more to her irritation than Monty's snoring. But given who he was talking to, damned if he knew what it was.

She took a step closer. "Oh, wait. Your grandmother didn't say a thing because she was too preoccupied fawning over my grand-father. My *married* grandfather."

Luke rocked back on his heels. Was she insinuating that something was going on between Gram and Harry Pearson? That was absurd. Except, he'd thought to himself that they made a cute couple mere minutes before. He was going to laugh it off, but one look at her mulish face had him on the defensive. "What the hell does that mean?"

"It means your grandmother needs to stay away from my grandfather." She annunciated each word forcefully.

"Are you even listening to what you're saying? They are neighbors. That's all. Two people whose grandchildren are—" *What?* And which of Harry's grandchildren was he even talking about? He glanced back at Harry and Gram. Their heads were together as they laughed about something.

For fuck's sake.

"Whose grandchildren are involved," he finished lamely.

Summer seemed to deflate before his eyes. "She's using you, you know."

Luke gave his head a quick shake. It did nothing to help him understand her. "Who?"

"Lizzie," she whispered. "She's using you to get more exposure on social media. Her contract is almost up, and she wants to move on to a bigger market. It's appalling." She sucked in a breath. "I thought you should know, that's all."

This was the last time he left the locker room before a game.

Ever.

He couldn't say he was shocked at what Summer just revealed. After all, he was doing the same thing. Most of the women he chose to involve himself with had an endgame that didn't include him. It was the primary reason he chose them in the first place. The relationships were purely for show. The less emotional involvement, the better for both parties.

What did surprise him, however, was Summer's reaction to her cousin's behavior. She seemed genuinely hurt on his behalf. Something in the vicinity of his chest squeezed.

She cared.

About him. About his feelings. And he couldn't have her doing that. There was too much peril down that path.

"I was using her, too," he admitted with a shrug.

Her eyes went wide for a long moment. Then a burst of staccato laughs escaped her mouth before she doubled over in near hysterics. Luke heaved a sigh. Would this woman ever behave like the rest of her species?

She eventually pulled herself back up and wiped her eyes. "Oh, that's rich."

He crossed his arms over his chest. "What?"

"You. Too macho to admit you got played. Instead, you have to save face by claiming you knew it all along."

It might be better to let her think what she liked. Except he needed her not to care for him. Not to like him. He needed to be that asshole. Anything to keep her from tempting him.

"Believe what you want. But it's the truth. Ask anyone I've ever dated." He met her gaze with a fierce stare of his own.

She scrutinized him carefully before her eyes filled with disgust. And maybe a pinch of pity. "You two deserve each other."

Luke wasn't prepared for the harsh sting of her words. He hated himself for not telling her the truth. That he was done using Elizabeth. That Summer had ruined everything. That he wanted her and only her. Lucky for him, Van Horn saved his ass before he could make a rash mistake.

"Kessler. I suggest you get in the locker room," the quarterback commanded. "Before the end zone spontaneously combusts with all the ... tension you both are throwing off. Unless you two need a moment alone back in the tunnel?"

"Puh-leaze. I never plan on being alone with this man ever again." Her words came out with conviction. Her eyes said something else though. They had that same crestfallen expression Monty got when Luke kicked him off the sofa. That look told him everything he needed to know. Ending things before they got out of hand was the right thing to do.

To hell with the sharp kick in his chest.

"Papa Harry will bring Monty home. Your dog is always welcome to come over. You, however, are not." Summer stormed over to the bandstand.

"Well, that's taken care of," Van Horn said.

A low snarl escaped Luke's mouth as he balled his fingers into fists. "Fuck you."

"Save it for the game, Kessler."

The two of them walked the rest of the way to the locker room in a charged silence.

At least Luke had forgotten all about his dad.

TWO WEEKS LATER, the plane ride back from Seattle was a subdued one. The Growlers lost a close one in overtime. Their win streak of three ended in the late hours of Thursday night. Fog delayed their departure an extra hour, which meant they'd be landing in Milwaukee just in time for Friday morning rush hour.

McGraff sighed from his seat next to Luke. "The refs made a bad call."

Luke didn't bother opening his eyes. "Shake it off. It won't be the last time that happens to you."

The rookie had been seeing more and more action as the season progressed. Last night, with the defense double covering both Luke and Jacobs every time they were on the field, Coach Gibson gave McGraff a shot during primetime. A short fade route into the end zone to win the game.

He'd run the route perfectly, using some fancy footwork to slip between two backs and across the goal line. Van Horn's pass was right on target. It was McGraff's reception that the refs questioned. They claimed he didn't have possession of the ball before going out of bounds. There wasn't enough video evidence to overturn the call, resulting in overtime. McGraff had been so upset about the no touchdown call that he'd dropped two passes in OT. The Growlers never stood a chance.

The rest of the team took it on the chin. No one held it against the rookie. All of them had been in his place at one point in their careers. In this case, though, it would have been the kid's first touchdown reception in the pros. Luke was sure the missed opportunity had to hurt.

"You're a talented receiver. You'll get plenty of more shots at it."

Luke's attempt at reassurance was met with a surly growl. "But it might not be in time."

The rookie's cryptic remark had Luke snapping his eyelids open. Before he could ask what the words meant, the lights went up in the cabin. A chorus of groans and off-color remarks filled the plane. The captain announced they were on the final approach to General Mitchell airport.

Luke put his seat up. McGraff had his face turned to the window, effectively cutting off any further conversation. Ten minutes later, they were taxiing up to the jetway. Coach Gibson and Coach Washington were heading down the aisle to the back of the plane. Both of them wore serious looks.

"I want everyone to remain seated," Coach Gibson announced. "McGraff, we need to take you off the plane first."

Coach Washington indicated Luke should get up and let McGraff past him.

"What's going on?" Luke murmured to Coach Washington.

The coach shook his head again, motioning for Luke to get up.

"It was a bad call," Luke protested as he unsnapped his seatbelt. "The kid did nothing wrong."

Coach Gibson looked at Luke like he had a screw loose. "It *was* a shitty call," he said. "But that's not what this is about." His expression softened as he turned to McGraff. "We need to get you through the airport quickly so you can catch a commercial flight to New Orleans. It's your dad."

McGraff didn't look surprised by the news. He nodded glumly as he unbuckled his seatbelt and slid to the aisle. The rookie's words from before suddenly made a lot more sense.

Shit.

Luke opened the overhead bin and pulled out the kid's go-bag. "Anything I can do?" he asked softly.

When McGraff looked up, the cocky attitude was wiped from his face. Instead, his eyes were wide and shiny with what looked like fear. He shook his head.

"If you think of something, I'm here." Luke clapped him on the shoulder, trying his best to convey he meant what he said. "We're all here for you."

The rest of the team silently looked on as McGraff headed to the front, flanked by both coaches. He stopped suddenly and turned to face Luke.

"Summer," he said. "I promised I'd be there this morning."

The mere utterance of her name had Luke's chest thumping. He had tried—and failed—these past two weeks to exorcise Summer from his thoughts. And his dreams. And his shower.

"Promised her you'd be where?" he asked stupidly.

"Career Day." The belligerence roared back into the rookie's eyes. "Your girlfriend was supposed to be the guest speaker. But she backed out yesterday afternoon. Something about advancing her career. She left her cousin high and dry."

Elizabeth and Luke had exchanged a few texts in the past couple of weeks. Mostly him wanting to get together so he could end things in person. As if she suspected what was coming, Elizabeth kept stringing him along. She still needed him to secure a new gig, it seemed.

McGraff's face deflated. "But after last night, I doubt those kids want to see me, anyway." He shot Luke a pleading look. "Summer wants to show the kids someone cares about them. She doesn't want to let them down. I can't let *her* down."

Luke nodded, knowing exactly how Summer had championed the rookie. "No one is letting her down. I've got your back."

"Antonio," Coach Gibson said. "We need to get you on that plane."

"Go." Luke waved a hand toward the door. "I'll take care of Summer."

And he would. Screw all of the warnings he kept giving himself to stay away from her. He was a grown-ass boy with a very hardened heart. She needed help, and he was in a position to give it. If doing so ignited whatever it was that kept sizzling between them, then so be it. It might be beneficial to get it out of his system.

Separating lust from love had never been a problem for him. It wouldn't be this time, either.

CHAPTER FIFTEEN

SUMMER PACED THE LIVING ROOM, the two dogs silently tracking her from their dog beds.

"Why isn't he picking up?" She shook her cellphone.

Monty let out an anxious whine in response.

"They should have landed by now. The Career Day assembly starts at nine-thirty." She dragged her fingers through her already riotous hair. Summer was surprised she had any hair left after the stress of the past twelve hours. "Where are you, Antonio?"

While she should be glad for Lizzie—she'd landed her dream job filling in for the pregnant meteorologist on the "Weekend Show"—the timing totally sucked. Summer had tried everything to reason with her to delay her flight to New York by a few hours. But even begging hadn't worked. Lizzie was moving on, the rest of the people in her orbit be damned. Even if it left her cousin in a tremendous lurch.

Of course, without Lizzie, there would be no "fluff piece" on the news, either. The local station was as peeved about her defection as Summer was. The principal wouldn't be pleased. There went any additional funding for the music programs. Still, it was the students Summer hated to disappoint. They were unaware of the prospect that extra publicity might bring. They'd simply been looking forward to having a real-life celebrity visit them.

The school was in a small, working-class neighborhood where there was not much chance to rub elbows with anyone famous. Having the plucky meteorologist whose image was plastered on half the billboards in town visit the school was sure to make them feel special. Not overlooked. Summer hated to think that Lizzie bailing on the assembly would reinforce that feeling of being worthless.

Desperate not to let the kids down, she'd coaxed Antonio to be the speaker instead. Or rather, the performer. Antonio said no way to giving a talk to students. But he would "talk" with his fingers on the piano keys. Not exactly the affirming presentation the principal had in mind, but the kids would enjoy it, and at this point, that was all that mattered.

If only he would show up.

She was checking the clock for the umpteenth time when a knock sounded on the door. Her "thank God" was drowned out by the chorus of joyful barks from both dogs. When Summer pulled the door open, however, she was stunned by the person standing there.

"Mom."

Looking at her mother was like staring into a mirror twenty-five years into the future. The two women mirrored one another in build, hair color, and eye color. Even their smiles were the same. But that was where the similarities ended. Despite having been up for what was likely a while before a two-hour drive north, Summer's mother looked immaculate in a navy DKNY pantsuit, a silk V-neck blouse, and her trademark pearl earbobs. Summer, on the other hand, looked like an unmade bed. She wasn't even sure her shoes matched, because they were mixed all together in the bottom of her closet, and she couldn't quite make out if one was navy or black.

The Judge handed Summer a coffee cup from her favorite donut shop. "Oh, fabulous. You haven't left for school yet."

"What are you doing here? Is something wrong with Sterling?" Now Summer was panicking about two people.

"Your brother is fine. He sends his love." She stepped across the threshold. "I came to help you out. My heavens, what is *that*?" The Judge swatted at Monty before the dog could bury his nose into her crotch.

Summer juggled the coffee as she rushed to corral the two dogs. "Monty! Off!" Both dogs started at the tone of her voice. Monty slinked back to his dog bed while Milli jerked her snout in the air and trotted off to the kitchen. Summer blew out a breath.

"Help me out with what?"

Her mother eyed Monty suspiciously. "Career day, of course. Harry said Lizzie left you in a bind." She clucked her tongue. "Not unlike Lizzie, I might add. The 'Weekend Show,' huh? There will be no living with her now." She glanced around the room and smiled softly. "I always loved this house. So kitschy and homey."

She was here to help with career day? Summer resisted the urge to pinch herself. Maternal wasn't in The Judge's personality, at least not since her husband had died. Her mother had never attended a single field trip for either of her children. Yet, suddenly she popped in unannounced to speak to a bunch of kids whose parents didn't vote in the city of Chicago. She wasn't buying it.

"Mom, what's going on?"

"I'm your mother. You needed help. So here I am." She peeked into the kitchen. "Maybe we can find you a cute homey place like this when you pass the bar. Someplace in Wicker Park would be nice."

Summer didn't have time to dwell on her mother's sudden character swing. She had bigger problems to address.

"Mom, I don't know what Papa Harry told you or even why, but I've got it covered." At least she hoped so.

Her mother's expression didn't change. Eight years on the bench did that to a woman. Summer and her brother called it their mom's "judge face." She could remain stoic in any environment or situation. Yet, it was the slight movement among the muscles in her throat that gave her away. Summer had hurt her. Nothing new. Summer was always hurting her mother.

Sighing, she checked her phone. Still nothing from Antonio. Hopefully he was at the school already.

"Well, in that case, perhaps I can come and watch?" her mom said, surprising Summer.

There was no way Summer could refuse, and she was astounded at how much she didn't want to. "You did come all this way," she said softly. "And the guy I got at the last minute to speak isn't very comfortable with actual public speaking."

The Judge arched a perfectly shaped brow.

Summer groaned. "I know. It's complicated. And a mess. I'll explain in the car. Please tell me you brought your robe and gavel."

Her mother's eyes sparkled. "Where I go, they go."

"You two behave," Summer called to the dogs as she and her mother headed out the door.

They were crossing the school parking lot when Papa Harry and two of his friends met them.

"The cavalry to the rescue," her grandfather said as he hugged his daughter-in-law. "This here is my friend, Fred. He used to be a ferry captain on Lake Michigan. He's got some great stories. The kids will eat 'em up."

Great. If Antonio was a no-show, at least Summer would have Judge Judy and the captain of Little Toot the tug boat to entertain the students.

They made their way into the school's lobby. Summer had

never seen so many parents milling about. One of them stopped her with a tap on the arm.

"Pardon me," she said. "I'm Elijah's mom. He's in your recorder chorus. He's so excited to be performing on television today. I want to tell his grandparents to watch, but I wasn't sure what channel and when."

Summer's mouth went dry. Not only would she have to disappoint the students, but their families would be crushed as well. She'd worked with the second and third graders for two weeks to learn a recognizable version of "Twinkle Twinkle Little Star"—a weather song, no less. She was proud they'd been able to master it so quickly.

"Um." Her mouth was suddenly painfully dry. "I'm so sor—"

"It will likely play on multiple channels," a male voice boomed behind her. "We'll film all morning, then put a package together and send it out to all the locals. You never know. Some of the networks might pick it up as well. They love stories about kids."

Elijah's mom beamed.

"We'll send out the info as soon as we know it," Papa Harry reassured the woman.

The other man extended his hand to Summer. "Patrick Conway at your service. I've got a crew to film today's activities, but I also thought if you need someone to speak, I could tell them about my career in sports broadcasting. We could also let the kids do a little sportscasting of their own, reading in front of a camera. I brought some fun scripts."

Stunned, Summer pumped his hand up and down, trying—and failing—to find words. She recognized the man's voice from a car dealership commercial and a radio spot for a local restaurant. But why was he here?

The school's receptionist was suddenly at her shoulder. "Miss Pearson?"

"Yes?"

"Where do you want the fire truck?"

"Excuse me?"

Mike strolled through the school doors, his helmet tilted slightly on his head. "I would have brought the ladder truck, but I wasn't sure how much room you had in the parking lot."

"I don't understand," Summer said. Because she didn't understand. Antonio was nowhere to be found, but a host of other people had shown up. None of whom she'd invited. Not that she wasn't grateful.

Mike wiggled his eyebrows. "Just answering the nine-one-one call."

She looked over at Papa Harry. "You called Mike?"

Her grandfather shook his head.

"I'm hurt you didn't call me yourself, Summer." Mike gestured toward the doorway where she was stunned to see Luke Kessler leaning against the wall. His eyes were twinkling despite the dark smudges shadowing them.

Summer gasped softly. "Oh."

Mike sighed. "But I see how the wind is blowing here." He beamed at the young receptionist, who responded with a shy smile. "Perhaps you could show me where to park my truck?"

Ignoring the ridiculous double entendre, Summer edged over to Luke. "You did this?" she whispered around the lump in her throat.

He nodded. "Antonio had to fly home. Family emergency."

"His dad?"

"It seems so." He gestured to the lobby. "I called in a few favors. There's a zookeeper coming with a cockatoo, too." He chuckled at the alliteration.

Summer was grinning so hard she felt as though her face might split in half. "You're amazing."

His hand moved through the air toward her before he quickly jerked it back into his pocket. "You're the amazing one, Summer."

"Lizzie?" As much as it pained her to ask, she had to know if he was doing this to ease her cousin's guilt for ghosting her today.

Or for some other reason that had her heart thumping.

He dropped his chin for a brief moment before lifting his gaze to hers and locking it there. "That's over. To be honest, it never really got started. All of this is because of you. Antonio wanted to help you out."

She held her breath.

"*I* wanted to help you out," he murmured.

A warm flush washed over her. He was here for *her*. She pressed her lips together to keep from bursting out in song or something equally ridiculous.

"Miss Pearson," the principal called out.

"I'll let you go." Luke pushed away from the wall.

"You're not staying?"

"I think you've got enough talent for one morning. I've got to get this thumb looked at by a trainer."

Instinctively, she reached for his hand, pulling back when a spark of static electricity sizzled between them.

"If you touch me while I'm standing here, I can't guarantee my response would earn a G-rating." His gravelly tone sent shock waves through her body.

She gnawed on her bottom lip.

"I'm going to get some rehab before taking a long nap. I'll be over after school to pick up my dog."

"You could stay for dinner. It's the least I can do to thank you for all your help."

The disarming, sensual smile he shot her instantly made her panties damp.

"I'll bring the wine," he said.

Summer chuckled, remembering his comments about her and wine. "Are you sure that's wise?"

"None of this is wise, Summer. But something tells me we're both way past caring."

"WHAT IF HE doesn't show up?"

Neither dog responded, both of them focused on the ground beef Summer was browning on the stove.

"Maybe he was delirious from lack of sleep when he said what he said earlier," she continued. "Oh, God. What if he fell asleep and doesn't wake up until tomorrow?"

The canines in the room remained silent.

"You two are no help." She pulled the beef from the burner, draining the fat off before scooping the meat into a pot of simmering marina sauce. "The one day when I really need Paige, she's off on a romantic getaway with her new boyfriend. It figures." She wiped her hands on a towel. "And what was I thinking offering to make dinner? It's not like I had time to prepare."

Career Day had been an overwhelming success. Summer was besieged by teachers and parents after the last bell rang. All of them were effusive in their thanks for the special day. Even The Judge lingered longer than Summer expected. Her mom seemed to be basking in the glow of Summer's triumph. Had she not been so preoccupied with thoughts of Luke, she might have wondered at her mother's odd behavior.

But her thoughts were singularly focused on the sexy man all day. More like fantasies than thoughts, if she was being honest. The same fantasies she'd been having since the moment they'd met. Only now, knowing that he and Lizzie weren't ever involved, she no longer had to feel guilty about them.

Both dogs sprung to life, barking frantically when a knock sounded on the front door. She dragged her hands along her jean-clad thighs in hopes of stopping their slight tremor. Shoving the dogs aside, she pulled open the door. Monty immediately launched himself into Luke's arms, slapping his tongue all over his best friend's face.

"Someone's glad to see you," Summer said with a smile, trying to appear cool and collected.

Luke's eyes met hers. "I hope he's not the only one."

Not to be ignored, Milli plopped down on his shoe, rolled over on her back, and demanded a belly rub.

"The ladies of the house are delighted to see you, also." She was impressed with her ability to keep things light when her stomach was twisted in knots.

His gaze grew heated, and he kicked the door closed behind him. Monty whimpered when Luke gently deposited him on the floor. He pulled out two Benebones from his jacket pocket, handing one to each dog.

Her stomach fluttered at the sweetness of it. "They're going to worship you even more, now."

Me too.

He grinned mischievously as he pulled a bottle of wine from his other pocket. "So you don't feel left out."

Her laugh was a bit shaky as she took the bottle from his hand and headed back into the kitchen. "I hope you weren't expecting anything gourmet for dinner." She set the wine on the counter, so she wouldn't drop it. Needing something to do with her hands, she headed for the stove and the pot of spaghetti sauce.

"It smells delicious."

Her stomach did a backflip at the feel of his body pressed against her back. His warm breath fanned her neck as he seemed to inhale her.

"Still, you should probably open the wine," she whispered. "It might help make dinner more palatable."

With a low, hearty chuckle, he backed away. She heard him taking off his leather jacket. Desperately trying to calm her nerves, she stirred the sauce with a bit more vigor than was necessary. Summer dropped the spoon at the sound of his groan.

"Oh my gosh." When she spun around, he was shaking out his left hand, the corkscrew halfway in the bottle. "I forgot about your thumb." She gently wrapped her hands around his sore one. "I'm so sorry."

He leaned down and touched his forehead to hers as she bent over his hand. "It's fine. I just jammed it." He brushed his lips along her hairline. "But if you want to kiss it and make it better, I won't object."

She bit back a lusty groan at his teasing. When she lifted her head, their gazes collided. The desire she saw shining in his stole her breath. Very slowly, he lifted his uninjured hand to cup her cheek. She could feel his pulse beating wildly in his wrist.

"Summer," he murmured.

She quickly put her fingers to his lips. Reaching behind her with her free hand, she turned off the burner before looping her fingers in the belt loop of his jeans and pulling his body flush with hers. A shudder rocked through her at the contact.

But he'd been right earlier in the day. She was past caring. Luke was here. With her. And she'd be a fool not to enjoy him.

"I don't want to talk about this," she whispered. "I only want to feel."

His wicked grin slowly engulfed his face. "Sweetheart, you can 'feel' whatever you like."

"Are you ever serious?"

And just like that, he was deadly serious, pulling her into his arms and kissing her senseless. His hands were suddenly everywhere, easing beneath her sweater to leave trails of heat along her back while his tongue plundered. Summer gasped into his mouth, her own fingers tugging at the hem of his shirt to get to his skin. His hips twitched unexpectedly when her hands breached the waistband of his jeans.

Emboldened by her power, she bit his bottom lip. He swore against her mouth. She rolled her hips, both of them groaning when she came in contact with his arousal.

"We are not doing this on the kitchen table," he growled against her neck.

Summer laughed at the image that came to mind. She teasingly reached out and tested the sturdiness of the table with her hand. Luke swore again, the words dirty and scintillating at the same time. He scooped her up, lifting her against him. She wrapped her legs around his waist, burying her face in his neck.

"Next time," he said.

She shivered at the promise in his words. He carried her down the hall to her bedroom. Monty barked joyfully, his toenails clicking on the wood floor as he lumbered after them. The dog whimpered when Luke closed the door in his face.

Dusk had fallen outside, and the single bedside lamp cast the room in shadows. Summer's body slid along his until her feet hit the floor. She kicked off her mule slippers. His eyes were dark and difficult to read. They both were breathing like they were poised to jump off a cliff.

"Tell me this is what you want." The command came out of his mouth more like a groan.

Summer nodded, saying a prayer he wasn't going to change his mind. "Is it what *you* want?"

His mouth gaped open. "Hell, Summer. Isn't it obvious? I've wanted you since the first moment I saw you. All indignant and prissy protecting your grandmother's dog. You were stunning in your fury. You've been the object of every one of my fantasies ever since. Every. Damn. One."

Heat lanced through her body at his words. She bounced up on her toes, trailing her palms along his chest. "You were kind of sexy yourself that day, as I recall."

"Only 'kind of?'"

"Well, your legs were all I had to go on." She shrugged coyly.

Her words hung in the air like the dare they were. Luke's chuckle sounded a bit diabolical as he stepped away from her. He toed off his shoes before reaching behind his head and tugging his sweatshirt off. His T-shirt followed, leaving her with an eyeful of perfectly sculpted chest. A narrow trail of hair formed a beeline from his belly button to his crotch.

Summer sunk her teeth into her bottom lip to keep from licking it. His nostrils flared as though he could read the lascivious thoughts swirling around inside her head. He reached for his fly and slowly slid the zipper down. The sound was obnoxiously loud in the quiet room. Before she could react, his jeans and his briefs were down around his ankles. A sigh escaped her lips despite her attempt to rein it in. He smiled with the arrogance of a man who knew precisely how perfect his body was. She was hit with a swift bout of shyness.

"Don't," he commanded. He cupped his hand beneath her elbows and pulled her against his hard body. "Don't shut down on me."

She pressed her lips against the warm skin on his shoulder, inhaling his familiar scent. "How do you always know what I'm thinking?"

His laugh rumbled in his chest beneath her hands. "You wear every emotion on your face. You're like an open book."

"Actually, one of us is more open than the other right now." She nipped at his shoulder.

In the blink of an eye, she was on her back on the mattress. Luke divested her of her clothes with impressive skill. His title of the man with the surest hands in the league was well earned.

"You're so fucking gorgeous," he whispered against her breast. "So beautiful."

"It's the poor lighting in this room," she replied self-consciously.

She instantly regretted her words when his lips left her skin. He mumbled something under his breath before pushing himself up on one arm and pinning her with a stern look.

"Listen very carefully, Summer Pearson," he growled. "You are beautiful in any and all light. Your wild hair, your sassy, lopsided mouth, your abundant curves. All of it makes you beautiful."

She was starting to get ticked at his laundry list of her faults. But then he traced his fingertips up her thigh before slipping a finger inside of her, effectively scattering all her thoughts.

"You're the most passionate woman I've met. And good God, how I've dreamed of unleashing that passion."

His tone was easygoing and hushed, incongruent with the fire his talented finger was stoking inside her. She tossed her head from side to side.

"That's it. I want to see that passion. Show me, Summer. Let it out."

Another finger joined the first one, and suddenly she was writhing beneath him. He leaned down beside her ear, where he coaxed her along with wicked words detailing all the ways he wanted to have her.

Her back arched off the bed, and she came in a powerful rush so unexpected she screamed. A chorus of barking outside the bedroom door brought her back down to earth. She opened her eyes to see Luke gazing down at her, a reverent look on his face.

Her limbs felt like lead, but the hummingbirds were trilling deep in her belly once again. She managed to lift her arms high enough to skim her fingers along his lower back and perfect ass. When she tried to pull him closer, he slid further down her body.

"Where are you going?"

"I'm not done having my way with you." His breath was warm against her belly.

She tugged on his hair. "It's your turn," she protested while her girl parts were doing a happy dance at the thought of an encore.

"Nope. I want to witness that passion again."

She had to be dreaming because no man had ever given her multiple orgasms on purpose. He spread her legs farther apart and grazed the tender part of her thigh with his teeth. *Not dreaming, then.* Turns out, his tongue was equally as talented as his fingers, finding her sweet spot in record time. Just like that, she forgot why she was even protesting in the first place. Her body exploded with pleasure, even more phenomenal than moments earlier.

There was no time to catch her breath, because Luke was finally wild to be inside her.

"You're so gorgeous when you come. I can't hold out any longer." His hand trembled as he sheathed himself with a condom. "I promise I'll try to make it good for you too."

Was he kidding? He'd made it good for her—*fan-freaking-tastic, in fact*—not once but twice. She almost laughed but seeing the grave expression on his face had her biting it back.

He was inside her with one swift thrust. Her head lolled on the pillow at the pure pleasure of it. Then he began to move, and her body was tight as a bow after only a few perfectly executed strokes. She wrapped her legs around his waist and dug her fingernails into his shoulders, unsure if she would survive a third time.

But it was perfect. *He* was perfect. She could feel the tension building inside her again.

"Luke," she breathed, unable to find any other words.

"Let go," he urged. "I want to take you with me. Please, Summer."

Oh. My. God. She was free-falling off the side of a mountain, and it felt spectacular. Moments later, Luke climaxed, releasing a string of unintelligible words, before collapsing on top of her. He buried his face into her neck and carefully rolled them both over so he was beneath her.

Both dogs whined from the other side of the door.

Luke chuckled. "I knew I should have splurged on the treats guaranteed to keep dogs occupied for hours."

CHAPTER SIXTEEN

A SOFT RAIN fell outside the snug Craftsman bungalow later that night. Inside, Luke and Summer were seated on the sofa, each with a plate of spaghetti on their lap. A fire burned in the fireplace, making the space cozy and warm. Across the room, the dogs were perched on their beds, anxiously lying in wait for a morsel of food to hit the floor.

Luke shoveled in another forkful of the pasta, a mash-up of corkscrew shapes and rigatoni, doused with a hearty meat sauce.

"I guess this isn't technically spaghetti, per se," Summer remarked. "But I didn't have any spaghetti noodles. This was all the pasta I had on hand."

He grinned at her. The meal was so totally Summer—unique, unpredictable, and delicious. "The sauce is fit for any kind of noodle."

She blushed prettily. "It's Grandma Bonnie's secret recipe."

Luke smothered a laugh. He'd seen the jar "Grandma Bonnie's secret recipe" came from when he went out back to grab some wood for the fire. Not that he minded. He'd eat dirt if it meant spending more time with Summer.

She was sitting facing him, her legs crossed to balance her

plate. The fuzzy pink robe she wore kept gaping open, providing a bird's-eye view of the fabulous breasts he hoped to press his mouth to again later tonight. He'd thrown on his golf shirt and jeans earlier, which he now regretted. His zipper was unbearably painful due to the peep-show she kept giving him every time she gestured wildly—which was often with Summer.

"She'd have a fit knowing we are eating dinner on the sofa," she said.

"Don't tell me she's one of those little old ladies who wraps her furniture in plastic," he teased.

"No!" She nearly dumped her pasta on the floor when she moved to swat him. "She was a stickler for eating meals at the table. As a family." She pressed her lips together as if she was composing her thoughts. "I need to apologize for the things I said about your Gram. I was so out of line. You were right. I was being ridiculous. It's just—" She covered her face with her palms.

Luke grabbed the plate off her lap and stacked it with his on the side table next to them. Monty let out a disappointed sigh that the food had been rescued.

"My grandparents have this epic love story," Summer explained. "Did you know they never spent a night apart in the sixty years they were married?" The muscles in her neck contracted as she swallowed. "Until the Alzheimer's took hold and she had to be confined in memory care."

He reached over and toyed with a strand of her hair as she talked.

"They communicate with one another with just a look. It's so romantic."

Luke wisely kept his mouth shut because one woman's romantic was another man's creepy. He really needed to stop watching the Sci-Fi Channel.

"My mom and dad would have had that, too," she said quietly. "But then they couldn't. My dad's death made Papa Harry and Grandma Bonnie's love story even more impressive to me. They set the relationship bar high without even trying." She offered him one of her lopsided smiles. "I know not everyone gets that kind of love in their lifetime. But it would be nice. Something to aspire to, you know?"

His mouth was suddenly dry. No, he didn't know.

"Anyway, I know my grandfather would never cheat on my grandmother. I'm ashamed of the ugly things I said about your Gram. I was overreacting to Papa Harry's kindness toward her."

He leaned in and kissed her nose. "I get it. Forget it ever happened."

Luke wasn't about to share with her that he'd picked up the same vibe when Gram and Harry Pearson were together. Nor did he agree with the idea that Harry was cheating on his wife. Summer's grandmother wasn't the same woman Harry married decades earlier. If anyone knew what it was like to lose someone's love while that person was still alive, it was Luke. He wouldn't blame the man for wanting companionship.

No way was he bursting Summer's romantic bubble though. If believing what she did made her happy, then Luke was happy. He'd keep an eye on the situation at Sunset Glen and warn both parties to be discreet.

She propped her arm up on the back of the sofa and leaned her head into her hand. "It's sweet that you moved your Gram all this way to be close to her."

He crossed his feet at the ankles on the ottoman. "She was starting to make some questionable decisions. And Boise is a long way from everywhere."

"There isn't anyone else to help look after her?"

"Gram and my dad are not particularly close."

"Because he wouldn't marry your mom?"

He jerked his head around to stare at her in wonder. She said the darndest things. "What makes you say that?"

She toyed with the fuzz on her robe. "There's no indication of them being married on Wikipedia."

He snorted. "Wikipedia leaves a lot of things out." He rested his head against the back of the sofa and stared at the dancing shadows the firelight created on the ceiling. "You're clamoring for the story, so here's the unabridged version. My mom and dad were both college athletes. Mom played volleyball, and dad was on the football team."

"Obvi," she said.

Luke pinned her with a look from the corner of his eye. She pantomimed zipping her lips and throwing away the key. Just looking at her mouth made him hard again. With a groan, he forced his eyes back to the ceiling.

"Being gay wasn't as accepted as it is today. Needless to say, my mom thought those feelings were something she could turn on and off. She figured she could suppress them by being in a relationship with a man. My dad was the lucky one chosen for her experiment." He shot her a cheeky grin. "Because what woman can resist the Kessler charm, eh?"

Summer rolled her eyes.

"After a few weeks, she figured out she'd made a mistake. Being an athlete, it took her a bit longer to realize she was pregnant. By then, she was involved with Karla. It seemed silly for my parents to marry simply to make me legitimate."

He swallowed the bitterness that always seemed to find its way into his throat when he dwelled on his lack of legitimacy. Adulthood, and hours of therapy, brought the situation into better focus. Their decision made perfect sense.

Still, clarity didn't make it hurt any less.

"But your father supported you?"

The indignant tone of Summer's question made his chest squeeze. She was championing him. Damn, if it didn't feel awesome having her in his corner.

"Early on, my dad was a huge part of my life," he told her. "He was there the day I was born. My mom and Karla both stayed in Boise to get advanced degrees. I told you Karla is a nurse. My mom is an athletic trainer. Those early years, it was always Gram and Dad and Mom and Karla for every event or holiday. I didn't know my family situation was unusual."

"Then?" she prompted.

He sighed heavily. "Then my dad became the most famous athlete in America. Kind of ironic since he never even expected to be drafted into the pros. He was taken in the eighth round. The first four seasons, he held a clipboard and wore a headset more than he held a ball and wore a helmet. Then their star quarterback went down. My dad jumped in and played better than anyone expected. The rest is history."

"He dumped you when he got famous?" She was getting riled up now.

"Not initially. We all went to Disney for his parade when he was MVP after they won the championship. But by then, Mom, Karla, and I were living in Canada. It wasn't until my father met his wife that he pared down his involvement in my life. A man with an illegitimate kid is nothing new. But when the baby mama is gay—" Luke whistled. "That was too much for her to handle."

"That bitch!"

Milli woke with a start and barked her agreement. Luke shook with laughter.

"I've only met her a few times, so I wouldn't know," he said when he sobered up.

"But she had no right!"

He pulled her onto his lap, tugging at the tie on her robe to expose her breasts. Her skin was flushed with fury.

"You are so hot when you're wound up about something," he murmured against her belly.

"I mean it, Luke." She shoved him away, much to his disappointment. "No sane woman would deny her son his father, especially one who didn't have a male in his life."

"Because I was being raised by two moms?"

She sunk her teeth into her bottom lip. "That was an ignorant and insensitive assumption of me to make. I apologize."

"Don't apologize. The situation still seems odd to a lot of people, but it's really no different." He traced a G on her stomach, groaning when she squirmed against his erection. "My moms were just like every other set of parents. It wasn't like I grew up in an anti-male environment. Quite the opposite. They made sure I had plenty of solid male role models to look up to. They made sure I had everything I needed growing up."

Almost.

He wasn't going to tell her about Karla's cancer and how it had changed everything. While only one woman was diagnosed with the disease, both of them fought it. The bond between the two became so intense that he was often left out of the picture. They never neglected him physically. It was simply they were so focused on pouring all their love into each other that there wasn't any love left over for him.

Her brow furrowed. "They haven't come to a game."

"They live in Australia now."

"Oh." She blinked a few times, but not quick enough for him to see the pity there.

Karla wanted a fresh start after surviving cancer. With Luke in Boise for college, she took a job in Sydney. His mother didn't bat an eye about going so far away from her only child. He'd been to visit once after his rookie season. It was the only time he'd seen his mom or Karla in person in the past twelve years.

She sat up and straddled his lap. Her hands cupped his chin. He took advantage of her position to press his hands inside her robe. This conversation was getting out of hand. He didn't want to think about his mixed-up family. He would much rather be moving inside her until she screamed with desire.

"But to suddenly be cut out of your father's life. That's unconscionable. It had to be devastating for a young boy."

It was pretty devastating the first time he looked up his dad on Wikipedia, and there was no mention of Luke in Jake Kessler's bio. None at all. The rest of the kids had laughed, figuring he was making up stories. Years of bullying followed as his resentment grew.

"I survived. And I'm better for it. I don't need my dad or anyone else to make me happy." He tugged the robe off her shoulders. He didn't want to go any further down this rabbit hole. "And right now, I want to make you happy. Multiple times."

She looked like she wanted to argue. The hint of pity in her eyes spurred him on. He hefted her over his shoulder and carried her to the kitchen. He was charged up enough to want to toss all the dishes off the table, but there weren't any on it. With a growl, he lowered her down until her back was pressed against the wood surface, her legs draped over the side. He spread the sides of her robe wide. The sight of her naked body laid out like a feast made his breath hitch.

"Luke?" she hiccupped.

He swatted her hands away when she tried to cover herself.

"Don't." He leaned over and blew on her nipples. "Unless you want me to tie you up."

Her caramel eyes went wide. "You-you'd do that?"

Damn, if she didn't sound like she wanted him to. His junk grew so tight he thought he'd explode on the spot.

"Don't tempt me." He hooked his foot around the leg of one of the chairs and tugged it forward before taking a seat between her legs.

She moaned but wisely didn't protest any further, which was perfect because Luke needed to lose himself in her. To savor her taste. To drown in her passion. To find oblivion with her. It was the only way to bury the pain talking about his past always dredged up.

Draping her legs over his shoulders, he plunged his tongue into her sweetness, teasing and toying with her until she was writhing on the table. He tormented her, bringing her to the brink several times before backing off. She swore beneath him, calling him all kinds of names and threatening bodily harm. He chuckled before putting her out of her misery. She bucked off the table with a silent scream.

He blew on the inside of her thigh, forcing a keening sob from her.

"Luke," she cried. "I need you. I need you right now."

She didn't have to ask him twice. He stood and shucked his jeans. Just as he stepped free of them, she sat up and shoved him back down into the chair. Climbing into his lap, she wrapped her fingers around him. He hissed at the pleasure of her touch as she guided him to her entrance.

With a toss of her hair, she bit her lip and began to move seductively on him. So slowly, at first, it was torture. But this was about satisfying her. His pleasure always came from watching a woman in ecstasy. And Summer in climax was something to behold.

"Too many clothes." She tugged at his T-shirt. "I want to feel you, damn it."

He would have laughed had his body not been so tight with need. A ripping sound filled the kitchen when he tore off the shirt. The noise spurred her on.

Her movements became more frantic, and he could feel her muscles growing tense around him. He was going to die right here in her kitchen if she didn't come soon. Reaching between their bodies, he flicked his thumb over that sweet spot he'd mapped out earlier. She climaxed a short moment later, burying her teeth into his shoulder to stifle her cry.

He held her through the pleasure and pain of it. His body coiled with tension as she came back to earth. And then she was kissing him. He forgot all about his father, his mothers, his loneliness. Everything. The only thing in this world was the woman wrapped around him and her contagious passion. He wanted to stay inside her and hold onto to this moment for a lifetime. To never have this night end.

With a low roar, he stood, lifting her from the chair and pressing her back into the stainless-steel fridge. Like an animal, he drove into her, angling their bodies to bring himself the most pleasure. She urged him on with sultry pants of "yes" and "please" even though the position couldn't be comfortable for her.

He should stop. This was no way to treat a woman. But it was as if something inside him snapped. Release was the only thing he could focus on in the moment. It raced through him with the force of every hard tackle he'd ever received. He swore violently before his body went slack.

Minutes that felt like hours later, Summer brushed a kiss beneath his ear. Her hands continued to gently slide up and down on his back.

"Luke," she whispered. "That was ah-mazing. No complaints at all. Except for maybe a tiny one. Um, my ass is getting a little chilly against this metal door."

Shit.

She giggled when he pulled her body away from the fridge. Her arms and legs tightened around him as he steered them toward the hallway.

"Sofa," she commanded, her words already slurring with sleep. "I want to sleep in front of the fire with you."

He pulled a blanket off one of the chairs and wrapped it around both of them like a human tortilla, before slumping down onto the sofa. She burrowed against him, waking up all the nerve endings he'd just managed to calm down.

"Don't let go," she whispered.

No worries there. Luke didn't plan on letting her go. But he was beginning to worry about the hit he'd take when, like everyone else, she decided to let go of him.

CHAPTER SEVENTEEN

THE RAIN CONTINUED off and on for the rest of the weekend. Not that Summer noticed. With the exception of walking the two dogs, she and Luke hadn't left the house since he arrived on Friday evening. They hadn't spent much time out of each other's arms during that time either.

She blushed as she glanced around the kitchen, thinking of the things they'd done in here. They'd behaved like bunny rabbits in nearly every room of her grandparent's home. It was shameful. *It was glorious.* Both dogs looked at her expectantly when Summer groaned with embarrassment.

"It's a good thing neither of you can talk."

Monty smirked at her.

Summer flipped the bacon she was broiling in the oven, the smell mingling with the scent of freshly brewed coffee, cinnamon, and nutmeg. It wasn't exactly Sunday brunch at Yolk in Chicago, but it would do. Besides, her French toast was always better. She had the brioche bread sliced and ready to be drenched in the egg batter as soon as Luke finished with his shower.

Thanks to their Thursday night game, the Growlers had the weekend off. The rain was supposed to let up by noon, and she was hoping to talk Luke into going to the local pumpkin patch with her. They could enjoy some cider while strolling the farm. Maybe they'd go on a hayride. She'd get a pumpkin for the front porch and another for Grandpa Harry while Luke could grab one for his Gram. Maybe there would be one of those mini ones she could buy for Grandma Bonnie's room.

She chewed on her bottom lip. *Gah!* She was such a romantic sap. They weren't living out a rom-com movie. He might have other plans. *Why wouldn't he have other plans?* Maybe the Growlers had practice or something.

Or worse, maybe he thought this weekend was simply a fling. It wasn't like they'd talked about where this was going. Or even if there was a "this."

She shoved one of the chairs from the kitchen table in frustration, accidentally slamming it onto her toe.

"Oww!"

Monty dropped his head into her lap when she sat down in the offending chair. She leaned down to snuggle the dog.

The self-doubt flooded over her like a tidal wave. Why couldn't she be perky and ooze self-confidence like Lizzie? Summer had worked so hard to get better at it over the years. Until Vienna happened. And now she was back to square one.

More like square negative one.

At some point, Luke was going to discover she was a poser. A woman who had managed to convince millions of people that she had talent when she didn't. A con artist who was going to law school because she couldn't think of anything better to do with her life.

The ringing of the doorbell put an end to her careening thoughts. Monty jerked his head up, bumping her on the chin. The dog ignored her cry, instead barreling toward the front door, barking like a gang-banger's mutt. Milli's high-pitched yip joined in as she scampered between the bigger dog's legs, trying to beat him to the door.

Summer pressed a dishtowel to her chin, hoping it didn't come away covered in blood. She didn't bother blocking the dogs when she opened the door. Whoever was interrupting her idyllic Sunday morning deserved to be licked to death by the two beasts.

"Sterling!"

For the second time in four days, she was surprised to see a family member standing on her front porch. It was uncanny how much her brother resembled their late father. It was almost as if the gods had decided to give each parent their own mini-me. Sterling had the same dancing blue eyes their dad inherited from Papa Harry. He'd been a towhead as a boy. As he aged, though, his hair had settled into a sandy-blond. Once down to his shoulders, he now kept it neat with a corporate cut. Today, however, the stubble covering his jaw gave him a bit of that bad-boy air he worked so hard to suppress.

Milli yipped frantically, trying to leap into her brother's arms. The little vixen always did love Sterling best. Monty gave her brother's hand a sniff, pronounced him safe with a low grunt, and ambled back into the kitchen, presumably to keep an eye on the bacon.

"Jeez, Mom wasn't kidding about that dog being butt-ugly."

"He makes up for it with his sweet temperament." Summer hugged her brother, partly glad to see him and partly relieved he hadn't shown up yesterday when who knows what she and Luke might have been doing. "What is going on? First mom drops in unannounced, and now you. If I didn't know better, I'd say you two don't trust me to live on my own."

"Or, it's possible we just missed you." Sterling scooped up Milli as Summer closed the door. "Please tell me that's coffee I smell. I could really use a cup." He followed her into the kitchen.

"They have coffee in Chicago, you know."

"Good to know, but I was in Lake Geneva. A colleague got married last night."

She handed him a steaming mug of brew. "Ahh. Let me guess.

You had to skedaddle before the post-wedding brunch to avoid the morning-after conversation with the bridesmaid you hooked up with. Am I right?"

"I'll never tell."

The tips of his ears were pink, however, telling Summer everything her disreputable brother hadn't. She leaned a hip against the counter and smiled at him over her coffee mug.

He mirrored her pose as well as her smile. "You look well. I was worried I'd never see that toothy grin ever again."

"You detoured forty minutes out of your way to see my smile? You could have Facetimed me for that."

"Stop being such a brat." He gave Milli a loud smooch and set her on the floor. The dog protested with a whine. "Same goes to you, dog." He pulled a folded envelope out of the back pocket of his jeans. "Mom said you're in a positive headspace again. I thought it was time we discuss getting back in the saddle."

The back of her neck grew tight. "'Back in the saddle?'"

"Here." He extended the envelope to her.

Summer gingerly took it from him. "What is it?"

"A list of people who have contacted me requesting the honor of your performance."

She tossed the envelope to the floor as though it had singed her fingers. Monty scrambled across the room to investigate, only to return to his post by the oven when he discovered it wasn't edible.

"What the hell, Summer?"

"What the hell, you, Sterling." She put her hand to her chest, trying to regulate her breathing. "What is it about the words 'I'm never performing again' that you don't get?"

His eyes narrowed. "All of it, since you won't tell anyone why."

"You. Were. There," she shouted.

He scoffed at her. "I was. And none of it made sense. But I'm sure every performer gets stage fright at some point. That's no reason to throw away everything you worked for. We can figure it out."

Stage fright. If only it were that simple. Just as she opened her mouth to argue, Luke raced into the room like a white knight coming to avenge her.

"Babe? Are you okay?"

A buck-naked white night.

The look on Sterling's face was so comical, Summer wished she'd snapped a picture to show Paige. Instead, she grabbed the dishtowel off the counter and flung it at Luke. Not that it would cover much. Of course, he caught it without looking, his eyes piercing into her brother's. He crumpled the towel with his hand rather than cover up any of his good parts.

Torn between laughing and knocking both their heads together, Summer stepped between the two men. "I'm fine." She gave Luke a reassuring pat on the chest. Sterling's eyes grew even wider. "This is my brother, Sterling. He was *in the area*." Her brother pursed his lips at the snarky tone she added to the "in the area" part. "Sterling, this is Luke, Luke Kessler."

Sterling started to extend his hand before pulling it back and giving Luke a wave. His eyes suddenly darted everywhere else in the room but at the chiseled naked man in front of him. Summer shook her head at the absurdity of the scene. She turned to Luke.

"Maybe you should—" she gestured to his nudity.

His expression relaxed when his eyes met hers. "Yeah." He turned on his heel and headed back the way he came.

Summer didn't hide the pleasure she got from watching him walk away.

"Jesus." Sterling smacked his forehead a few times with the heel of his hand. "Mom had it all wrong. Your positive headspace is post-coital bliss. And correct me if I'm wrong, but weren't he and Lizzy a thing?"

The pan sizzled when she dropped a hunk of butter into it. "Briefly."

"Huh. And now you two are a thing?"

With a shrug, she dredged the bread through the egg wash before dropping it into the frying pan. Because she didn't know the answer to Sterling's question herself. She wanted them to be a thing, didn't she? Doubt swirled in her stomach again.

"I'm going to take the dogs for a walk."

She turned to see Luke standing in the doorway dressed in his jeans and wearing Papa Harry's Growler jacket. Both dogs ran to him at the word "walk."

"I'll give you two some privacy," he said.

She didn't want privacy. As far as she was concerned, the subject of her performing again was moot. And she didn't want Luke to leave.

Like, ever.

"Sure," she managed to push out past her lips. "I made breakfast. Enough for all of us."

He was across the room before she could blink. Cupping the back of her neck with his long fingers, he pulled her in for a possessive kiss that had her sighing with relief as she pressed her body into his.

"It smells delicious," he murmured against her lips. "I'll be thinking about it the entire walk."

And then he winked at her. With a nod to Sterling, he disappeared out the front door, both dogs happily following.

"Wowza." Sterling sank into one of the chairs and guzzled his coffee.

Summer pulled the bacon from the oven. She flipped the French toast, slapping it on the plate along with two pieces of bacon. A hefty dousing of powdered sugar followed, then she loudly put the plate down in front of her brother.

He looked up at her sheepishly. "Syrup?"

She retrieved the bottle from the pantry and set it down on the table more gently than she had his plate. After refilling her coffee, she took the seat beside him. He sighed as he inhaled the food. She sipped her coffee while he ate. The companionable silence helped to diffuse the mood from earlier.

"Look, Sum," he said after wiping his face with a napkin. "I'm trying to understand, that's all. You know I'll support you in whatever you choose. It's just . . ."

"Just what?"

He leaned back in the chair. "You have a gift. And the delight on your face every time you stroked the bow across the strings of your cello gave me and everyone else listening as much enjoyment as the music you made. I don't want to see your joy disappear, that's all."

She swallowed painfully around the boulder that had formed in her throat. "It's over, Sterling."

"I don't get it," he argued. "Papa Harry said you played at his place, and were fantastic. Lizzie sent me the video of you performing at someone's engagement. And the joy, it was there on your face, Summer. Plain as day."

Damn Lizzie.

"She was not supposed to be filming that. No one was." She gripped the handle of her mug tightly.

"Yeah, well, we all know Lizzie does whatever the hell she wants." He reached for her hand. "Help me out here. Help me understand what happened."

She wanted to. She really did. But it was too mortifying. Besides, he wouldn't understand. He'd slough it off with some placating remark about the guy being an idiot who didn't know what he was talking about. Except music wasn't Sterling's business. And there were likely plenty of people who thought the same way as the man she'd overheard in Vienna.

Worst of all, she could never unhear it. And she'd always wonder if someone was thinking the very same thing every time she performed. Sterling wouldn't understand how devastating that feeling was to her psyche. Very few people could.

She shook her head. "There's nothing to understand. I'm going to law school like I'd always planned."

He slapped a hand on the table. "You were in kindergarten when you decided that! What did you know at five years old?"

"You don't think I'll be a decent lawyer?" she challenged.

Sterling held both hands up as if she'd drawn a gun. "There's no way for me to answer that and not be crucified. Besides, if I said I didn't think so, you'd make it your life's mission to prove me wrong whether being a lawyer brought you joy or not."

He wasn't wrong.

She eyed him smugly over the rim of her mug. "Mom supports my career direction."

"Mom wants us both to be settled. And content. She's kind of uptight about it, in case you hadn't noticed." He scraped his fingers over the stubble on his chin. "I think it's because she doesn't want to let Dad down. She's got it in her head that if we don't turn out perfect, she's somehow failed him, you know?"

Summer slumped back against the back of the chair. "I never thought of it that way." The silence stretched as they both pondered his theory. She eyed her brother carefully. "Are you doing what you want to do?"

He barked a laugh. "I'm doing what I excel at."

The perfect non-answer if she ever heard one. Not that she was going to call him out on it. Especially since she wasn't exactly being honest with him herself.

He blew out a frustrated breath. "I should go." Pressing his palms to the table, he pushed himself up.

She followed him. "You don't want to stay and meet Luke?"

Sterling laughed humorlessly. "It's been a crazy weekend already. I think I'll skip making small talk with the naked man my sister is entertaining for brunch, thank you very much."

They walked to the front door.

"Besides, I need to get back so I can ask if anyone in my fantasy league wants to trade for Kessler."

She gave him a quizzical look.

"I've seen the dude's junk," he explained. " And now that's the mental image of him that will pop into my head every time he scores me points." He practically shuddered. "I don't need that happening every week."

"Oh my, God, men are so stupid." She shook her head.

"Yeah, well, it's usually women who make us that way." He gripped her shoulders, pulling her in to press a kiss to her forehead. "You know I love you, right?"

"Right back at ya," she whispered.

He stared at her a moment longer before giving her shoulders a quick squeeze. "Say hi to Papa Harry and Grandma Bonnie for me." And then he was gone.

Summer padded back into the kitchen, jumping when she saw Luke standing at the back door drying off the dogs.

"Your brother left?"

"Mmhmm," she replied, adding more butter to the frying pan. "He said something about three's company." She gave him a sly smile over her shoulder.

He poured himself a cup of coffee and came to stand next to her at the stove. "Call me a curious only child. Do you two always yell at each other?"

"No. We're actually pretty close. He was being ridiculous about something, that's all." When he didn't reply, she glanced up at him. He was studying her quizzically. "What?"

"What's ridiculous to you might not be to him."

Something told her if Luke and Sterling ever decided to gang up on her, she wouldn't stand a chance. She glanced around the floor for the envelope. It wasn't there. Sterling must have taken it back with him. Hopefully, he'd burn it when he got home.

"He's not the boss of me."

He laughed loudly as he wrapped his arms around her and pressed his body into her back. Her nerve endings danced at the contact. His lips traced her neck. "I believe I once told you that you needed a keeper."

You can be my keeper, she wanted to shout. Instead, she busied herself with making his French toast. She cleared her throat. "So, what do football players do on Sunday when they don't have a game?"

His lips stilled on her skin. "Trying to get rid of me, Summer?"

She spun in his arms, her muscles relaxing when she saw the teasing glint in his eyes. "Definitely not. I have plans for you, buster." She pressed a kiss beneath his chin.

"Whatever they are, I'm up for them. But first, you're going to have to feed me, woman. I'm pretty sure I'm going to need my strength to keep up with your demands."

Laughing, she served him his French toast, then cooked some for herself.

"I was thinking we could go pumpkin picking," she said.

His fork hesitated slightly before heading to his mouth.

"I mean, if it stops raining. Or not. Maybe you want to watch football or something? I could always study."

He put his fork down and picked up her hand.

"Rain or shine, going to the pumpkin patch with you sounds like the perfect day to me."

She was pretty sure he was lying, but that only made her heart sing louder. He leaned forward and brushed a kiss along her hairline, the same spot her brother had. A surge of emotion cascaded through her. She felt cherished.

And she liked the way that felt. Very much.

CHAPTER EIGHTEEN

"How are you holding up, Dare Devil?" Palmer punctuated his question with a slap to Luke's back.

It was Wednesday, and their teammates were filtering into the locker room to get dressed for practice. On a normal week, Mondays were quiet around the training facility. Mostly, players dropped in for treatment of their various injuries. Unless a position coach specifically called a player in to watch game film, most guys prepped for their next game on their own time. On Tuesdays, players caught up on community activities, promotional work, or hung out with their families. The pads came back on the next day as everyone got down to business preparing for that weekend's opponent.

Luke wiggled his thumb. "Right as rain."

Palmer scoffed at him. "I wasn't talking about that, hoser. Everyone knows an injury would have to be major to sidetrack you. I'm talking about your love life."

Luke paused with his fingers gripping the hem of his Henley. He glanced around the locker room hoping that no one was paying attention to the punter. No such luck.

"I spent the last year in a long-distance relationship with my girl," Palmer continued. "I know what it can do to a guy if you get what I'm saying." He shot Luke a wink.

It took Luke a tense minute to figure out what the guy was babbling about. With a pang of guilt, he realized Palmer was referring to Elizabeth. He'd never properly ended things with her before becoming involved with Summer. Much of the blame lay with Elizabeth. She was the one who had taken off without a word. Still, his moms had taught him to always take the high road —especially when it involved a woman.

Not that he could help himself where Summer was concerned. They'd been on a collision course since the moment their paths crossed. And damn, had it been one cataclysmic explosion when they both gave in to their baser desires.

One that could very well knock him off his axis.

Up until this weekend, he believed he'd had great sex before. With Summer, though, it was damn near a religious experience. There was another level to them coming together. It touched his soul.

And that made him nervous.

He'd always been able to separate sex from love. He was an expert at it, in fact. Some shrink could probably write an entire book about him.

Somehow, though, Summer had wiped-out his well-fortified defenses. From the moment he'd kissed her on opening day, he'd been like a drug addict trying to score his next hit. The more he tried to deny it, the more his body craved her. Worse still, his need for her seemed to grow every time he had her. Despite knowing the painful withdrawal he was bound to suffer when she left him, Luke wouldn't give her up.

He couldn't.

"Gonna share your porn subscription with him, Kessler?" one of the guys called out from across the locker room.

"Maybe you could take him to the strip club for a lap dance," another player added. “Do they even let you in the clubs with that baby face of yours?”

“Are you kidding? The ladies love boys,” one of the linemen said.

“Watch yourself, men,” Fletcher’s voice boomed. “His lass is handy with a hatchet.”

The room was practically vibrating with laughter now. Palmer skulked off to his locker. Grateful for the distraction, Luke tugged off his Henley. A whistle pierced through the row of lockers.

“Well, that explains why Dare Devil ditched out on our card game Sunday afternoon, fellas. Check out those scratch marks.” Jacobs pointed a finger at Luke’s bare back. “Damn, is that a bite mark near your ass?”

A chorus of catcalls erupted. “I always knew that girl would be stormy in bed,” someone shouted.

The laughter escalated. Jacobs bumped shoulders with Luke. “I went by your place looking for you yesterday. I should have figured you’d skip over to the Big Apple to hook up with your meteorologist.”

“Yeah,” one of the other receivers said. “We were concerned that having the Seasonal Arm Candy out of town would mess with your mojo. Everyone knows how you like to be locked down with a woman during the season. I’m glad you two are making it work. We won’t have to deal with the fallout on the field.”

Shit.

The last thing Luke wanted was for the guys to think he and Elizabeth were together. Deceiving them didn’t feel right. Trust was important among a team. Except, what was going on between him and Summer was too new, too confusing to explain to his teammates. He wasn’t ready to share her with this group of nosy boneheads. Not yet, anyway. It was easier to let them think what they wanted.

He grinned at Jacobs. "Everything is working out fine."

Jacobs clapped him on the back and headed outside to the practice field. Luke was pulling on his cleats when he felt the uncomfortable weight of someone's stare on him. He glanced up to see Van Horn shake his head.

"What?"

"I hope you know what you're doing." The quarterback picked up his helmet and followed the others out of the locker room.

Luke snatched up his helmet and trailed after him. He knew exactly what he was doing. Having the greatest sex of his life with an unpredictable, one-of-a-kind, sexy-as-hell woman who made him laugh. Who made him feel alive. Who made him feel worthy.

LATER THAT EVENING, Summer was poring over her note cards. The dogs played tug-of-war with a knotted piece of rope while Luke was studying film on his tablet. A fire crackled in the grate.

"This is nice," Summer said softly.

He glanced up to see her smiling shyly at him. "It is." And he meant it. He'd been back to his place for some clothes and food for Monty, but otherwise he'd decamped to Summer's house. It surprised him how seamlessly he slid into her life.

Every morning, he and the dogs walked her to school. While she was working, he was either at practice, taking care of his charitable commitments, or hanging out with Gram and her cronies at Sunset Glen. Harry and the guys even invited him to join their poker game—complete with those gin-soaked raisins. The geezers claimed they were good for their constitution. The only thing Luke thought they were good for was obliterating the taste of Fred's gnarly cheese curds.

"Antonio is getting back tomorrow. I'll still be in school when his flight lands. I hate that no one will be there to pick him up."

He dropped his head back against the sofa. “Is that your not-so-subtle way of asking me to do it?”

She scooted closer. “Well, he is a member of the team. Shouldn’t someone pick him up?”

“We have practice and position meetings all day tomorrow. I’m sure they’ll send a car for him.”

“His father just died.” She smacked him on the shoulder. “How would you feel if you lost your father and someone you didn’t know was there to greet you?”

He cocked an eyebrow at her.

Her face softened as she seemed to deflate. “I get it.” She toyed with the collar of his shirt. “You lost your dad years ago. But he’s still here. There’s still a chance—” She bit her bottom lip in response to his sharp intake of breath. “Never mind. Antonio handles his emotions better than I do. He’s a tough football player. He’ll be fine. Practice comes first.”

Talk about sucker punches. In all likelihood, the rookie would come back with an even bigger chip on his shoulder. Apparently, that was how McGraff handled his emotions. He sighed. It wouldn’t be the first time he took one for the team, he told himself.

“Fine. Give me his flight info, and I’ll let Coach Washington know I’m picking him up.”

She threw her arms around his neck and crawled onto his lap. “I knew there was a sweet man inside there.”

“Mmm. You want to see what else is inside here?” He pressed his mouth to her neck, reveling in the taste and scent of her.

She threw her head back and laughed. “We’re supposed to be studying.”

He tugged at the sweatshirt she’d stolen from him and dragged it over her head. “I am studying. Right now, I’m going for some extra credit with the teacher.” He scraped his thumb over her pebbled nipple, confined in one of those thick sports bras. “Poor babies. We need to set these free.”

Sighing, she arched at his touch. "You are such a bad influence on me."

"I can't help it if you're easily distracted by my sex appeal."

A throaty laugh escaped her lips. Luke contemplated how best to get them both undressed without moving from this spot when her phone pinged. Summer groaned when she looked at the fitness tracker on her wrist.

"It's your Scottish friend's wife. She wants to meet before the game Sunday to talk about her grand opening." She slapped him on the chest. "This is all your fault."

"Mine?" He did his best to look innocent even though he'd known precisely what he was doing when he goaded her into saying yes to Andi.

Summer sat up, tugging his sweatshirt back over her body. "Don't play dumb with me. You know you keyed me up so I'd do the opposite of what I wanted to do."

"Let's see if that will work this time."

She swatted his hand when he reached for the sweatshirt again.

"I mean it, Luke. You know I don't play in public anymore. Yet you pushed me into it. Now I have to find a way to back out graciously."

He tried to make sense of what she was saying. "It's partly your fault for being so amazing at the engagement party."

She squinted at him. *Wrong answer.*

Luke sighed. "You don't have to think of a gracious way to get out of it. I'll let Andi know you won't be able to do it."

Her shoulders slumped. "You'd do that?"

He reached over and gently traced a finger along her cheek. "Of course." *I'll do anything for you.*

Something twisted in his chest when he saw her eyes misting up. "Hey, it's all good. Andi is a reasonable woman. She'll understand." He maneuvered her back into his lap. "No need to stress over it any longer."

Summer was quiet for several moments, the only sound in the room Monty's snoring and the snap of the wood in the fireplace. He brushed a kiss on the top of her head.

"I wish you'd tell me what this is all about."

"It's not a big secret," she murmured. "I get stage fright, that's all."

He wrapped his arms around her and pulled her tighter against his body. She leaned her head on his shoulder. "Did you always get stage fright?"

She shook her head. "Just once."

Some of the puzzle pieces fell into place. "And you haven't performed since then."

"No," she whispered.

"Except for at Sunset Glen and Palmer's engagement."

"Yes. But those don't count."

"So you keep saying."

She tried to jerk away from him, but his hands were way quicker.

"Hey." He tilted her chin toward him. "Those do count. You know why? Because you played in front of people, and you were magnificent. Do you know what I saw when you were playing?"

"If you say joy, I'm going to slug you!"

Thank goodness for her warning, because he was going to say joy. He'd unpack her response later. Right now, he needed to try a different tact. "I saw a very sexy woman who turned me on."

She relaxed within his hold. "You're only saying that."

"No, I'm not. I was jealous of a freaking wooden instrument. Of the way you were caressing it." He stroked low on her back, gently caressing her ass through her leggings. "Of the way you plucked the strings." He flicked his tongue below her ear. "Of the way you held it between your legs," he whispered.

She shivered. "There's nothing sexy about playing the cello."

Luke snorted. She pulled back so she could study him. He arched both brows. She sunk her teeth into her bottom lip, her tell that she was up to something. Then she was off his lap, making a beeline to her cello leaning in its stand in the corner of the room.

"You think *this* is sexy?" Her tone was incredulous.

He propped his feet on the ottoman and leaned back, tucking his hands together behind his head. "Oh, yeah."

She shot him a cynical look, then glanced back at the cello. Gingerly picking up the bow, she made a show of deliberately wiping it with rosin, stroking it slowly up and then down. With a groan, Luke shifted on the sofa.

The corners of her lips twitched, the little wench. She straddled the wooden chair, spreading her legs wide for a tortured moment before settling the cello between her knees. Shooting him a coy smile, she pulled the bow across the strings. Slowly, the room filled with sound, and Summer was lost.

She played Chris Isaak's "Wicked Game," and Luke would have laughed at the irony of it had he not been too busy watching her masterfully make magic before him. He'd lied when he said she was sexy. Sexy didn't capture what she was. She was a goddess.

"Is it hot in here?" she asked once she'd finished the song. Without waiting for an answer, she tugged off his sweatshirt, leaving her in her bra and leggings. She cued up for another song. "This is for the Hosers in the house."

She launched into Shawn Mendes' "Mercy" before transitioning to Leonard Cohen's "Hallelujah." Her head lulled from side to side, and the image of her writhing beneath him made him restless on the sofa. Summer seemed immune to his predicament as she continued with Bryan Adams' "Breathless."

When she closed her eyes and tossed her head back, exposing her long neck, Luke couldn't take it anymore.

"Summer!" he shouted.

The bow stilled on the strings, and she blinked several times, seeming to remember where she was.

"Come here," he commanded.

She blinked again. Her mouth opened, no doubt to make some sassy comment. But Luke was so aroused, his brain was no longer doing the thinking.

"Come. Here."

Seeming to understand he was deadly serious, she did as he asked. Of course, she took her sweet time returning the cello and its bow to the corner before sauntering back to the sofa.

"Here?"

He wrapped his hands around her waist and hauled her into his lap. "Here."

She giggled when she came in contact with the part of him most anxious to get her naked. "You weren't kidding when you said the cello turns you on. Go figure."

Her giggle turned to sighs minutes later when Luke stripped them both of their clothes. He spent the rest of the evening doing whatever he could to put that same look of bliss on her lips that she wore when she was playing the cello.

CHAPTER NINETEEN

THE FOLLOWING DAY, Luke stood with his back to the wall while waiting in the airport arrival area. It turned out Wash was more than okay with him ducking out from practice to pick up McGraff. The coach even rescheduled their position meeting to later in the day so both players could be present.

"I'm glad you're m-making an effort with the k-kid," Wash said. "He'll need someone to l-lean on these next few weeks."

"He can't just lean on you? You've got more fatherly experience than I do."

Wash gave him the side-eye and dismissed Luke from his office. "Go get Antonio. And call your dad. He's looking for you."

No shit.

He had four missed calls from his dad this week. That was three more calls from the man than he averaged in a year. He always let his dad's calls go straight to voicemail. That way, he had time to gird himself for whatever nonsense his father was about to lay on him.

Right now, though, Luke had time to kill. More importantly, he needed to look busy before the two men bearing down on him with phones in their hands arrived. He punched in his father's number and put the phone to his ear, hoping his dad was on the golf course or something.

It wasn't Luke's lucky day.

His old man picked up on the second ring.

"Shouldn't you be at practice?" Jake Kessler asked without preamble.

The thing about having a dad who'd spent eighteen years in the pros was the guy knew exactly how Luke spent his days. It annoyed Luke to no end. His dad hadn't cared when Luke was younger to know what grade he was in. Yet, now the guy felt he could micro-manage his son's life.

"Wash switched things up today. I'm picking up McGraff at the airport."

"Ah. It's a shame about his father. But it'll do him some good to be back on the field this weekend. He needs to get his confidence back after last week's fiasco."

Luke shook his head at his father's insensitivity. "I think he'll have more on his mind than the game. The kid just lost his dad. I'd say that's more important."

"Why must you twist around everything I say? Of course that's more important. I was merely suggesting that one way to deal with his grief is to continue living his life. As a dad myself, I know I'd want my kids to do that if something happened to me."

It was on the tip of Luke's tongue to ask if he was included in that sentiment, only he didn't want to engage with the guy today. Not when he still had a satisfied glow from the past few days with Summer. The last thing he needed was to have his relationship with his sperm donor souring the positive things in his life right now.

"I have several missed calls from you. What's up?" he asked instead.

"I have the signed footballs you texted me about."

To say that Luke was surprised at how easy it was to get his father to agree to sign the footballs for him was an understatement. Jake Kessler was very protective of his image and the money his name could generate. Heaven forbid the market be flooded with memorabilia signed by him. He liked his swag to bring in top dollar. It helped him maintain his cache within the sports world.

"Great." Luke said. "The return box was in the package with the balls. The postage is prepaid. All you have to do is stick them in and ship them back to me."

"I've got a better idea."

Somehow Luke doubted that.

"I'm covering your game in Kansas City in two weeks. How about we meet for dinner the night before, and I can give them to you then."

He should have known there'd be a catch. Now that Luke had proved himself worthy in the football world, his dad couldn't resist trotting his son out to show off to his cronies what a successful father he'd been. It started at the players' combine before the pro draft. There'd been rumors Luke would go in one of the early rounds, finally giving him street cred with his father. Of course, the media was eating the story up. The prodigal son of the world's most beloved quarterback was joining the game. Jake swooped in, taking Luke to dinners with team owners, reporters, and anyone else who could further his career.

Luke had been ecstatic. He'd finally gotten his dad's attention. Until reality bit him in the ass. It turned out the recently retired quarterback was trying to further his *own* career. Luke was the perfect news item to keep him relevant.

"I have a carefully scripted routine the night before a game," Luke replied. "I don't deviate from it. I'm sure you can remember how that goes. You were the one who taught it to me."

It was a lesson he had learned the hard way. Following a particularly rough round of trouble in school, Mom and Karla decided it might help if he could spend an afternoon with his dad. They took him to watch Jake play a game in Buffalo, but the weather was snowy, and his dad's plane was late getting in from Dallas. It was only seven-thirty when the team arrived at their hotel. Jake informed them that it was too late in the day for him to meet. It would mess up his "carefully scripted routine." The playoffs were on the line, after all.

From then on, Karla repeated the words "carefully scripted routine" whenever she was pounding out chicken breasts. It took Luke several years to find the humor in her actions. Hell would have to freeze over before he forgave his dad, however.

He heard his father sigh. "We're staying in the same hotel. Wash confirmed that with me, so it's no use denying it. I'm sure you can find a few minutes to drop by my room to pick the balls up then."

A few minutes Luke could handle. Especially if it benefitted the Humane Society.

"Sure. I'll text you when I'm free."

As he disconnected the call, he spied McGraff traipsing toward the kiss and ride. If the rookie was trying to appear inconspicuous, he had failed miserably. He wore an oversized bright yellow LSU hoodie pulled over his head. With his Growlers go-bag draped over his shoulder, he was like the Pied Piper for football fans throughout the airport. A line of people trailed behind, trying to overtake him, including a sports talk radio jock who was a snarky jerk.

Luke quickly intercepted the rookie. "Over here," he said, steering him by the elbow toward the parking garage.

McGraff looked at him in surprise. "Where's the fire, man?"

"Unless you're prepared to give an interview, you might want to pick up the pace."

He didn't have to tell McGraff twice. They made it to the parking garage in record time. A few minutes later, Luke steered his truck onto the highway and headed north to the practice facility without incident.

"Thanks, man," McGraff said, his tone begrudging. "And

thanks for taking care of Summer. She told me you saved career day."

"I made a few calls, that's all."

He slumped in the seat. "Just as well. Those kids would have been bored out of their minds listening to me play."

"I doubt that. You're practically their age," Luke teased. "They would have thought it was hip."

The kid flipped him off.

Luke chuckled. "Although, it would be hard to compete with a cockatoo that crapped on the principal's head."

McGraff tried not to react. Luke could hear it in his breathing. It was no use, though. His belly laughs filled the cab of the truck. Luke glanced at him out of the corner of his eye. With his face relaxed, he looked like a young kid. Hell, at twenty-one, he *was* practically a kid. And now the major breadwinner for his family, to hear Summer tell it. McGraff was responsible for his mother, his great-grandmother, and four siblings. Losing his father had to be a blow in more ways than one.

"How you doing?"

McGraff relaxed his head against the headrest and closed his eyes. "Fine."

"What about your mom? Does she have someone to help her with all the details?"

He grinned. "Yeah, that agent of mine who gets fifteen percent of my signing bonus. I'm the one putting my body on the line every week. So the shark should do something to earn his pay, right?"

"Smart move." Luke meant it. "Still, if you need more time, I'm sure the team would support that."

McGraff snorted. "And give Jacobs more reason to dog me? No way. Besides, between my mom, Granny Pearl, and the little kids, I had to get out of there."

Luke laughed. "Jacobs is a hard nut to crack, but you've got mad skills on the field. He's got to respect that."

"You think so? I mean, the part about the mad skills?"

"I wouldn't say it if I didn't mean it."

His face lit up in a sly smile. "Awesome. Cuz I'm gunning for your playing time, too."

Luke pulled into the parking lot of the practice facility. "I wouldn't respect you if you weren't," he said. "But don't think I'm going to make it easy on you, Tony-O."

They walked to the locker room with a newfound sense of solidarity. Luke silently thanked Summer for pushing him to pick the kid up. He made a mental note to thank her properly later that night.

"Hey, I bet we can talk Van Horn into buying us dinner tonight. Our reception rate is one of the highest in the league. I believe he owes us some compensation for making his stats look nearly perfect," he said. "Don't you?"

A mischievous twinkle lit up the rookie's eyes. "You think we can talk him into that place with the pie?"

"Van Horn doesn't eat sugar, which means we are absolutely making him take us to the place with the pie."

"THE DOCTORS TOLD us to expect a more rapid decline in her motor skills over these next few months," Summer whispered to Paige. "The disease is progressing more quickly now."

The two were hovering outside the sunroom in the memory care building at Sunset Glen. Grandma Bonnie sat in her wheelchair, stroking Milli's back while the dog snoozed. At her feet, a flock of dust motes danced in the sunshine streaming in from the wide windows.

Her grandmother's shoulders were slightly hunched, something the teacher in her would never have tolerated from her students. Three other residents were also in the sunroom. A woman was working with an occupational therapist. A man was dozing in a recliner. In the corner, a woman was arguing with an inanimate object.

Paige linked her arm through Summer's. "I know this is difficult for you. In her heart, though, she knows you're here."

Summer squeezed Paige's hand. "I didn't realize until I moved up to Milwaukee how important this time with her and Papa Harry would be to me. It hurts seeing her like this, but at least she's still her happy-go-lucky self. Some dementia patients become easily agitated and a danger to themselves." She gestured to the woman in the corner, now babbling about Scotland. "Or they slip into a world of their own."

"Well, Bonnie did set off the fire alarm the other day." Paige chuckled. "Who would have guessed that Alzheimer's would turn your sweet grandmother into a prankster?"

That was one of the many things Summer cherished about her friend. Paige could always find a way to lighten the mood. Until Paige showed up on her doorstep this morning, Summer hadn't realized how much she'd missed her.

"She told the staff she did it because it had the word 'pull' written on it."

Paige clapped a hand over her mouth as her eyes crinkled with mirth.

"I know. It sounds like an excuse one of your kindergartners would give," Summer said.

"What's got you two girls giggling?" Papa Harry strolled up to them, his eyes twinkling and cheeks ruddy from being outside. He was wearing his Elmer Fudd jacket, with its big red and white checks and fleece collar. The coat was as ancient as the man wearing it, but both always made her smile. He shifted Summer's cello between his hands. "Don't tell me Leslie thinks she's Queen Elizabeth again?" He winked at both of them before popping his head into the sunroom. "Ah, there's my girl. She likes to spend her days soaking up the sun when the weather is pleasant. You don't mind playing for her in here, do you, Sunshine?"

"Not at all," Summer said. And she was surprised at how much she meant it. A few weeks ago, she would have gotten the shakes performing before anyone she didn't know and trust. Of course, it made it easier that the occupants of the room were relatively harmless to her tattered reputation. "I've always wanted to play for the queen," she joked.

Papa Harry's eyes twinkled. "Atta girl."

Summer took a seat in a chair opposite Grandma Bonnie. If her grandmother noticed, she didn't acknowledge her. The pain of her ignorance had dulled these past two months. That wasn't to say it didn't hurt. Summer was sure it always would. She did her best to quash it by immersing herself in music.

She opened with one of her grandmother's favorites, Etta James' "At Last". Grandma Bonnie closed her eyes. She began to sway slightly when Summer moved on to tunes from the Carpenters and others from her grandparents' early days as newlyweds. When she began a Chopin sonata, her grandmother's eyes shot open. It was a piece Grandma Bonnie had played on the piano to lull her twin boys to sleep at night when they were young.

"I'm teaching my granddaughter that piece," she said.

Summer stilled the bow on the strings. "It's lovely. I'm sure she'll cherish having you teach it to her." She was amazed she could even speak the words, but she wanted her grandmother to know how much those lessons meant to her. How much music had saved her from those dark years after her father died and the mother she knew became another woman entirely.

Out of the corner of her eye, she saw Paige dabbing her cheeks.

"I taught her how to read music within a week," Grandma Bonnie continued. "And she has the gift of relative pitch. The little mimic can hear a tune and play it back perfectly. She's one of those rare people who doesn't need classical training to be a successful musician. Took to the cello like a lamb to water." Her grandmother's face scrunched up. "No. That's not right. Not a lamb to water. What is it? Why can't I remember it? Grayson, what is the saying? I need to get it right."

Papa Harry wrapped an arm around his wife's shoulders. He murmured something in her ear, gently rubbing her back until she calmed down. Trying not to call attention to herself, Summer packed up her cello. Minutes later, she and Paige were out the door.

"I never thought I'd say this, but after today, I can't blame the Princess for jumping ship," Paige said an hour later when they were seated at Summer's kitchen table, nibbling on nachos and drinking wine. "It takes someone with a lot of fortitude to watch a person decline like that. And Lizzie never had it."

"It's not her fault. Besides, I'm not sure our grandparents ever factored into her decision."

"My point exactly." Paige refilled both their wine glasses. "Does she know about you and Luke?"

Summer dropped her head into her hands. "No. Both she and Luke told me there was nothing to their relationship. Still, I have no idea how to even broach the subject. And there is no telling how she'll react. Thankfully she's been so busy reporting for affiliates that we've only exchanged a few texts since she left."

"Oh, please, please, *please*, let me be the one to break the news to her," Paige begged. "Pretty please."

"I would rather keep things quiet for the time being, especially since I have no idea where any of this is headed. Or if it's even headed anywhere."

Paige wiggled her eyebrows. "You two are definitely on the map. This is the first night you've been apart in more than a week. And that's only because he has to stay in a hotel with his teammates before a game." She leaned forward. "Do you think it's because they don't want the players having sex?"

Summer stared wide-eyed at her friend. "Huh?"

"You know." She swatted Summer's arm with her napkin.

"They say male athletes shouldn't have sex before they compete. Something about altering their testosterone. They won't perform as well on the field if they're, you know, *performing* the night before."

"How do you know this stuff?"

Paige shrugged. "Just because I spend all day with kindergartners doesn't mean I don't read up on other subjects."

"Like sex," Summer teased before taking a sip of her wine.

"Well, I did have to live vicariously for the past couple of dry years."

Summer propped her elbow on the table and dropped her chin into her hand. "But not anymore?"

Paige blushed.

"I want to hear everything about you and Jon."

"You *have* heard everything about Jon and me. At least I kept you updated on my love life while you were being all stealthy."

Summer sighed. "It all happened so fast. And truth be told, I still don't believe it's real."

"Oh, it's real." Paige fanned herself. "At least his dog is. And what the heck did you feed him today?"

Summer's phone pinged while she was herding the odorous dog outside.

"Ooo. Is that him? Maybe he's sexting you because he's going through withdrawal or something." Paige grabbed Summer's phone and opened the home screen. "Who's Darren? Jeez, Sum, how many guys are you talking to?"

"Give me that," Summer said. "Darren is the custodian at school." She glanced at the message and smiled. "Another delivery arrived today. A xylophone! Can you believe it?"

"Really? You didn't even have one of those at Preston."

"Yeah. Isn't it awesome? I'm stunned by the generosity of people. All from a two-minute human-interest story." One that wouldn't have happened had it not been for Luke. She sighed happily as she forwarded the text to him.

"But will the kids appreciate it?"

"The kids at this school soak up everything you give them like a sponge. And they're so appreciative. They don't take anything for granted," Summer said. "Several of the kids have what it takes to get into one of the magnet schools. I want them to have as much opportunity to succeed as the kids at Preston do."

"But you're only here for a couple more months," Paige reminded her. "You're coming back to Chicago at the end of the semester, remember?"

Paige had the right of it. When the music teacher's maternity leave ended, Summer would be superfluous. The LSAT was next month. She had an internship lined up after that. There was no reason for her to remain in Milwaukee.

Was there?

Monty barked to come back inside. Summer's phone pinged with a text from Luke.

> A xylophone! Are you freaking kidding me? Antonio wants to play it. Those kids don't know how lucky they are to have a gorgeous musical genius looking out for them. BTW, I spoke with Andi. You're off the hook. All is well. Have fun on your girls' night, babe. I'll be thinking of you while I listen to Antonio snore.

He signed off with a kissing emoji.

She looked up to see Paige scrutinizing her. "Mmhmm," her friend said as she got up to let the dogs back in. "You." She pointed to Monty. "Give a girl a break and take it downwind, please."

But Summer wasn't paying attention. Instead, all she heard was her grandmother's words whispering in her head.

. . . one of those rare people who doesn't need classical training to be a successful musician.

Her grandmother believed in her all those years ago. If she could see Summer now, would she be ashamed? *She'd be angry at you for giving up,* a voice that sounded a lot like her father's, jumped into the internal debate she was having with herself.

With a sigh, she reread Luke's text. She glided past his "musical genius" comment because really, he was merely being sweet.

But he believes in you, just like Grandma Bonnie.

Ignoring her dad, she scanned down to the part about Andi. It was simply a store opening. A soap store, for that matter. How risky could it be? Did people even go to those things? If they did, they wouldn't be recording the cellist. Besides, she'd liked Andi immediately. It would be a shame to let her down.

"Sum?" Paige tapped the table lightly. "If you're done sexting with number eighty-one, maybe we can get dinner before the wine goes to my head."

"Oh, sure. Sorry. I need to send one more text to someone else." She scrolled through her messages to find the one from Andi.

> Ignore whatever Luke told you. I'd be happy to play at your opening. Sorry for being such a ditz.

She hit send before she could change her mind. Less than a minute later, Andi replied with a series of emojis and a request to meet at the stadium before the game the next day. Summer responded with a thumbs up.

Paige handed Summer her coat. "You okay?"

Surprisingly, she was. She smiled at her friend. "You bet. Come on. You haven't had a butterburger until you've eaten at Solly's."

CHAPTER TWENTY

LUKE'S ragged breath wafted over Summer's cheek as he glided in and out of her. His relentless teasing was driving her wild. She pounded on his back, begging him for release. He reached between their bodies, his finger connecting with the spot guaranteed to make her fly. Seconds after, he followed her into oblivion.

"Am I crushing you?" he asked several minutes later.

She dragged her fingertips down his spine. "Mmm. I can think of worse ways to die."

Chuckling, he slowly pushed himself up on his forearms and began nibbling on her shoulder. "Have I told you that I missed you?"

"I think you've shown me how much you missed me four times since we got back from the game last night." She sighed when his lips made their way up her neck.

"Then I'm glad today is a holiday, and there's no school. I'll have plenty of time to show you a fifth and a sixth time. And that's all before lunch."

"As thrilling as that sounds, we can't. It's your Gram's birthday, remember? We're meeting her and her friends at the diner for breakfast."

He swore roughly before nipping at her ear. She smacked his chest in retaliation. With a groan, he extended his arms fully and stared down at her, wearing a bemused expression. It was as though he didn't know what to make of the situation or what to do with her.

She could relate. Reaching up, she brushed back a lock of hair hanging below one of his eyes. His pointed stare was starting to make her uneasy. "What?"

His lips slowly molded into one of his irresistible smiles. "I can't believe how lucky I am to be here with you."

Well.

She smiled back at him with cheeks that were growing warm beneath his gaze. She was pretty sure *she* was the lucky one. Not that she would concede that point to him. "You know it, buster," she said as she slapped him on his sculpted ass.

He tugged her out of bed with him. "If we hustle, I can show you how much I missed you while we are in the shower."

An hour and a half later, they arrived at the Oak Creek Diner. Several of the regulars called out to Luke as he and Summer navigated the traffic jam of walkers to get to the back room where Gram and her friends were seated. The Growlers won their game by a field goal the day before, and it seemed the entire town was still basking in the victory.

"Way to walk the tightrope along the sideline, Kessler," one man shouted. "That catch you made to end the half was incredible."

Luke waved his thanks. He posed for a selfie with another group of diners before he and Summer arrived at the long table housing what seemed like half of Sunset Glen. Papa Harry was there with his friends Pete and Fred. The three men were at one end of the table playing some sort of game with the sugar packets.

The newly engaged Sharon and Gary were also there, making eyes at each other like two middle-schoolers. Summer had to bite back a laugh at the ridiculousness of it. Not surprisingly, Mrs. Hilbert was seated at the center of the group. Two other women Summer had seen around the senior community flanked Gram at the other end of the table. A birthday balloon was tied to the back of her chair. A paper crown that had seen better days was sitting a bit cockeyed on her head.

Gram shot Luke an amused look and shrugged her shoulders as if to say, "If you can't beat 'em, join 'em."

Luke grinned back at her. "You look pretty hot for a woman seventy-seven years young." He brushed a kiss on her flushed cheek.

"You are a rascal," she said.

He held a chair for Summer, then took the one across from his gram. The waitress filled their cups and took their orders.

"I have something for you." Summer reached into her purse and pulled out an assortment of bath bombs, soaps, and lotions she'd gotten from Andi the day before. Andi was determined that if she couldn't pay Summer using currency, she would pay her in product. As a result, she was now the proud owner of a decade's worth of scented soaps and other assorted bath products.

She passed Grace the gift bag she'd put together.

"You didn't have to get me anything," Grace said.

"Nonsense. Every birthday is deserving of a gift."

A delighted smile settled on Grace's face as she dug through the bag of soaps. Mrs. Hilbert launched into a description of every piece. To hear the woman tell it, she and Andi were like mother and daughter. The revelation surprised Summer.

She turned to Luke to confirm the older woman's claim. He had that slightly stunned look on his face again. His hand found hers beneath the table, and he locked his fingers through hers. If he picked up that the gift for his grandmother was more of a peace offering, then so be it. Summer still felt awful about the things she'd said about his grandmother. She wanted him to know she was sorry. He gave her hand a squeeze, seeming to read her mind.

"Since we're all together, we need to finalize the plans for the wedding," Mrs. Hilbert announced.

"Wedding?" Wide-eyed, Luke looked around the table. His hold on her hand grew tighter.

"Gary and Sharon's, I presume," Summer murmured.

"Oh. Yeah, right." He relaxed against the back of his chair.

"Will you two be tying the knot soon?" Summer asked.

"Next month," Sharon replied.

Gary made dopey eyes at his fiancée. Beside Summer, Luke shook slightly, trying to suppress a laugh.

"You better tell her the date, Sharon," Mrs. Hilbert said. "She needs to get it on her calendar if she's going to be providing the music."

Now it was Summer's hand doing the squeezing. "Pardon me?"

"They wanted to play recorded music. Pfft." Mrs. Hilbert rolled her eyes. "I told them they need to zhush it up a little. Have some real music when they walk down the aisle. And who better than you? You've been in on this since the beginning."

Since the beginning?

Unless this was one of those "90-Day Fiancé" things, Summer highly doubted that. She glanced over at Papa Harry. He had an incredulous look on his face. He opened his mouth to say something. Only Luke beat him to it.

"Don't you think that's a tad presumptuous even for you, Mrs. H?" His words cracked through the air like a whip.

Mrs. Hilbert didn't appear the least bit insulted by his tone. In fact, she eyed Luke critically before transferring her gaze to Summer. The corners of her mouth turned up into a knowing smile.

"I told you recorded music would be fine." Sharon smiled

tenuously at her groom-to-be. "We just want to be married. We don't want to impose on you, Summer."

"It's not an imposition," Summer said. After all, she'd already played at Sunset Glen once, and social media hadn't blown up. A second time couldn't possibly hurt anyone. Heck, if this is what her career came to, she might have to embrace it. *Lawyer by day, musical love doctor for seniors on weekends.* She gave Luke's thigh a reassuring pat. "As long as it's not the same weekend as the LSAT, I would be delighted to perform the wedding music."

Gram and her friends sighed with delight. Mrs. Hilbert smiled smugly. At the opposite end of the table, Papa Harry groaned.

"You might want to hold off on agreeing until you hear the logistics of their wedding," he warned with a chuckle.

Summer glanced around the table. "The wedding won't be at Sunset Glen?"

Gary shook his head. "I'm giving this woman the nuptials of her dreams." He leaned toward Summer and lowered his voice to a stage whisper. "Her first wedding was a shotgun affair. She always dreamed of getting married near the water. We're doing the deed smack dab *on* Lake Michigan."

Fred murmured something about Gary and Sharon doing "the deed" everywhere and anywhere, but they all ignored him because Luke suddenly commanded all their attention.

"What does that even mean?" He asked the question loud enough that it rose above the din of the restaurant.

"It means we're renting a ferry boat and riding down to Chicago for the wedding at her former church. Then we'll have the reception on the ferry on the way back." Gary looked like a man who'd promised his fiancée a yacht cruise on the Riviera rather than a ferry boat ride on the Great Lakes.

"In November?" Luke looked over at Papa Harry. "On Lake Michigan? A bunch of seniors on a ferry boat."

They all nodded.

"We're calling it the Free Love for All Ferryboat," Pete announced.

Summer swallowed a stunned laugh.

"Are you all *nuts*?!" Luke shouted.

A hush fell over the diner.

"Now, son," Papa Harry said. "It's a legit ferry boat, captained by a professional crew. The company rents it out for these types of occasions."

"Like a party boat? A booze cruise for the geriatric set, you mean? Do you know how many of those trips end up as hour-long news docudramas when things go south?" Luke aimed a finger at his grandmother. "You're not going." He turned to Summer. "And neither are you."

Summer tugged her hand free from his. As much as his concern thrilled her, she never liked being told what to do. "I can make my own decisions, thank you."

He narrowed his eyes at her.

"So can I," Grace chimed in. "And I'm going. It sounds like a lot of fun."

"Atta girl," Papa Harry repeated the exact words he'd used with Summer a few days before. The same twinkle was in his eyes, too. Only this time, it was directed at Luke's gram. Summer did her best to ignore the twisting in her stomach.

Luke glared at Papa Harry. "You're not the one responsible for her. I am."

There was a collective intake of breath at the table.

His grandmother cleared her throat. "Pardon me. While I'm in my right mind, I'm the only one responsible for me."

The seniors sat silently in solidarity. Luke murmured a few words that would likely have his grandmother washing his mouth out with soap had anyone, but Summer, heard them. He slumped back against the chair.

"Apologies, Gram. It's just . . ." He raked his fingers through his hair.

Summer rested her hand on his thigh once again.

"It's just that you are a good man, Luke Kessler," Mrs. Hilbert said. "Isn't that right, Summer?"

He was. He was sweet, generous, and caring—even if that caring came off as overbearing sometimes. A wave of warmth bubbled up in her chest as she realized he'd lumped Summer in with his precious grandmother when he'd wrongly issued his ultimatum. Knowing a part of his story, she knew how important his grandmother was to him. Grace was the one constant in his life. She always had been. It could only mean one thing. He cared about her as much as he did Grace.

"He's better than a good man, Mrs. Hilbert." Summer turned to him, regretting that they had an audience but not wanting to miss an opportunity to tell him what she really thought. "He is one of a kind."

A line of waitstaff arrived with all their breakfast orders at once. The smell of bacon and sweet rolls immediately diffused the tension at the table.

"Luke," Papa Harry said. "If it will make you feel better, you and I can go to the marina to check out this boat and meet with the crew. We can make sure it's all on the up and up."

"Gary and I already did that," Fred protested. "I spent forty-five years ferrying boats across Lake Michigan. I think I know a seaworthy vessel and crew when I meet 'em."

Mrs. Hilbert laid her hand on Fred's shoulder. "Of course, you do, dear. No one's questioning you. Harry's simply trying to reassure Luke, that's all. Although, it's not like we need permission slips from our children or grandchildren to have a weekend of fun." She aimed a demure look at Luke. "But we can't have the Growlers' best receiver distracted, can we? Think of the damage it would do to your fantasy football stats."

Shaking his head, Luke dug into his breakfast. Summer met Papa Harry's eyes and mouthed "thank you." He saluted her with his coffee mug. Out of the corner of her eye, she noticed Grace smiling serenely at her grandfather, as well. When Summer looked back at Papa Harry, he was buttering his toast, oblivious to heated stares from any women.

She was being ridiculous again. Grace was simply grateful to Papa Harry for easing Luke's nerves as much as she was. That was all there was to it. The twisting in her belly could easily be chalked up to hunger pains. After all, she had worked up an appetite this morning.

"This French toast has got nothing on yours," Luke murmured beside her. "I told you we should have stayed home."

Stayed home.

Did he mean that? Or was it just an expression? She didn't have much time to ponder his words further before Mrs. Hilbert was at it again.

"Summer, we should get together to discuss what you're going to play at Andi's store opening. It's going to be a very chic event," the older woman announced. "We all need to put it on our calendars. Clive is importing champagne."

Over my dead body. There was no way Summer was taking musical direction from the old bird.

Luke chuckled beside her. "She's a force of nature. But my money is on you."

Buoyed by his compliments, she tuned Mrs. Hilbert out and enjoyed the rest of her breakfast.

THE REST of the week was a blur for Summer. When she wasn't teaching, she was sorting through the instruments and sheet music donated to the school as a result of career day.

"I have a box of handbells, Paige. These are perfect for the younger grades." She pointed her phone toward the open box. "Can you believe it? Grandma Bonnie's legacy will live on in this school."

"I think you mean your legacy," Paige said.

Summer turned the phone screen back so she could see her friend's face. "Nonsense. I'm carrying on her dream, that's all."

"Whatever you say."

Something in her friend's voice caught Summer off guard. "Why are you being so glum today?"

"I'm sorry," Paige said. "Jon had to cancel our dinner tonight. He has to cover for another salesperson in Arizona. He won't be back in town for another two weeks."

Some friend Summer was. She was gushing on and on about all the wonderful things going on in her world when her best friend was trying to navigate a long-distance romance. Clearly, things weren't going so well with Paige's love life.

The same certainly couldn't be said about Luke and Summer's relationship. With the exception of Saturday night, they hadn't spent a single night apart in two weeks. He and Monty were practically living at her house full-time. Everything was still new and exciting, yet at the same time, easy and relaxed. Being with Luke was like crawling beneath a favorite blanket. It felt familiar and comfortable.

Like where she belonged.

Of course, she didn't bother telling Paige any of this. She couldn't. Not when she wasn't sure if she was living in a fantasy that—like every other positive thing in her life—could implode at any moment. Talking about it might jinx things. So she kept her happiness—and her fears—to herself.

"What kind of sales work did you say he did?" she asked Paige.

"Something about selling access to satellite time for television stations to broadcast. It all sounds very complicated and demanding. There are always lots of balls in the air, from what I can gather."

"That sounds stressful. Not only for him, but on a relationship as well."

Paige sighed. "Yeah. But when we are together, things are so awesome, Summer. Perfect, actually. Sum, I think he could be The One."

The One?

Summer sat down in one of the student chairs. "Seriously?"

How many nights had the two of them sat in front of the fire and talked about "The One?" Whether they'd ever find him. How they would meet. What he would be like. What their weddings would be like.

Neither of them had dreamt up a guy who sells satellite air time or a football player.

A football player?

Summer suddenly felt light-headed. Where had that come from? Paige had found The One. Not her. Except…everything Luke said or did was what Summer would want from The One. He made her laugh. He made her ache for him. He made her feel precious.

"I'm not good at being patient," Paige was saying. "You of all people know that."

"Um, yeah, sure."

"Jon likes my impatience." Paige laughed. "He says it means I have structure in my life. I know where I'm going. I don't have time to wait."

Summer tried to focus on her friend, but so many thoughts were swirling around in her head. Could Luke really be The One? Did she even want him to be? Her insides vibrated with a resounding "yes" just thinking about it.

But did he feel the same?

"Maybe I should tell him how I feel. Or do you think it's too early?"

Paige's question snapped her thoughts back into focus. "Way too early." Summer wasn't sure if she was answering Paige's question or her own internal one. "And it's probably something you should discuss in person."

Could she tell Luke how she felt? Should she?

"You're right. This is why you are my best friend. You keep me from being impulsive." Paige grinned at her from the screen. "Hey, maybe you can come down here this weekend?"

"I can't. I have Monty and Milli, remember?"

"You mean you're picking the canine stink bomb over a weekend with me?"

Summer laughed at her description of Monty. "I have a better idea. The Growlers have a game in Chicago next month. It turns out I'm coming down for it. I got talked into playing at the wedding of two of Papa Harry's friends."

"A store opening and a wedding? Wow, Sum, I can't tell you how thrilled I am to see you out there performing again."

"It's technically not performing."

"Hey, justify it however you want. I'm glad it's happening."

Summer was starting to feel glad about it, too. But she had grander ideas to discuss right now.

"I'm sure Luke can get us tickets. Maybe you can bring Jon. The four of us could meet for drinks at the team hotel the night before. Wouldn't that be fun?"

"Oh my gosh, yes. If I give Jon enough of a head's up, he can hopefully make it work with his schedule." Paige let out a little squeal. "Finally, we get to double date with our guys. The first of many, I'll bet."

Summer was surprised at how much she wanted Paige's words to be true.

CHAPTER TWENTY-ONE

The Growlers lost a tight one to their division rivals that weekend. The mood in the locker room was testy despite the team having a winning record for the season so far. Their starting running back had developed a case of turf toe, making him questionable to play in Sunday night's game against Kansas City. Jacobs was nursing a twisted ankle, and two starting offensive linemen were out with knee injuries.

"Our offensive game plan needs to be adjusted," Coach Gibson told the team after a longer-than-usual practice Thursday night. "We'll go over the changes tomorrow morning. Practice will be in full pads in the afternoon. Have a good night, gentlemen."

"You boys be sure to s-study the game film I sent," Wash reminded the receiver corps huddled in the corner of the locker room. "I don't have to tell you we can't afford any m-mistakes Sunday. K.C. will pounce on them in a hot minute." He turned to Luke. "Kessler, Coach wants to run some things by you. I need you to stay tonight."

"Uh, oh. Kessler's getting sent to the principal's office," one of the tight-ends teased.

If the guy only knew how many times that had happened during Luke's misspent youth. At least they weren't going to call his moms. The way Jacobs was eyeballing him though, he might rather deal with the two women. The receiver likely understood the game plan was being modified to work around his bum ankle. Luke would be shouldering the workload this week.

Both men had incentives built into their contracts, guaranteeing them bonuses based on the number of catches they made per season. Every ball Van Horn threw Luke's way was potentially money out of Jacobs' pocket. Too bad if the father of four didn't like it. At the end of the day, the only thing that counted was the score and a W for the Growlers.

Luke was flattered he was included in the planning. He hadn't given much thought to his career after his playing days ended. Coaching wasn't out of the question, though. Having former players like Coach Gibson and Wash show him a few tricks would benefit him.

He shrugged at Jacobs. "Sure, Coach."

A few minutes later the offensive coaches reassembled in the conference room at the back of the building. Most of the team referred to it as the "War Room" because the game plan for each week was drawn up inside its four walls. Two sixty-inch monitors were mounted on each side of the room. The coaches used them to review game films.

The counter along the back wall was home to an assortment of snacks. Nuts, protein bars, fruit, and a huge container of Twizzlers that gave Van Horn the sweats every time he entered the room. Coach Gibson was addicted to Twizzlers. He claimed he kept them there for his two young kids when they visited him at work. No one dared call him out on his lie.

Luke pulled a vitamin water from the glass fridge stocked with sports drinks and assorted waters. Then he took a seat next to Wash.

"Both my kids were carrying on about something when I

called Merrit to tell her I'd be late," Coach Gibson said to the rest of his staff. "That means I'm going to have a lot of making up to do tonight. Let's see if we can get this knocked out quickly." He turned to Luke. "I'll start with you, Kessler. I gotta know where Notre Dame ranks with your brother, Brady. He'd look excellent in a gold helmet next fall."

For the love of shit.

Luke dug his fingers into the arms of his chair. Was that the reason he was invited? The disappointment stung. He didn't have a clue which schools Brady was considering. Nor did he care.

Coach Gibson, it seemed, did care. Probably because the man was once an All-American for the Fighting Irish. The coach had a vested interest in seeing his alma mater get the best recruiting class.

"I'm yanking your chain. Your dad wouldn't let him come to a school where he'd have to sit behind another QB for at least a year, if not two," Coach Gibson said. "Even if you did know where Brady was headed, you wouldn't tell me. Brothers stick together like that. I respect that."

Luke's chest suddenly felt like it was too tight. He and Brady Kessler shared DNA. That was all. He forced out a laugh. None of the men in the room seemed to notice the lack of humor behind it, however.

Coach Gibson unwrapped a Twizzler. "What I really want is to get your read on McGraff."

"McGraff?"

"Yes. I need to know what his mental state is right now," Coach Gibson explained. "He's a young man who suddenly lost his dad. He's also very adept at letting people see what he wants them to see. Can he handle the increased workload we are about to throw at him?"

"We need to know if we c-can count on him having his head in this g-game," Wash added. "You know him the best out of anyone on the team."

Luke leaned back in his chair. It was true the rookie was more relaxed with Luke than when the season started. But that didn't mean they had heart-to-heart talks in their hotel room each week. As far as he could tell, Antonio was handling his father's death well. The kid showed up to practice early, stayed late, and knew the playbook backward and forward.

The person Coach should be consulting was Summer, however. She'd been checking in with him daily. Luke knew they'd met for coffee several times in the past few weeks since his dad passed away. If anyone had an accurate read on the state of the rookie's mental health, it would be her.

Except she was with her study group tonight, and Luke didn't want to interrupt her.

"I take it you plan on giving him Jacobs' kick return duties?"

Coach Gibson nodded. "I realize it will create some tension in the locker room, but McGraff is this team's future. I'm counting on you to smooth over any ruffled feathers."

"We've got the right man for that j-job," Wash said.

Luke glanced around the coaches seated around the table and went with his gut. "Adversity makes a lot of athletes perform at a higher level. I honestly believe that will be the case here. Antonio came in here wanting to prove himself. He gets paid an exorbitant amount of money to play this game. You should let him play it."

The faces of every coach at the table relaxed.

"That's what I hoped you'd say." Coach Gibson signaled to the offensive coordinator. "Sonny, let's run through the plays. Kessler, chime in on the routes you think are best suited for McGraff."

It was after eight when Luke pulled into Summer's driveway. She wasn't due home for another half hour. That gave him just enough time to walk the dogs, then start a fire to make the house warm and cozy for her after a long day. There was also the added bonus that she liked to make love in front of the fire.

Looking forward to getting Summer naked, he practically skipped up the front steps—only to collide with someone sitting on the darkened porch.

"What the hell!"

"Damn it, you hoser. You spilled her custard."

"McGraff?" Luke clicked on the flashlight on his phone and pointed it in the rookie's direction.

"Hey!" McGraff shielded his eyes. "Do you have to blind me with that?"

Their yelling had Monty and Milli barking wildly inside. Luke punched the code on the front door, pushing it open and clicking on the porch light. Monty was already scrambling to lick up the custard McGraff had dumped on the painted wood surface. Milli made a beeline to the rookie, flirting with him in hopes he'd pick her up. McGraff had his back pressed against the Hardy board siding. His eyes were wide as he watched Monty lap up the custard.

"You better keep that beast of yours under control, Kessler," he said.

Monty looked up as if just noticing they had company. He gave his chops one last satisfied lick before trotting over to inspect McGraff's sneakers.

"I mean it, Kessler. Dogs and I don't get along."

"Don't tell me you're afraid of dogs, Tony-O?"

McGraff glared at him. "You would be too if you'd seen what people use these dogs for where I come from."

The kid had a point. "Monty. Milli. In the house." Both dogs stared at him blankly. Luke should probably watch some of those training videos the shelter suggested. "Go inside or no cheese before bedtime."

Cheese being the magic word, the dogs trotted back into the house. Luke followed, leaving the door open for McGraff, hoping he'd be too scared of Monty to come in. The rookie was made of sterner stuff, it seemed, because the door closed with him inside. Luke turned to face him.

"What are you doing here, Antonio?"

"I was about to ask you the same thing."

I live here.

The words were on the tip of Luke's tongue before he quickly bit them back. He didn't *live* here, per se. A fact McGraff knew all too well. Although, it had been nearly a month since Luke had slept in his own bed.

Not that he was going to share that bit of intel with his teammate. Or any of his teammates, for that matter. What he had with Summer was different than previous seasons. And he wasn't ready to examine the reasons why. He simply wanted to let things go on as they were—he and Summer in their private bubble.

That was going to be hard to do with McGraff staring him down.

"You first," Luke demanded.

The rookie's lip curled. "I thought I'd surprise Summer with some of her favorite custard. I know how hard she's been working. She hasn't had a free night for dinner in weeks."

That's because she's been with me. He tamped down on the possessive smirk he wanted to give the kid.

"But, thanks to you, she won't get a treat tonight."

That was where the rookie was wrong. Summer would be getting plenty of treats tonight. Just not from McGraff. "I'll let her know what happened. I'm sure she'll appreciate your thoughtfulness."

The rookie's chin rose a notch. "I can speak for myself." He slumped down on the living room sofa.

The same sofa where Luke planned to worship her later this evening.

"I'll wait for her to get home. Kopp's doesn't close 'til ten. I can take her out to get one."

Like hell.

"Your turn," McGraff said. "The talk in the locker room is you hook up with your Seasonal Arm Candy in New York each week. What are you doing popping into Summer's house when she's not at home?"

None of your damn business.

Monty tried to get Luke's attention by playing air hockey on the kitchen floor with his water dish. Ignoring McGraff's question, Luke went to give his dog water. Unfortunately, the rookie followed.

"I thought you were afraid of dogs?" Luke snapped.

"That thing seems too dumb to do any real harm. And both of you look awfully at home here. What gives?"

Luke was about to ream the rookie a new one when McGraff's eyes darted to a sheet of yellow legal pad stuck up on the fridge. It was a note Summer left for him this morning. Signed with a damn giant heart and two rows of x's for kisses.

Shit.

"You and Summer?" The question was followed by a snarl. "You've got to be shittin' me. I thought she had better sense than that."

Luke didn't appreciate the guy's comment. "What's that supposed to mean?"

"Does she know?"

"Does she know what?"

McGraff was suddenly in Luke's face. "Does she know that you're gonna dump her as soon as the season is over?"

Luke almost laughed. In all likelihood, he would be the one who got dumped. It was the story of his life. It didn't matter if he couldn't see a scenario where he'd ever willingly walk away from Summer. Whatever they had was doomed from the start.

"My relationship with Summer is none of your fucking business."

The scouts weren't exaggerating about the rookie's reflexes, because the kid had Luke by the throat in less than a second.

"She's not like the other women you've used, Kessler," he hissed. "She's a got a heart of gold, but that doesn't mean it's unbreakable. Her confidence had been badly shaken this year. It's taken her months to find her balance, and I won't have you messing her up, ya hear?"

He wasn't telling Luke anything he didn't know. That didn't mean he had to take it from some punk rookie. "I told you it was none of your business."

Luke shoved McGraff's hands off him. A second later, the two of them were grappling with each other until they were on the kitchen floor. McGraff's elbow connected with Luke's chin. Luke kneed him in the gut. They grunted and groaned as each man tried to pin the other to the slick tile. Monty and Milli were providing the excited play-by-play when cold water suddenly landed on Luke's back.

"Hey!" Summer yelled.

Luke froze with his fingers in McGraff's hair. The rookie quickly released his fingers from Luke's earlobe.

"Both of you, off the floor. Now."

Summer was using her teacher voice. Now was probably not the time for Luke to tell her how sexy it made her sound. The two men got to their feet.

She glared at both men. "What is going on here?"

"He started it," McGraff whined.

"He started it," Luke said at the same time.

Not a muscle in her face moved. "Out. Both of you."

Luke's pulse began to race. *Out?* What did she mean by that? "You don't—"

"No talking," she snapped. "If you're both going to behave like school boys, you can be treated like school boys. The dogs need to be walked. You'll do it together. Don't come back until you've resolved whatever this—" She waved her hand between them "—is about."

Neither man moved.

"Go!" she shouted.

Monty and Milli shot out of the kitchen. McGraff followed, wearing his signature sulk. Luke opened his mouth to say something, only stopping when Summer shook her head and pointed to the front door.

"That's gross," McGraff complained when they started down the front walk. "That was the dog's drinking water she tossed on us."

"At least you're wearing a freaking jacket. It's thirty something degrees, and I'm covered in cold dog slime."

Monty tugged on the leash, crossing paths with Milli and tangling the leashes.

"Give me the tiny one," McGraff said. "At least her poop will be the size of Tootsie Rolls."

Men and dogs walked in silence for a block until McGraff had to go and ruin it.

"I meant what I said back there. Hurt her, and I'll mess you up."

This time Luke did laugh. He was genuinely glad Summer had a stand-up guy like Tony-O in her corner. "Deal." If he wasn't going to be there with her, he wanted her to have someone else to lean on. "Lean on" being the key phrase. Because the thought of Summer actually with another man had the blood roaring in his ears.

McGraff's head snapped around. "Seriously?"

"Yeah. If I hurt her, I deserve it."

They covered another block without speaking. Once again, McGraff couldn't keep his mouth shut.

"Wow, man. You're in love with her."

Luke tripped on a crack in the sidewalk, righting himself before he faceplanted on the concrete. *In love with her?* The blood was roaring in his ears again. Love wasn't for him. It didn't matter that he loved being around her. That he loved being inside her. That he loved watching her so passionately live her life. That would never be enough.

It never was.

Yet, Luke had survived that kind of pain before. This time, he'd be ready for it. Ready for the gut-wrenching agony that would accompany losing Summer. He wouldn't ever let himself be in love with her. But he would love her in every way he could until things came to the inevitable end.

"I get it. You don't want the ladies in the locker room gabbing about your love life. Don't worry. Your secret is safe with me," McGraff continued. "I won't let on about you and the meteorologist being over. Or you and Summer. Mostly because I respect Summer's privacy. I couldn't care less what you do with your private life. But it's gonna cost ya."

"If you mean to blackmail me to get Wash to give you more playing time, you can forget it. I already recommended you for kick returns and half the receiving assignments this week."

"Dude, I don't need your help getting more playing time. My hands and feet can do their own talking."

Luke sighed. They turned the dogs back toward Summer's.

"But thanks," McGraff added. "I appreciate the vote of confidence. I need something else from you though."

"What?"

The kid was quiet for several steps. "I want to adopt a cat. I went to the shelter, but apparently you've got to have references and all that bullshit. They know you there. I figure you can speak for me."

Luke gaped at him. That was not even on Luke's radar of things McGraff might ask. "You want to adopt a cat?"

"Yeah, man. It's lonely in my place with just me. I grew up in a small house with a big family." He shrugged.

When Luke didn't immediately respond, McGraff scuffed his sneaker on the concrete. "Forget it."

"We'll go tomorrow," Luke replied. "You can pick one out and fill out the paperwork. You're not bringing it home until Monday, though. That way you can spend a couple of days with it before you have to leave it for hours at a time."

"Yeah. That makes sense. Thanks."

"Don't mention it. Know this though, if you hurt that animal, I'll mess you up."

The kid's laughter echoed throughout the quiet neighborhood.

CHAPTER TWENTY-TWO

ANDI'S SHOP was chic and stunning with its exposed brick walls and antique grocery store bins. The bins were filled with an assortment of soaps and bath bombs, creating a kaleidoscope of colors. There was a cute retro makeup table in one corner housing a display of lip balms Andi created herself. Even the cash register was vintage. Summer fell in love with the eclectic space the moment she stepped inside.

"I thought you could set up over there." Andi pointed to a pink bistro table and chair in the corner.

"That'll be perfect." Summer glanced about the room, already crowded with several of the Growlers' WAGs, Mrs. Hilbert and her friends from Sunset Glen, as well as the staff and clients from the salon next door. Her nerves were racing. For the first time in months, however, she felt excitement more than terror. She was surprised at how much she was looking forward to playing. "Let me know when you want me to start."

"There's no real agenda tonight." Andi tilted her head in the direction of Clive, the salon owner Summer had just met. "He wanted the Chamber of Commerce to do a ribbon-cutting, but I put my foot down. I don't need a stampede of people coming through the store because of who I married. I'd rather people find me by word of mouth."

Someone called Andi's name.

"Go ahead," Summer said. "I'll get started."

Andi gave her hand a squeeze. "Thank you again for this."

Summer leaned her cello against the bistro table and began to unzip its case.

"Here, let me help."

She turned to find Antonio beside her. Appearing unusually bashful, he took the cello from its case and carefully handed it to her.

"I owe you an apology," he said. "About last night. I should never have lost my cool like that."

He looked so young and sincere, like one of her students who'd had a meltdown in class. "Apology accepted. Besides, it wasn't entirely your fault. It takes two to tussle."

"Yeah. He better have apologized, too."

"Mmhmm," was all she said.

Her anger at coming home to find Antonio and Luke rolling around on her kitchen floor faded quickly, thanks to some expert coaxing from Luke's talented hands and tongue. Summer could feel the blush on her face remembering all the ways he'd "apologized" the night before. She nearly laughed watching Antonio respond with a blush of his own. He likely could guess how she and his teammate made up.

"I am mad at you for something else though," she said.

His eyebrows shot up to the top of his forehead.

"Perhaps I wanted to go see the kittens today."

Antonio's face lit up with one of his toothy grins. Of course, she wouldn't have intruded on Luke and Antonio's male-bonding expedition today for all the money in the world. But she didn't need either of them knowing that. Besides, pouting reaped some fantastic benefits from Luke.

"You can come over to meet them on Monday. I need help

naming them."

"Them?"

"Yeah, it didn't make sense only taking one. Cats get lonely, too."

"That's sweet." She leaned in and kissed his cheek.

The back of her neck tingled. She looked over at the door. Luke was striding in, Grace and Papa Harry with him. He stopped short, glowering, when he saw her standing so close to Antonio.

"Uh oh, I better vacate before he burns a hole in the wall with his nasty stare." Antonio's smile turned mischievous. "Although, we could have some fun with him."

She rolled her eyes. "Both of you are on the same team, you know. Now scram."

Chuckling, he wandered off. Summer took a seat in the chair. She set the cello against her leg before pulling the bow and rosin from the case. Holding the bow at the frog, she rubbed the rosin swiftly back and forth along the bow hairs going from top to the bottom of the bow, repeating the process several times. Then, she checked the screw at the end of the bow to make sure it was tight enough. By the time she was ready to play, the shop was overflowing with people. All of them milling around, sipping champagne, and chatting loudly.

Summer had acquired a rapt audience of one. A little girl with enormous blue eyes sat quietly on the floor in front of her. She reminded Summer of herself at that age, perched on the piano bench as Grandma Bonnie played.

"What would you like to hear?" Summer asked her.

The young girl shrugged shyly.

Summer warmed up with "Three Blind Mice." By the time she'd finished, a little boy was sitting next to the girl, both of them wide-eyed. Ariana Grande's "Positions" was next, followed by a Harry Styles song, then something from Taylor Swift. Her audience had grown in size, but the two kids were still frozen to their spots on the floor in the front row.

"Max only sits this still when 'Bob the Builder' is on TV," a woman said as she knelt between the children. Judging by her stunning blue eyes, she was the young girl's mother. "You must have magical powers."

"Music will do that," Summer replied.

"Well, certainly when you're playing. I was sad to miss Palmer's proposal to Shaina, but now having heard you play, I see I missed a whole lot more than him popping the question." She offered her hand to Summer. "Merrit Gibson. My husband is the coach of the Growlers. These are our children." She placed a hand on the boy's head. "Max and Harper."

"Is she a princess, momma?" Harper asked.

Laughing, Summer shook her head.

"It takes one to know one." Luke emerged from the crowd carrying a bottle of water.

Harper jumped to her feet, holding out her arms to him. He picked her up effortlessly with his free hand. They were apparently very familiar, because the girl wasn't shy about hugging his neck.

"She looks like a princess to me." Luke winked at her as he placed the bottled water on the bistro table. "For you, Princess Summer."

"Your name is Summer?" Harper clapped her hands together. "That's a princess' name!"

"See? What did I tell you?" Luke said.

"More!" Max demanded of Summer. "More music."

She was pleased to oblige, diving into an Ed Sheeran tune. Luke swayed from side to side while Harper hung on like a monkey. Her giggles of delight blended in with the music. Max tugged at Luke's legs, demanding the same treatment as his sister.

Summer was so enthralled watching Luke dance around the shop with two laughing children in his arms, she nearly lost her place in the song. Despite not growing up with the best paternal role model, his compassion and generosity were perfect traits for a doting father. Any kid would be lucky to have him as their dad. Any woman would be lucky to have children with him.

Her breath hitched at the thought. She wanted to be that woman. The desire was so sudden and intense, she had to take a break when the song ended. Applause filled the shop as she took a sip from the water bottle Luke had left for her. His concerned gaze found hers in the crowd. She pasted on a reassuring smile and soldiered on with a Maroon Five favorite.

Mrs. Hilbert and Fred joined in on the dance party Luke had started, doing a little swing dance together in the corner. Summer decided to liven things up with "Time of My Life" from *Dirty Dancing*. Gary and Sharon were dancing now, albeit a tad inappropriately.

Every time Summer caught a glimpse of Andi, the shop owner was smiling from ear to ear. The festive mood in the shop emboldened Summer to move into a set of swing songs that had more people dancing. She spied Papa Harry twirling Grace Kessler in his arms. The image reminded her of all the evenings he and Grandma Bonnie had cut a rug in their living room while Summer plunked out a tune on the piano. Papa Harry likely missed those evenings as much as Summer did. She wouldn't fault him for dancing with a friend.

"Brava!" A woman clapped when Summer took another break. "You are even better in person than you are on YouTube."

Her words sent a lick of panic up Summer's spine. *Crap.* Just when she thought she'd banished it completely. She dragged in a deep breath, hoping the woman wasn't waiting for a coherent response any time soon.

The other woman's face relaxed but without a trace of pity. Summer was grateful for that, at least. "I'm glad to see it didn't break you."

If she only knew.

"And while you might not believe it now, you will emerge stronger." She reached into her purse and extracted a card emblazoned with the Growlers' logo. "I'm Chris Ciaciura, the owner of the Growlers. I also happen to be a patron of the Milwaukee Philharmonic."

Summer couldn't stop her body's wince.

The other woman nodded in empathy. "I know. That's the last thing you want to discuss. But when you do—and I believe a young woman with your chutzpah won't let what happened to her keep her down too long—you get in touch. You've got to start back somewhere. You're already making our Growler band better." Leaving Summer with a gracious smile, she slipped back into the crowd.

Summer studied the card for several seconds before tucking it in her cello case. Not that she'd ever use it. She was going to law school. But it would be a pleasant reminder of someone who appreciated her talent.

THE FOLLOWING NIGHT, Luke was in Kansas City, taking the hotel elevator up to his father's room. The weird thing was that he didn't dread their meeting as much as he usually did. Maybe it was discovering that his teammates had his back where his old man was concerned. Or the knowledge that other people saw right through Jake Kessler. Whatever it was, the overwhelming need to prove something to his father wasn't screaming as loudly as it once did.

Of course, his overall good mood could also have something to do with it. He could thank Summer Pearson for that. When he was with her, he felt—whole. She filled up all the missing pieces inside of him. Her smile, her passion, chased away much of the bitterness he'd been carrying around for the past twenty years.

The crazy good sex didn't hurt, either.

The doors opened on the concierge floor. Directly across from the elevator was a lounge enclosed by soundproof glass doors. The room was filled with network and advertising execs in town for the Growlers' nationally televised game the following night. A college football game played on the big screen while the guests enjoyed late-night cocktails. Not surprising, Jake Kessler was front and center. He likely invited Luke up to his room at this time of night knowing the suits would see the two of them together.

Whatever.

His father gestured for him to come in. Luke may be relaxed, but he wasn't letting his old man dictate how this meeting would go down. Shaking his head, he pointed to his wrist, the universal signal for time. He'd agreed to the time Jake suggested because curfew was in fifteen minutes. That way, he was guaranteed their face time would be short, if not sweet.

After slapping a few people on the back, Jake emerged from the lounge. "It wouldn't hurt you to come in and say hello," he said as they walked toward his room. "You aren't going to play football forever. You need to think about life after the game."

"Right now, the only thing I've got on my mind is tomorrow's game."

Judging by his father's nod, Luke gave the correct answer. Not that he wanted to score any points with the guy. He wanted to grab the footballs and go back downstairs.

"Good man. First rule of football, keep your head in the game." His father headed for the mini-bar as soon as they entered his room. "The network must think I have the prostate of a twenty-something. They stock this thing with enough fancy water to hydrate a kid's soccer team." He held up a bottle of mineral water. "Want one?"

Luke shook his head, wondering how soon he could ask for the footballs without being rude.

"Wash says you're happy."

When Luke raised an eyebrow in response, his father got defensive.

"What? So I keep tabs on you? It's what a father does."

Luke channeled his inner therapist and let that one pass, because, really.

"He says it's the weather girl you're seeing."

"Meteorologist," Luke interjected. "Weather girl is blatantly sexist." He didn't bother correcting him on the more important fact. It was the cellist who was making him happy.

His father waved a hand through the air. "No reason to rat me out to your mother and Karla for my slight against the female gender. It's not like I talk that way in public. She's perky, that one. She'd make a great wife."

For fuck's sake. "Because she's 'perky?'"

"She's cute, yeah. But she's also a wholesome Midwesterner. No one can quibble with that. Plus, she's a celebrity in her own right. She won't need you for media attention. She'll have her own." He sighed. "Trust me when I tell you what a bonus that is. And, since she's in television, she'll have lots of connections for you when you retire."

Luke was growing more and more uncomfortable with the conversation. For years, he'd been living a false narrative just so he could prove something to this guy. Dating women who "looked good on paper." Women who made Luke look good in the media. And for what? To impress his dad?

Meanwhile, Jake Kessler was encouraging him to pick a wife based on the woman's resume. He didn't care about Luke. All he cared about was how Luke's decisions might impact the old man's legacy.

He was done trying to make himself worthy of this idiot.

"I need to get back downstairs before night check. Can I get the footballs and head out?"

His father pulled a laundry bag from his closet. "I'm assuming this is for some pet charity event."

"The Humane Society."

"You're never going to get over that, are you?"

Of all the nights for his dad to go there.

"How many times do I have to tell you?" he continued. "I didn't know the dog was yours. Your grandmother had pneumonia. By the time they got in touch with me, she was in bad shape. She couldn't tell me what was what. The dog had been neglected for days. I had no idea if she was even going to recover. The only choice I had was to take it to a shelter."

The memory made Luke's chest burn. The yellow Lab, Rowdy, had been a gift from Gram during one of his turbulent preteen summers. Karla was allergic, so they agreed Rowdy would stay in Idaho. Luke would see the dog when he visited, which was becoming more and more frequent. Knowing the dog was keeping Gram company made it slightly easier each time Luke had to leave him.

Of course, his dad had another choice that fateful winter night. He could have taken care of the dog himself. Except it was easier for him to walk away. After all, Jake Kessler excelled at that.

"You might have checked whether or not it was a kill shelter first."

The air in the room seemed to crackle. Luke reached for the bag of footballs. His father pulled them back.

"Wait," he said. "I need something from you in return."

Why wasn't Luke surprised?

"I need help with your brother."

Luke scoffed. The Golden Boy seemed to be dogging him everywhere these days.

"Half-brother," Luke said dryly.

Jake ignored the snipe. "He won't listen to anything Denise or I tell him."

"Welcome to eighteen. Had you bothered to participate in my life back then, you would know that sort of behavior is typical."

A vein in his dad's neck pulsed. As usual, though, he made no apology for skipping out on Luke. "Well, in his case, he could screw up everything he's been working for his entire life. He's practically daring colleges not to recruit him with his attitude and his behavior."

"I'm still trying to see how this involves me."

"Damn it, Luke! He's not like us!"

Us.

He'd heard the phrase "stuck in my craw" before. Now he knew exactly what it meant. The word "us" seemed to be lodged in his chest, blocking air from coming in or out.

It didn't matter, because Jake hadn't finished with his tirade. "You and I had to work for everything in this game. Neither of us was supposed to make it. Yet, we did. And not only to the sidelines but onto the field. Into the record books. Brady, though—" He shook his head in wonder. "Everything—every aspect of the game—comes easy to him. He's got this incredible gift. Except for the damn passion. The stick-to-it-ness that made Kessler a household name." There was a look of desperation in his eyes. "He can't fail. We can't let that happen. Think of the legacy we would leave. Me. Brady. You. We could be bigger than the Mannings. A football family dynasty."

"You're forgetting one thing," Luke said quietly. "We're not a family."

He turned and left the room. The footballs be damned.

CHAPTER TWENTY-THREE

"YOU GOOD, MAN?"

Luke looked up from his locker to see McGraff watching him. "I will be when you stop shoving cat videos in my face."

The idiot spent much of the night before torturing Luke with videos of cats doing ridiculous things. Something else to blame on his sperm donor. If Luke had been able to sleep, he wouldn't have had to see a cat take a dump on an actual toilet. He shivered. It was an image he was never going to be able to unsee.

"Excuse me for trying to cheer you up, man."

"Oh, no. Is Kessler mopey?" one of the linemen called out. "What's a matter, Canuck? Not getting enough *candy* from your Seasonal Arm Candy, eh?"

A round of chuckling broke out amongst his teammates.

This was ridiculous. Why had he even let this go on? Because he was trying to impress a man who wasn't worth impressing. Well, no more. Time to rip that particular band-aid off.

"There's no Seasonal Arm Candy," he announced to a suddenly stunned group of half-dressed football players. "We aren't together."

"Shit, Kessler, what did you do?" one of the guys asked.

"I didn't do anything. She moved to New York," he replied.

"We all assumed you saw her there," the Growlers' center said. "You never show up to poker nights. We figured it was because you were in New York."

"Nope. I had other commitments." *Named Summer.*

McGraff coughed beside him. Luke ignored him. He also ignored their quarterback, staring him down from across the room.

"Damn," one of the other guys said. "This is bad karma, man."

"What's bad karma?" Wash strolled into the locker room.

"Kessler's single. He's never single during football season. It's a bad omen." The enormous Samoan linebacker stalked toward the training room. "Prepare yourselves for some stinky juju out there," he called over his shoulder.

A murmur rose among his teammates. They were all a bunch of fickle old ladies. There was no such thing as juju on the playing field. Talent, stamina, and passion won games. Luke didn't have time for any woo-woo bullshit.

"You aren't d-dating Elizabeth Pearson any longer?"

Luke shook his head tersely at the coach.

"Who is p-putting that smile on your face, then?"

The locker room seemed to still. Luke could feel all their eyes on him. The question was inappropriate. Even more unusual, it came from Wash, a firm believer in minding his own business.

There was no way he was revealing his relationship with Summer to these guys. Especially his position coach, who would be snitching to Luke's dad before the whistle blew for kickoff. What he and Summer shared was unlike any other relationship he'd been in before. It was too special, too precarious, too important to mess up by letting these nosey gossip mongers in on it. Besides, the less agency his teammates had in their relationship, the more likely he'd be able to lick his wounds in peace when the inevitable happened, and she dumped him.

Except...

The confrontation with his father the night before unleashed feelings he'd thought he'd locked up tight, never to be examined. Never to be wished for. Thoughts of a family had unexpectedly seeped into his head. Not the family he'd never been allowed to be a part of. Instead, images of Summer kept dancing before his closed eyes. The idea that maybe, just maybe, she could be his family. Along with Monty, Milli, and—whatever else came along. His heart was racing at the very idea. An idea he hadn't ever allowed himself to float before.

It scared him, and it thrilled him at the same time.

McGraff shifted beside him. Luke shook his head, warning the rookie to keep his pie-hole shut.

Luke stared down Wash. "Living my best life, that's all. I'm enjoying the game. Enjoying being on the greatest team in the league." He grinned widely.

Wash's gaze was skeptical, but he didn't press further. Still, Luke did what he always did to divert the attention whenever anyone got too close. He changed the topic by tossing out a dare.

"In fact," he said. "Tonight's dare involves our toques."

A collective groan went up around the locker room. Luke signaled for the equipment manager. He began handing out knit caps with the Growler logo to each one of the players. Luke turned his inside-out and pulled it onto his head.

"I double-dog dare anyone to wear their toque like this tonight," he said.

"What do I get if I do?" Palmer asked.

"A close-up on national television and a million memes featuring your idiotic picture tomorrow," Fletcher murmured.

Luke ignored the kicker. "Fifty bucks for the charity of your choice."

"You're on." Palmer yanked the toque over his ears and strutted out of the locker room.

Fletcher shook his head. "I didn't even have to up the ante to get the fool to bite." He pulled something shiny from his duffel. "I have my ma's Saint Christopher medallion. Shall I wave it over ya for good luck?"

Van Horn laughed when Luke flipped the kicker off. They started toward the tunnel.

"Kessler," Wash said.

It was then that Luke noticed the coach was carrying a familiar laundry bag.

"Where do you w-want me to put these?"

Luke didn't bother repeating the first thought that popped into his head. Instead, he quietly took the bag from Wash and shoved it into the bench seat of the locker.

"You ready to shine tonight, Crime Dog?" Wash asked.

The rookie squared his shoulders. "Damn straight. I'll be stealing so much of the TV time that no one will ever see Palmer's big head."

"Well, amen for s-small favors."

McGraff proved to be prophetic. He took the opening kickoff thirty yards leading to a score on the Growlers' first possession. Van Horn grew more comfortable checking down to the rookie as the game wore on. By halftime, McGraff had sixty yards receiving and close to that in kick returns. Still, the game was tied.

The players were all amped up on their way into the locker room at halftime. Each position had its designated quadrant staked out. Wash gathered the receivers around his laptop to go over the adjustments they would make when they returned to the field.

Jacobs hobbled around them, begrudgingly offering advice to McGraff. Even more astounding, the rookie seemed to be lapping up the constructive criticism. Van Horn gave Luke one of his "who knew" looks. Luke grinned and pulled his inside-out toque back on his head.

Man, he loved this game. He loved being a part of this band of brothers. He could feel the joy pulsing through his veins, fueling his adrenaline for the second half. He hadn't lied earlier when he told Wash he was living his best life. He'd succeeded in a sport where everyone doubted him. And, making things even sweeter, for the first time in his life he had someone to share his happiness with off the field. And, he dared to hope, well into the future.

The Growlers took the lead thanks to one of Fletcher's field goals. Kansas City tied it back up with less than two minutes to go. Van Horn led the Growlers back down the field, but with twenty-one seconds left, they were still nine yards from the end zone. And it was fourth down. Coach Gibson chucked his headset and signaled for the team to gather around him on the sideline.

"Kessler," Coach said. "How would you like to show your dad he isn't the only one in the family who can throw a touchdown pass?"

The coach was taking an enormous risk. It was a squib kick for Fletcher. One he could make with his eyes closed. One that would tie the game. Yet, the Growler's coach was calling a trick play that would potentially give the team a win.

"Hell yeah," Luke replied. His arm wasn't as powerful as his father's—or Brady's—but every time they'd run this play in practice, Luke's pass was dead on. He had every confidence it would be tonight, too. And he was pretty jazzed that his coach was equally as confident.

"We'll send the regular formation in and hope they call a time-out to ice you, Fletcher. When they do, everyone huddle up back here, and we'll substitute Kessler in to hold."

Van Horn let out an angry sigh.

Luke slapped him on the back. "Don't be grouchy that I'm stealing a completion from you."

"All I care about is that you get the completion," the quarterback growled. The man detested losing about as much as having the game taken out of his hands.

"When I do, I'll be sure to give you all the credit during my post-game presser."

The other team did try to ice Fletcher with a time-out. When the Growlers reassembled in field goal formation a second time, it was Luke kneeling to receive the snap. The opposing players realized he was in the game just as the ball was hiked. Luke jumped to his feet and cast his eyes toward the end zone where not one, but two Growler players were open. Too easy. Sporting a gigantic grin, Luke rocketed a spiral downfield. The ball had just left his hand when a helmet collided with his ribs.

"You shouldn't be carrying that," Summer admonished Luke as she grabbed the bag of dog food out of his hands, nearly tumbling backward from the weight of it.

"I'm fine," he said, repeating the same two words he'd been uttering since he'd returned to Milwaukee four days earlier.

The gingerly way he'd been carrying the kibble told her otherwise. The hit Luke took was vicious in real time. The slow-motion replay streaming on every sports channel made it look even more gruesome. He'd taken a helmet to the chest, his body exposed while he extended his arm to throw the game-winning pass. The image of him lying limp on the field still nauseated her. Of course, he had to be a he-man and pretend he was "fine" despite the grimace on his face whenever he turned a certain way.

Jocks, she thought to herself as she settled the bag in the pantry.

He'd been lucky. His ribs were only bruised, and no internal organs were impacted. The way he was sulking around the house, however, one would think he'd been told he couldn't ever play football again rather than miss a couple of games.

"Our receiving corps is already depleted," he grumbled whenever the subject came up. "I shouldn't be on the IR when my hands and legs work perfectly well."

Obviously, his brain wasn't working "perfectly well," Summer would murmur to herself before smiling and giving him a patronizing kiss on the cheek. She should have made him the Tin Man for Halloween rather than giving that part to Antonio.

"If you're so fine, why don't you get into your Scarecrow costume. The trick-or-treaters will be here soon." She slipped her feet into the ruby slippers that completed her Dorothy outfit.

"Tell me again why I can't put on my jersey and go as myself for Halloween?"

"Because that doesn't fit with the Wizard of Oz theme. Milli is Toto. Monty is the Cowardly Lion." Monty picked that moment to try to shake off the black mane around his neck. Summer grabbed him before he could fling it across the kitchen. "No, Monty!" She gave the dog a kiss on the nose. "You look handsome with it on." The dog sat down with a thump, but Summer swore he smiled at her.

"Traitor," Luke said to the dog.

Summer moved closer to Luke, trailing her fingers down his chest. "Truth? I can't let all these cougar moms see you in your jersey. I don't want to risk them waylaying you while you're out walking the dogs. In case you haven't noticed, I'm not very good at sharing." She stretched up on her toes and pressed a kiss to his lips.

His arms circled around her like a vice as he pulled her in to deepen their kiss. She melted into him. He winced. She quickly shifted away, afraid of hurting him. He swore violently.

"Do NOT say you're fine," she told him.

"I miss you," he said, the expression on his face similar to that of a lost young boy.

Summer got the feeling this was about more than just the sex the doctor had advised them not to have for the next couple of weeks. She carefully leaned back in. "I'm right here," she whispered against his neck. "I'm not going anywhere."

He lowered his forehead to her shoulder. "Promise?"

Something shifted inside her. She wasn't going anywhere tonight. Or tomorrow. But she was leaving Milwaukee at the end of the semester. Would that be the end of this? Or would they somehow, someway, continue as they were? They still hadn't discussed it. Both of them tiptoed around any discussion of the future while enjoying living each day in the moment. Yet, it was suddenly painful to realize how much she wanted that scenario. How much she wanted Luke.

"Promise," she replied, hoping against hope she could keep that promise.

The dogs barked when Antonio clanked through the front door.

"Why does Van Horn get to play the Wizard?" Antonio groused.

"Because he'd be too tall to be a Munchkin," Summer replied.

"And too handsome to be the Wicked Witch," the Growler quarterback said with a cheeky smile when he followed Antonio into the house.

Summer pressed her palms to her cheeks. "Lord, save me from all this testosterone." She turned to Luke. He was wearing that mystified look again. "Go put on your costume," she ordered.

"So bossy." He sauntered closer, sporting a roguish grin. "Have I told you that's one of the things I love about you," he whispered near her ear.

Her heart skipped a beat. Did he really mean the L-word? She met his gaze. He cocked an eyebrow at her.

"Ask me later, and I'll give you a list." He leaned in and kissed her soundly.

She swayed on her feet when he walked away. Embarrassment made her cheeks warm when she turned to find Trey Van Horn studying her intently. She glanced around for Antonio.

"He's rifling through the candy bowl," the quarterback said, seeming to know her thoughts. "The kid has the nutritional sense of a gnat."

Suddenly uncomfortable with the other man's scrutiny, Summer went outside to light the pumpkins she and Luke had carved. Unfortunately, Trey followed her.

"How is he?" he asked.

She didn't bother pretending she didn't know who he was asking about. "Restless," she replied. "He's not very patient with the healing process."

Trey chuckled. "You've described most men and all professional athletes."

"Mmm." She wrapped her arms around her midsection, rubbing her biceps against the chilly evening. Dusk was falling. Shouts of the children beginning their trick-or-treating the next block over floated through the air. Summer felt guilty discussing anything about Luke with the quarterback. Despite the constant back and forth of smack-talk though, the teammates seemed to genuinely care about each other.

"You're good for him, you know," he remarked.

Her head jerked involuntarily toward him at his unexpected comment.

His teeth flashed briefly in the fading light. He reached up and pinched the bridge of his nose. "That's the second time I've told a woman that regarding one of my teammates." He shook his head as though he couldn't believe it himself. Then he shrugged. "But contented teammates make winning teammates. And frankly, that's all I care about."

"Is it?" she couldn't stop herself from asking.

He nodded adamantly.

She didn't believe him. Still, she let it slide, preferring to play Devil's Advocate instead. "What if I don't think Luke is good for me?"

Trey leaned back against the railing, crossing his arms over his gladiator's chest and calling her bluff. "Luke is good to everyone. Especially women. Too good, if you ask me."

Summer didn't disagree. Not that she was going to tell the arrogant quarterback so.

"He may seem affable and devil-may-care on the outside, but deep down, he cares," he continued. "He cares a lot. And I'm pretty sure all he wants is to find that someone who will care back just as much."

This conversation was making her throat increasingly tight.

"He's a bit like one of those wounded dogs he likes to rescue, though," Trey said. "A little gun-shy where love is concerned."

"What are you trying to say?" she managed to croak.

"Don't give up on him."

His words flabbergasted her. She wouldn't give up on Luke. Ever. She loved him.

Shit.

She loved him. Of course she did. What was not to love? He was perfect. The quarterback had nothing to worry about. Nothing could make her give up on Luke.

Antonio poked his head out the front door. "Hey, Summer. I thought you told me you bought Milk Duds?"

CHAPTER TWENTY-FOUR

It had been nearly two weeks since Luke's injury, and the painful sting every time he drew in a breath was long gone. The team doctors cleared him for every activity except football. He was frustrated not to be returning to the field that weekend when the Growlers played their rivals in Chicago. At least he would be able to seek relief from the other pain he'd been suffering these past few weeks. Unfortunately, he had to endure a four-hour ferry ride with the Geezer Squad before he could get Summer naked in a Chicago hotel room.

"Welcome aboard the Free Love for All ferry boat," Pete announced when they boarded.

Summer giggled beside Luke.

"Do not encourage him," Luke said.

She looped her arm through his. "I hope when we are their age, we still have the same *joie de vivre* as they do." She squeezed his arm. "The same passion."

Luke's pulse began to beat so hard against his temple that he was sure everyone on Lake Michigan heard it. He couldn't imagine the passion he felt for Summer ever tapering off. And as long as she was by his side, he would absolutely love life. He ached to tell her that, surprised at the ferocity of the feeling. Surprised at how easily the words would come after all these years of keeping his love locked tight inside. It was a risk opening himself up like that, but the risk was worth the reward if it meant a lifetime with her.

Tonight. He'd tell her tonight.

Once the ferry arrived in Chicago, it would dock at Navy Pier. The Geezer Squad had dinner plans that they thought included Luke and Summer. But he had other plans for the two of them. Plans that didn't include a dozen geriatric chaperones.

Everyone was staying in a nearby hotel ahead of the wedding the next day. The reception on the ferry would follow. Sunday, Luke had arranged for the crew from Sunset Glen to go to the Growlers' game at Soldier Field. A charter bus would return them to Milwaukee later that night.

"Let's get this party started," Harry Pearson said once the ferry was in motion.

The cabin was emptied of the wooden benches once used for passengers and was now retrofitted with a small dais, a parquet dance floor, and multiple round tables. In addition, there was a buffet line where the caterer would serve food during the reception. Despite his earlier reservations, Luke had to admit this was a solid venue. Unique, but then so was this crowd of crazy seniors.

Gram and her friends spent the last few weeks crafting flower arrangements for the tables. They laughed together as they began to decorate the cabin. The pleasure he felt watching her thrive in her new home never ceased to amaze him. He didn't think he could ever repay her for the years of unconditional love she'd given him, but at least he'd given her this.

"Summer," Mrs. Hilbert called. "How about some music while we work."

What a difference a few months made. Summer didn't hesitate to open up her cello case and rosin up her bow. Before long, she was playing show tunes that had the elders singing along. Her grandfather joined in with his trumpet. Fred and Gary jumped in with their horns.

Gram came over and pulled Luke onto the dance floor. He wasn't much of a dancer, but he managed not to embarrass himself.

"It's so wonderful to see you happy," she surprised him by saying.

"Me? I'm always happy."

"No. You *pretend* to be happy, but you're not all the time. You forget I've known you since you were a baby."

He wasn't sure what startled him more: her perception of him, or the accuracy of it.

She glanced in Summer's direction and smiled. "I don't think you are pretending now, though."

He followed her gaze. Summer was laughing at Mrs. Hilbert's attempt to limbo.

"Jesus, someone's gonna break a hip," he said.

Gram laughed. "Maybe. But one thing you realize when you get older is that life is fleeting. You can't be afraid to live. You can't be afraid to fill the years you have left with as many experiences as you can. As much love as you can."

The music ended, and he pulled Gram in for a bear hug. "That might be the best advice you ever gave me."

Pretty soon, the Chicago skyline was in sight. Gram and her friends bundled up and went up to the deck to soak up the late afternoon sunshine. The weather forecast called for snow the rest of the weekend.

"Admit it," Summer teased. "That was fun."

"They could put a locker room to shame with some of their jokes," he said.

She carefully wiped down her bow. Luke picked up the cello and went to lay it in the case. A card tucked in one of the side straps and bearing the Growlers' logo caught his eye.

"Why do you have a business card from the team's owner?" he asked when he picked it up.

Summer reached for it. "I meant to throw it away."

Luke held it out of her reach. "But why do you have it?"

"Mrs. Ciaciura gave it to me when I played at Andi's opening." She shrugged. "She's a patron with the Milwaukee Symphony, and she seemed to think I'd be interested in playing for them."

"Are you?"

"You know the answer to that."

"No, I don't. I know you love making music. I know you're amazing at it. So amazing that a million people followed you on YouTube. I don't know why you stopped."

She wrenched the cello from his fingers and placed it in the case. "I told you why," she said. "I get stage fright."

"One time, by your own admission."

"Why are you doing this?"

Because he wanted her to live life to the fullest. He wanted her not to leave anything on the table. Gram's words spurred him on. He would love Summer no matter what, but that didn't mean he would stop encouraging her to give her dream one more shot.

He reached between them and took her hands. "Because spending time with Gram and her friends has taught me something. You said it yourself earlier. It's the *joie de vivre*. Joy. You've got to take it where you can get it, every chance you can. You don't want to waste it."

She tugged her hands-free and dragged her fingers through her hair. "It's not that simple."

"Actually, it is."

"Says the super-star athlete," she quipped.

"Except I wasn't supposed to be one, remember? All the odds were stacked against me. I didn't listen to the negatives. Instead, I outperformed them."

She gave him a pensive look. "It's impossible to shut it out."

He took her hands again. They were chilly. "Tell me."

A long, fraught minute later, she opened her mouth. "In Vienna," she began, her voice hoarse with emotion. "I overheard the chairman of the board telling the director that I wasn't fit to perform because I lacked classical training. That I hadn't paid my dues when the other members had. He said I was nothing but a gimmick."

It took everything he had not to explode into a rage against the guy. To want to hunt the bastard down and make him pay for sabotaging Summer's confidence like he had. He squeezed her fingers gently.

"The thing is…he was right," she continued. "It wasn't fair to all those others who had put the work in. I got on stage, and I couldn't face them. I didn't feel worthy of the opportunity."

He brought her fingers up to his lips. "You're worthy of that and so much more."

She crawled into his lap, burying her face against his neck. "You think I'm being silly," she murmured against his skin.

"No," he answered right away. "But I think you know it's only one man's opinion. You've had this card in your case for weeks now, and you haven't thrown it away. There's a part of you that doesn't want to give up."

She was quiet for what felt like an eternity before she said quietly, "I'm scared it will happen again."

I can relate, he thought as he rubbed her back. He was scared shitless that she might reject his love. Yet, suddenly he was willing to take that risk because he had to let her know how much she meant to him. "You won't know until you try," he whispered in her ear.

Luke wasn't sure if he was telling Summer that, or himself. *Screw it,* he thought. He didn't want to wait until tonight. He didn't want another moment to slip by without her knowing that he loved her.

"Summer…"

"Hey, you two, we have docked at Navy Pier. We're going out for deep-dish pizza. Get a move on."

Damn Mrs. Hilbert and her impeccable, lousy timing. Summer scrambled off Luke's lap, swiping at her eyes.

"We are not going to dinner with them," Luke announced, his tone making her wide-eyed.

"We're not?" Summer said.

"No. The only place we are 'getting a move on' to is the hotel. When we get there, we're hanging out a do not disturb sign. We'll get room service if we get hungry."

She sunk her teeth into her bottom lip, making his already raging libido scream louder. He grabbed her cello and swatted her on the behind with his free hand. "Hustle, Pearson. We've got lost time to make up for."

SUMMER NEARLY SQUEALED with delight as she grabbed the handle of her rolling bag and hurried out of the cabin ahead of Luke. Somehow, she felt lighter for confessing her fears to him. He didn't ridicule her for feeling the way she did. Instead, he'd held her. Comforted her. Supported her. He'd shown her something that felt a lot like love, and her heart was singing at the prospect.

They dashed down the gangplank and steered around the opposite direction from the wedding party. He hailed an electric pedicab rickshaw bike. The wind whipped as the driver pedaled the bike in the direction of their hotel. Luke pulled her in close and warmed her with his body and his lips.

She was in such a sensual fog that she barely registered them checking in. Luke smiled devilishly when they found themselves the only occupants of the elevator. He pressed her up against the wall while his hands and his mouth roamed her body. She was panting with need when the doors slid open. They raced with their luggage down the hallway, nearly colliding with another couple locked in a passionate embrace.

Summer's embarrassed laugh turned into a shocked gasp when she realized who the two people making out in the hallway were.

"Papa Harry?" Her throat was so choked with emotion, the words were painful to push out.

Grace quickly jumped away from her grandfather. Nausea rolled through Summer's stomach at Papa Harry's sheepish look.

"Sunshine..." Her grandfather took a step in her direction.

Summer took a step back, only to collide with Luke. "Don't 'Sunshine' me. What the hell, Papa Harry?" Her eyes began to burn with unshed tears. "How could you do this to Grandma? How could you do this to your *wife*? Your terminally ill wife of *sixty years*?"

"Summer." Her grandfather's tone had morphed from placating to stern.

"No!" she shouted. "I don't want to hear your excuses. I don't care. This is disgusting." She turned to Grace. "And you. You think you can swoop in and steal another man's wife? How dare you? How dare you do that to my defenseless grandmother, who gave him the best years of his life. How dare you do that to my family." The last word came out as a painful sob.

Grace went ghostly white. She swayed against the wall. Papa Harry reached for her, but she shooed him away. He turned back, scowling at Summer as if the situation was somehow her fault.

Luke stepped in front of Summer and put his hands on her shoulders. A disappointed look shadowed his eyes. Good. At least he now saw his precious Gram for what she was—a home-wrecker.

"That's enough, Summer." Luke gave her shoulders a shake. He looked like he wanted to say more, but he sighed heavily and turned to face his Gram and Papa Harry. "This is not what I meant when I said to be discreet."

The breath stilled in her lungs at his words. A shiver ran up her spine. "What did you say?" she croaked, surprised she could muster any sound at all.

She watched as Luke's entire body tensed. He slowly spun around on his heel. "Summer," he began.

A painful ache began at the back of her throat. She knew instantly there wasn't an explanation he could give that would make this better. "No." She grabbed her cello and her roller bag and took a giant step back.

He followed her. "Summer, I need you to be reasonable about this."

A shrill laugh escaped. "Me? The one who was being ridiculous when I brought this up weeks ago? The one who was imagining things? I'm the unreasonable one?"

"That's not what I meant."

"How long? How long have you known?" She took a few more steps back. "How many times have you listened to me rhapsodize about my grandparents and their storybook romance while you laughed behind my back?"

"It wasn't like that," he said through gritted teeth.

"You knew how much they mean to me. How important they were to my life. Yet you condoned this anyway."

"I didn't condone anything."

"It doesn't look that way from where I'm standing."

He heaved a sigh. "Let's go inside and talk about this in private."

She barked a laugh. "I'm not going anywhere private with you. I'm done having my trust and my feelings trampled on. I can't believe I wasted my love on you."

It must have been divine intervention, because the elevator doors opened behind her. Summer dashed in. Luke remained in the center of the hallway, hands on his hips and a shellshocked look on his face. She didn't allow herself to cry until she got to the apartment she shared with Paige.

PAIGE HANDED Summer a cup of tea. "Are you sure you don't want anything stronger?"

Summer dabbed at her eyes with a tissue. "It seems a shame to waste good alcohol when I'm already numb."

"Oh, sweetie." Paige plopped down on the sofa beside her. She wrapped her arm around Summer's shoulders and pulled her in.

Summer let her head loll onto her friend's shoulder. "I don't know who hurt me more, Papa Harry or Luke."

Best friend that she was, Paige didn't offer up an opinion.

"I can't believe I let Luke's charming smile and buff body suck me in."

Paige stroked Summer's hair. "You're not one to be swayed by a smile or a bodacious body. I'm sure there's a lot more to him that you fell in love with."

There was. So much more. She hiccupped a sob. "Do you think I'm being unreasonable?"

Silence descended. Paige's hand stilled on Summer's hair. Summer sat up and looked at her friend. Paige pressed her lips together in a rueful way.

"Am I?" Summer said.

Paige turned and drew her legs up underneath her on the sofa. "Unreasonable about Papa Harry, maybe a teensy bit."

"Really?" Summer's chest squeezed.

"Ask yourself this," Paige said. "You go and see Grandma Bonnie every day, but you haven't accepted the reality that the woman you know and love isn't there anymore. Lizzie refuses to visit your grandmother because she can't bear to see her like she is now. You're both avoiding the inevitable." She took Summer's hand. "Papa Harry has been left behind with someone who doesn't recognize him. Is it fair to condemn him to a companionless existence for the rest of his life? For him to have no joy?"

Joy. Summer was getting sick of that word. She shook her head. "It was just such a shock."

"I'm sure it was. You've held their relationship to such a high standard. Maybe even an impossible one?"

Summer buried her face in her hands. "I'm such an idiot. I said some awful things."

Paige wrapped her up in a hug. "Give it time. Your grandfather loves you. He'll forgive you."

"I don't know if I can forgive Luke though. He lied to me."

"That boy has got some 'splaining to do."

"I'm sorry to barge in here and ruin your weekend plans with Jon," Summer said.

"First of all, it's not barging in if it's your own home. And the impending snowstorm put the kibosh on Jon's visit."

"Maybe I should take up my old position on the sofa."

"Not happening," Paige replied adamantly. "You're going to take the LSAT and then come home when the semester ends."

"The thing is…" Summer turned to her friend.

"Oh, I don't like when you get that look on your face," Paige said.

"I was thinking of calling Mrs. Ciaciura."

"Oh my gosh, seriously?" Paige clapped her hands.

"Not for me to do an actual performance. I don't think I'm ready for that. I may never be. When I played at the shop opening, there were these two precious kids who were mesmerized by the music. I was toying with the idea of a youth orchestra performance of Peter and the Wolf. We could live stream it to gin up more interest."

Paige was smiling ear to ear. "Our girl is back."

"Baby steps," Summer said. "I don't want to freeze again."

"You won't. I know you won't. What can I do to help?"

"Let's start with some wine. The numbness is starting to wear off, and my heart feels like it will never be whole again."

CHAPTER TWENTY-FIVE

I CAN'T BELIEVE I wasted my love on you.

Right when Luke had begun to believe he wouldn't be burned by love any longer. *Wham.* Summer hit him with a sucker punch more painful than any from his childhood. At least he hadn't done the unthinkable and told her he loved her.

Not that it made him feel any better. Just because he hadn't voiced his emotions didn't mean they weren't real. He would survive though. He always did.

Luke needed to face the facts. Love wasn't for him. Family wasn't for him. Gram was the extent of his family. He wasn't even going to consider what his life would be like when she was gone.

Monty dropped a rubber ball at Luke's feet. The dog had been moping for the past two weeks. Not that Luke had been much better.

He reached down from where he was stretched out on the massive leather sofa and plucked the ball from the ground. "It's just you and me again, pup. Get used to it." He tossed the ball across the family room. Monty didn't chase it. Instead, he lowered his head onto Luke's hip and sighed.

"Yeah. Me too, buddy."

As if his love life falling apart wasn't enough, the Growlers were also in a tailspin. They'd dropped their last two games. One in a snowstorm in Chicago. The other had been Luke's first game back last weekend. Neither game had been close. But at least he'd had something to keep his mind off Summer during the day.

The nights, however, seemed to be endless. Even worse, the Growlers had a bye this weekend. Rather than one free day, Luke found himself staring down four days with nothing to do.

He rubbed the dog's ear. "She's taking the LSAT today. You wouldn't have gotten to see her or Milli anyway. I had reservations at this incredible B & B lined up in Door County. I was going to surprise her after she finished with the test."

Instead, he was lying on his sofa, watching college football and conversing with his dog. He'd kept busy yesterday doing promo work with Patrick Conway and his wife in preparation for the charity auction benefitting the Human Society. The holiday gala would take place the week after next. He'd coerced most of his teammates to either contribute or buy tickets. At least he could feel positive about doing something worthwhile.

His phone pinged. He reached for it with a lazy groan. "If this is Tony-O again with instructions about Thanksgiving, I'm uninviting Gram and me from dinner."

With Thanksgiving on Thursday, most of the Growlers took advantage of their weekend off to escape snowy Milwaukee and celebrate early with family. Antonio's family, however, decided to bring the holiday to him. His mother, sisters, brother, and even Granny Pearl were all marveling at the winter wonderland they'd found themselves in. Mrs. McGraff was hosting a Thanksgiving dinner with all the trimmings, and the kid insisted that Luke and Gram be a part of it.

Luke was fairly certain the rookie was aware that he was no longer living at Summer's house. For whatever reason, Antonio had made it his mission to look after Luke, including checking up on him at all hours of the day. Luke let it go because he knew the kid was doing the same with Summer. Evidently, he was a textbook masochist because he wasn't ready to sever that last tie to her.

Sure enough, Antonio sent a picture of his kittens playing with a football.

what kind of pie do you like? mama wants to make sure you don't go hungry :)

As if Luke was a lineman or something and was going to devour three pies.

Whatever she's serving will be fine.

Antonio typed back.

you sure?

Luke responded with a thumbs up, hoping that would appease his teammate for the rest of the day.

Monty whined at the patio door.

"You want to go out and make yellow snow?"

Luke hauled his ass off the sofa and padded over to the doors leading out to the snow-covered yard. He really should start a fire. It would make the place feel a bit cozier. Like the fires they'd enjoyed at Summer's bungalow.

"For fuck's sake, now I'm trying to make this place cozy. It's a bachelor pad, right?" he said to the dog. "We don't need cozy." Monty looked like he might argue the point, but Luke pulled open the door and pointed outside. "Out. Go annoy the squirrels."

With a gleeful bark, the dog leaped into the snow. Luke watched him play for a minute before heading into the kitchen.

Had he eaten today? Antonio's text about pies suddenly had his stomach growling.

He finished putting together a hoagie fit for a lineman when his doorbell rang. Luke debated not answering before sighing heavily and heading for the foyer.

"Van Horn, I told you I don't need a babysitter today," he said as he pulled the door open.

Except it wasn't the quarterback standing on his porch. At least not *that* quarterback.

"What the hell?" Luke murmured.

"Hey." Brady Kessler nervously shifted his duffle higher on his shoulder with one hand while giving Luke a small wave with the other one.

Luke glanced behind his half-brother. "Is he with you?"

Brady shot him a sheepish look. "Nah."

"You're here by yourself?" Luke asked. "Why? How?"

Monty barked playfully. A feminine laugh followed it.

"Layla came with me," Brady said.

What the ever-loving hell?

Brady's sister raced around the corner of the house, Monty in tow. She laughed again when the dog tugged at her backpack.

"Monty!" Luke yelled. "Leave it."

The dog whimpered in annoyance before sitting on Layla's foot.

"I like your dog," she said.

The girl had her mother's smile, only much warmer. She had hair the same color as Luke, not quite brown, not quite blonde. On her, it looked pretty. Pale green eyes studied him, unsure of their next move. Luke remained where he was, filling up the doorway.

"Do you mind telling me what's going on?" he asked. His tone was a bit testy because, hell, what were his two teenage half-siblings doing a thousand miles from home, unchaperoned?

Brady's face closed up, his lips forming a mulish line. "You know, forget it." He turned on his heel. "I told you this was a stupid idea, Lay."

"No!" Layla cried. She hurried to block her brother's path. "We're not leaving. At least not until we see Gram."

Say what?

"You're here to see Gram?"

Luke's shock quickly evaporated. These two were the answer to his prayers. Gram had been devastated by the scene in Chicago. So much so that she broke things off with Harry Pearson. Her smile had been noticeably dimmer ever since. But a surprise visit with Brady and Layla would go a long way toward cheering her up. She would be thrilled to see them.

"We're here to see you, also," Layla announced, hands on her hips. "But we'll settle with Gram if you're too busy for us."

She looked so much like a younger version of Summer, so full of attitude and sass that Luke almost laughed. Also, like Summer, Layla's eyes betrayed her confidence. She was nervous and scared of being rejected.

It was a look Luke knew all too well.

"Are we busy, Monty?" Luke asked the dog.

Monty responded with a bark.

"He says no." Luke stepped out of the doorway and waved them inside.

Layla's grin engulfed her face. *Jesus, she would be a heartbreaker one day. If she wasn't already.* She grabbed her brother's hand and tugged him into the foyer. Monty barked a chorus of hellos as he circled the legs of both teens. Luke led them to the back of the house.

"You can leave your coats in the mudroom. It's through the kitchen," he said.

He noticed Brady looking longingly at the sandwich on the counter. If the kid was anything like Luke was at eighteen, he was hungry every thirty minutes. Luke grabbed some plates and cut the sandwich into thirds. He dug through his pantry for a bag of chips and his emergency pack of double-stuff Oreos. After laying the spread out on the island, he reached into the fridge and pulled out some bottles of Vitamin Water. He considered grabbing a beer to calm his nerves but thought better of it. The least he could do was set a good example.

"Help yourself," Luke said when they emerged from the mudroom and took a seat at the island.

Monty sat down, his tongue lolling to the side as he stared down both teens hoping for a handout. Layla was the first to go soft, ripping a piece of turkey from her sandwich.

"Don't even think about feeding him," Luke warned. "He's on a diet."

Layla giggled.

Luke leaned a hip against the counter. "So now that we've established I'm not busy, why don't you tell me what's going on, starting with how did you two get here?"

"Having fun isn't hard when you've got a platinum card," Brady sang.

Luke shook his head in disbelief. He did pretty well in life with a multi-million-dollar contract. But these two had been born with trust funds ending in at least six zeroes thanks to their mother.

"Do your parents know you're here?"

Brady and Layla exchanged an anxious glance.

"One of our parents is your parent, too," Brady said, neatly sidestepping the question.

"On paper," Luke replied.

Layla's eyes went wide.

Luke pinched the bridge of his nose. "Tell me this, are the cops going to show up at my door looking for you?"

They both shook their heads.

"Dad's in San Diego doing a game this weekend," Brady said. "I was going to go with him, but he was all pissy about us losing in the state quarterfinals. I didn't need those kind of vibes."

"It wasn't Brady's fault they lost. Their defense was like Swiss cheese."

Something stirred in Luke's chest hearing Layla stick up for her brother. Still, he needed to get to the bottom of this. Brady was eighteen, but Layla was only fourteen. Gram could take care of letting the old man know where his beloved progeny were. The less Luke was involved, the better.

"What about your mom?" he asked.

"She's at some health spa for the week with her friends." Layla shrugged. "It's their annual tradition."

"During Thanksgiving week?"

It was Brady's turn to shrug. "Dad is always gone for Thanksgiving, broadcasting the game. We don't do the whole family holiday thing."

Huh. All this time that Luke felt left out, Jake Kessler wasn't even celebrating holidays with his own family. Massive trust funds or not, he was beginning to feel a lot of empathy toward the two teenagers in his kitchen.

"And they just leave you both at home. Alone? For a week?" *Weren't there laws against that?*

"They think we are with friends," Layla said. "But it gets old butting in on other families' holidays. We want our own family."

Luke thought his heart might have stopped. Was she saying what he thought she was saying?

"He's probably got plans with his girlfriend and her family. She's from Milwaukee, you know." Brady sounded churlish.

Layla looked at Luke expectantly.

"No girlfriend. It's only Gram and me."

"Seriously? You're alone just like us?" she asked.

Not once in his life had Luke ever considered Jake's other kids to be "just like" him. Apparently, he'd been wrong. He wanted to rage at their father for the way he'd mistreated these two cool teenagers. But his words would only fall on deaf ears. The loser was only out for himself. Luke could be the real winner here.

"You're not alone, Layla. You've got Gram and me."

With a squeal that had Monty scrambling for cover, she jumped from the barstool into a dumbfounded Luke's arms.

"Oh, this is going to be so awesome. We've wanted to get to know you for forever."

Her words shocked him even more than her hug. He glanced over at Brady, but the kid did his best to avoid eye contact. Something warm and light was beginning to unfurl inside of Luke. Something that felt really nice.

"Can we go see Gram?" she asked.

Luke nodded.

"I have to change first."

Brady groaned. "She changes clothes ten times a day." He gestured to the giant duffel he'd carried into the house. "That thing weighs fifty pounds."

"I didn't know what the weather would be like."

"There are two guest rooms upstairs. Take your pick," Luke said.

She hurried up the backstairs. Monty galumphed behind her.

"Gram will insist you let your parents know where you are," Luke told Brady.

"Yeah, I know." Brady tore at his napkin, balling each piece up. "We're not lying when we say they won't care though."

"I think your dad cares. He was worried about you when we spoke in Kansas City last month."

"You keep saying *my* dad. Must be nice to shut him out like that."

Luke didn't think it was relevant that the kid should know who exactly had shut out who. Brady already harbored enough resentment for his parents.

"He's worried you're sabotaging your chances to be the top high school recruit."

Brady dropped his head into his hands. "That's all he cares about."

Preaching to the choir, little brother.

"I'm not like you guys though."

He's not like us. Jake's words from their meeting in Kansas City ricocheted through Luke's head.

"I know this might sound like sacrilege to you, but I'm not sure I love the game as much as you and Dad do." Brady's shoulders slumped.

Luke wasn't sure how to respond to that, so he went with a platitude. "You're young. Maybe it will come."

Judging by Brady's reaction, he'd chosen the wrong words.

"I'm so sick of hearing that. What if I'm into something else? Another sport? Music? Gaming?"

"Are you?"

"How would I know?" he shouted. "I've never been allowed to try anything else. All my life, it's been football this and football that. Don't do that; you'll ruin your arm. Don't eat that; it will mess up your metabolism." He paused to suck in a breath. "You were lucky. You didn't have to grow up in the shadow of the GOAT Jake Kessler's limelight. You got to play football for the fun of it. You experienced college without any of the pressure of knowing you had to perform, or else. I doubt I'll enjoy a single minute of it." He scowled. "Dad wants me to commit next month. Then I can gray-shirt and start college next semester. I'd miss prom and graduation and everything else. For what? The whole thing blows."

The expression on Brady's face was so raw that Luke could feel his pain as if it were his own.

"What's the point?" Brady asked, his voice sounding broken.

These days, there were too many stories of young athletes succumbing to the pressure to perform at a certain level. Luke barely had a relationship with the kid, but that didn't matter. He was going to rectify that starting this week.

Right then, he made a solemn vow to protect his brother, no matter what. Their father would likely regret asking Luke for his help with Brady. *Too bad,* Luke thought. Someone needed to advocate for him. And who better than his big brother.

"Brady, you know you don't have to do anything you don't want to."

"Tell that to Dad."

"Oh, I will. I've got your back, Brady. Don't you worry about a thing."

A look of surprised relief came over Brady. Mimicking his sister, he leaped from his chair and pulled Luke in for a fierce hug.

"I'm so glad we came," Brady said.

Luke was suddenly so overcome with emotion, he couldn't get any words past the boulder in his throat. The best he could manage was a thump of agreement on his brother's back.

"Aww. Aren't they cute, Monty?" Layla flounced down the stairs. "My two big brothers hugging it out. Maybe save your bromance for later though. I want to go see Gram."

Luke grabbed his keys and his jacket.

"I don't know why you had to get so dressed up, Layla," Brady said. "It's a community of old people."

"Who may have grandsons visiting." She batted her long lashes and cocked her hip.

Brady groaned. "She's all yours now, Luke."

They both were. And for the first time in weeks, he felt hopeful again.

"Whatever you do," Luke warned. "Do not eat any raisins while you're there."

CHAPTER TWENTY-SIX

SUMMER SLEPT for eighteen hours after taking her LSAT. It was Sunday afternoon before she felt human enough to face the world. She'd been burning the candle at both ends while preparing for the exam.

Not that she could sleep anyway. Her bed was cold and lonely without Luke's body intertwined with hers. Even the sofa where they'd slept in front of the fire didn't feel all that comfortable any longer.

"Not that it matters," she told Milli. "I'm headed home in a month."

Home.

Silly how she'd begun to think of the cozy Craftsman as home. Home was in Chicago. In an apartment with Paige. Going with Sterling to Bulls' games in the winter and Cubs' games in the summer. Even shopping with The Judge on the Miracle Mile. This house belonged to Papa Harry, who likely couldn't wait to evict her.

She hadn't been to Sunset Glen in two weeks. Summer told herself it was because she was too embarrassed at skipping out on Sharon and Gary's wedding to show her face there. The truth?

She was avoiding the place because she was too afraid to face her grandfather.

How he must hate her. Her mouth went dry at the memory of that night. He came by during the school day to pick up Milli for her visit with Grandma Bonnie, avoiding Summer altogether.

She needed to put on her big girl panties and apologize. Today. Her hands trembled at the thought. But she couldn't put it off any longer. And she shouldn't have ignored Grandma Bonnie all this time. Although, she didn't know how she could look the woman in the eye knowing what she knew.

Summer poured the dregs of her tea into the kitchen sink with a groan.

"Okay, Milli, let's do this."

The sun was out, melting away the couple of inches of snow that fell the day before. On the drive over to Sunset Glen, Summer put on a Meghan Trainor song hoping to give herself a boost of courage. Milli panted with excitement when they pulled into the complex.

"You want to see your momma, huh, girl?"

An ambulance was idling at the entrance to the main building. It was not an uncommon occurrence, given the population. Still, Summer always felt a heightened sense of alarm whenever she saw one.

She clipped on Milli's leash and headed for the memory care unit. The woman at the reception desk looked harried. She took one look at Summer, and her face fell.

"That was fast," she said.

"Excuse me?" Summer asked.

"Summer. You're here." Mrs. Hilbert came charging toward her. Her face looked drawn.

Darn it. She'd hoped to get in and out of here without seeing anyone other than her grandparents. It looked like she'd have to make all her apologies this visit.

"Mrs. Hilbert, I'm so sorry about missing the wedding. Something came up."

The woman waved her hand. "Never mind about that. Your grandfather needs you. Come with me."

She steered Summer toward the memory care wing.

"My grandfather's apartment is in the other building." Summer started to change direction.

"No." She pointed to the locked door accessing the memory care apartments. "He's in there. You need to go in. Punch your code."

Something about Mrs. Hilbert's demeanor had alarm bells ringing. Summer unlocked the door and hurried inside. Several of the staff were crowded at the end of the hall, peering into the apartment across from Grandma Bonnie's.

The only thing Summer saw, however, was her grandfather crouched down along the wall, his head in his hands. A sense of dread surged through her.

"Papa Harry?" she whispered.

He looked up then, his beautiful blue eyes damp and red-rimmed. "She's gone, Sunshine. My Bonnie is gone."

She sank to the floor beside him, trying hard to drag in a breath. "No," she croaked.

Milli tried to shove her way between them.

Papa Harry pulled the dog to him. "She's gone," he repeated. "She left us, Mill."

Tears blurred Summer's vision. The EMTs pushed a gurney out of the open apartment. Milli suddenly went still before jumping out of her grandfather's arms and barking manically. Papa Harry slowly got to his feet, lifting the little dog with him. He laid her on the sheet-draped gurney.

"She's gone, Milli," he said, his crocodile tears dripping on the dog.

With a whimper, Milli curled up next to Grandma Bonnie. Unsure of what to do, Summer got to her feet. A keening sound rose from the apartment, and a man came to the door. Summer had seen him several times when she visited her grandmother in the solarium.

"We were taking a nap," he cried. "Why won't she wake up?"

One of the medical staff murmured something at the man.

"Wait," Summer said. "Grandma Bonnie was taking a nap in his room?"

Her grandfather avoided her eyes. Instead, he patted the man on the shoulder. "I'm so sorry for your loss, Edward."

What?

"I don't understand," Summer said.

Except she did.

Dear God.

What had she done? All the awful things she'd said in Chicago that night roared through her head. The humiliation of it all had her slumping down onto the floor again. Without warning, gut-wrenching sobs wracked her body. How could she have been so wrong? And so foolishly cruel.

Papa Harry hauled her into his arms. "Hush, child."

"But-I-I didn't know," she cried. "I only saw what I wanted to see. I'm so s-sorry for everything I said. I messed everything up so badly. I don't blame you if you h-hate me."

He rocked her gently. "I couldn't ever hate you, Sunshine. And don't ever apologize for loving someone as fiercely as you loved your grandmother. You might have taken the time to hear me out that night, but I knew you'd come to your senses soon enough."

"How-how long?"

"How long has she been with Edward? About nine months. Not long after she forgot who I was."

Summer was sure her heart was in a million pieces in her chest. How could she have so totally misjudged this beautiful man? "But you moved here anyway."

His smile was grim. "I didn't want to give up hope. It was only recently that I could let her go."

She gulped a sob. "Because of G-Grace."

He nodded solemnly.

"I can't believe I accused you the way I did when all this time it was—it was—" Summer couldn't get the words out.

"Don't you dare blame your grandmother. She left us long ago," Papa Harry ordered. "And this version of Bonnie died knowing great love. Twice. I couldn't have asked for anything more than that for her."

THE FUNERAL WAS HELD the day before Thanksgiving. A beautiful Indian summer day that Grandma Bonnie would have adored. Summer was so hollow inside she wasn't sure if it was her going through the motion of living or a ghost. Paige had taken over the moment that she arrived in Milwaukee, making sure Summer, Papa Harry, and even Milli were cared for.

"It isn't so much that she's gone," Summer had told her friend. "I knew that was inevitable. I can't get over what a fool I made of myself. I seem to be making a habit of that."

Thankfully, Paige didn't utter so much as one "I-told-you-so." She simply listened with a sympathetic ear.

At the gravesite, flanked by The Judge and Sterling, Summer was selfishly relieved that Edward wasn't invited to the internment. Things were awkward enough without having to explain things to the rest of the family. The last thing she expected was for Luke to show up, however. She felt his presence the minute he entered the church, Grace on his arm. Now, if she looked just the right way out of the corner of her eye, she could see him standing behind the crowd, head bowed reverently.

It was sweet of him to come. It was also sheer agony. She missed him. So much that she felt the ache deep within her bones. But she didn't know how to begin to apologize.

Or if he'd even accept it.

Don't give up on him, Trey Van Horn had warned her.

Except she had. Appallingly. She doubted he was waiting around for her to come to her senses like her grandfather. Why would he? He'd never told her he loved her. According to Trey, Luke was very stingy with his love. Besides, after the way she behaved, she wasn't sure she deserved it.

A tear rolled down her cheek. Her mother pressed a tissue into Summer's hand. She wiped her eyes, risking another peek at Luke. But he was already gone.

"What did you do to Luke?" Lizzie asked when the family returned to the house.

Summer fumbled the tray of cookies she was holding, only to have Paige rescue it before its contents were all over the kitchen floor.

"I'll take those out," Paige said. She mouthed "Holy shit" from behind Lizzie before moving to the living room.

"I—what do you mean?" Summer asked.

Lizzie dropped her head back. "Don't play dumb with me. You two were a thing. Papa Harry confirmed it."

"He did? You knew?"

"Of course. I knew before you did. He certainly never looked at me the way he looked at you."

Summer was flabbergasted. "And you're okay with it?"

"I was kind of hurt you didn't tell me. I told you there wasn't anything to the two of us. He's a standup guy. You deserve someone like him, Summer."

Tears pressed against the backs of her eyes, despite Summer thinking she'd cried them all out these past several weeks.

"He is an amazing person," she managed to say. "But it didn't work out. I'm going back to Chicago. To law school."

Lizzie shook her head.

"What?" Summer demanded.

"Do you remember when we were kids, and we'd play games with the boys?"

Summer nodded. Those summers spent here with Grandma Bonnie and Papa Harry were some of the most precious times of her life. Lizzie, Summer, and the three Pearson boys were like their own pack trying to best each other at everything.

"You never gave up," Lizzie said. "Even when winning was impossible. You never quit. I envied you that fierceness. Your passion for being the best. I was so worried about everyone liking me that I sometimes lost on purpose. But not you."

Summer swallowed around the lump in her throat.

"I miss that Summer."

Lizzie's brother stuck his head inside the kitchen. "Ready, Lizzie?"

"Yep." She hugged Summer tightly. "I have to go. I'm working the Thanksgiving parade tomorrow." She bounced up on her toes. "I have to keep pinching myself to believe my life is real."

Summer needed air. She headed out the back door only to nearly trip over The Judge seated on the back porch while playing tug of war with Milli. Her mother scooted over on the step to make room for Summer.

"She's a little cutie. Maybe I ought to take her to Chicago with me."

Summer stared at her mom incredulously. "You never let Sterling and I have a dog, and now when we're gone, you'll get one?"

Her mother shrugged. "Maybe it's because you and Sterling are gone that I want some company."

Milli lost interest in the rope toy and began chasing after a leaf. Summer rested her head on her mother's shoulder.

"She was a lovely woman," her mother said.

"Grandma Bonnie?"

"Who else would I be talking about today?"

Summer was silent for a few beats. "Did you two always get along?"

"Did we always love one another, or did we always agree?"

"Do you always have to be such a judge?"

Her mother chuckled. "The semantics matter, Summer. Learn that early."

Summer sighed.

"We mostly disagreed over you," her mother surprised her by saying.

She sat up. "What?"

"Mmm. If you must know, I was incredibly jealous of the relationship you two had. Or, more explicitly, the talent you both shared. I would have killed to have an ounce of the talent Bonnie possessed. And you? Oh my. You're a whole other level."

It was as if aliens had taken over her mother's body.

"Don't look at me that way. It's the truth. Bonnie wanted you to go away to a school for the performing arts. I didn't want you to. It was too soon. Too soon after your father—" Her mother looked away. "After your father left us. I barely saw you as it was. So yes, I was selfish, and I kept you home with us." She brushed her palms together. "There. Now you have loads to talk to a therapist about."

A maelstrom of emotions cascaded through Summer. Shock and a touch of anger that she was denied such an opportunity. Sorrow and guilt that she had been the cause of a rift between her mother and grandmother. Most of all though, she felt a sense of peace knowing that her taciturn mother truly loved her.

"I wouldn't have wanted to leave you." The words slipped out unbidden. But they were the truth. "Or Sterling."

Her mother's lower lip quivered ever so slightly. She nodded. "And you became a superstar anyway."

Summer snorted a laugh. "A superstar failure, you mean."

"Nonsense. You had an off day."

"Hardly."

Her mother faced her, the stern judge's mask firmly in place. "Summer Pearson, if you didn't want it, you shouldn't have pursued it."

"What? I wanted it!" Summer shouted. "I wanted it with every fiber of my being!"

"Then why aren't you still pursuing it?" her mother asked calmly.

She felt like she'd had the wind knocked out of her. "Because I'm going to law school."

"I would love nothing more than for you to take the safe route and become a lawyer like me. It's a respectable profession."

"But?"

Her mother shrugged. "But if you're simply taking the safe route because it's, well, safe, then I hope you won't regret it later on. Life is short, Summer. If losing your father taught us anything, it was that."

Summer's head felt like it was going to explode. "Mom, what are you trying to say?"

"I'm trying to make amends with the beautiful woman we just laid to rest. The wonderful mother of my husband and your father. She saw something in you long before the rest of the world got to see it. I should have listened to her and tried to make something work." She cupped Summer's face with her hands. "You're an amazing teacher. If that's what you love, do that. You'll be an incredible lawyer because no one has more passion for righting injustice than you do. But if it's the music in your blood, fight for it." She pressed her forehead to Summer's. "Whatever you choose, you'll make me proud. You always do."

CHAPTER TWENTY-SEVEN

THREE DAYS LATER, Summer hesitated in front of Grace Kessler's door. She drew in a deep breath. This conversation was long overdue. And not only so she could ease her conscience, but for Papa Harry's sake, too. He'd put on a brave face, trying to enjoy the holiday with his family as if his heart hadn't been broken.

Twice.

The blame for the second heartbreak lay squarely at Summer's feet. She had botched all of it up when she unleashed her wild accusations at Grace and her grandfather. The shame was still so intense, her knees nearly buckled. Summoning courage from a reserve she didn't know until recently existed, she shook it off. It was time for her to fix this.

When she raised her hand to knock, the door swung open. A pretty teenage girl gave Summer a startled smile.

"Oh my gosh. That could have been awkward," the girl said with a laugh.

There was something about her amused eyes that looked eerily familiar.

"Gram," she called over her shoulder. "You've got company."

Gram?

Summer's stomach did a backflip. Grace's smile faltered slightly when she came to the door.

"Summer," she said softly. "This is a surprise."

"This must be your week for surprise guests." The girl kissed Grace on the cheek. "I'd better go before Brady blows a gasket in the Uber. He wants to see Luke at the hotel before our flight. We'll be back Friday night for the gala. Don't forget I'm doing your makeup."

With another pleasant smile for Summer, she dashed out the door and down the hall.

Brady wants to see Luke?

"Was that who I think it was?" she asked Grace.

Grace nodded. "She and Brady surprised us last weekend. It's been wonderful getting to know them."

Summer's cheeks hurt, trying to contain her smile. *Luke must be so thrilled.* She was delighted for him. Overjoyed, in fact. He'd always talked a big game about not caring that he wasn't a part of his father's family. Except Summer knew the real Luke Kessler. The vulnerable one hiding behind a façade of affable *bonhomie.* That guy cared. A lot. And she was thrilled he didn't have to deal with that hurt any longer.

"That's wonderful," she said wistfully.

A door opened farther down the hall.

"Come inside," Grace insisted. "Unless you want to have this conversation with an audience."

"Heck, no." Summer didn't have it in her to deal with Mrs. Hilbert today.

Grace led her past the kitchen to the airy living room with its wide windows that stretched almost to the ceiling. A fire was flickering in the gas fireplace. She cleared off one of the chairs so Summer could sit.

"Oh, Brady forgot his hat." She shook her head and placed the knit cap adorned with the Growlers logo onto the dining table.

"Not that he'll need cold-weather gear in Dallas. It will be here waiting for him when they come back next weekend."

If Luke's brother and sister were returning to Milwaukee next week, there must have been a true family reconciliation. No wonder Grace had let Summer through the door. The woman was still riding high from the joy of having her family back together. And Luke could finally make peace with his father.

"Will their dad be coming with them next week?" Summer asked.

"Not unless there is something in it for him." Grace waved at Summer to sit. "I'm afraid I won't win any parenting awards."

"The fact that your grandson adores you says otherwise."

"You're sweet to say so." Grace turned to stare out the window. "I'm not even sure where I went wrong. Nothing was ever good enough for Jake." Her eyes were shiny when she turned back to Summer. "We lived a simple life. My husband was a private pilot. He flew many celebrities on hunting and ski trips throughout the northwest and into Canada. Jake was always fascinated by his father's passengers. He begged to go along so he could rub shoulders with the wealthy, always wanting more than he had. I'm not sure what he thought it would get him." She sighed. "Eventually, he was one of the famous ones, thanks to football."

"Fame can be a powerful obsession," Summer said.

Grace nodded in agreement. "But it can also be fleeting. I'm afraid the man doesn't know how to live without it." She smiled warmly. "Fortunately my grandchildren seem to have dodged their father's character flaw."

Summer let Grace's revelations about Luke's father sink in.

"But I doubt you came here to listen to the Kessler family's dirty laundry. How is Harry?" Grace asked when she took a seat in a chair across from Summer.

"He's putting up a brave front."

"He's lucky to have all of you." Grace began to wring her hands.

"I think he'd rather have you."

Grace's hands stopped moving. Her mouth opened briefly before snapping closed. Summer leaned forward.

"There are no words for the way I behaved that night. I had no right to say the things I did to you." She dragged her fingers through her hair. "I didn't have all the facts. Not that that gives me an excuse for any of it. The facts were none of my business."

The other woman remained silent.

A lick of panic raced up Summer's spine. She pressed her case. "Even if you can't forgive me, please don't take it out on Papa Harry. You make him happy. I'm pretty sure he makes you happy."

Grace dipped her chin.

"He deserves to be happy," she continued. "You both do. If you never want to see me again, that's okay. I'll stay out of both your lives forever. Just don't stay out of his. Please."

Summer held her breath waiting for the other woman to say something. *Anything.*

"Are you planning to stay out of Luke's life forever, as well?"

That was not what she expected Grace to say. She rubbed her sweaty palms over her jean-clad thighs. "I'm taking my apology tour one person at a time," she said. "Besides, I'm not even sure where to begin with him."

A slow mischievous smile formed on Grace's face.

"I might have some ideas about that."

THE HOTEL BALLROOM was crowded with people dressed in their holiday formal wear. Even Wash had donned a tuxedo for the charity auction.

"Wife made me get it just in case I decided to do 'D-Dancing with the Stars,'" he joked with the Growler players congregated near the dessert tables.

"Look at you, Crime Dog." Jacobs clapped Antonio on the back. "Looking all slick in Armani. Hard to make out the color with all that cat hair covering your ass."

Antonio began furiously wiping his pants. "Shit."

"Too bad Fletcher is at home with his new baby tonight," Jacobs said. "Everyone would be so busy looking at his hairy legs and wondering what's beneath that damn kilt of his. No one would notice your furry tux."

Luke looked over at his brother. Brady was taking in all the banter with an amused look. Their father was not pleased with his son and daughter's sojourn in Milwaukee last week. Surprisingly, however, Jake Kessler had appreciated Luke's intercession on Brady's behalf. Luke told his father in no circumstance was Brady graduating early. Instead, Brady would take his time looking at schools, likely choosing a program where he could be a backup for a year or two.

Coach Gibson came over to chat up Brady. The coach was practically giddy at the news that Notre Dame was still in the running.

"Hell. Stanford doesn't stand a chance," Van Horn said at Luke's shoulder.

"I don't know. Brady complained about the cold the whole time he was here last week," Luke replied. "It gets pretty chilly in South Bend, too."

Van Horn shook his head. "Nah. I think now that he's found you, he's going to want to stay close."

Luke looked at his friend. The quarterback shrugged. "Where else is he going to get tips from the best QB in the league?" He winked at Luke and wandered over to the table housing the mayor and his wife.

Patrick Conway made his way to the microphone on the

stage. Luke looked at his watch. He still had fifteen minutes before he was to begin emceeing the auction.

"If I can have everyone's attention," Pat was saying. "Before we get into the auction in earnest, we have a very special treat for you tonight. I urge you to find your seats and enjoy this extraordinary musical talent."

The lights dimmed, and the crowd made their way back to their dinner tables. Gram was seated next to Harry Pearson, who hadn't left her side all evening. The two of them were holding hands and looking like prom dates who were about to get lucky. The Ciaciura's teenage grandson had taken over Luke's seat. The kid was hanging on every word Layla was saying.

Luke was still standing when a murmur filtered throughout the ballroom. He looked up to see a woman in a glittering gold gown take the stage. And she was carrying a familiar cello. His feet were instantly glued to the floor.

Summer gifted the crowd with that beautiful off-kilter smile he knew and loved so much. Applause broke out as she took her seat. The stage went dark except for a single spotlight beaming down on her. The lights from several cellphone cameras appeared throughout the audience.

Luke's heart was racing. He considered hurdling the tables to get to her. She had to be a nervous wreck.

But then she began to play a calming song he remembered his mom and Karla listening to after yoga. Vivaldi, he thought. Her fingers and the bow danced on the strings. She moved her head when the music would crescendo, closing her eyes when the tune grew lighter.

"Dude, down in front," Palmer hissed behind him.

Luke stumbled into an empty seat at a table full of strangers. Thunderous applause filled the ballroom when she finished. Her smile was rapturous now. She stood and made a silly curtsy to the crowd before launching into a John William's movie tune.

"Thank you," she said a bit breathlessly. "This one goes out to a very special person, without whom I would never have been able to be on this stage tonight, outperforming the negative."

A collective sigh went up when the first notes of Cohen's "Hallelujah" flickered through the room. Luke sprung from his seat, nearly plowing over a waiter to get backstage. The crowd was on its feet when Summer finished. She stood and took a bow. He signaled her from the wings, but she remained onstage. Patrick joined her.

"We have one more item to add to the auction items. This one isn't listed in your programs," Patrick announced. He smiled knowingly at Summer. "Miss Pearson is donating a one-hour private performance."

The audience cheered. Luke was having trouble catching his breath.

"Let's start the bidding at twenty-five hundred," Patrick said. "Do I have twenty-five hundred?

"Twenty-five hundred," Coach Gibson shouted from the back of the ballroom.

"Five thousand," Palmer followed up quickly. The punter turned to the head coach. "Sorry, Coach, but my girl would love to hear Summer play when she walks down the aisle."

A resounding "aww" rose up among the crowd. Coach Gibson nodded in agreement. Summer put both hands over her heart.

"Seven thousand dollars," a man Luke didn't recognize called out.

Sweat began to form on the back of Luke's neck. He didn't have time for this. He needed to talk to Summer now.

"Ten thousand dollars!" The audience gasped, then applauded when one of the pitchers from Milwaukee's baseball team bid on Summer.

This was getting way out of hand. A slow burn was building inside Luke's chest, watching other men bid on his woman. And she was his woman. He'd let her walk away once without telling her how things were. He'd be damned if he did it again.

"Fifteen thousand," Van Horn shouted.

Oh, hell, no.

Luke stormed the stage.

"Twenty-five thousand dollars!"

This from Brady. The crowd went wild. Luke froze and glared at his brother.

"Really, Brady?" he scolded.

His brother shrugged. "Having fun isn't hard when you've got a platinum card."

Luke leveled a stern look at Patrick. "Do not accept a single bid from him." He turned to Summer, who was doing that sexy thing with her lip that never failed to make him wild. "And the bidding is closed at one hundred thousand dollars."

Summer slapped her hand over her mouth. Amid catcalls from his teammates and boisterous applause, Luke wrapped his fingers around her wrist and tugged her backstage. They ended up in a small storage room filled with tablecloths and centerpieces. He pressed her up against the door.

"Hi," she whispered.

"Hi, yourself."

Her face glowed. "I did it," she said. "I actually performed. For real this time."

His chest swelled with pride for this unpredictable, wildly talented, desirable woman.

"You did, babe."

She cupped his face and pressed a kiss to his lips. He leaned in for more, but she pushed him away.

"Not yet. Not until I tell you what I need to tell you."

He placed his finger on her lips. "Only if you're going to tell me again that you love me."

Her eyes went wide. He was suddenly panicked that she would say she didn't love him. But then, she slipped her arms around his neck and gave him a sultry grin.

"Number eighty-one in my program, but always number one in my heart."

He heaved a sigh of relief and leaned his forehead against hers. "I'm sorry about the whole thing with Gram and Harry. I didn't think it was—hell, I didn't think. It was so wrong of me to keep it from you. I knew how hurt you'd be and only wanted to spare you from any pain."

Her skin brushed against his as she nodded. "I reacted very poorly. I'm sorry, too."

"No," he told her. "Your commitment to what's right is one of the things I love about you, Summer."

She pulled back. "You love me?"

"God, yes." He sealed his lips over hers, giving her a kiss that was equal parts needy and wild. He'd been too long without her. Never again. Her grandparent's story of never spending a night apart was beginning to hold some appeal.

Pulling her mouth away, she banged her head against the door. "You said one of the things you love about me," she said between breathy pants. "Are there more?"

Damn, she was a sassy minx. And he loved it. He loved her. "Allow me a little show and tell, Summer Pearson."

He was reaching for the zipper of her sexy dress when he heard voices on the other side of the door. Van Horn's voice, specifically.

"I'll check in here."

Luke swore violently before pulling the door open a half an inch and giving his quarterback a look that would kill a lesser man. Van Horn had the nerve to chuckle. He backed away slowly. Luke pressed the door closed and locked it.

"Nothing back here," they heard Van Horn say. "I'm sure they're fine, Layla. Let's go back to the auction. There's a racehorse you should bid on."

Son of a—

Summer pressed her fists to his chest. "Oh my gosh, Brady

and Layla, Luke. They are awesome. I'm so glad you three are connecting. You have a family."

"Yeah, well, hold that thought because the two of them might become as annoying as your brother."

She threw her head back and laughed. He took advantage and reacquainted himself with the slender column of her neck that always turned him on.

"Mmm," she sighed. "We should probably get back."

"Oh, no. I paid a hundred grand for an hour, and I'm taking my full hour."

"That was for a performance, silly."

"Yes, but the type of performance was never specified, sweetheart."

Her mouth gaped open.

"By my watch, we have fifty-four minutes left."

She bit down on her bottom lip before pressing her body against his. "I hate to break it to you, number eighty-one, but you're stuck with me for a lot longer than fifty-four minutes."

His heart soared at the thought. But he kept her busy for fifty-four minutes anyway.

EPILOGUE

"I ALWAYS WANTED TO BE A BRIDESMAID," Layla gushed as she fiddled with the knot on Luke's tie. Her French-manicured fingers moved over his chest to straighten the already smooth lapels of his charcoal suit. "There. Now you look *hawt*."

"Wait, are you implying that I don't always look hot?" Luke teased his sister.

Her lips twitched as she tried, and failed, to contain an impish smile. "And to think I wished for an older brother whose ego I wouldn't have to constantly stroke. You're no better than Brady."

Luke winked at her. "But I'm much better *looking* than he is."

"Hey, I'm right here, you know." Slouched in the leather chair in the corner of Luke's bedroom, Brady didn't bother looking up from his phone.

"Brady!" Layla cried. "Get up. You're wrinkling your suit!"

The urgency in her voice startled Monty from his nap. The dog jumped off the bed with an alarmed bark.

"Not you, sweet boy." Layla made kissing noises at the dog while she secured his bowtie for the umpteenth time. "I meant the other beast."

Heaving an exasperated sigh, Brady slowly got to his feet. Layla moved to furiously adjust the shoulders of Brady's jacket just as Mrs. Hilbert burst into the room carrying two small plastic containers.

"There you are, young lady," she said to Layla. "The photographer wants to get pictures of you with the bride before the ceremony. And you boys need to put on your boutonnieres." She handed one of the containers to Layla. "Here, help me get them gussied up."

Minutes later, with their wedding look complete, Mrs. Hilbert stepped back to admire her handiwork.

"You are certainly a handsome family," she said.

Family.

Luke still got a lump in his throat every time he heard the word. It had been seven months since Brady and Layla had shown up on his doorstep. Luke couldn't believe how easily the two teenagers fit into his life. They quickly filled up that part of him that he thought would always be empty.

And Summer filled up the rest.

She made him whole, in fact. As much as he appreciated the unconditional love of his newfound younger siblings, he couldn't imagine his life without Summer. *Without her love*. She made him believe things he never thought possible. And, this afternoon, with a small ceremony in his backyard, their families would be joined together officially. From here on out, his future—and his heart—would be full.

Even more exciting, in another week, Brady would be three hours away in South Bend, Indiana, for football camp and, later in the summer, his freshman year at Notre Dame. Layla was spending June and July in Chicago interning for a designer friend of her mother's. Luke and Summer would be switching off with Gram, chaperoning Layla in the apartment she was sub-letting from Summer's former roommate, Paige. For the first time in his career, the long months between the end of one football season and the start of another were something Luke was actually enjoying.

"Now, you need to skedaddle, Layla. We don't want to keep the bride waiting," Mrs. Hilbert commanded.

"Wait." Layla grabbed for Brady's phone. "Will you take our picture first?"

Mrs. Hilbert beamed when Layla handed her the phone. "Stand between your brothers."

Luke and Brady exchanged a look over Layla's head before leaning in and kissing her cheeks at the same moment. She giggled as she squirmed between them.

"Stop it! You'll mess up my hair," she said between laughs.

"You've got some weeds stuck on your head," Brady joked. "Here, let me pull them out."

Layla smacked Brady's hands away, her fingers immediately going to her head. Not a hair was out of place in her elaborate updo, however, and the Baby's breath she'd adorned it with was still intact.

"You look beautiful, Layla," Luke told her.

And she did. The vintage lavender dress she wore made her look older than her fourteen years but in a tasteful way. The soon-to-be heartbreaker swished the full skirt flirtatiously.

"Someone has to provide the fashion sense in this family," she quipped. "Ooh! Wait until you see Summer's dress, though." Layla sighed reverently. "It's stunning."

Luke swallowed roughly at the thought of Summer in a "stunning" dress. He couldn't wait to see it. He couldn't wait to see *her*. The last few days leading up to the wedding were a blur. Her relatives were all in town, and there had been so many demands on her time that the two of them hadn't had a moment alone. The situation left him very frustrated. Hell, as much as he was looking forward to seeing her in the supposedly "stunning" dress, he was looking forward to seeing her out of it. The zipper of his pants grew painfully tight.

He glanced at his watch. *Damn.* He had at least five hours before he could get her alone and naked. And when he did, he had something very important he wanted to ask her.

"Stop taunting the boy," Mrs. Hilbert said. "It's time to get those pictures so we can get this wedding moving. My Spanx are starting to cut off my circulation. Fred will be up to get you boys in five minutes," she instructed them.

"THE GUESTS ARE ALL SEATED," The Judge said. "It's time to begin."

"You're not going to wear your robe to perform the ceremony?" Summer asked. The Judge wore an elegant sleeveless, tea-length Carolina Herrera dress in orchid. A stunning pearl broach was its only embellishment.

Her mother rolled her eyes like a teenager. "Only if you want me to. But the sun is beating down on the backyard, and black is a little stifling."

"Is this wedding even official if you're not carrying your gavel?" Sterling teased.

Their mom shot him a withering look, making him laugh.

"Mom, you look *ah-mazing*. No wonder the district attorney always asks to meet you in your chambers."

The Judge shocked Summer by blushing.

"What?!" Summer cried.

Sterling winked at her. "I'll fill you in later. But for now, it would be a crime—" He made air quotes with his fingers "—to cover up that outfit with your dumpy judicial robe." He turned to Summer. "And you, my wunderkind sister, are rocking that dress."

Summer glanced over at her mom. "He's just trying to butter me up, so I'll play the Labor Day concert in Grant Park."

"Is it working?"

"You've already got me over-scheduled this summer as it is," Summer replied. "Luke and I want to take the kids to Idaho before the season starts."

She'd returned to performing slowly. A fundraiser for the local SPCA was first, followed by a set during the local public broadcasting station's pledge drive. The city of Milwaukee schools had been all in for the "Peter and the Wolf" performance with the symphony. It was such a success that the school system offered her a job as a consultant, asking her to liaison with the symphony for future concerts with students. Her professor at Northwestern convinced her to take an adjunct position teaching a class on promoting the arts through social media. And just last weekend, she'd played at Kane Palmer's wedding. Things were going well, but she wasn't ready to rush back into her earlier days of social media fame.

Sterling looked askance at The Judge. "Will you listen to that? The *kids*?"

Their mother smiled serenely. "I'm looking at an accomplished woman who is living her best life. And I couldn't be prouder."

Mrs. Hilbert poked her head into the room, Millie in her arms. "Frenchie here says it's show time." The little dog barked her agreement. She was barely tolerating the purple fascinator Layla had attached to her head. Time was definitely of the essence.

The Judge hurried outside, taking her place under the arbor of white roses and violet peonies. Sterling took Summer's arm.

"Mom and the DA?" she asked her brother.

He nodded and squeezed her arm. "Looks like both my girls are going to get their happy ever after."

The guests "ahhed" when he escorted her down the aisle. Standing next to The Judge, Papa Harry put his hand to his chest before blowing Summer a kiss. Her smile felt a bit wobbly as she took her seat beside the arbor. She settled her cello between her leg and began to play the song Papa Harry, and Grace requested, "Can't Help Falling in Love."

Brady came down the aisle first, barely getting a rambunctious Monty to heel. The big dog lunged for Summer as soon as he saw her, but Brady was able to restrain him before disaster struck. Luke's brother shot Summer a sheepish grin as he and Monty took their places.

Layla was next, with Millie strutting beside her, the dog reveling in the attention and the sighs from the crowd of Sunset Glen residents. Summer's vision blurred slightly when Luke came into view, Grace on his arm. She dazzled in an ecru tea-length gown similar in style to Layla's. But it was Luke who had Summer's heart skipping every other beat. She could feel his eyes on her the moment he entered the backyard.

It was always that way with them. That intense feeling of connection. That feeling like they were the only two people in the world—even in a stadium full of fans. She never imagined she could love anyone the way she loved Luke. And she certainly never dreamed of being loved the same way in return. That sort of magical relationship was something she thought only existed between her grandparents. But she'd been wrong about a lot of things. And she was delighted to be wrong about this thing, too.

Somehow, she made her way through the song just as Luke handed off Grace to Papa Harry. Luke must have sensed her emotions because he bypassed his seat next to Layla and came to stand behind Summer instead. He gently rested his hands on her shoulders. Together they watched The Judge perform the marriage ceremony of two of their favorite people. Summer serenaded them out with "I'm a Believer," much to the crowd's delight.

"Remember all those months ago when you said you didn't want me to be a part of your family?" Luke reminded Summer while they watched Grace and Papa Harry cut into their wedding cake an hour later. "You're stuck with me now."

She pressed her back into his chest. He wrapped his arms around her waist. Embarrassment and guilt washed over her as she remembered that day in the Sunset Glen atrium. Then, she hadn't known his backstory and she wasn't aware how hurtful her offhanded comment was to him. "I couldn't stand the thought of you marrying Lizzie," she admitted.

He nuzzled her neck. "Ah ha, so you admit you were falling for me even when you were playing hard to get?"

"And feed your ego? Never. But technically, Grace is the only one with the Pearson last name."

"Ah, so for us to be family, you'd have to change your last name to Kessler, then?"

Summer's breath stilled. Was he saying what she thought he was saying? She slowly turned in his arms. He was smiling. But she knew him well enough now to know that behind his daredevil grin, there was a young boy who just wanted to be loved. And she did love him. She really, really did.

"That's usually the way it works," she whispered. Her heart felt like it might explode.

His mouth relaxed into the sexy grin reserved just for her. He brushed his lips over her forehead. "Maybe we should go back to your place and discuss this further?"

Yes!

"Summer!" Lizzie screeched. "It's time for the bouquet!"

Layla linked her arm through Summer's and pulled her out of Luke's embrace. "Come on, Summer. Let's do this."

Were they kidding? She didn't want to tussle for the bouquet. She wanted to go home with Luke and "discuss" things.

"Whoa, Layla," Luke protested. "Aren't you a little young to catch the bouquet?"

Seriously? That's what he was objecting to?

"Do they even toss the bouquet anymore?" Summer said as Layla dragged her into a crowd of women in sensible shoes, jockeying for position. "Someone could get seriously hurt here."

"Speak for yourself, missy," Mrs. Hilbert said. "The bouquet toss is a time-honored tradition, and I, for one, am going to catch it." The woman aimed a conspirator's wink at Grace.

Lizzie snorted. "Bring it on, sister." She waved at Josh, whom she'd reconciled with last Valentine's Day. He gave her a thumbs-up.

Still clutching Summer's arm, Layla edged to the front of the crowd. Summer was shocked when The Judge filled in the space beside her. Her mother shrugged. Summer looked over at Luke, glaring when he cupped his hands and mouthed, "Soft hands, babe. Soft hands."

Grace turned her back to the women, counted to three, and tossed the bouquet. A scrum ensued, complete with squealing and shouting that included an obscenity or two. No one, however, counted on Monty's four-foot vertical leap. The dog snagged the bouquet while it was in mid-air, racing off with it, Millie in hot pursuit.

Much later that night, Summer and Luke decided to exclude all dogs from their upcoming wedding reception.

I hope you enjoyed Luke and Summer's story. Would you like a playlist from the book? Or a peek at the prologue of Paige's story? Scan the code to sign up for my newsletter and I'll send you a link for both. By subscribing, you'll get all the scoop on all my books long before anyone else.

If you want more day-to-day action where you can get sneak peeks at covers, name characters, participate in my advanced reader group, get the recipes in my books, or just have fun, scan the code to join my reader group, the X's and O's, on Facebook.

And please, don't forget to tell other readers how much you enjoyed ***Double Dog Dare*** by leaving a review on the site where you purchased this book, on Goodreads and/or on BookBub. It's the best way to get the word out about favorite reads and I ALWAYS appreciate when readers take the time to post some kind words about my books!

Have you read Declan Fletcher's marriage of convenience story, ***Just for Kicks***? You can pick up a copy at any of your favorite retailers.

Are you curious about the Growlers' coach Heath Gibson and his wife Merrit?
Read their story for free! Simply scan the code below.

Want more football? Meet the Baltimore Blaze:
Game On – Quarterback Shane Devlin's story
Foolish Games – a secret baby story
Risky Game –a fake relationship story
Sleeping with the Enemy –a second chances story

Do you enjoy books about small towns and big families? Be sure to check out my Chances Inlet series.

Back to Before
All They Ever Wanted
Second Chance Christmas

Coming soon: Paige's Story! Yep, she's going to Chances Inlet.

ACKNOWLEDGMENTS

Writing a book is, for the most part, a solitary journey. Never more so than the early 2020s. I'm so grateful to all of you readers who reached out and connected via social media during that time. It means so much to me that you want to read books I've written. I couldn't have written this book without your support.

As always, a huge shoutout goes to the home team. Thanks for putting up with me during my writing "process." Thank you to Lauren Rico for schooling me on all things orchestra related. Summer suffered a huge plot twist before the story was written and I didn't get to use what Lauren shared, but who knows what Summer will be up to next. Thank you to my dear friends, Jeannie Moon, and Anna Doll for their editing expertise. Lee Hyat, thank you for another gorgeous cover. And Rachael Brown, thank you for having PA superpowers!

ABOUT THE AUTHOR

After years of writing reports and testimony for Congress, **Tracy Solheim** decided to put her creative talents to better use. The recipient of the 2020 Georgia Author of the Year Award, she's the *USA Today* best-selling author of contemporary sports romance, romantic suspense, and small-town second chance novels. Tracy lives in the heart of SEC country, also known as the suburbs of Atlanta, with her husband, two adult children who frequently show up at dinner time, and a neurotic Labrador retriever who keeps her company while she writes. See what she's up to by subscribing to her newsletter at TracySolheim.com.

CPSIA information can be obtained
at www.ICGtesting.com
Printed in the USA
LVHW102014210722
723964LV00002B/66